Pe
PROPOSALS
WEAR MY RING

Perfect
PROPOSALS
COLLECTION

March 2016

April 2016

May 2016

June 2016

Perfect
PROPOSALS
WEAR MY RING

Ally
BLAKE

Lindsay
ARMSTRONG

Kate
HARDY

MILLS
BOON

First Published in Great Britain 2016
By Mills & Boon, an imprint of HarperCollins*Publishers*
1 London Bridge Street, London, SE1 9GF

WEAR MY RING © 2016 Harlequin Books S.A.

The Secret Wedding Dress © 2013 Ally Blake
The Millionaire's Marriage Claim © 2005 Lindsay Armstrong
The Children's Doctor's Special Proposal © 2009 Pamela Brooks

ISBN: 978-0-263-92152-6

09-0316

THE SECRET
WEDDING DRESS

ALLY BLAKE

In her previous life Australian author **Ally Blake** was at times a cheerleader, a maths tutor, a dental assistant and a shop assistant. In this life she is a bestselling, multi-award-winning novelist who has been published in over twenty languages with more than two million books sold worldwide.

She married her gorgeous husband in Las Vegas— no Elvis in sight, though Tony Curtis did put in a special appearance—and now Ally and her family, including three rambunctious toddlers, share a property in the leafy western suburbs of Brisbane, with kookaburras, cockatoos, rainbow lorikeets and the occasional creepy-crawly. When not writing, she makes coffees that never get drunk, eats too many M&Ms, attempts yoga, devours *The West Wing* re-runs, reads every spare minute she can and barracks ardently for the Collingwood Magpies footy team.

You can find out more at her website, www. allyblake.com

For Deb.
For your imagination, your encouragement, your
friendship.
And for the bit about the lift.

CHAPTER ONE

PAIGE DANFORTH didn't believe in happily ever afters.

So it was a testament to how awesome a friend she was that she stood freezing her tush off outside a dodgy-looking Collingwood warehouse in the grey half-light of a misty Melbourne winter's morning with her best friend Mae who was there to buy a wedding dress.

Wedding Dress Fire Sale! Over 1000 new and used dresses, up to 90% off! read the massive hot-pink banner flapping dejectedly against the cracked brown bricks of the old building. Paige wondered if any of the other women in the line, which by that stage snaked all the way around the corner of the block, saw the irony of the hype masking the depressing reality. By the manic gleams in their eyes they all bought into the fantasy, for sure. Each and every one of them convinced they were the ones for whom the love songs and sonnets rang true.

'The door moved,' Mae whispered, grabbing Paige's arm so tight she knew it would leave a mark.

Paige lifted her long hair out of the way so that she could loop her thick woollen scarf once more around her neck and stamped her boots against the pavement to get her sluggish blood moving. 'You're imagining things.'

'It jiggled. Like someone was unlocking it from the inside.' Mae's voluble declaration spread up and down the line like wildfire, and Paige was almost pushed over in the sudden surge of bodies.

'Relax!' Paige said, prying her friend's ever-tightening claw from her arm while glaring at the rabid-looking woman pressing close behind her. 'The doors will open when they open. You will find the dress of your dreams. If you can't find yourself a dress in a thousand, then clearly you're a failure as a woman.'

Mae stopped twitching to glare at her. 'I should rescind your Maid of Honour duties for that alone.'

'Would you?' Paige begged.

Mae laughed. Though it was short-lived. Soon she was jogging on the spot like a prize fighter seconds from entering the ring, her usually wild red hair pulled into a no-nonsense ponytail, her focus fixed, as it had been since the moment her boyfriend had proposed.

All of a sudden the flaky wooden doors were flung open with a flourish, the mixed scents of camphor and lavender spilling into the air with a sickly sweet rush.

A tired-looking woman in skinny jeans and a T-shirt the same hot pink as the sign above yelled, 'No haggling! No refunds! No returns! No sizes bar what's on the floor!' The words echoed down the narrow lane, and the line of women mushroomed towards the doors as if she'd announced Hugh Jackman would be giving free back rubs to the first hundred through the door.

Paige barely kept her feet as she pressed forward into the breach, and then grabbed Mae by the shoulders as she screeched to a sudden halt. Like Moses parting the Red Sea, waves of women poured around them.

'Holy moly,' Mae said.

'You're not wrong,' Paige muttered, as even she was impressed with what she saw.

Sweetheart necklines by the dozen, beaded corsets as far as

the eye could see, sleeves so heavily ruched they made the eyes water. Designer dresses. Off the rack dresses. Second-hand dresses. Factory second dresses. All massively discounted. Every last one of them to be sold that day.

'Move!' Mae cried out as she came to and made a beeline for something that had caught her now frantic eye.

Paige quickly tucked herself in a corner in the shadow of the door. She waved her mobile phone in the air. 'I'll be over here if you need me!'

Mae's hand flapped briskly above the crowd of heads and then she was gone.

What followed was a lesson in anthropology. One woman near Paige who wore an immaculately tailored suit squealed like a teenager when she found the dress of her dreams. Another, in a twin-set, glasses, and tidy chignon, had a full-on temper tantrum, complete with stamping feet, when she discovered one didn't come in her size.

All for the sake of an overpriced dress they'd only wear once at a ceremony that forced people to make impossible promises to love, honour, and cherish for ever. In Paige's experience it was more like bicker, loathe, and cling on for dear life until there was nothing left but lost years and regret. Better to love, honour, and cherish yourself, Paige believed. For the chance to dress like a princess one time in your life the relentless search for love couldn't possibly be worth it.

The scents of hairspray and perfume mixed with the camphor and lavender and Paige soon had to breathe through her mouth. Her fingers curled tighter around her mobile, willing Mae to ring.

Mae. Her BFF. Her partner in crime. They'd had one another's backs for so long, since their parents had gone through simultaneous messy divorces and had left them both certain that happy ever after with some guy was an evil myth—one that had been perpetuated by florists and bakers and reception hall owners. Mae, who'd forgotten it all the moment she'd found Clint.

Paige swallowed. She deeply hoped Mae would be perfectly happy for ever and ever. She really did. But a hot spot of fear for her flared in her stomach every time she let herself think about it. So she decided to think about something else.

As brand manager for a luxury home-wares retailer, she was always on the lookout for locations in which to shoot catalogues, and, while the Collingwood warehouse was near decrepit, at a pinch the crumbling brickwork could be considered romantic.

Not that she wanted to shoot there any time soon. The next catalogue had to be shot on location in Brazil. Period. Such a big expense for a single catalogue was as yet unheard of at Ménage à Moi, which was a boutique business, but Paige *knew* in her bones it would be worth it. Her proposal was so dazzling her boss had to say yes. And it was just the shake-up her life needed—

Paige shook her head. Brazil was the shake-up the *brand* needed. *She* was fine. Hunky-dory. Or she would be when she got the hell out of the building.

Breathing deep through her mouth, she closed one eye and imagined the massive windows draped in swathes of peacock-blue chiffon, the muted brickwork a total juxtaposition against the next season's dazzling, Rio-inspired, jewel-toned decor. Weak sunlight struck the glass which was in dire need of an industrial wash, made all the more obvious when compared with one incongruous clean spot that let through a single ray.

Dust mites danced in the sunbeam and Paige's eye naturally followed it all the way to a rack of wedding dresses, most of which boasted ridiculously excessive layers of skirt that would struggle to fit even the widest chapel aisle.

She made to glance away when something caught her eye. A glimpse of chiffon in dark champagne. The iridescent sheen of pearls. Impossibly intricate lacework. A train so diaphanous it was lost as someone walked by the rack, blocking out the ray of light.

Paige blinked. And again. But the dress was gone. And her heart skipped a beat.

She'd heard the expression a million times, only had never experienced it until that moment. Didn't realise it came complete with a tightening of her throat, a sudden lightness in her head, and the complete cessation of thought.

Then someone moved, the ray of light returned, and there it was. And then she was standing. Walking. At the rack, her hands went to the fabric as though possessed by some otherworldly force. The garment came to her from between the tight squeeze of dresses as easily as Arthur had released Excalibur from its stone prison.

As her eyes skimmed over the softly twisted straps, the deep V, a torso of lace draped in strings of ocean pearls that cinched into the most exquisite silhouette before disappearing into a skirt made of chiffon that moved as if it breathed, Paige's heart galloped like a brumby with a horse thief hot on its heels.

'Wow,' a voice said from behind her. 'That's so cute. Are you just looking or do you have dibs?'

Cute? That was the best word the woman could come up with for the sliver of perfection draped over Paige's shaking hands.

Paige didn't even turn around. She just shook her head as the words she'd never thought she'd hear herself say escaped her lips:

'This wedding dress is mine.'

'Paige!'

Paige looked up from her position back near the doors to find Mae literally skipping towards her.

'I've been trying to call you for twenty minutes!'

Paige's hand went to her phone in her pocket. She hadn't felt a thing. In fact, by the intensity of the light now pouring into the building, much of the morning had passed by in a blur.

Mae pointed madly at the heavy beige garment bag hooked over one crooked elbow. 'Success! I wanted you to see it but I couldn't get hold of you and this skinny brunette was eyeing it up like some starving hyena, so I stripped down to my bra and knickers and tried it on in the middle of the floor. And it's so freaking hot.'

Mae's eyes were now flickering to the fluorescent white garment bag with the hot-pink writing emblazoned across the front that was draped over Paige's thighs. 'Did you find a bridesmaid's dress?'

Paige swallowed hard and slowly shook her head. Then, unable to say the words, she waved a wobbly arm in the direction of the sea of white, ivory, and champagne frou-frou.

'Oh. For a catalogue shoot? You're doing a wedding theme?'

And there it was. The perfect out. The exorbitant dress was a work expense. That would even make it tax deductible and less taxing on her mortgage payments. But panic had clogged her throat shut tight.

Mae's eyebrows slowly slid skyward. Then after several long seconds, she burst out laughing. 'I thought I was the one who made bizarre shopping decisions when I wasn't getting any, but this takes the cake.'

Paige found her voice at last. 'What's *that* supposed to mean?'

Mae's spare hand went to her hip. 'Tell me quick, without having to think about it, when was the last time you went on a date?'

Paige opened her mouth to say when, and who, and where,

but again nothing came out. Because for the life of her she couldn't remember. It had been weeks. Maybe even months. Rather than worry that she hadn't even noticed she hadn't been on a date in an age, she clutched onto the hope that there might be a reasonable reason for her moment of shopping madness.

'You need to get yourself a man and soon.' Mae tucked her hand through the crook of Paige's arm and dragged her to her feet. 'But until then let's get out of here before the smell of spray-tan and desperation makes me pass out.'

Paige stood in the single lift of the Botany Apartments at New Quay at Docklands, staring blankly at the glossy white and black tiled lobby floor, the decadent black paisley papered walls, the striking silver sun-bursts framing every door, all lit by the diffused light of a half-dozen mother-of-pearl chandeliers as she waited for the doors to close.

Was Mae right? Had her wholly daft purchase been the result of a recent spate of accidental abstinence? Like a knee-jerk reaction in the opposite direction? Maybe. Because while she had no intention of following Mae's path down the aisle, she liked dating. Liked men just fine. She liked the way they smelt, the way their minds worked, the curl of heat when she was attracted. She liked men who could wear a suit. Men who paid for drinks and worked long hours as she did and weren't looking for anything more than good company. The kind of men downtown Melbourne was famous for.

So where had they all gone?

Or was it her fault? Had all the extra energy she'd put into the Brazilian catalogue proposal taken it out of her? Or was she bored with dating the same kind of guy all the time? Maybe she was emotionally sated by the *Gilmore girls* re-runs on TV.

Groaning, she transferred the heavy white garment bag

from one hand to the other, flexed her empty hand, and waited for the lift doors to close. And waited some more. It could take a while.

The lift had a personality all of its own, and as personalities went it was rotten to the core. It went up and it went down, but in a completely random fashion that had nothing to do with the floor she chose. Telling Sam the Super hadn't made a lick of difference. Neither had kicking it. Perhaps she should next try kicking Sam the Super.

Until then, all she could do was wait. And remind herself that a tetchy lift was a small price to pay for her little slice of heaven on the eighth floor. She'd grown up in a huge cluttered house filled with chintz and frilly curtains, and smelling of Mr Sheen and dried flowers and tension you could cut with a knife. And the first time she'd seen the sleek, open-plan opulence of the Botany Apartments she'd felt as if she could breathe fully for the first time in her life.

She closed her eyes and thought about the minimalist twenties decor in her apartment, the sliver of a view of the city, the two great-sized bedrooms—one for her, the other her home-office-slash-Mae's-room when Mae was too far gone after a big night out to make it home. Though it had been an age since Mae slept over. Not since around the time Clint proposed, in fact.

Paige shook her head as if shooing away a persistent fly. The point was the lift was a tiny inconvenience in the grand scheme of things. Except those times when she was carrying something that weighed the equivalent of a small car.

Okay. If datelessness had led to the *thing* currently giving her shoulder pain, then she needed to do something about it. And fast. Or who knew what she might do next? Buy a ring? Hire the Langham? Propose to herself in sky-writing?

As her spine began to crumple in on itself Paige muttered, 'I hereby promise to throw myself upon the mercy of the next man who smiles at me. He can buy me dinner first. Or I can buy him a coffee. Heck, I'll share a bottle of water from the third-floor dispenser. But I need to get some man time and fast.'

An absolute age later, when the lift doors *finally* began to close, she almost sobbed in relief. Until at the last second a row of fingers jammed into the gap.

'Hold the door,' said the deep male voice on the end of the long brown fingers.

No-o-o! Paige thought. Once those doors opened, the wait for the perverse damn lift to head skywards would start over, and she might never get the feeling back in her shoulders again.

'No?' the male voice asked with a low note of incredulity, and Paige blanched, realising she must have said it out loud. It seemed years of living on her own had made her a little too used to talking to herself.

Feeling only the slightest twinge of guilt, she jabbed at the 'close door' button. Repeatedly.

But the long brown male fingers had other ideas. They prised that stubborn door open with what was a pretty impressive display of pure brute strength. And then he loomed into view, a stranger, a great big broad one, his bulk blocking her view of the foyer entirely. Head down, brow pinched into a frown, he stared intently at the shiny smartphone in his spare hand.

Something about him had Paige pressing herself deeper into the small lift. Something else entirely had her eyes flickering rapidly over a well-worn chocolate-brown leather jacket with thick dark hair curling over the wool-lined collar. Over soft denim, lovingly hugging masses of long hard muscle, the perfect lines broken only by a neat rectangular bulge where his wallet sat against his backside. Down to huge scuffed boots. *Huge.*

Any calm and soothing thoughts the view of mother-of-pearl chandeliers and silver sun-bursts had inspired were swept away by the raw and unadulterated impact of the man. The sweet curl of heat she'd been thinking about earlier rushed into Paige's stomach like a tidal wave and colour rushed into her skin with a whoosh she could practically hear.

Then, before she even had a chance to collect herself, a husky voice inside her head sent the stranger a silent plea: *Smile.*

Paige all but coughed on her own shock. *He* was not what she'd meant when she'd decided to get herself a man. A comfortable re-entry was just the ticket. Honestly, who needed such a breathtaking expanse of male shoulders, or such thick dark hair that looked as if no amount of product could completely ever tame it? Or fingers strong enough to open a lift door? As for the hint of hooded dark eyes she could make out in profile and stubble long past designer? That kind of intensity wasn't comfortable. It was overkill.

She was staring so hard at the man's lips—thinking that they were too ridiculously perfect to be hidden amongst all that rough stubble—there was no missing it when they twitched, as if they might be about to actually smile.

Oh, God, Paige thought as the man slid his phone into the inner pocket of his jacket. She'd been caught staring. And the pink warmth turned into a red hot inferno beneath her skin.

'Thanks for holding,' the stranger said in a voice that was deep and rich, like how the devil ought to sound if he hoped to be any good at tempting people to the dark side.

'My pleasure,' said Paige, eyes flickering up to his, which was why she didn't miss a millimetre of his eyebrow raise, reminding her he was perfectly aware of her attempt to sabotage his ride.

Quitting while she was behind, Paige shut her mouth and made room, plastering herself as far to one side of the small lift as possible. The sooner he got to wherever he was visiting, the better.

Naturally the lift was narrow, complementing the dinky design of the boutique apartment building, and the sizeable stranger seemed to fill every spare inch of space all by himself. Even the bits he didn't physically invade seemed to pulse with his energy. Every time he breathed in the hairs on Paige's arms stood on end.

'What floor?' he asked.

'Eighth,' she said, her voice gravelly as she waggled a finger at the number-eight light that was lit up all hopefully.

The stranger ran a hand across the back of his neck and then the corner of his mouth lifted.

Paige held her breath while her hormones whooped up a series of cat-calls deep in her belly. But it wasn't a smile. Not officially. Even though it sure hinted at the kinds of eye crinkles that had a habit of turning her knees to water.

'Long flight,' he said, his deep voice rumbling through the floor of the lift and all the way up her legs. He lifted one ridiculously broad shoulder over which a leather satchel and a laptop bag hung. 'Not all here.'

Not all here? Any more of him and Paige would be one with the wall.

When the stranger leaned across to press the button to shut the doors Paige's skin tingled and tiny pinpricks of sweat tickled down her neck and spine. She breathed in and caught the scent of leather. Of spice. Of fresh chopped wood. Of sea air. Sweat that wasn't her own.

Outside it was the depth of winter, yet she yanked her scarf away from her neck and thought about ice cream and snowball fights to counteract the certainty that she was about to overheat. Yet something about him, something dark and dangerous dancing in his eyes, in the way her skin hadn't stopped thrumming from the moment she'd laid eyes on him, made her quite sure, no matter how many snowballs she imagined, it would never be enough.

He pulled back and grunted when the lift didn't move, and finally Paige's brain caught up with her hormones. 'Oh, no, no, no,' she said, 'there's really no need to press that button. Or any button. This lift is completely contrary. It rises and falls as it pleases, with no care at all for—'

With its usual impeccably bad timing, the lift doors slid neatly closed, the box juddered and after an infinitesimal drop it took off. Paige glared in disbelief at the indicator light above the doors, which lit up in actual sequential order as it rose smoothly towards the sky.

Rotten, stinking, little—

'You were saying?' the stranger said.

Paige's eyes cut to his to find humour now well and truly lighting them, creating fiery glints in the dark depths. As if he was about to smile at any second.

Okay, so that deal she'd made earlier to herself, it had been more like a set of guidelines than a promise. What if some pimply sixteen-year-old on a skateboard had smiled first? Or if it had been the guy with the scraggly beard and the rat on his shoulder who walked up and down the Docklands promenade yelling at seagulls? Clearly her deal needed tweaking before it went into *official* effect.

She lifted a shoulder, trying for nonchalance as she said, 'This lift has it in for me, clearly. While you, on the other hand, have the touch. Want a job as a lift operator? I'd pay you myself.'

The stranger's expression warmed. No, *burned*. As if the temperature of the glint in his eye had turned up a notch.

'Thanks for the offer,' he said, 'but I'm set.'

And had he moved closer? Or merely shifted his weight? Either way the lift suddenly felt smaller. The hairs on the back of Paige's neck now joining the party as they stood to attention.

'Oh, well. It was worth a shot.'

When the beautiful bow of his top lip began to soften sideways, Paige smartly turned to watch the display as the floor numbers rolled over all too slowly.

'You live in the building?' the stranger asked.

Paige nodded, biting her lip so as not to shiver as that dark velvety voice rolled over her skin in delicious waves.

'That explains your…relationship with the lift.'

Before she could help herself, her eyes slid back to the stranger, fully expecting to find him looking at her as if she might wig out at any second, as Sam the Super always did when she made a complaint. But the stranger's gaze was making its way over her hair, the curve of her neck, pausing a beat on her mouth, before coming back to connect, hard, with her eyes.

Her next breath in was long and deep, and once again filled with the scents of spice, and all things deeply masculine. Maybe she wasn't hallucinating. Perhaps he was a fighter pilot/lumberjack/yachtsman by trade. It could happen.

'It started out slow,' she said, sounding as if she'd run a mile in a minute flat, 'a missed floor here and there. But now it's all the time. I keep pressing the button knowing it'll make not a lick of difference, as I refuse to stop hoping it will one day simply start acting like a normal lift. While it won't stop refusing to be one.'

'Such friction,' he said, laughter lighting his eyes. 'A clash of equal and opposite wills. Like something out of a Doris Day and Rock Hudson flick.' He glanced at the computerised electronic display of her nemesis. 'With a sci-fi bent.'

Completely unexpectedly, Paige laughed out loud, the sound bouncing off the walls of the tiny lift. And this time when her eyes snagged back on his they stuck. Such dark eyes he had, drawing her in so deep, so fast, she wouldn't have noticed if the lift started humming *Pillow Talk*.

The only explanation she had for her reaction to him was her dating drought. He was so against type. She normally gravitated to men who were so clean cut they were practically transparent. Men who'd not have blinked had she slipped them a dating contract: three nights a week, split checks, no idealistic promises.

Whereas this man was so dark, enigmatic, and diabolically hot every nerve in her body was fighting against every other nerve. His big body that made her palms itch, and his scent that made her want to lean in and bury her face in his neck. 'Getting back on the horse' with a man like that would be akin to falling off a Shetland pony at the fair and getting back on a stallion jostling at the starting gate of the Melbourne Cup.

And yet… She wasn't after a dating contract. She needed a springboard from which to leap back into the dating world. And there *he* stood, beautiful, sexy, and glinting at her like nobody's business.

She stuck out a hand. 'Paige Danforth. Eighth floor.'

'Gabe Hamilton. Twelfth.'

'The penthouse?' she blurted before her tongue could catch up with her brain. That was how addled she was; she hadn't even noticed which floor he'd pressed. The penthouse had been empty since the day she'd moved in. Meaning… 'You're *not* visiting.'

'Not.' How the guy managed to make one word evoke so much she had no idea, but he evoked plenty. The fact that he would be sleeping a mere four floors above her being the meat of it.

'Renting?' she asked, and his eye crinkles deepened, making her wonder what she'd evoked without meaning to.

'Mine,' he drawled.

Paige nodded sagely, as if they were still talking real estate, not in non-verbal pre-negotiations for something far less dry. 'I hadn't heard it had been sold.'

'It hasn't. I've been away. And now I'm back.' For how long he didn't say, but the glint sizzling in his dark eyes and making her feel as if steam were rising from her clothes told her he believed it was long enough.

The lift dinged, as lifts were wont to do—normal lifts, lifts that weren't demonically possessed—right as she was gaining momentum to do something rash. Rash but necessary.

And then the doors opened.

'Of course,' Paige muttered as she recognised her own floor by the dotted silver wallpaper, a Ménage à Moi staple. What could she do but step out?

The back of her hand brushed Gabe's wrist as she shucked past. The lightest possible touch of skin on skin. When little waves of his energy continued crackling through her as she stepped out into the hall, Paige turned back. It was on the tip of her tongue to ask him in for coffee. Or offer to show him the sights of Melbourne. Or any other number of euphemisms for breaking her dating drought.

Then he stifled a yawn.

Like the dawning of the sun it occurred to her that the glint in his eyes had probably been the effect of jet lag the entire time, not some kind of extraordinary instant mutual chemistry between herself and the vision of absolute masculine gorgeousness gracing the lift before her.

If her complexion had been tomato-esque earlier, she'd bet right about then she resembled a fire engine.

Please, she silently begged the lift as they stood facing one another, *close now. Just this once. Close.*

And it did. The two great silver doors slid serenely towards one another, Gabe's dark figure growing darker by the second. Until his hand curled around the edge of one door, stopping it in its tracks. Mere mechanics no match for his might.

'I'll see you 'round, Paige Danforth, eighth floor,' Gabe said, before his fingers slid back away.

Then, as the doors came to a close, he smiled. A dark smile, a dangerous smile, a smile ripe with implications. A smile that sent the dancing hormones inside her belly into instant spontaneous combustion.

Then he was gone.

Paige stood in the elegant hallway, breathing through her nose, feeling as if that smile would be imbedded upon her retinas, and messing with her ability to walk in a straight line, for a long, long time.

The gentle whump of the lift moving up inside the lift shaft brought her from her reverie and she blinked at the two halves of her reflection looking back at her in the spotless silver doors.

Or more specifically at the huge, great, hulking, fluorescent-white garment bag hanging from her right hand. The one she'd completely forgotten about even while her right hand now felt as if it would never feel the same again.

The one with the hot-pink words 'Wedding Dress Fire Sale!' glaring back at her in reverse.

CHAPTER TWO

'I'LL be damned,' said Gabe to the dark wood panelling on the inside of the lift doors as he rubbed at the back of one hand with his thumb where the heat from the touch of his new neighbour's skin still registered.

During the endless trudge through Customs, the drive from the airport with its view over Melbourne's damp grey cityscape, then with the winter wind blowing in off Port Phillip Bay and leaching through his clothes to his very bones as he'd waited for the cabbie's credit card machine to work, Gabe had struggled to find one thing about Melbourne that had a hope in hell of inducing him to stay a minute longer than absolutely necessary.

Then fate had slanted him a sly wink in the form of a neighbour with wintry blue eyes, legs that went on for ever, and blonde tousled waves cool enough to bring Hitchcock himself back to life. Hell, the woman even had the restive spark in her eye of a classic Hitchcock blonde; fair warning to any men who dared enter it would be at their own peril.

Not that he needed any such warning. Three seconds after he signed whatever his business partner, Nate, wanted him to sign he'd be on the kerb whistling for a cab to get him back to the airport. Not even the kick of chemistry that had turned the small space of the lift into a travelling hothouse would change that.

Gabe rehitched his bags, then shoved his hands into the deep pockets of his jacket, closed his eyes and leant back into the corner of the lift. As the memory of where he was, and why he'd left in the first place, pressed against the corners of his mind he shook it off. And, merely because it was better than the alternative, he let his thoughts run to the cool blonde instead.

About the way she'd nibbled at her full lower lip, as if it tasted so good she couldn't help herself. And the scent of her that had filled the small space, sweet and sharp and delicious, making his gut tighten like a man who hadn't eaten in a week. As for the way she'd looked at him as if he was some great inconvenience one moment, and the next as if she wanted nothing more than to eat him up with a spoon...?

'Wow,' he shot out, eyes flying open, hands gripping the railing that ran hip high along the back of the lift, feet spread wider to combat the sudden sense that his centre of gravity had shifted. The lift had rocked. Hadn't it? Try as he might he felt nothing but the gentle sway as it rose through the shaft.

Jet lag, he thought. *Or vertigo.* He sniffed out a laugh. He had Hitchcock on the brain. The guy was no dummy and was also clearly terrified of cool blondes. Did one thing inform the other? No doubt. If a woman looked like trouble, chances were she'd be trouble. And Gabe was a straight-up guy who preferred his pleasures the same.

He pulled himself to standing and ran both hands over his face. He needed sleep. Clearly. He imagined his custom-built king-sized bed which a week earlier he'd had shipped back from South America. The deal there was done anyway, and he'd ship it out again the second the next investment opportunity grabbed him. He imagined falling face down in the thing and sleeping for twelve hours straight.

For some, home was bricks and mortar. For others it was family. For Gabe it was where the work was. And wherever in the world he got wind of an exceptional business idea in need of someone with the guts and means to invest, that was where he sent his bed. And his pillow—flattened to the point he probably didn't even need the thing. And his mattress with the man-shaped dint right smack bang in the middle that fitted his spreadeagled body to perfection.

Moments before he fell asleep on his feet the lift deposited him neatly at his floor. Exactly as it was made to do.

Gabe yawned till his ears popped, fumbled for the keys to the apartment he'd never seen. The apartment he'd bought to shut Nate up, when Nate had maintained he needed a place in Melbourne considering the company they jointly owned was based there.

He stood in the open doorway. Compared with the barebones hotel room that had been home the past few months it was gargantuan, taking up the entire top floor of the building. And yet somehow claustrophobic with its dark colour palette and the huge grey windows along one wall that matched the drizzly grey world outside them.

'Well, Gabe,' he said to his blurry reflection, 'you're certainly not in Rio any more.'

He slid the carry-on and laptop bags from his shoulder onto the only piece of furniture in the whole room, a long L-shaped black lounge that cut the space in half. Only to be met with a loud 'Arghuraguragh!'

Jet lag and/or vertigo gone in an instant, Gabe spun on his heel, fists raised, heart thundering in his chest, to find a man reposing on his couch.

'Nate,' Gabe said, bent at the waist, hands on his knees as he dragged his breath back to normal. 'You scared me half to death.'

Gabe's best mate and business partner sat up, his hair sticking up at the side of his head. 'Making sure you got here in one piece.'

'Making sure I arrived at all, more like.' Gabe stood, cricked his back. 'Tell me you went one better and filled my fridge.'

'Sorry. Did get doughnuts though. They're on the bench.'

Gabe glanced at the familiar white box as he passed it on the way to the silver monolith of a fridge, opening it to find it was empty bar the maker's instructions. A frisson of disquiet skittered down his spine. If that wasn't ready...

He strode across the gargantuan space towards the great double doors he could only assume led to the bedroom, whipped them open to find—

No bed.

Swearing beneath his breath, Gabe ran his hand up and down the back of his neck so fast he felt sparks.

Nate's hand landed upon his shoulder a half-second before his laughter. 'Your couch looks a treat but it's not in the least bit comfortable.'

'You didn't seem to mind a moment ago,' Gabe growled.

'I can power-nap anywhere. It's a gift born of chronic insomnia.'

Gabe slowly and deliberately shut the bedroom doors, unable to even look at the space where his bed ought to be.

'Hotel?'

'The thought of going back out into that cold is making my teeth ache.'

'I'd offer my couch, but it's my decorator's cruel joke. God-awful leather thing with buttons all over it.'

'Thanks, but I'd be afraid I'd catch something.'

Nate grinned and backed away. 'I have seen with my own two eyes that you're here, so my work is done. Catch you at the office Monday. Remember where it is?'

Gabe's answer was a flat stare. He was lucky—or unlucky more like—to end up in Melbourne once every two or three years, but he knew where his paychecks came from.

Nate clicked his fingers as he wavered at the front door.

'Almost forgot. Need to make a right hullabaloo now you're back. Housewarming party Friday night.'

Gabe shook his head. He'd be long gone by Friday. Wouldn't he?

'Too late,' said Nate. 'Already in motion. Alex and some of the old uni gang are coming. A few clients. Some fine women I met walking the promenade just now—'

'Nate—'

'Hey, consider yourself lucky. I'm so giddy you're here I contemplated dropping flyers from a plane.'

And then Nate was gone. Leaving Gabe in his dark, cavernous, cold, empty apartment. Alone. The grey mist of Port Phillip Bay closing in on his wall of windows like a swarm of bad memories, pretty much summing up how he felt about the possibility that he might still be there in a week's time.

Before he turned into a human icicle, Gabe tracked down the remote for the air-con and cranked it up as hot as it would go.

He found some bed linen in a closet, then, back in his bedroom doorway, looked glumly at the empty space where his bed ought to be. He stripped down to his smalls and made a pile with blankets and a too big pillow and lay down on the floor, and the second he closed his eyes fatigue dragged him into instant sleep.

And he dreamt.

Of a cool feminine hand stroking the hair at the back of his neck, a hot red convertible rumbling beneath his thighs as he eased it masterfully around the precarious roads of a cliff face somewhere in the south of France. When the car pulled into a lookout, the cool owner of the cool hand slid her cool blonde self onto his lap, her sweet sharp scent hitting the back of his mouth a half-second before her tongue followed. Gabe's dream self thought, *Hitchcock, eat your heart out.*

* * *

That night at The Brasserie—one of a string of crowded restaurants lining the New Quay Promenade—when Mae told her fiancé, Clint, about Paige's little purchase, he choked on his food. Literally. A waiter had to give him the Heimlich. They made quite a stir, ending up with the entire restaurant cheering and Paige hunching over her potato wedges and hiding her face behind both hands.

Clint recovered remarkably to ask, 'So what happened between us pouring you into a cab after drinks last night and this morning to have cured you of your no-marriage-for-Paige-ever stance? Cabbie give you the ride of your life?'

Paige dropped her fingers to give Clint a blank stare. Grinning, he put his hands up in surrender before smartly returning to checking the footy scores on his phone.

She didn't bother telling him there had not been any curing her doubt as to the existence of happily ever afters. But she neglected to say that there had been one ride she couldn't seem to wipe from her mind. A ride in a lift with some kind of tall, dark and handsome inducement that got a girl to thinking about all sorts of things she wouldn't admit out loud without the assistance of too many cocktails.

She dropped her hands to her belly where she could still feel the hum of his deep voice.

As she'd done a dozen times through the day, she brought her thoughts back to the fluoro white bag covered in hot-pink writing currently hanging over the back of her dining chair.

The fact that Gabe Hamilton had got his flirt on while she was carrying a wedding dress made him indiscriminate at best. And the kind of man she wouldn't touch with a ten-foot pole. Fidelity meant a great deal to Paige. She'd worked for the same company since uni. Had the same best friend since primary school. She'd drive twenty minutes to get her favourite Thai takeaway. She'd watched her own mum crumble be-

fore her very eyes as her father confirmed his own disloyalty
again and again and again.

'Humona humona,' Mae murmured, or something along
those lines, dragging Paige back to the present. 'Move over,
Captain Jack, there's a new pirate in town.'

Clint glanced up. Whatever he saw was clearly of little
interest as he saw his chance to sneak a pork rib from Mae's
plate then went back to his phone.

Paige gave into curiosity and turned to look over her shoulder, her heart missing a beat, *again*, when she found Mr Tall,
Dark and Handsome himself warming his large hands by
the open fire in the centre of the room, his dark hair curling slightly over the collar of his bulky jacket, feet shoulder
width apart.

'Look how he's standing,' Mae said, her voice a growl.

As if used to keeping himself upright in stormy seas, Paige
thought.

Mae had other ideas. 'Like he needs all that extra room
for his package.'

'Mae!'

Mae shrugged. 'Don't look at me. Not when you could be
looking at him.'

Paige tried not to look, she really did. But while her head
knew it was best to forget about him, her hormones apparently
had fuzzier principles. She looked in time to see him push a
flap of his leather jacket aside and glide his phone from an
inside pocket, revealing a broad expanse of chest covered by
a faded T-shirt. Paige wasn't sure which move had her sali-
vating more—the brief flash of toned brown male belly as
his T had lifted, or the rhythmic slide of his thumb over the
screen of his phone.

And then he turned, his dark eyes scouring the large space.

'Get down!' Paige spun around and hunkered down in
her seat until she was half under the table. It was only when

she realised neither of her friends had said anything that she glanced up to find them both watching her with their mouths hanging open.

'Whatcha doin' down there?' Mae asked.

Paige slowly pulled herself upright. Then, wishing she had eyes in the back of her head, she muttered, 'I know him.'

'Him? Oh, *him*. Who *is* he?'

'Gabe Hamilton. He's moved in upstairs. We met in the lift this morning.'

'Annnnndddd?' Mae said, by that stage bouncing on her chair.

'Sit still. You're getting all excited for nothing. I tried to shut the door on his fingers. He suggested the lift and I were trapped in a passive-aggressive romantic entanglement. It was all very…awkward.'

Mae kept grinning, and Paige realised she was squirming on her seat.

She threw her hands in the air. 'Okay, fine, so he's gorgeous. And smells like he's come from building his own log cabin. And there might have been a little flirting.' When Mae began to clap, Paige raised a hand to cut her off. 'Oh no. That's not the best part. This all happened right after you dropped me off. While. I. Was. Carrying. The. Wedding. Dress.'

'But didn't you explain—?'

'How exactly? *So, sexy stranger, see this brand new wedding dress I'm clutching? Ignore it. Means nothing. I'm free and clear and all yours if ya want me.*'

'That'd work for me,' Clint said, nodding sagely.

Mae smacked him across the chest. He grinned and went back to pretending he wasn't listening.

'I blame you, and your man-drought theory,' Paige said. 'I would have been hard pressed not to flutter my eyelashes at anyone at that point.'

'Like if Sam the Super had turned up she would have

wanted to ravage him in the lift?' Mae muttered, shaking her head as if Paige had gone loco.

Paige couldn't stop feeling as if the world was tilting beneath her chair. Mae, of all people, should have understood her need for absolutes. The old Mae would, what with her own father's inability to be faithful. This new Mae, the engaged Mae, was too blinded by her own romance to see straight.

Paige fought the desire to shake some sense into her friend. Instead she reached for her cocktail, gulping down a mouthful of the cold tart liquid.

'It's all probably moot anyway,' Mae said, sighing afresh. 'That man is from a whole other dimension. One where men date nuclear physicists who model in their spare time. Or he's gay.'

'Not gay,' Paige said, remembering the way his gaze had caressed her face. The certainty he'd been moving closer to her the whole ride, inch by big hot inch. Jet lag or no, there'd been something there. She took a deep breath and said, 'Anyway. It doesn't matter either way. A man who flirts with a woman holding a wedding dress ought to be neutered.'

'Well, my sweet,' said Mae, perking up, 'you'll have the chance to tell him so. Because he's coming this way.'

Gabe had been about to leave when he'd seen her.

Well, he'd seen her dinner companion first—a redhead with wild curls and no qualms about staring at strangers. After which he'd noticed his fine and fidgety neighbour's blonde waves tumbling down a back turned emphatically in his direction. If she'd given him a smile and a wave he might well have waved and gone home. But the fact that the woman he'd planned to ignore was ignoring him right on back tugged at his perverse gene and sent him walking her way.

'Well, if it isn't Miss Eighth Floor,' he said, resting a hand on the back of her chair.

Paige turned, her eyebrows raised, her smile cool. But the second her deep blue eyes locked onto his, his blood thickened, his lungs got tight, and he felt a sudden surge of affection for the hard floor of his room.

Hitchcock be damned, he thought as the memory of those cool blonde waves tickling his chest as she'd ridden him in his convertible slammed into his head. It might only have been a dream but his libido clearly didn't give a lick. 'When I said I'd see you around I wasn't expecting it to be quite so soon.'

'Living in the same building we'll be bound to run into one another.'

'Lucky us.' He gave her a smile, the kind he knew gave off all the right signals. Her eyes flared, but she physically pulled her reaction back. In fact from her pale pink fingernails gripping the table, to the ends of her gorgeously tousled hair, she screamed high maintenance. Complication. Trouble.

And yet the smile tugged higher at the corners of his mouth.

Maybe it was the challenge. Maybe it was the dream. Maybe it was that he suddenly had time on his hands, time he'd rather spend in doing than thinking. But as Gabe looked into those hot and cold blue eyes he knew he was going to get to know this woman.

A loud clearing of the throat sent them both looking to Paige's friend.

Paige said, 'Gabe Hamilton, this is my friend Mae. Her fiancé, Clint.'

Leaning across the table to shake hands with enthusiasm, Mae said, 'I hear you've just flown in from overseas.'

When the table shook and Mae scrunched up her face, Gabe got the feeling she'd been duly kicked under the table. So Little Miss Cool had been talking about him to her friends, had she? Perhaps this would be easier than he thought. Though

rather than that taking the edge off the challenge, the energy
inside coiled tighter still.

He sourced a spare chair at the next table and dragged it
over, sliding it next to Paige, who pretended she'd suddenly
found a mark on her dinner plate fascinating.

'Brazil,' he said to Mae, pressing his toes into the floor
as Paige sat straight as an arrow in the seat beside him. 'I'm
just back from Brazil.'

'Seriously?' said Mae. 'Hear that, Paige? Gabe's been to
Brazil.'

Paige glared at her friend. 'Thanks, Mae. I did hear.'

Mae leant her chin on her palm as she asked, 'Back for
good, then?'

'Not,' he said. Not that he was about to tell these nice
people that given the choice he'd rather be neck deep in pi-
ranha-infested waters than stay in their home town. 'Here on
business for a few days.'

'Pity,' said Mae, while Paige said nothing. Those bedroom
eyes of hers remained steadfastly elsewhere. Until Mae added,
'Paige has a total thing for Brazil.'

'Does she, now?'

At the low note that had crept into his voice, Paige's eyes
finally flickered to his. He smiled back, giving her a silent
'hi' with his eyes. She saw it too. Her eyes widened, all simmering heat trapped beneath the cool surface, and her chest
rose and fell at the same time as his, as if she was breathing
with him.

Gabe's libido, which had been warming up nicely since the
moment he'd spied her, went off like a rocket. He gripped the
back of her chair, his thumb mere millimetres from the dip
between her shoulders. When Paige breathed deep, arching
away from his almost touch, her nostrils flaring, her throat
working, he swore beneath his breath.

'Why, yes,' said Mae cheerfully, seemingly oblivious to

the sexual tension near pulsing between her tablemates. 'In fact she's spent the past few months trying to convince her boss she has to shoot their summer catalogue there.'

'Really?' Gabe said, dragging his gaze to her friend in an effort to keep himself decent. 'So what kind of work does Paige do?'

'I'm brand manager for a home-wares retailer,' Paige shot back, a distinct huskiness now lighting her voice. *Oh, yeah, this was going to be fun.* 'Most of next summer's range is Brazilian. In feel if not in actuality.' Then, as if the words were being pulled from her with pliers, 'And what were you doing in Brazil?'

If he'd been in need of a bucket of water to cool the trouble brewing in his pants, Paige asking about his work was a fine alternative. He'd learned the hard way that the less people knew about his business, the better. *What big information you have! All the better to screw you with, my dear.* 'This time around, coffee,' he allowed. 'You like coffee?'

'Coffee?' She blinked, the change of subject catching her off guard. She shifted till she was facing him a little more. Her eyes now flitting between his, the push and pull of attraction working up the same energy he'd felt at their first meeting. Then she slid her bottom lip between her teeth, leaving it moist and plump as she said, 'Depends who's making it.'

Gabe felt the ground beneath him dip and sway as it had in the lift and he gripped the back of her chair for dear life. *Vertigo,* he thought, *definitely vertigo.* Hitchcock had been a glutton for punishment to keep going back to his twitchy blondes. Yet Gabe made no move to leave, so what did that make him?

'Why coffee?' Mae asked.

'Hmm?'

'The reason you were in Brazil. Do you grow it? Pick it? Drink it? Brew it?'

Gabe paused again, calculating. But the deal was done.

He'd gone over every full stop, met every employee, vetted every business practice to make sure the product line was legitimate and above reproach. And profitable, of course. Nothing, and nobody, could ruin it now.

'I'm investing in it. Or in a mob called Bean There, to be more specific,' he said.

But it was too late. Paige had sensed his hesitation and, for whatever reason, her knees slid away from his and back under the table. Hot and cold? The woman ran from fire to frost quicker than he could keep up.

At that point Gabe seriously considered cutting his losses. But at his heart Gabe was a shark. When he got his teeth in something it took a hell of a lot for him to let go. It was why he was the best at what he did, why he'd never met a deal he couldn't close. She didn't know it yet, but the longer she sat there shutting him out, the deeper she sank her hook beneath his ribs.

A voice from across the table said, 'Oh, I love those places! Those little hole-in-the-wall joints, right? One guy and a coffee machine.'

'That's the ones.'

'Ooh, how exciting,' Mae said, 'insider information! From our very own corporate pirate.'

Gabe flinched so hard he bit his tongue. It was as though the woman had the book on which buttons to press to make his jewels up and shrivel. 'It's common knowledge,' he avowed, 'so feel free to spread the word. The more money they make, the more steak dinners for me.'

Clearly the time had come to retreat and regroup. He pulled himself to standing.

'Stay!' said Mae.

'Thanks, but no. Beauty sleep to catch up on.'

He looked to Paige to check if she was even half as moved by his imminent departure, only to find her sitting primly with her fingers clasped together as if she didn't give a hoot. Yet her gaze had other ideas. Beginning somewhere in the region of his fly, it did a slow slide up his torso, pausing for the briefest moments on his chest, his neck, his mouth, before landing on his eyes.

'Friday,' he heard himself say in a voice that was pure testosterone. 'Housewarming party at mine. You're all welcome.'

'We'll be there,' said Mae.

Gabe reached out to shake Mae's hand. Then Clint's. He saved Paige for last.

'Paige,' he said, and he lifted her hand into his. His dream had been wrong on that point at the very least. Her hand was as warm as if she'd been lying in the sun. As for her eyes... As if touching him had unleashed all that she'd been trying to hold back, desire flooded them, then exploded in his chest like a bonfire, before settling as a hot ache in his groin.

Damn.

She pulled her hand away. Her brow furrowing, as if she wasn't sure what had just happened. He knew. And hell if he didn't want more.

'Friday,' he said, waiting until she nodded. Then he shot the table a salute before walking away, his entire body coiled in discomfort, his field of vision a pinprick in a field of red mist as blood pounded through his body way too fast.

He headed back to his apartment. To his hard floor. The ache lingering deep in his gut. And this time as he stared at the ceiling in his big empty bedroom, sleep eluded him.

He wondered how his neighbour might react if he showed up at her door asking for a bed for the night, carrying his box of doughnuts and wearing nothing but boxer shorts and a smile. The only thing keeping him from finding out was her patent determination to remain cool. If he read her even slightly wrong, boxer shorts might be not quite enough protection.

CHAPTER THREE

LATER that night, when the lift doors closed several minutes after Paige had pressed the button for the eighth floor, she leant against the wall, getting herself comfortable for the ride ahead of her.

The second she closed her eyes, the picture projected onto the backs of her lids was the view of Gabe Hamilton as he'd walked away. All long strong legs and loping sexy strides. The thought of him made her tingle all over. Like static, only...hotter.

As it turned out, whatever she thought of Gabe Hamilton's scruples about flirting with a possibly engaged woman, she hadn't imagined the spark. It was there, in the directness of his gaze. The purpose in his smile. He knew he was gorgeous and wasn't above using it to get what he wanted. And if she had even half a sense about such things, he wanted her.

Paige crossed her legs at the ankle and slid her thumb between her front teeth and nibbled for all she was worth.

She'd never been one of those girls who went after men who looked as if they sinned a dozen times a day and twice on Sundays. Sure, she could appreciate the appeal. The desire to tame the untameable. But she'd seen the emotional destruction a man with that kind of concentrated charm left in his wake. And while she wasn't a big believer in happy endings, more than that she was determined never to act in such a way as to have an unhappy one.

Unfortunately, she hadn't dated any good guys of late either. The why of it niggled at a shadowy corner of her brain, as if it should be more obvious. But while her head filled with thoughts of Gabe Hamilton, and his hot hand and hotter eyes, she was finding it hard to think straight at all.

She pulled herself upright, shook out her hands, and paced around the lift.

The sorry truth was, she'd met enough 'good guys' who turned out to be jerks in the end anyway. So wouldn't it be better to know a guy was trouble from the outset? Wouldn't it be easier to protect herself if she knew up front exactly what she was in for? Wouldn't it be something to let go and open up to all that sinful, seductive intensity just once?

Her eyes scrunched tight and she stopped pacing.

Despite evidence to the contrary, Gabe Hamilton didn't seem like a jerk. He seemed…focused. Sexy as all get out. More than a little bit intimidating. And by his own admission, he was only in town for a bit. Which was a plus. Maybe the biggest plus of all. She wasn't after a relationship with the guy. Just a safe place to dip her toes into the dating pool. A kiss. Maybe a little messing about. Or a good and proper tumble.

She sucked in a deep breath and let it go.

Anyway, she didn't have to decide that night. She had till Friday at the very least to think about it, so long as they never shared the lift in that time. Not that it had ever done right by her before.

When the lift made its first stop she twirled her hair over one shoulder, stifled a yawn, glanced at the number to check which floor besides the eighth she'd landed on, then realised the lift had taken her to the top. To the penthouse.

She slowly stood to attention, her hands tight on her purse in an attempt to get a grip on the sensual wave rising through her knowing Gabe Hamilton was close. And with everything she had she willed the lift to descend.

But the lift being the lift, the doors slid open, and stayed open, leaving her standing staring into a large dark entrance boasting two shiny black double doors leading to the only apartment on the floor, one of which bumped as the handle twisted.

Paige shrank to the back of the lift, but there was no hiding. Every last wisp of air bled from her lungs as Gabe stepped through the doorway.

He looked up, saw her, and stopped. A muscle worked in his jaw. It was a testament to how her senses were working nineteen to the dozen that she even noticed that tiny movement, considering what the guy was wearing. Or not wearing, to be more precise.

Pyjama bottoms. Long, soft, grey-checked pyjama bottoms. And nothing else. After that it was like a freeway collision inside her head, the way the gorgeous bits of him piled on top of one another. The deep tan that went all over. The large bare feet. The hair, all mussed and rugged. Arms that looked strong enough to lift a small car. A wholly masculine chest with the kind of muscle definition no mere mortal had the right to possess. And a happy trail of dark hair arrowing beneath his pyjama bottoms...

'Paige?' he said, his devil-deep voice putting her knees on notice.

'Hey,' she croaked back.

'I heard the lift.'

'And here it is.' Going for unflappable, she cocked a hip and waved a hand towards the open doors like a game-show hostess. She failed the moment the heat rising through her body pinked across her cheeks.

A hint of a smile gathered in Gabe's dark eyes, tilting his gorgeous mouth. 'Did you want me for something?'

'Did I want you—? No. *No*.' She laughed only slightly hysterically. 'I was heading home, but the lift, it—'

'Brought you here of its own accord.'

'It's contrary that way.'

'So you've said,' he said, planting his feet and crossing his arms across his chest, a broad, brown, beautiful mass of rises and falls that brought a flash flood to the desert that had been her mouth.

Paige dragged her eyes to the huge starburst on the ceiling as she said, 'It's late and you must have things to do, bags to unpack, sleep to catch up on.'

He slowly shook his head. 'I'm used to living out of a bag. And for some reason I'm not all that tired right now.'

'I could be here a while.'

He leaned against the doorjamb. 'Or you could come in.'

The blood thundered so hard and fast through her she couldn't be sure she'd heard him right. 'Come in?'

'I can tell you everything I know about Brazil.'

Paige blinked. Simply unable to find the words to—

'And I have doughnuts.'

And at that she laughed. Loud. Nervous energy pouring from her in waves. 'Well, that's original. I mean, I've been offered "coffee" before of course. Even a good old-fashioned nightcap on occasion. But never doughnuts.'

He watched her, all dark, and leaning and so much man. Her mouth now watering like Niagara Falls, she swallowed again before saying, 'What is a nightcap anyway? Sounds like it should be one of those Wee Willie Winkie hats with the pompom on the end—'

'Paige.'

'I…' Her eyes slid to his naked chest as if they'd stayed too long away. 'I feel overdressed for doughnuts.'

'Only one way to fix that.'

She realised then that he'd moved aside so that the way through his open front door was clear. Inviting.

Her body waved towards the open lift doors, gripped with a desire to step across that threshold and into the arms of one big hot male, but she caught herself at the last second. She couldn't. Could she? She'd met him that morning, for Pete's sake. Knew nothing about him other than his name, address and occupation— Okay, so that was pretty standard. As for the way he made her feel—as if she were melting from the inside out—by looking at her?

The lift binged, the doors began to close, and Paige slipped through the gap, the bump and hum of the lift descending without her echoing through her shaking limbs. Other than that the dark foyer was perfectly quiet. No music. Just the sound of her shaky breath sliding past her lips.

She'd have a doughnut. Get to know him a little. Maybe even grab him at the last for a goodnight kiss. She could handle a guy like Gabe for one night if that was what it took to find her dating legs again; legs that wobbled like a marionette's as she made her way to his door.

She held her breath as she slipped past him but there was no avoiding that complex masculine scent radiating from his warm naked skin.

Inside, the apartment was darker still. When he went towards the raised kitchen, Paige headed in the opposite direction where cloud-shrouded moonlight spilled through the wall of ceiling-to-floor windows. And he hadn't been lying when he'd said there was nothing to unpack. In fact there wasn't much of anything at all.

No lamps, only the light of an open laptop on the kitchen bench. No pictures on the walls. Not even a big-screen TV. Just a couch, a long, sleek L-shaped thing that could fit twenty. And it looked out over the stunning water view, as if the inside of the apartment was irrelevant.

Which maybe, to him, it was. In her experience a man who refused to stamp his own personality on a place wasn't connected to it. Or those living in it with him. Hence the unrestrained frippery of the home she grew up in. If a home was where the heart was, then Gabe Hamilton's heart was most definitely not in that apartment. Probably not even in her home city. And while in the past that would have been enough to turn her on her heel without looking back, her heart began to race.

'Not a big fan of decor?' she asked, glancing across to find him in the raised kitchen where a single muted down-light now played over his naked torso, making the absolute most of his warm brown skin. He loomed over a huge white box that did, in fact, contain doughnuts. 'Or furnishings in general?'

He looked around as if he hadn't noticed how bare the place was. 'I don't spend my weekends antiquing, if that's what you mean.'

'You don't have to go that far, but you could do with a dining table. Some kitchen stools. A throw cushion or two.'

'I'd bet my left foot that no man ever looked back on his life and regretted a lack of throw cushions,' he rumbled.

'But they're like garnish on a dinner plate. You don't need it to make the meal, but that splash of colour makes your mouth water all the same.'

To that he said nothing, just watched her across the darkness, and her own mouth had never watered as much in her entire life.

'Is it just me, or is it hot in here?' she asked, peeling off her shirred blazer, her knobbly scarf, and throwing them over the back of a couch.

'Air-con's on heat blast. I'm acclimatising.'

Her eyes fell onto a plate of doughnuts he was piling high. She edged towards the scent of sugar. And him. 'Turn the heat down and put on a sweater. Much more comfortable.'

'For who?'

For her clearly. She'd been inside his place for less than two minutes and already a drop of sweat slid between her shoulder blades, trickled down her spine, and pooled in the dent at the bottom of her back.

As for him? His gaze lingered on her cream silk top, hovered over the minuscule spaghetti straps, then swept down her bare arms. Paige fought the urge to cross her arms across her chest, as even in the sweltering room her nipples contracted to aching peaks.

'Nah,' he said as his eyes moseyed back up to hers, 'I like the heat.'

Leaving the doughnuts to the elements, Gabe edged around the island, his dark eyes locked onto her. Heart pounding, she backed up a step, and her backside hit the couch.

'Would you prefer I turn it down?' he asked, his voice dropping as he neared.

God, no, she thought. By the twitch at the corner of his beautiful mouth, she realised she'd clearly said it out loud. *Bad habit. Must break.*

He moved closer, and, breathing deep, she caught his wholly masculine scent that made her certain he could change a tyre, and build a fire, and wrestle a shark all before breakfast and not break a sweat.

And she knew. There would be no doughnuts that night. There would be no lines drawn, or contracts agreed upon. Her world contracted until all she knew was moonlight, heat, breath, her throbbing pulse. And Gabe. Half naked, his dark gaze searing into hers.

Then, right when she thought she might die from the tension coiling within her, he took one last long step and his big hand was in her hair, and his hot mouth was on hers.

Explosions went off behind her eyes, beneath her skin,

deep in her belly until her whole body was awash with heat that had nothing to do with the sweltering air.

Her hands were in his hair gouging tracks in the lush softness. Her leg was wrapped around his. Her body arcing into him as every part of her that could meld with his did.

She felt his smile against her mouth. A smile of pure and utter conquest. She nipped at his bottom lip. *Take that.*

He stilled, all that strength bunching, waiting, compounding. In the stillness his heat beat against her skin. The energy coursing through his veins found a matching beat in hers. Every sense was on a delectable high.

When the wait for retribution became too much, she rolled against him. Softly. Fitted herself along his length. Purposefully. Slid her hands to the back of his head, and her tongue across his bottom lip, tasting the tender spot she'd bitten.

This, she thought. This was what she'd needed. This raw release. Who needed promises? Who needed commitment? Of all times for her friend to pop into her head, this was not a winner. Clint joined Mae as they smiled at one another in that gooey way they had when they thought nobody was watching. In fact, they didn't really care who was watching, they were too busy watching one another.

Paige shook her head in an effort to remove the image from her mind, and the usual dull ache it had created deep in her belly.

As if he sensed her retreat, Gabe closed his big strong arms around her, wrapping her in heat and muscle and might. He pressed her back and kissed her slow and deep until she was nothing bar a flood of sensation pouring hot and thick through her whole body. His scent curled itself about her, warm, spicy, mouth-watering, until she couldn't remember what her mouth tasted like before it tasted like him.

This. The word whispered through her again.

And things only got better from there for a really long time.

As he found the sweet spot below her right ear, sucking her skin into his hot mouth. The hollow at the base of her neck with his tongue. The line of lace where the edge of her bra met swollen sensitive skin. Until her mind was a haze. Her body pure vibration.

She groaned in frustration as his lips were gone from hers, but then his arm slid beneath her legs and he lifted her as if she weighed nothing. She wrapped her arms around his shoulders and held on tight, her breath shooting from her lungs as light, bright, startled laughter.

When her eyes found his, dangerous and intense, the laughter dried up in her throat, the pleasure of it trickling down to her toes.

She bumped in his arms as he kicked open what must have been the bedroom door. Then he stopped so fast she gripped on tighter so as not to fly out of his arms.

'Dammit,' he said. Followed by a whole slew of words worthy of any pirate.

'Problem?'

He slid her down his body, his hardness giving her no doubt he was as deep in this thing as she was. Then he took her by the shoulders and turned her so that she could see into his bedroom.

It was huge, half the size of her whole apartment. Gorgeous window mouldings and cornices, with another fabulous art deco sun-burst in the centre of the high ceiling. Occupational hazard, it took her half a second to imagine a reading lamp and great chair in the near corner. A small antique desk with enough room for his laptop below the wide window. Lush dark curtains pooling on the shiny floor. None of which were there.

But decor and character weren't the only things the room was lacking.

It had no bed.

A small sound of desperation escaped her lips as her eyes

roved quickly over the scrunched-up blankets on the floor, none of which looked terribly conducive to the kind of action her poor neglected body was screaming for.

She swore beneath her breath. Or at least she thought she had. The rumble of laughter at her back told her she'd said it out loud. Again.

Then his hand slid around her waist, tucked beneath her top, and found her sensitive stomach. She melted against him, against the hardness pressed against her backside. He swept her hair aside and his teeth grazed her shoulder and if she hadn't pressed her thighs together she'd have orgasmed on the spot.

She spun in his arms, her hands finding his firm chest. His body filled her view, blocking out any light that dared come between them. His face was all darkness and shadows, his skin like a furnace, his scent like pure testosterone. Instinct had her swaying back, only to find herself up against the doorjamb.

'Gabe...' Paige said, her spine merging with the line of the doorway.

His hand landed on the doorjamb above her head. She breathed out. Slow, shaky, every ounce of oxygen leaving her body until she was weak with desire. Heat licking and trembling at her core. She couldn't feel her feet. Could feel the beat of his heart against her palms all the way in the backs of her knees.

Her chest felt tight, her lungs dysfunctional. She wasn't sure how much longer she could hang onto her self-control. But if she pulled back now, how long till she had such a chance again? If she turned away from *this*, she might as well buy a cat, get a blue rinse and be done with men for ever.

She curled her fingers and traced her nails through the crisp dark hair of his chest. Pressed her lips gently to his flat nipple, before tracing it with her tongue. Her hands, getting greedy now, roved over the bumps of his six-pack, the hard muscles at his hips, over what turned out to be a damn fine example of male backside.

Something close to a roar escaped Gabe's mouth as his fingers curled into her hair and tugged, sending her head sliding down the vertical strip of wood. Then his mouth found hers, any gentleness or exploration gone, his lips and tongue making a joke of any last resistance she might have had.

He tucked his fingers beneath the strap of her top, sending it cascading down her arm, revealing the lacy half-cup of her bra. His eyes, dark as night, watched as his palm cupped her breast, then his thumb ran over the dark centre. Chills running up and down her body, she pressed her feet into the floor and she bit her lip so as not to cry out.

His hand found her hip, his thumb swirling over her belly button. Then before she knew it her jeans were unbuttoned, the zip sliding open one tooth at a time. Paige's hands went to Gabe's hips, grabbing on for dear life as his big hand slid inside her pants, cupping her. Then he slid a slow, strong finger along the seam of her underwear.

She bucked as a shot of the most exquisite pleasure pierced her, blocking out every other sensation.

Then his mouth was on hers again, taking her blissful agony and doubling it. Trebling it. Turning her thoughts to mere threads swirling in a wash of liquid heat as a finger curled beneath the hem of her underwear, dipped inside her, sending wave after wave of shock and awe through her.

Her body no longer her own, she strained towards him. The perfect insistent slide of his finger. Then two. Melting from the inside out as blood roared in her ears, all sensation rushed to her centre, and, with a cry stifled as her mouth pressed against his shoulder, she came. A riot of hot waves buffeting her from scalp to toes, again and again, before finally diffusing to a warm delicious hum.

Her skin was slick with sweat. Her lips tasted of salt. Her knuckles ached from the clench of her fingers at Gabe's hips.

Her eyes opened sluggishly as her top slid back up her torso, at the scrape of a fingernail as her strap hooked back over her shoulder. No. No! What was he doing? Even through the haze of afterglow she knew they weren't *done*. Not by half!

Her focus landed on his eyes to find them lit by a slow burn that turned her mouth dry. She traced her thumbs into the waistline of his pants and he stopped her, his expression almost pained. His voice was subterranean when he asked, 'Do you have protection?'

And she felt the floor drop out from under her.

It had been months, literally, since she'd needed a condom. Or even thought to put it on her shopping list; that was how dry her spell had been. She was on the pill of course, but she'd known this guy less than a day.

She must have looked as disappointed as she felt as Gabe's forehead thunked against the wood, his breath shooting hot and hard over her shoulder, creating fresh goose bumps in its wake. 'The closest chemist is three blocks from here.'

'If I go outside in this state I'll be arrested.'

'Or there's the stacked brunette on six.'

With palpable effort, Gabe pulled back. His dark eyes connecting with hers, the intensity coming at her making her knees buckle. 'What about her?'

'She looks the kind of girl who might have a permanent stash of such…accessories.'

After a few moments of quiet, Gabe burst out laughing. 'Not quite the impression I want to make on the neighbours, door-knocking at one in the morning with a hard-on and a request for condoms.'

Condoms, she thought. *Plural. Good God.*

'No,' she said, licking her suddenly dry lips. 'I suppose not. Even if you are only in town for a little while?'

Gabe's dark eyes seared into her as if he was actually considering it. Then after one hard breath in and out, he took her by one finger and dragged her in his wake, away from the cruel temptation of his under-utilised bedroom and back into his big under-decorated home where he gathered her clothes.

'Gabe?' she said, half apology, half despair.

He shooshed her with a glance that told her he was barely controlling himself as it was. She bit her lip and kept quiet.

Once at the lift he redressed her until she had a semblance of decency. 'In case the lift stops on another man's floor,' he said, the gleam in his eyes making it clear he didn't believe her story for a second. 'Wouldn't want him to get the wrong idea.'

'But—'

The lift opened. His jaw tightened and Paige was sure he was about to kiss her again. Her lips opened, her breath hitched, her skin came over all hot and tingly. But he turned her on the spot and gave her a little shove inside. 'Scram. Before I start something neither one of us will be able to stop.'

Compared with his apartment, the inside of the lift was freezing cold. She crossed her arms across her chest to hold in the warmth. To hold in the delicious fizzing in her blood. The wonderful heaviness between her legs.

What to say? *Sorry? Thanks? See you around?* In the end neither of them said anything, they just watched each other as the lift doors closed.

She slumped against the wall—her legs no longer able to support her—slapped a hand over her eyes and shook her head. What had *happened*? She'd broken her drought, that was what. And how! As the lift took her to the lobby and back a half-dozen times Paige relived every hot, rash second of it to make sure.

When the lift finally opened at her floor, she breathed out

a long shuddering sigh of relief. Considering how her day had begun, she couldn't possibly have hoped to negate that disaster so soon. But she had.

Hopefully now her life could get back to normal.

CHAPTER FOUR

PAIGE's phone rang, but no matter how hard she reached, how hard she tried, it was never enough. She couldn't connect.

She woke up with a start, her heart thumping in her chest, her legs entangled in a mess of sheets, to find light pouring through her bedroom window. A quick glance at her bedside clock told her it was after ten. Once she realised it was a Sunday she relaxed. Wow, she hadn't slept in that late in—

The buzzing of her landline told her she hadn't dreamt that part at least.

She reached out, grabbed the phone, lay back on her bed with the back of her hand over her eyes to block out the light. Expecting it to be her mum, she sighed, 'Hiya.'

'Sleep well?'

Words became impossible as her mouth fell wide open. She had to swallow, twice, before saying, 'Gabe?'

'Making sure you got home okay last night.'

Her head was spinning. How did he get her number? She hadn't given it to him. He'd looked her up? He'd looked her up! *Oh, calm down. It doesn't mean anything. He's just being gentlemanly.* Though what he'd done to her up against the doorjamb the night before was so far from gentlemanly she had to cross her legs to keep from suffering a relapse.

'Paige?'

'I hardly had to brave the night. I'm four floors down.'

'As I well know.' The heat in Gabe's voice had Paige slid-ing deeper under her sheets. Until he added, 'By way of a lift that, according to you, is contrary.'

'You still think I'm making it up, don't you?'

'Don't get me wrong, I'm not complaining. In fact I've de-veloped a soft spot for the thing.'

She could all but see his seductive smile down the phone. Feel his warm breath on her neck. His hot hands on her skin. How had she convinced herself a night with Gabe Hamilton would be enough? Maybe it would have been, if either of them had come with protection. And maybe she'd turn into a monkey at the next full moon.

Whatever might have been, after last night he'd been left wanting, and she was left wanting more. And not just getting out there and dating again more. Him more. Big dark Gabe Hamilton more. That was what came of diving in head first when she'd meant to test the water with a tentative toe. But it was too late to think about what she should have done. She was in this thing now. Why not make the most of it?

'Where are you?' she asked. Her body began to feel hot and soft by turns at the hope he would say he was outside her door.

'Why?'

'No reason.'

'Liar,' he rumbled. Not only did the man have a voice that could send a nun into a fit of hot trembles, he knew what to do with it. 'I'm at Customs. Tearing the place down in search of my bed.'

'Couldn't sleep?'

'Not so much. You?'

'I slept fine.' Deep, dreamy, delicious.

The low notes of Gabe's laughter vibrated down the phone. And Paige bit her lip so as not to say anything else incrimi-nating.

'Glad to hear you're safe and sound. And well slept. Now

I've gotta see a man about a bed. See you 'round, Eighth Floor.' And then he was gone.

Paige pressed the phone to her hot ear a moment longer before she let her arm flop sideways, the phone dangling from her hand. She stared at the ceiling, at the bouncing blobs of sunlight reflecting off the prism dangling from the corner of her dressing-table mirror.

He'd checked to see if she made it home. Which was actually quite lovely. Kind of a good guy thing to do, in fact. But then he'd made no noise about when, or even if, she'd see him again before Friday's party. Which was a decidedly bad boy thing to do.

She rolled onto her tummy and pressed her face into her pillow. If only he were outside her door with a condom tucked in the back pocket of his old jeans. Then he could have his wicked way with her, and they'd be even, and that would be that. Perhaps. Probably not.

It was a Sunday, she had nowhere else to be, so she closed her eyes and pictured herself flinging open her front door to find him standing there after all, though this time in her head he wore black leather trousers, a loose white shirt open to the navel, an eye-patch. He was so big and tall he'd fill her small kitchen—

Her eyes flew open and she sat up with a start as she remembered the wedding dress in its fluorescent bag still hanging over her dining chair.

She rubbed the heels of her palms against her eye socket and breathed out hard. Then she caught a glimpse of herself in the dressing-table mirror. Her eyes were smudged with old eyeliner, her hair a scrambled mess. And her mouth? It tasted like three-week-old bread.

Looking as she looked, with a wedding dress in her kitchen, hearing one note of that voice and she would still have let him into her apartment in half a second flat. No, she would have dragged him in. Had she completely lost her self-control?

That was that. Until his party Friday she was using the stairs.

As Gabe leaned against the wall of the lift transporting him silently to the fifteenth floor offices of BonaVenture Capital he couldn't help comparing it with the one at the Botany Apartments. Light, bright, luxuriously spacious and prompt as this one was, it hadn't the added benefit of having deposited pure temptation in the shape of a leggy blonde at his door two nights before. He knew which he preferred, hands down.

He was quite sure this casual dalliance would end up being a most welcome postscript to the unwelcome trip. Casual being the key word.

He liked women. Downright adored some of them. He'd been raised by a strong woman—his gran, after his parents died a week before his tenth birthday—so he respected the hell out of them. But his work kept him on the move, which made casual more workable. That, and the fact that the one and only time he'd attempted a hearts and roses relationship he'd been burned to a crisp.

He shifted his stance, but the discomfort that had settled over him remained. He preferred not to look back to that time. It was a big black hole in his past with the capability to suck him in if he gave it half a chance. Being back in Melbourne, heading into the BonaVenture offices where it had all come to a head made it nearby impossible *not* to remember, but he was determined to try.

And if losing himself in the warm, willing arms of Paige Danforth every now and then helped, then who was he to argue?

He was rubbing at the bite marks she'd left on his shoulder when the lift dinged. He pressed his feet into the floor and held his breath, only to lose it in a rush when the doors opened to an expansive foyer with a shining dark wooden floor, blood-red walls, and sunlight seeming to pour from every corner of the place even though he couldn't see a single window.

He glanced back at the floor number to make sure lifts all over the city hadn't suddenly gone mad.

It was only when he looked up that he saw a sign twice as long as he was tall advertising *BonaVenture Capital* in elegant white type that he was sure he was in the right place. This was his company, only nothing like it had been when he'd last been in Melbourne. Two years before? Three? Now he remembered Nate carrying on about paint swatches during a lot of emails and calls at one point. He'd agreed to Nate spending whatever he liked on the refit so long as he didn't have to read another memo about the critical difference between Egg White Omelette and Alabaster Dream. Whichever way Nate had gone, it worked.

'Wow,' he bit out, shocked laughter rumbling in his chest.

Shrugging his laptop bag higher on his shoulder, Gabe slowly walked through the foyer dodging the hive of men and women in sharp suits bustling back and forth to and from hallways hidden away to the sides. To think it had been less than ten years since they'd started their venture capital firm with Nate's trust fund, Gabe's hard-earned savings from every job he'd had since he was twelve years old, and a business plan mapped out on a handful of beer napkins in a dark corner of their favourite pub while their college mates downed shots at the same table.

He remembered like it was yesterday, walking through the city the next morning, while the grey city turned gold with the magic touch of sunlight, feeling as if his life was finally about to begin. As if he literally had the whole world at his feet. As if brilliance was within his grasp.

And then a smidge under three years later he'd nearly lost it all. And he'd spent every second of the last seven years of his life making up for it.

He pressed his boots into the expensive floor and for the first time since that time he let himself wonder if they might have finally pulled through.

'Buddy!' Nate said, appearing from nowhere as if by osmosis. He must have noticed the surprise on Gabe's face as he laughed loud enough to turn heads. 'So what do you think? Gorgeous right?'

'Egg White Omelette?' he asked, pointing a thumb at the company name.

'Plain old White,' Nate said.

'Who'd have thought?'

'Want to see your office?'

'Hell, yeah,' Gabe said. Though for half a second he wondered if he deserved anything more than a hole in the wall considering how often he used the place. But Nate's excitement soon had him feeling a glimmer of anticipation at what lay beyond the doors Nate had led him to. 'So what does a partner in a schmancy joint like this get for his buck?'

Nate grinned as he opened the doors with a flourish to reveal a corner office big enough to host a pool tournament. Huge gleaming glass desk. Acres of lush dark carpet so thick you could swim in it. And that was it.

Gabe found himself forced to school his face so as not to show his intense disappointment at its lack of...something. Nate had decked it out exactly the same as his apartment. Bare. Static. Distinctly lacking *garnish*.

Nate slapped him on the back. 'I'll give you a minute to settle in. Take a lap or ten. Spin around like Julie Andrews on the hilltop.'

Then he was out of the door, leaving Gabe alone in the big empty room.

Feeling tight and antsy, he whipped the beanie off his head and ran his fingers hard through his hair, realising it needed a cut. At the rustle of his leather jacket sleeve it occurred to him he was probably the only person on the entire floor not in a suit.

'And this is why I don't come back here,' he told the walls, which could only be Light Grey. Turned out slapping on a fresh coat of paint didn't nullify his history with the place after all. He could feel it pressing in on him from every angle.

The only time he hadn't felt the pressure was when he was with Paige. Deep in the rush he got when a blush rose up her elegant neck. In pounding lust every time he witnessed the love-affair her teeth had with her bottom lip. Drunk on the taste of her sweet skin. Unleashed by the bottomless wells of desire clouding her big blue eyes.

That was that. When he wasn't doing what he came to Melbourne to do, he'd bury himself to the hilt in a most agreeable leggy blonde. And once the job was over, he wouldn't be seen for dust.

His relief was short-lived when he saw Nate's arms were filled with a pile of daunting-looking binders. Throwing them on the desk with a hearty thump, Nate said, 'No need to tell you, I'm sure, how hush-hush this has to be.'

Gabe merely stared at Nate while he waited for the irony to sink in that he was telling that to the one man who'd learned that lesson the hard way.

'Right,' Nate said, with the good grace to look sheepish. 'Now read up. And then I need your take. Are we going to list BonaVenture on the stock market, or what?'

Paige walked along the promenade, the heels of her ankle boots clacking rhythmically against the cobblestones, her long skirt clinging to her tights with static, her wool scarf flapping behind her. No wonder she loved winter. It had been nearly two days since her sexual jump start, and still every shift of fabric on her skin felt like a caress.

Her stomach rumbled expectantly at the scent of warm food flowing from the open doors of the run of restaurants below the apartment buildings lining the waterside. What the heck? She'd order The Brasserie's melt-in-your-mouth steak and chips to go.

It had been a good day. The girl who delivered morning tea had brought her favourite raspberry and white-chocolate muffins. The first product for Ménage à Moi's summer line arrived into the warehouse and looked gorgeous; all luscious fabrics and rich decadent colours, as sexy and sensuous as Carnival itself.

In fact she couldn't remember enjoying her work so much in a good while. The past few months she'd found herself growing frustrated there too, hence the hyper-motivation to get the Brazil proposal off the ground. Discontent seemed to have crept into more parts of her life than she'd realised, which made no sense. Her life was *exactly* as she'd always planned for it to be. A great apartment, a great job, a great social life, and all of it on her own terms. What more could she want?

She shook her head. What mattered was that things were looking up. At work, and in the bedroom if the number of men who'd smiled at her that day was anything to go by. She'd felt so many eyes on her it was as if she were surrounded by a cloud of flirtatious energy. She'd smiled back but kept on walking. Happy to take her time, now her wheels were back on the track.

Her mobile beeped. For a brief second she imagined a naughty message from Gabe, not that she'd heard from him since that phone call the morning before. The one that had left her with so much idle sexual energy she'd cleaned her entire kitchen, oven included.

Until she remembered he didn't have her mobile number, as only her home number was listed. He didn't even know which apartment was hers as far as she knew, only her floor. Enough to track her down if he wanted to. Which in nearly forty-eight hours he hadn't.

Why hadn't he? Unless his phone call the day before had really been about making sure she'd made it home all right and nothing more.

She shook her head again. They weren't dating. They were barely even lovers. She'd taken this thing as it had come so far and would continue to do so until it faded. Or he left. And that was that.

Nevertheless, when she checked her phone it was with a level of anticipation that left her knees quaking so much she had to pull over to the side of the cobbled path. When she saw the message was from her mum Paige's good mood took a little trip sideways.

Miss you, darling, the message read. Paige grimaced. She knew that tone. It was the one where her mum was feeling sorry for herself, and wondering, even all these years later, if divorcing Paige's dad had been the right thing to do.

Miss you too! Paige tapped into her phone, looking up every second or two to make sure nobody barrelled into her. *Want me to come over for dinner?*

You're busy. You probably have plans.

Paige bit her lip at the thought of the steak and chips for one she had planned. But her day really had been so good. And if she had any intention of retaining the new lightness in her step she really needed it to stay that way.

Next weekend, then, she tapped in. *Shopping. Last of the big spenders.*

Perfect. Love you, baby.

Paige slid her phone into her huge bag with a sigh.

She loved her mum. They'd always been close. They'd had

to be. When her dad was home, it felt as if he was biding his time till his next tour. And when he was off overseas playing cricket it was for months at a time. And as it had turned out most of that time was spent shacked up with some girl or another while her mum looked the other way...

Paige would never let herself be taken advantage of in that way. Never let someone mean so much it would be to the detriment of her own dreams. Never be made a fool of for love. Not for all the raspberry white-chocolate muffins on the planet.

When she felt the deepening evening crowd parting around her, Paige shoved her hands under her armpits to get the feeling back into them as she walked a little more slowly home.

Her recent malaise really made no sense at all. Her life was perfect because she was in complete control.

And she knew how to prove it.

Gabe lounged on his huge uncomfortable leather couch; still in his jacket and boots, legs splayed in front, neck resting against the hard back, eyes closed to the cool moonlight spilling over him.

He'd read so many memos, reports, and projections regarding taking BonaVenture public there was no doubt the company was in better shape than he and Nate could ever have dreamed it could be. He should be feeling damn proud. Vindicated. Relieved. Instead he was so restless he could barely sit still.

Gabe reached for his keys, suddenly needing to go...somewhere, anywhere but the big, empty, cold, lifeless room in which he sat. In which his every thought seemed to echo. Tracking down the one thing that seemed to quiet those thoughts seemed as good a place to start as any.

He paused at his front door when he realised he had no

idea which apartment number was hers. To hell with it—he'd knock on every door till he found the right one.

He opened his door, the lift dinged, and the doors slid open. And as if he'd conjured her from thin air, there Paige stood, soft and pink-cheeked, her blonde hair gathered off her face in a wind-tousled knot.

He opened his mouth to joke about the errant lift being his new best friend for having brought her to him again, but at the slow lift and fall of her chest, the quick swipe of her tongue over her plump bottom lip, his throat came over too tight and every muscle in his body was hit with a sudden dull ache.

If he'd had any illusions that the lift *had* brought her there by accident, they went up in flames the moment Paige lifted her right hand and unfurled a row of condoms. The silver foil wrappers swung from her fingers, glinting at him and sending tracks of fire through his veins.

A growl rose in his throat, and along with it the urge to throw her over his shoulder and drag her back into his cave. But it seemed she had ideas of her own.

She stepped out of the lift, tucked the edge of a condom wrapper between her teeth, and slid a pin from her hair, allowing it to tumble over her shoulders.

She dropped a couple of inches of height as her boots hit the floor with a double *klump klump*. Next came her scarf, uncoiling from around her neck far too slowly before it pooled at her feet. Then, as she watched him from beneath her long lashes, her breaths coming harder again, her fingers moved to the top button of her cardigan. Gabe had to dig his toes into his shoes until they hurt in order to stand still, knowing he'd never forgive himself if he didn't let this play itself out.

The long strip of silver foil still dangled from her teeth as she padded his way, and slowly, achingly slowly, undid each button until she opened it to reveal beautiful soft skin and a pale pink lace bra, the dark circles of her nipples drawing his hungry gaze.

As she came level with him she slid the demure cardigan from her shoulders, her breasts pressing forward, her back arching. When she hooked the cardigan on the end of one fine finger and twirled it over her head, at the aroma of her hot skin wafting past his nose his patience finally gave out.

Gabe lifted her off her feet and threw her over his shoulder fireman style and a whoosh of her laughter filled his lofty apartment.

The second he'd seen her all the blood in his body had headed for his groin. The second he touched her he was rock hard, ready. It took every ounce of self-control he possessed to place her down gently. Her stockinged feet landed with a soft touch on his hard floor.

She took the row of condoms from between her teeth, tucked them into the back pocket of his jeans, her hands lingering on his backside a moment. He gritted his teeth to keep from exploding on the spot as her soft hands moved up his torso to press his jacket aside. She shoved it down his arms and to the floor, and then she was on her toes, her hands beneath his T-shirt, his muscles clenching at the firm touch of her determined fingers.

And then her mouth was on his. Hot, lush, bliss. He wrapped his arms around her and lifted her bodily off the floor to feel her body against the length of his. All he could think was so hot, so soft, so beautiful. The urge to get her horizontal was getting harder to push back, when he remembered belatedly that he *still* didn't have a bed.

Irrelevant. His apartment might be stark, but his imagination was not.

He backed her into the pool of light by the kitchen, needing to see her, to live through her every reaction. Her breath hitched as he bunched her skirt in his big hands, only to come in contact with a hard man's worst nightmare. Tights. He glanced down. Dark pink, they were, like the colour of her skin when she blushed. Hell. Was she trying to kill him? When she started to shimmy her skirt down, her body rubbing against his, he was sure of it.

He thanked everything that was good and holy that the tights were going south as well. Like a man in trouble, he sank to his knees to worship those legs. Drinking in the tiny V of her G-string, her pale thighs. His hands were so dark against her pale skin as he circled her lean calves, traced her fine ankles, spent extra time on the soft spot behind her knee when he saw it made her shake.

When her fingers slid into his hair, hard and reckless, he placed a single kiss at the juncture of her thighs, marking his place, before he kissed his way up her beautiful body. The curve of her stomach, the dip of her navel, the jut of her hip, the shadow of her breasts and back to her mouth, hot, ready, waiting. The gates of heaven.

When he lifted her and plonked her on the kitchen bench, she cried out and flinched as her warm bottom met the cold granite. He swallowed her gasp, and it turned into a groan. Her lovely long legs hooked around his waist, pulling him to her with an urgency he understood.

When the heat at her centre bore against him and his tether ran out.

Pants off. Condom on. He hooked her underwear to one side and nudged the head of his penis against her centre. The swift intake of breath as he stretched her killed him just a little more.

His eyes met hers to find them wide. But hungry. Her nostrils flared with every intake of breath and her cheeks were so pink with desire he couldn't stand it any longer. He plunged into her. She cried out, pleasure and shock twisting on her face before she tilted her hips to take him deeper, tighter.

If he'd thought her mouth the gates of heaven, deep inside her was heaven itself. So hot, and tight, her muscles clenching around him as together they found a perfect rhythm.

He opened his eyes to find hers on his. Like twin blue flames, hypnotic, drawing him in until he felt the ache build deep inside. He needed every last effort to hold back, even as he rocked into her, deeper, harder. He stopped breathing altogether when her mouth dropped open, her eyes turned to liquid, her breaths to short sharp gasps, and her fingers to talons in his back as she came. Then, after a moment of the most gripping stillness, his world crashed around him in waves of hot, hard, liquid heat.

He came to and found her shaking in his arms. The chill of unheated air touched his skin, turning his sweat to ice. He lifted her off the bench, wrapping his long arms around her until their combined body heat warmed them both.

Her eyes caught his and he took her in. The cool blonde exterior. The wild heat pulsing so close to the surface. Just what he needed. For now.

He opened his mouth to say…who knew what? But she silenced him with a kiss. Soft, sensual and steadying.

Then with a light scrape of fingernails across the stubble of his cheeks, she moved away, stepped into her skirt. Padded through his still-open front door to find her clothes, putting them back on as she went before twisting her long, dishevelled hair back into a makeshift knot.

And then she was in the lift and gone, leaving him with his pants still around his ankles.

'Dear God,' Gabe said, running his hands over his face. That had been hot. Scorching. And they hadn't said a single word to one another the entire time.

He pulled up his jeans, leaving the fly undone, and leant his weary self against the kitchen bench, imagining her in the lift, skin pink from ravishing, clothes rumpled, lips swollen, pretty blue eyes as dark as night. And impossibly he found himself getting hard for her again.

Gabe pushed himself away from the bench, and padded into his bedroom on the way to his shower. He nearly tripped over his laptop bag, which had remained unopened since he'd walked in the door. In fact it had remained unopened all day.

He couldn't remember a day in the past several years he hadn't spent glued to the thing, searching out the next big idea. Collating, researching, and filling his head with every nuance of it so that he would not fail to land it. His gran had raised him to work hard, and make her proud. And since the time he'd failed her so spectacularly on the latter, he'd re-doubled his efforts at the former. And while he'd never quite managed to regain that flicker of brilliance he'd felt the night BonaVenture was born, he'd never seen failure since.

But rather than feeling antsy at not working himself to exhaustion, he felt smug as hell. BonaVenture was so healthy it was radiant. And he'd had himself some mind-blowing sex with a beautiful woman who seemed so in tune with his preference to have a good time and not push for anything more, finding her was nothing short of serendipitous.

If he didn't let himself enjoy the spoils of his labour every now and then, what the hell was the point?

As Paige waited in the foyer for the lift the next afternoon, she was still in a bit of a daze, wondering where she'd found it inside her to head to a man's apartment, strip for him, have her way with him, then leave.

She'd never done anything like that before, but she liked it. After years of being so categorically careful, a little reckless-ness was a revelation. Even a relief. The world seemed that bit brighter, colours richer, the spring in her step springier. She'd even had an even more awesome day at work. Probably something to do with great sex being good for the blood vessels or some such thing.

Maybe she should indulge in a fling every now and then from now on; find some stranger to give her life the occasional splash of panache. Airports could be the new bar. Find someone looking lost and lonely and bam! Her next date.

She was laughing out loud when the lift doors opened, but all her confidence turned to mush when she got in the lift that afternoon to find Gabe already on board, lounging resplendently in the back corner. His dark eyes connected with hers, lit, burned, and it was all she could do to keep blushing from head to toe.

Funny, because now they were even, or nearabouts. Though perhaps she still owed him an orgasm. She stepped inside the lift, feeling his dark eyes on her, and thought it seemed as good a time as any to remind him as much—

'Good afternoon, Ms Danforth,' a female voice said.

And Paige leapt fair out of her skin. Her gaze jumped sideways to find Mrs Addable from the ninth floor tucked into the front corner, stroking Randy, her Russian Blue whose hair was the same solid dark grey as his owner's.

'Mrs Addable, hi,' Paige mumbled as she slipped into the gap, behind Mrs Addable, and beside Gabe, who looked straight ahead even while his body heat reached out to her like an invitation. 'Randy okay?'

Mrs Addable rolled her eyes. 'He's decided he's too good for his litter tray. We now have to take a constitutional down to the garden near the parking lot four times a day.'

Mrs Addable's eyes slid over lounging Gabe to Paige, who was standing as still and upright as a tower. The older woman's sharp eyes softened to a dull gleam.

'You're Gabe Hamilton,' Mrs Addable said.

'That I am,' Gabe's deep voice rang out.

Paige had to swallow hard so as not to tremble as the sound

reverberated deliciously through her bones. She remembered all too well the feel of his breath against her cheek that came with the exquisite sensation of having him inside her.

'Gloria Addable. 9B. I heard Sam the Super talking to Mr Klempt the other day about your arrival.'

'Pleasure to meet you, Gloria.'

'Likewise, Gabe.'

No *Mr Hamilton*, Paige noticed. She'd lived in the building for two years and had yet to progress from polite surnames from anyone in that apartment bar the cat.

'Sam said you'd had some trouble with your bed?' Mrs Addable added, eyes now front, watching the movement of floor numbers, the slow strokes to Randy's back causing the cat to purr.

'True, yet I've managed remarkably well,' he said, pulling himself upright, bringing him closer.

Paige looked directly ahead, not daring to meet his eyes. Yet she felt a beat pulse between them. Two. Three.

'I have a spare mattress I can send up,' Mrs Addable tried again. 'It's only a single, but…'

While Mrs Addable droned on about the history of her single mattress, Paige felt Gabe move closer still. Close enough when she breathed the sleeve of his jacket brushed against the sleeve of hers.

Then he said, 'My bed arrived this morning.'

Forgetting propriety completely, Paige shot her gaze straight to his. 'It did?'

Mrs Addable's snort of triumph barely touched the edges of her sub-conscious. Gabe's dark and dangerous eyes had a funny way of blocking out everything else.

His voice was low as he said, 'The service lift, it seems, is less touchy.'

'That's great,' Paige said, adding a belated, 'For *you*.'

Gabe's cheek lifted in the beginnings of the kind of smile that meant big trouble for her. 'I'm glad—for me—too.'

The lift binged and when Paige and Mrs Addable both turned with expectation towards the doors, Gabe took the chance to slide his finger down the edge of Paige's. The shock of his touch shot through her like a bushfire, spreading in half a second flat to the whole of her chest and the ends of her curling toes.

The door opened to the fourth floor. Where nobody was waiting. And stayed there.

Mrs Addable sighed. 'It's okay, Randy. We'll get there eventually.'

As the lift went up and down the next ten minutes, Paige locked her knees, and bit her bottom lip, and prayed for the strength not to moan out loud as Gabe's thumb traced circles over the wildly fluctuating pulse at her wrist, making her so woozy she saw spots.

And for the first time since she'd moved into the building she was thankful she had a Machiavellian lift.

CHAPTER FIVE

IT TOOK more than fifteen stupid minutes for the stupid lift to open at Paige's floor on the night of Gabe's party. Way too much time in which to wonder if she ought to change her dress. Her hair. Her mind.

She felt edgy. Hyper-aware. As if she could feel even the slightest shift of air dancing across her skin. Because after several days of living out the most hot, illicit, exciting affair of her life under cover of darkness in the privacy of Gabe's moon-drenched loft, the real world was about to impose on their heretofore perfect little bubble of secret sex.

The lift doors began to close and she slipped inside at the last second, squeezing into a gap amongst a group of bright shiny young things, none of whom she'd ever met. Why would she have? She and Gabe knew hardly anything about one another outside the bedroom.

Which was fine. Perfect really. It kept things super casual.

She wished she'd brought up the party once, at least to get a gauge of what she might be about to walk into. Would she and Gabe treat one another as virtual strangers? As friendly neighbours? Or would they simply avoid one another all night?

This, she thought. *This* was why she liked things to be simple, straightforward, with all the cards on the table from the very beginning. This nervous tumbling in her stomach was awful. And horribly familiar. Surely it was a symptom that something wasn't right.

As the lift rose the deep *whump whump whump* of music pulsed in her bones, lifting the energy throbbing deep within her to screaming point. The lift opened, and the sounds of party chatter and, ironically, Billy Idol singing 'Hot in the City' spilled into the lift as the inhabitants tumbled out.

Paige took a deep breath, smoothed a hand over her new dress, ran another over her hair, then with chin tilted she walked into Gabe's penthouse.

As it turned out, Paige knew plenty of people. Mrs Addable and several other inhabitants of the building huddled by the windows checking out the view. She saw a few girls from uni, and even a couple of guys she'd dated. She felt an odd surge of disappointment. She shook it off. She wasn't special to Gabe and she didn't want to be.

She nearly managed to convince herself as much when a quick glance around the jam-packed room revealed a massive red and grey rug now covering the lounge-room floor. A large red urn bursting with a tall spray of stripped willow. And chairs and tables in every place they ought to be. A half second after she got over the surprise of Gabe having *decorated* she realised every item was from that season's Ménage à Moi catalogue. The bubbles in her stomach went haywire.

Then the hairs on the back of her neck began to prickle, as though she was being watched. In a party that size someone somewhere would be smouldering at someone, and it was likely she'd been caught in the crossfire. And yet…

Rolling her shoulders to fend off the scratchy sensation, she turned, eyes searching the crowd until they landed on a pair of familiar dark eyes.

Gabe stood on the far side of the large room, his back to the floor-to-ceiling windows, a near full moon and a million stars twinkling in the inky black sky his backdrop. He was so deliciously handsome, so unsettling, so *much*. And his eyes were focused entirely on her. Dark eyes of a man who was near addicted to doughnuts, knew more about Doris Day movies than she did, and who remembered where she worked even though she was sure she hadn't mentioned it since the day they first met.

She liked that he was leaving. Liked that he was discreet. Liked that every time she saw him he could barely keep his hands off her. But the riot of sensation ripping through her in that moment was so beyond mere *like* she hadn't a hope of naming it.

She clutched her silver lamé purse in one hand, and the small box she'd brought with her, so hard they left imprints on her palms.

'Paige!' Mae's voice rang sharp in her ear.

Paige blinked, the noise and energy and light and life of the party rushing in on her as if she'd burst from a tunnel. Then the crowd shifted, and Gabe was gone.

Paige turned to find Mae shoving through the crowd and bundling up to her like a ball of energy, Clint lolloping in her wake.

'How cool is this?' asked Mae. 'And my godfather, this apartment! You must be dying to get stuck into it.'

Paige opened her mouth to tell Mae this was Gabe's version of decorated, until she remembered that according to Mae this was the first time Paige had been there too. She hadn't meant to keep the thing with Gabe from Mae, but they'd barely seen one another in the past week, and she'd been so busy at work— And it had been so intense, so unlike anything she'd ever done before, she hadn't wanted the bubble to burst.

She'd fill Mae in on all the juicy details the first moment they had some girly time together, just the two of them. She glanced across at the ever-present Clint and wondered when that might be.

'Where is that delicious pirate of yours?' Mae asked. 'The guy was clearly into you at The Brasserie last week, and he looks like the kind of guy who doesn't need a flashlight and a map to find your treasure, if ya know what I mean.'

Paige rolled her eyes even while she knew it to be the absolute truth. Gabe Hamilton had found her treasure no problem at all. In fact, her treasure was so attuned to him she was doing her best to ignore the heavy ache in her treasure just thinking about him.

'Drinks!' Mae said and Clint looked as if he was reminded again why he wanted to marry her. Then hand in hand they made a beeline for the bar.

Leaving Paige to pretend every fibre of her being wasn't paying intense heed to their host, wherever he might be.

Gabe ran a finger beneath the V of his sweater for about the hundredth time since a bunch of strangers had piled into his apartment.

He'd be pushing it to say he knew even a tenth of them, and a half of *those* he'd met in the lift at one point or another that week. The rest were a blur of hair and teeth that Nate had introduced to him, talking each and every one up as though they were the next big thing. He got it, Nate was trying to make him feel at home. Yet the only thing keeping him from making a hasty exit in search of fresh air, no matter how cold, had been brief glimpses of a familiar head of cool-blonde hair.

He'd known the moment Paige had arrived—some shift in the air, some call of the wild to his hormones had him sniffing the air for her scent. And then she'd appeared through the crowd in a white dress that looked as if she'd been poured into it and revealed enough leg to give a less vital man palpitations.

His gaze found her again, this time talking to some guy. Her hair shifting across her back as she talked. When the guy moved in, placing a hand on her upper arm, waving his big watch in her face, something clenched hot and hard deep inside Gabe. Something primal and not pretty.

'It's the legs,' said a voice cutting into his thoughts.

He turned to find a group of men in sharp suits standing beside him, all cradling half-filled glasses, all looking in Paige's direction.

'What's that?' asked Gabe.

'They're like something out of a forties detective movie,' said another of the men. 'I've spent more time than I dare admit imagining myself as Sam Spade, walking into a smoke-filled room, sunlight pouring through slatted blinds, to find those legs crossed as she sits waiting on my desk.'

'Hamilton, right?' asked the third. 'We're friends of Nate's.'

'Right,' said Gabe, brushing off the fact that Nate seemed to have more friends he didn't know than friends he did. There were more pressing matters. 'You know Paige?'

At the dark tone of his voice three pairs of male eyes turned his way. Turned, and softened. He could all but hear them thinking, *Poor mug, thinks he's in with a chance.*

Never in his life had Gabe felt a stronger urge to kiss and tell. *I've had her up against a wall, on the kitchen bench, crying out my name so loud the whole damn building must have heard.* But he lifted his glass and filled his mouth with Scotch before his foot landed there instead.

'Dated her one time,' said the first, 'before she introduced me to my wife.'

'Cool move,' said the second with a laugh.

'Cool creature,' said the third.

Gabe's gaze drew back to Paige. He caught her profile as she smiled and waved at someone across the room. Her smile was calm. Understated. He could see why people might think her cool, he'd thought so himself at one point, but now he understood it was a mask, a mode of self-protection. Something tickled the back of his mind, as if he were trying to catch the disparate threads of a dream.

Familiarity, perhaps. Maybe even a recognition of his own natural reserve.

Or déjà vu.

Another cool blonde of his acquaintance came crashing into his mind, right along with the tightness in his gut as he'd first spied that long ago blonde smiling at him from across the room at BonaVenture's first big party, and the smile that never quite reached her eyes unless they met his.

'No,' he said, out loud, turning heads. Grimacing, he downed the last of his Scotch before slamming the glass onto a passing tray.

This wasn't the same as that. For one thing he'd been young, and cocky, and ruled by his libido. He was older, wiser now and kept that part of him on a short leash. And yet his subconscious wouldn't let it lie. This thing with Paige was… intense. And it had ignited exceptionally fast. Who could blame him? The woman was so lush and lovely she kept him half hard half the day and all the way all night.

He ground a thumb and forefinger into his eyes, but the memories continued to knock against the inside of his brain.

He'd met Lydia right as BonaVenture had hit the crest of its first wave of success. The business that had been a mere dream a few years before had gone stratospheric right after his gran had died. And it was as though he'd gone to sleep one night himself, and woken up to find the world as he'd always known it was simply no more.

Lydia had been his port in the storm, and it had never occurred to him that her motivations in being with him might have been anything less than romantic. In the end that error of judgement had all but destroyed everything he and Nate had worked so hard to build.

And here he was, set to make the biggest financial decision

of his life, and he'd gone and entangled himself in a blonde distraction once again.

'Having fun?' Nate said, slapping Gabe on the back, rocking him back on his heels.

A dark cloud hovering about his ears, Gabe shoved his fingers hard into the front pockets of his jeans. 'So much so I barely know how to contain myself.'

Nate snorted. 'Now quickly, I have a thing in Sydney this week. A meet and greet with an upstart encryption software company. Looks schmick. I was going to send Rick, but I'm not sure that he's as net savvy as— Gabe?'

'Hmm?' A sliver of white glinting through the crowd had snagged Gabe's attention. 'What now?'

'I was being about as subtle as a woman in red lipstick. I'm offering you a lifeline, mate. An actual prospective client to sound out while you're here. Thought you'd jump at the chance to sink your fangs into an actual real live deal.'

Normally he would, but he was in a questioning type of mood, and even while Nate's face was a picture of innocence, so far everything he'd said or done that night had screamed ulterior motive.

'Unless you have other plans? More decorating perhaps? Like what you've done with the place so far. Very...pretty.'

Gabe cut him a glower. 'Considering your flair for interior design I take that as a compliment. When's the flight?'

'Daybreak tomorrow. And you're welcome.'

Gabe caught the glint of light on blonde hair move through the swarm and heard himself say, 'Make it a day later and I'm there.'

He felt Nate's incredulous stare. Pretended he didn't.

Nate said, 'Am I missing something here? I've had people manning the lifts at work in case you slipped out and were never heard from again— Ri-i-ight. I see.' Nate grabbed a tiny pastry from a passing tray and threw it into his mouth. 'So who's the blonde?'

Gabe breathed out long and slow. He'd been quietly concerned about the ever-decreasing degrees of separation between Paige and Nate and confirmation that Nate wasn't a paid-up member of the 'I Fantasise About Paige's Legs' club was more of a relief than he cared to admit. Gabe set his vision at the middle distance, and drawled, 'Any blonde in particular you need me to soften up for you?'

Nate grabbed him by the ears and turned his head the half-inch to face the blonde in question. 'The one who has you dancing about like you have ants in your pants. The one making you think twice about getting out of bed early tomorrow.'

Gabe swiped his hands away. 'For starters, I don't dance. And secondly she lives in the building and…' She what? Wasn't the reason why he was actually considering shucking off work? The dark cloud surrounded his whole head. 'She all but shut the lift doors on my fingers when we first met.'

'That's it? Well, then you won't mind if I head that way and—'

Gabe's hand shot out and grabbed Nate by the back of the neck.

Nate laughed as he ducked out of Gabe's grip. 'Been so long since I've seen you even look twice at a blonde, it's bloody reassuring. Like you're really back. Not just here, but *back*. Now, seems I have to go tell poor Rick he has an early start in the morning.'

With that, Nate headed off, leaving Gabe silenced. And shrouded in more grey clouds than ever. Of all times for Nate to slant a reference at Lydia… He'd dated blondes since her, surely? Lydia hadn't screwed him over *that* much.

Sure she'd sold their pillow talk with the competition, leading to an investigation by the Australian Securities Commission for insider trading, which had meant the near undoing of the business into which he and Nate had poured their hearts and souls, the repercussions of which had sent him careening off to all four corners of the globe in an effort to wrench BonaVenture from the grips of obliteration—

But it wasn't as if it affected him any more. Unless you counted the fact that he was more vigilant when it came to his business dealings. Perhaps even a little zealously so. But his dating habits were peachy. Or at least they would be once all the monkeys finally left his apartment.

All bar one.

Paige sensed Gabe a good second before his deep dark voice said, 'Miss Danforth, how good of you to come.'

She took a quick heartening gulp from her champagne, then turned and said, 'Why, of course.' At least she planned to. But nothing came out.

In leather and a three-day growth Gabe Hamilton looked like a sexy pirate. In pyjama bottoms and nothing else he was every woman's fantasy. In a cool pin-striped jacket, navy cashmere sweater, and dark jeans he looked so delectably tactile he was more dangerous than ever.

When he leant to place a soft warm kiss on her cheek she had a fair idea of what oxygen deprivation must feel like— all breathless and weak and woozy, with a touch of delirium thrown in.

'For you,' she said, shoving the small box between them. 'Housewarming present.'

He took the package, his brow furrowing as he stared at it. And suddenly she felt silly for bringing anything at all.

She flapped her hand at him. 'On second thoughts, give it back. It so won't go with your gorgeous new decor.'

Pulling the gift out of her reach, he glanced up under his thick dark lashes. 'You noticed.'

'I'd be pretty sucky at my job if I didn't. It looks great. You did good.'

He cocked his head in thanks. Then brought her gift to his ear and gave it a little shake. 'So long as it's not a throw cushion I'm sure it'll do fine.'

All she could do was shrug, while she felt more and more sure that what was meant to be a funny little trinket was too ridiculous, too overfamiliar, too obvious he'd made an impact on her. But then she thought of the big changes he'd made to his apartment, because of her, and didn't quite know what to think any more.

He opened the box, a wash of surprise, bewilderment, and laughter playing over his beautiful face as he stared at the hot-pink flamingo in his big dark hands.

'For your phone,' she explained, sliding her hand to the inside pocket of his jacket, knowing that was where his ever-present phone would be. She drew it out and placed it neatly into place in the crook of the bird's bent leg. Tilting her head for him to follow, she slipped through a gap in the crowd to put the phone holder on the kitchen bench.

She turned and, with a ta-da move, said, 'To keep the doughnut crumbs away.'

Gabe blinked at the kitsch splash of pink adorning his sleek dark kitchen, then back to her. His silky dark eyes looking *right* into her. She knew how Lois Lane felt knowing Superman's X-ray vision meant he could tell what colour undies she wore. She felt the same desire to hide behind something big and solid for protection.

Waving her hand in front of her dramatically pinking face, she said, 'It's a silly little—'

'It's perfect,' he said, placing a hand over his heart. 'Thank you.'

'My pleasure.' And it was. *He* was. Her complete and utter

pleasure. A pleasure she'd actually thought might fizzle in the glaring light of a public outing.

The crowd jostled and she bumped against him. He gathered her with a strong arm until she was flush against his big strong front, the heat of him bleeding through her barely there dress. Again she wondered how she'd gone so long without a man in her life. Without the mouth-watering ache inside her. How? Because it had never felt like this before.

'Let's get the hell out of here,' Gabe's voice rumbled through her.

Paige laughed. 'But the party's just started.'

'Really? Feels like it's been going on for days.'

When it began to dawn on her he might not be kidding, she glanced over his shoulder at the party going great guns behind him. 'But don't you need to—?'

'Not so much.'

Her eyes swung back to his to find them drenched with desire. For her. The hot ache sank and spread until she would have collapsed in a quivering puddle of pure need had Gabe not been holding her.

When the urge to grab his hand and run, dispatching a coat-hanger tackle on anyone in her path, swelled hot and fast inside her, Paige knew then that she'd gone past the point of curing her dating-drought.

She'd cracked.

Relinquishing a degree of control had seemed a worthy price to pay to find her feet again. But the raging desire to give in and do whatever Gabe asked of her was so strong it scared her. It felt like a heck of a short trip from that to becoming her mother, watching the clock, marking off the calendar, blushing hopefully every time the phone rang. And living a life of perpetual disappointment.

She locked her knees and pressed her hands into his chest,

steadfastly ignoring the urge to curl her fingernails against the hard planes. 'Gabe, you have to stay.'

He slowly shook his head. 'I have to have you.'

Good God. Paige licked her lips, preparing to explain why he'd have to wait but there were simply no words. She bit her bottom lip to stop from whimpering. His dark gaze honed in on the movement, a muscle jumping in his cheek. The hastening of his heartbeat beneath her palms was her undoing.

'Okay. Let's go,' she said.

Apparently that was all Gabe needed. He grabbed her hand and drew her through the crowd, parting it like a hot knife through butter.

'Gabe!' a voice broke into her buzzing sub-conscious.

Fully expecting Gabe to accelerate into a sprint, Paige was so surprised when he actually stopped she banged into his back, and had to grip his arm in order to steady herself. He wrapped his arm around her in order to steady her, so she was all wrapped up in him when she found herself the subject of some shrewd attention from a man she'd never met.

'Now what?' Gabe said, his impatience clear as day.

The party guest, handsome in a clean-cut jock kind of way, smiled patiently at Gabe, and then at her.

Gabe sighed, then said, 'Nate Mackenzie, Paige Danforth.'

Nate grinned as he held out a hand. 'The infamous lift monopolist. Pleasure.'

Paige laughed in surprise. Then glanced at Gabe to find him quietly fuming at his friend. A friend he'd talked to about her. While she'd never said a word to Mae. Mae who was somewhere at the party, clueless she was about to do a bunk. Her stomach clutched more than a little.

'One last thing before you depart,' Nate said to Gabe. 'The men in grey by the window. Go say "hi".'

Gabe growled so low Paige winced. 'Another time.'

Paige felt Nate's attention focus on her even as he held

Gabe's dark gaze with his deceptively smiling eyes. 'This is the only time. We need them. For the…deal.'

Gabe's grip tightened on hers and she prepared to make a dash for the door. But when her eye slid to his it was to see a muscle clenching in his cheek.

To her he'd always seemed basically untouchable. As if nothing could topple him. In that moment he looked like a fish on a hook. A fish who could have thrown the hook with little more than a jerk of his great head if he'd decided to do so. But a fish who was currently chewing on the hook instead, gritting it between his teeth, before he squared his shoulders, apologised to her for a momentary change of plans, and took off.

'Sorry,' Nate said, clearly meaning it. 'Business, you know.'

'That's fine,' she said, even though she hadn't a clue. She barely knew what Gabe did for a living. It involved travel, a phone that might as well be permanently attached to his hand, and…men in suits, apparently.

'I'm his partner at BonaVenture,' Nate said. 'And by the look in your eyes he's never mentioned me to you.'

'Sorry.'

They'd never talked that much about her work either. Which added to growing worry gnawing at her innards, because her work was pretty much the most significant thing in her life. Only the past week that distinction had been usurped by the man standing stiff-backed amongst a group of men who were grinning and fawning, shaking his hand as if he were some kind of rock star.

'If only he wasn't one of a kind.'

'Hmm?'

Nate ran a hard hand up the back of his neck, eyes zeroed in on the conversation on the other side of the room. 'Gabe. He's brilliant, you know.'

She didn't know that either, actually. Oh, she knew the

man had skills, but she was fairly sure she and Nate were thinking of quite different ones.

'I have a good line in spin,' Nate continued, 'but Gabe? He's a superstar. He can smell potential from a continent away. He can seduce even the most timid ideas men to let him in. Nobody else out there like him. My life would be a hell of a lot simpler if there were.'

Nate's astute gaze slewed from Gabe and back to her, his mouth lifting into a smile so self-confident it completely belied his previous words. She could see in that look why the two men got along. They were both forces of nature. And even while she had no idea what was going on behind Nate's clever hazel eyes it gave her goose bumps.

Then Nate said, 'If you have any kind of influence over him—'

She held up her hands and waved them frantically enough to stop Nate in his tracks. 'I don't. Honestly. We're…friends.'

For a perfectly nice term, 'friends' sounded such a lame description for what they were, and Nate's raised eyebrows told her he wasn't buying it either.

But he backed down. 'Apologies. Clearly I'm getting desperate.'

'For?'

'Him to stay, of course.'

The worries that had been little fissures splintered to form the Grand Canyon. 'He's *considering* sticking around?'

'You tell me.'

She swallowed past the tightness in her throat. Like a good many things, they hadn't talked about when he was leaving as an actual couple would, because they weren't an actual couple. They were…flinging. And to protect herself from any damage the act of flinging might incur, she'd done a lot of assuming. And you knew what they said about assuming?

She *needed* him to go. The only reason she was taking

chances where she'd never taken them before was because
it had an end date.

As if he knew she was thinking about him, Gabe looked
back across the room. As their eyes connected she could practically see the energy arcing between them.

Gabe shook his head once, promising he wouldn't be long.
Or was he saying, *Don't get any ideas, now. Don't make the
mistake of falling for me*? On any other man the warning
would be conceited. Gabe ought to have had it tattooed on
his bicep at birth.

It seemed she'd been right to try to protect herself from
fling damage. Only problem was, it hadn't worked.

CHAPTER SIX

THE sound of the party spilled through the closed front doors of Gabe's apartment as Paige pressed the lift button, her finger shaking, whether from anticipation of what was to come or aftermath of the conversation with Nate. Probably a mixture of both.

She glanced up, and caught Gabe's eye. Remembered the warmth that had flooded her the night she'd caught him smiling at her over a doughnut while he leant against his kitchen bench in unbuttoned jeans and felt a tiny stab of fear that Mae wasn't the only one she was hiding things from any more. So she blurted, 'When are you going back to Brazil?'

'I'm not,' he said, and Paige's stomach fell to her shoes. Then, 'That deal's done. But I will be leaving as soon as I'm done here. I follow the work, and ninety per cent of the time it's many *many* miles from here.'

She breathed out a sigh of relief so loud she closed her eyes tight against the embarrassment of it.

'Wrong answer?' he asked, and she was surprised to find humour in his voice.

She screwed up her eyes. 'Will it sound callous if I say that's the right answer?'

'It does a bit,' he said, his smile growing. He gathered her to him, sliding his hands over her hips, his thumbs trailing hot and tempting spirals over her lower back. 'But then it seems I'm into callous women.'

The lift binged. Opened.

Paige let out a huge 'Whoop!' as Gabe's hands slid to her backside, lifted her and carried her into the lift. Then, before the lift doors closed, his lips were on her neck, his fingers sliding into the edge of dress, caressing the outer edge of her breast.

This, she thought. This was what mattered. Not all that thinking, and wondering and second-guessing. It was exhausting. And unnecessary. Thank heavens. Because she'd much rather be doing *this* instead.

Goose bumps sped across her skin as Gabe's warm breath shot across her ear. 'Although it's not manly to admit as much, I'm strangely looking forward to learning what real garnish might look like.'

'Why's that?'

'I finally get to see your place.'

Paige's eyes flung open. The wedding dress! It was still hanging over the chair in her kitchen. She'd never got around to putting it away. As though if it went into her cupboard that would be the final evidence of ownership.

In one second flat, Paige kicked off her shoe and with a naked toe jabbed the emergency stop button. The lift juddered to a halt with such suddenness she gripped Gabe's jacket for dear life.

In the sudden silence their intermingled breaths sounded overly loud. Her heart rocking against her ribs sounded even louder.

Though she was clueless as to how she was going to explain that little move, her eyes went back to Gabe. Surprise lit the dark depths for a moment before one dark eyebrow rose, and his smile kicked up at one corner. And relief flowed through her like an injection of pure heat on a cold winter's day.

Then with a growl that spoke to something deep and primal inside her, Gabe pressed her back into the wall of the lift. Their hands were all over one another, urgent, desperate to find skin.

Her skirt was up, his pants down, he was sheathed and inside her. Hard, solid heat filling her until she cried out with the pleasure of it. She flung a hand over her eyes as sensation pummelled her every which way.

So hot, so right, she thought. Whatever else was going on, however short a time they had, they were made for this and that couldn't be denied.

Sensation pounded through her like a perfect storm as she tightened around him, pleasure pulsing until she couldn't stand it any more. And with a cry that must have echoed up and down the lift shaft every last tension fell away in waves of perfect heat, until it ratcheted right back up again as Gabe's powerful release followed right on top of hers.

The storm inside her quieted slowly as she leant her forehead on his chest, letting the deep rhythm of his breaths calm her.

When she finally lifted her head it was to find his eyes were closed. His lips parted as he found his natural breath. The bright lights of the lift created shadows beneath his brows, highlighting every crinkle around his eyes, every hair on his jaw, the curve of his Adam's apple.

He was so much man it made her chest hurt just looking at him.

He opened his eyes, gave her a small smile, tucked a stray lock of hair behind her ear, and then his eyes left hers to drift over her face. Hovering momentarily on her hair, her neck, her lips.

This, she thought, swallowing hard.

Raging attraction plus wedding-dress-purchase-recoil had

sent her into his arms in the first place but *this* was why she wasn't yet ready to walk away. The way she felt when they were alone together. Work, family, Mae; they didn't come up because they didn't matter. He stilled her mind. Made everything feel simple. Let her live in the moment.

She reached up and traced the backs of her knuckles along the hollow of his cheek. Ran a thumb softly over his bottom lip. Smoothed a stray hair in his eyebrow. And he let her. His eyes gave nothing away, but his nostrils flared at her quiet touch.

When the feeling inside her began to swell so large she struggled to find a full breath Paige curled her fingers into her palm and pressed herself against the wall so that they could disentangle themselves. Gabe fixed his pants, she fixed her dress, both of them flickering sly glances at each other, before they both burst out laughing.

'You, Miss Danforth, are a revelation,' he said.

'Would you believe before you came along I was a bit of a good girl?'

His dark eyes connected long and hard with hers for long enough that her breath caught in her throat. Then, as he reached for the emergency button, he said, 'Nah.'

And Paige laughed again, light, free. Happy. Even as she revelled in the feeling, she knew it was dangerous.

Gabe didn't notice as he was jabbing and jiggling the emergency button. Yet the lift refused to budge.

Giving her dress a last fix, she joined him. 'You're kidding me, right?'

Gabe spared her a flat glance, before reaching into his jacket pocket for his mobile to call for help. Only to find it was missing.

'The flamingo,' they said as one, and Paige laughed so hard she clutched her stomach.

'This isn't funny. There are over a hundred people stuck up there.'

'And it'll only take one to leave early to notice the lift's not working.' Paige put a finger to her bottom lip. 'If not for the fact that the lift is a total diva at the best of times.'

A muscle jumped in Gabe's cheek and she realised he was beginning to look kind of stressed. Poor love.

'Here,' she said, pressing him aside to pop the hatch to find the lift's emergency phone. It was busted. Seriously, at the next tenants' meeting she was bringing out a whole bag of whoop on Sam the Super's ass.

Gabe ran a hand through his hair as his gaze shot up, down, and at the seam in the lift's doors.

And something occurred to Paige. 'Gabe. Are you claustrophobic?'

He tugged at the V of his sweater. 'Of course not. But neither am I keen on feeling trapped in a small space for an extended period of time. This rotten, stinking, no good—' Gabe said, his voice now not much more than a growl as he banged at the control panel with enough force to bruise. Still the lift didn't budge.

Paige lost it. Laughing so hard now she hiccuped. 'See!' she managed to get out. 'It's not just me. This is fantastic. And I was so sure he'd fallen under your spell.'

'He?'

Paige blinked up at Gabe, whose eyes were narrowed dangerously in her direction. She was the one who'd hit the button in the first place after all.

Her bottom lip slid straight between her teeth and his gaze slid straight to her mouth, his eyes darkening, his breath lengthening, as she said, 'Rock Hudson, of course.'

Then his eyes shot back to hers, and the corner of his mouth lifted in a dangerous smile.

Silence stretched between them, only broken by the occasional creak of the lift. They were left with nothing to do but wait.

'So,' Paige said, crossing her arms, cocking her hip, 'what now?'

'What kind of name is Gabe?'

Gabe's thighs burned from being on his haunches the past ten minutes as he tried to rewire the phone and get them the hell out of the box. He could sniff out creative accounting in a company report from a mile away, but he knew less than nothing about electrical engineering.

'Just Gabe? Or short for Gabriel?' Paige added when it became clear he wasn't about to answer.

'Short,' he said.

'That's sweet,' she said, clearly not as concerned as he was about the thinning of the air. 'Like the angel.'

Gabe's knees creaked as he pulled himself to standing. He turned to find Paige standing in the far corner of the lift, one bare foot on top of the other, her hair now up in a makeshift knot, the ends of his sports coat rolled up at her wrists. Despite the stale air all sorts of parts of him stirred for her again. He shot them down. He was conserving air. 'You having fun over there while I try to get us out of here?'

'Tonnes. I'm used to being the one swearing under my breath at this thing. It's nice to watch someone else have a turn.'

'Nice ain't the word I'd use.' Gabe looked around the small space. No way was he something so pansy-assed as *claustrophobic*. Though time spent in parts of the world with less than exemplary examples of modern vertical architecture had left him with an ever so slight discordance with elevator travel.

'Now back to your name—'

'It's a family name,' he said, rubbing his fingers across the stiff back of his neck.

'Mother's side? Father's?'

'Aren't you hot?'

Paige blinked her big blue bedroom eyes at him and wrapped herself tighter in the cosy warmth of his jacket. Then she slowly shook her head.

'The air-con's been turned off,' he said. 'When did that happen?'

'I haven't been paying attention. But we'll be fine here for hours. I read a book about a guy in Brussels who was stuck in a lift for like a week. Lived off detritus he dug up from the carpet. Hugh Jackman was going to play him in the movie.' She seemed to go far away for a second before she snapped back. 'Compared with him we have it pretty good.'

'Hugh Jackman, or the guy in Brussels?' Gabe asked, trying his best not to imagine being stuck in what amounted to a luxury coffin for days. 'Don't answer that. In fact no more talk.'

Her cheek lifted as she held back a smile. He hadn't realised she was a sadist but she was enjoying his discomfort way too much. Proving it, she slid one foot to the wall, cocking a sexy knee in his direction, drawing her tight dress right up her thigh. Then she took a big deep breath before saying, 'So, Nate seems like a good guy. Great hair. And that dimple? Adorable!'

Gabe clenched his teeth so hard he was sure he heard something crack. 'Are you kidding me?'

She blinked several times over. 'I'm sorry, did you want me to stop asking questions about *you*, or to stop talking altogether?'

He raised one telling eyebrow.

She did the same, and began to swing her knee side to side, drawing his gaze to those legs. Legs that could make a grown man get on his knees and thank God he'd been born. She asked, 'Is Nate single?'

'My father's,' Gabe ground out.

She cupped a hand to her ear. 'I'm sorry?'

'My name comes from my father's side.' He checked the ceiling, wondering at what point he should kick out a panel, climb onto the roof, and shimmy up the metal cord—

'He was a Gabriel?'

Gabe shook his head. 'Frank.'

'*His* father, then?' Paige pressed. 'No? His father's best friend's war buddy's pet llama?'

And whether it was the fact that she was apparently willing to suffocate them both before giving up, or the way she looked so soft and smudged in her pretty bare feet and his big jacket, Gabe gave up something he'd never even shared with Nate. 'My father's mother was a Gabriella.'

It was a small confidence, but the surrendering of it was felt. He was more than surprised when places inside him seemed to shift to accommodate the newfound space.

Paige's knee stopped mid-swing and her bottom lip tucked between her teeth, probably to stop herself from grinning at his namesake, but he didn't much care. The sheen her teeth left in their wake brought on a blood rush of attraction with a vengeance. Screw it. If he was going to die here, he might as well die smiling. Eyes locked onto her mouth, he ambled her way.

She asked, 'This was the grandmother who made sure your Doris Day knowledge was up to snuff?'

'Amongst other things. Gabriel had come through several generations, and Gran had no brothers, so…'

'So not a girlie name, then.'

'Not.' He lifted his eyes to hers, to find them darkened. As if she knew exactly what she did to his blood. And his nerves. And the tempo of his breaths. So long as she never realised she had the ability to shake things loose inside him as well.

She shook a lock of hair from her face and the knot tumbled free over one shoulder. 'Well, I think it's…sweet.'

'Do you, now?'

'Sweet as pie. Sweeter than how my name came about.' She laughed, but there was no humour in it. And when she frowned and looked down at her bare toes curling and uncurling against the floor Gabe stopped in his tracks.

He wasn't adept at deep and meaningfuls. In fact they had the tendency to bring him out in hives. But stuck in the lift, their personal space overlapping, it simply felt decent to ask. 'How's that?'

Several beats pulsed between them before she flicked her hair from her eyes again and said, 'Dad was a cricketer. International. Away eighty per cent of the year. Mum figured he'd be away when I was born—which he was. So, in an effort to include him in my birth, she gave him the job of naming me. Carte blanche.'

Her voice was even, but he felt the cool in her as she spoke. Saw the chips of ice in her warm blue eyes. They echoed inside him, banging painfully against the raw edges of the new space there.

'Want to know who I was named after?' Paige's shoulders lifted as she wrapped her arms tighter around herself, and flicked her hair again.

'More than life itself.'

She laughed even as she frowned at herself for doing so, the husky sound washing over his skin like waves of warmth. 'The maid who'd turned down his bed at the hotel when he'd got the phone call.'

God. What a prick. Instinct had Gabe wanting to run his thumb across the vertical lines above her nose. Circumspection had him pressing his feet hard into the floor.

She tucked the wayward lock behind her ear. 'I think Mum

had been hoping to rouse some kind of connection in him. Hoping it would encourage him home more. To us.'

'Did it work?'

Her smile remained, only now it was bittersweet. 'Not so much. He cheated any chance he got, and she scrubbed the kitchen till it shone. Until one day she had enough, and asked for a divorce. He had the gall to be shocked. And even while she took him for plenty, he left her broken.' She shook out her shoulders, and scraped her teeth along her tongue as if trying to get rid of a bad taste in her mouth. 'Anyway. Bygones.'

Bygones, Gabe thought. *Things we pretend don't matter any more. But sweeping them under the rug only creates a lump to be tripped over time and again.* He pushed the thought away.

'Do you see him much? Your dad?'

'Never. Mum and I are pretty close, though. She's a good woman, way more forgiving than I could ever be. Yours?'

He should have seen it coming, but he'd been concentrating so hard on Paige the question came out of left field. And he was caught, looking into her big blue bedroom eyes, all liquid, hurting, wanting, patient.

He could practically feel his heart beating in his neck as the words spilled from his lips. 'They died when I was young. My gran raised me.'

'Gran Gabriella,' she said, nodding, even smiling a little, as if the pieces of him slipped into place.

'She was an amazing woman. Tough. Stubborn. Thank God too. I was a wild kid. Impatient. First to climb the tree. Fastest to the top of the hill. She had a choice to either let me go feral or guide me with a firm hand. All of my focus I owe to her.'

'Is she in Melbourne still?'

'She passed several years back. Right about the time my career took off. It broke my heart that she wasn't around to see it.' As he breathed out he felt another shift, this one so significant he could practically feel air swirling inside him in the place where he'd harboured that regret for so long.

Paige's next breath out was long and slow, as if she too was letting things go. He could have kissed her for leaving it there. Hell, he could have kissed her either way. Her hair falling in wisps about her face. Her lips pink from the nibbling.

'Paige—' he said, but that was all that came as he wasn't sure what he wanted to say.

He actually shook his head at the realisation that she'd rendered him speechless. The rainmaker. The silver-tongued seducer of innocent creatives.

No matter the mistakes he'd made in his life, he'd done something right for her to have come into his life at the right moment. This woman who'd looked so relieved earlier when he'd reiterated that he'd be leaving soon, that their affair had a use-by date, even he'd been a little taken aback. Until he'd given himself a swift mental slap.

Paige was warm, sexy, astute, and gorgeous as all get out, but there was a limit to what he could offer. It was a good thing that he'd been forced to remember what a destructive illusion *feeling* for someone could be. He'd remember with even more biting clarity once he was no longer surrounded by air that smelled so thickly of warm, soft, edible, feminine skin.

He stepped forward and placed his hands on her upper arms. Her warmth seeped from the fabric of his too-big jacket into his skin. Her delicious scent curled beneath his nose. Her big blue eyes looked unblinking into his as her chest rose high and fell hard.

Yes, he thought. *That.* The touchy-feely stuff had made him feel unexpectedly raw, but it had nothing on pure and simple sexual hunger.

He placed a hand on the wall above her head, and heat

arched through him as her lips parted, soft and moist and practically begging for his kiss.

When she licked her lips, and tilted her head, the *wanting* that swept through him was thick and consuming. Unrelenting. And limitless, filling all the newly shifted places inside him. He closed his eyes on that thought. Gritted his teeth against the insinuation.

Then at the slide of her hand into the back of his hair, the press of her hips to his groin, the sweet shuddering sigh as her breath whispered across his neck, he thought, *Oh, to hell with it—*

Then the lights flickered. And the lift began to move.

The lift binged, the doors opened, and Paige knew that if she snapped her eyes left she'd see the silver wallpaper of the eighth floor. But she couldn't snap her eyes any which way, not for all the coffee in Brazil.

Not with Gabe looking at her that way. As if he was looking not at her, but into the very heart of her. She wondered what he saw. If it was a disappointment, all cold and uninviting. Or if it flickered with any of the heat freefalling through her body. If he had any inkling any warmth glowing inside her had been put there by him. She looked away then, and hoped she hadn't left it too late.

'We should probably get out of here before the thing changes it mind,' she said. 'You're way too big for me to carry out of here if your claustrophobia gets the better of you.'

'Funny woman,' said Gabe, though it was apparently enough to get him to move, as he grabbed a door and ushered her through. Without all that concentrated heat burning a hole right through her, Paige somehow managed to put one foot in front of the other to scoop up her heels and purse and exit the lift.

The recessed lighting made the hallway overly bright to

Paige's eyes, as if she'd spent a year in a cave, not an hour in a perfectly well-lit lift. As if the confidences she and Gabe had shared had all been a crazy dream. She shucked his jacket from her back and held it out to him on the end of a finger. He took it and tucked it over his crooked elbow.

He angled his head towards the ceiling. 'I'd better head back up, check everyone's okay. Make sure Nate hasn't invited everyone to sleep over.'

'You're braver than I am.'

'You kidding? I'm taking the stairs. You?'

She wrapped her arms about herself, missing Gabe's jacket, missing his nearness. It was enough to have her take a step back as she shook her head. 'I think I've tempted fate enough tonight.'

His mouth lifted into the beginnings of a smile, though it never quite eventuated. In fact he looked downright serious. Heart beating so loud she was certain he could hear it too, Paige took a breath to say goodnight, but Gabe cut her off, eating up the space between them with three long strides. Barefoot, she had to look up so far to meet his eyes.

'When will I see you again?' he asked.

Paige's breath hitched in her throat. Apart from the party invite, it was the first time either of them had even come close to suggesting making actual plans. 'Soon enough, if the past few days are anything to go by,' she said, trying for sassy, but when her voice came out all husky she failed miserably.

'Good point. But I was thinking more along the lines of dinner.'

'Dinner?' Paige asked, her voice rising in her complete surprise. 'Like a proper date?'

Gabe nodded, serious face well and truly in place.

A date? A *date*. A date. Experience said no way. Gabe was a nomad. She'd recognised the impatience in his eye the moment she'd first seen him. If she hadn't learned to keep a man like that at arm's length from watching her mum watch her dad walk away, time and time again, then she was an out and out fool.

Of course, there was the small fact that Nate was in the process of trying to get Gabe to stay...

'Paige,' Gabe said, the tone of his voice making it clear he wanted an answer.

While her subconscious argued back and forth, all she could do was go with her gut. And it turned out that her gut, like the rest of her body, wanted Gabe.

'Okay. Let's do it.'

'Good,' he said on a hard shot of outward breath. 'I'll call to set it up.'

Gabe slid a finger beneath her chin, and kissed her gently. Tenderly. Then his tongue swept into her mouth and she curled her fingers into his sweater and held on for dear life.

Then with a shake of his head, and a growl that told her it took everything he had to leave it at that, he turned and disappeared into the stairwell, a flash of dark clothing, and huge shoulders, and powerful strides. Leaving Paige blinking into the bright empty hallway.

At the start of the night her biggest hope had been that their sizzle didn't fizzle in public. Now he'd asked her on a date. She'd wished for a guy to end her dating drought. She had nobody to blame but herself.

CHAPTER SEVEN

Paige had just sat down to cocktails with Mae and Clint at the sparkly pink Oo La La bar on Church Street when she got the call she'd been telling herself she hadn't been waiting for all day.

She held up a finger to excuse herself, slipped off the stool, and headed out into the icy Melbourne night. She stuck her spare hand under her armpit and banged her feet against the ground in an effort to keep warm as she answered her mobile.

'Hey, Gabe!' Paige scrunched up her face. Even in the age of number display, she should have at least feigned nonchalance.

As Gabe's rich laughter rumbled down the phone she realised she needn't have worried about the cold; every time she heard that voice a wave of heat followed in its wake.

'What's up?' she asked. As if she didn't know that either! She bit her lip to stop herself from saying anything else daft.

'I do believe I promised you dinner,' he said.

'Right. So you did.' There, that was better. Now she might get away with him not guessing she'd spent much of her Saturday daydreaming about where he might take her. Or what she might wear. If Gabe's sweet tooth was enough to make them last till dessert. Or if his taste for her was stronger still.

A tram thundered noisily down the street, sparks flinting off the overhead cables and disappearing into the inky blackness above. Paige pressed the phone to her right ear, and a finger in the left. 'I'm sorry, I missed that last part.'

'I said we'll have to have a rain check.'

Her feet stopped stamping and she came over all still.

'I'm in Sydney for work. Flew down first thing this morning. Not sure when I'll be back.'

He was in Sydney? A thousand miles away and he hadn't even told her he was going? He hadn't even had anything like this on the cards as far as she knew. Because she didn't known much of anything? Unless he'd simply changed his mind. Maybe his claustrophobia was so bad he'd only asked in the aftermath of post survival euphoria!

'Paige? Can you hear me?'

'Yeah. I got that,' she said. She rubbed at a spot under her ribs where she suddenly felt as if someone were poking her with a chopstick. 'Cool. I understand. I've got so much going on at work this week as it is. I guess I'll catch you when you get—'

'Paige.' He cut her off, his deep drawl pouring through her like melted chocolate.

'Yep?' She closed her eyes and slapped herself several times on the forehead for good measure. When she opened her eyes it was to see a couple, arms linked, scooting as far around her on the footpath as possible. She sent them a sorry smile but they were jogging too fast to see.

'I'll be back in a couple of days, and then I'm sure we can squeeze in a night out if we both try real hard.'

He didn't say, *'before I leave for good,'* but it was out there, like a big black piano waiting to fall down on her head. Paige pressed the heel of her palm to her chest as the chopstick beneath her ribs grew thorns.

'I'll call when I know more,' Gabe said.

'Sure. Fine. Or not. Whatever. Honestly, I'm cool either way.'

Gabe laughed again, the smooth deep sound vibrating

down her arm and landing with a warm thud deep in her belly. 'I'll call,' he promised, 'even if you're cool either way.'

'Okay,' she said on a long drawn out breath.

'Goodnight, Paige.' He rang off.

Paige turned towards the bar, but there her boots stopped short. She tapped her phone against her front teeth, her eyes misting over to the soft pink light spilling through the windows of the funky cocktail bar as she forced herself to think.

Good God, had she really floated the idea that Gabe was in Sydney avoiding her? She needed to get a grip. A man she wasn't attached to had merely postponed a date that till the night before had never even been on the cards. And yet her heart thumped at triple its normal pace. That wasn't her. She did not obsess about men she couldn't have. She was *not* her mother...

No. Time apart was the exact wake-up call she needed. Her life had been plenty satisfying before Gabe Hamilton moseyed into her lift and into her life, and she could do with a few days without him to remind her of that.

She breathed deep, the thin cold air slipping into her bloodstream, and she felt far less wobbly than she had a minute earlier. In fact she felt positively urbane. Then the extreme mixed scents of Richmond's Asiatic restaurant row hit the back of her throat and hunger followed in its wake. Teeth chattering, she hustled back inside the bar.

'Trouble in paradise?' Mae asked as Paige plonked herself back on her stool.

Paige opened her mouth to say everything was fine, but Mae's open palm stopped her in her tracks.

Mae said, 'Let me tell you a little story while you consider your answer. There I was the other night, enjoying my miniquiche at your gorgeous neighbour's housewarming, when I spotted you and the hot pirate, looking all cosy. I barely had time to jab Clint in the ribs when you were off, running for the door as if you couldn't wait to find somewhere private in which to tear one another's clothes off.'

Paige blinked down into her milky cocktail as the heat rose in her cheeks; a healthy mix of mortification that if Mae had noticed there was a good chance others had too, and regret that Mae knew she'd been keeping her fling with Gabe a secret.

'So what's going on with the two of you?' Mae asked.

'Nothing,' Paige insisted. 'Okay, something. But not what you think.'

'Why didn't you tell me?'

'It all happened so fast.'

'So fast you couldn't send me a text? Preferably with image attached.'

Paige frowned at Mae's pink cocktail, and tried to find an answer her best friend might understand, and couldn't. 'Honestly, I don't know why I didn't tell you. Maybe because I wasn't quite sure what to say. I'm still not.'

'Sounds serious.'

'Lord, no! It's a fling. That much I am sure of.'

'You've had flings before, Miss Paige. Before Clint came along the two of us were the queens of the no-strings fling and you never kept it from me before. So what made this one different?'

She risked looking at Mae, and saw the one person in the world who knew her best. Her next breath out felt awash with relief that the truth was out, tempered by a little stab of heartache that she'd found it so hard to tell her.

She leaned forward, and wrapped her fingers around her cold glass. 'Maybe it's that from the moment I met him it *felt* different. Which has been thrilling, but also kind of terrifying. I might be struggling a bit with remembering where my limits lie.'

'Maybe you're struggling because, with him, you don't want limits.'

Paige let herself wonder for about half a second before she remembered the unbearable feeling of the chopstick jabbing her under the ribs. She shook her head. 'Oh, no. With this one I want them more than ever.'

Mae nibbled at the inside of her cheek a few moments as if she was grappling with some inner turmoil, before leaning over and wrapping cool hands around Paige's. 'I know you like putting your life into neat separate little boxes, Paige— work, home, friends, lovers—and I get why. Having them in boxes makes them feel like they're under your control. I used to be the same way. And then I met Clint.'

Paige got her usual tummy ache at the mere mention of Clint's name, only this time the jab of the chopstick under the ribs joined it. Which made no sense at all.

Oblivious, Mae went on. 'I thought he was goofy and shy and way too sweet for the likes of me. I could have put him in that easy-to-ignore box on day dot and that would have been that. But I took a chance instead. I let him see me, and let myself see him. And look at us now.'

Paige wriggled on her stool, not liking talking about Clint any more than she had about Gabe. Because she hoped so hard that Mae could rise above the statistics, and genetics, and history and be happy for ever after? All of a sudden that theory didn't hold water.

She gave herself a mental shake. One thing at a time. This current dilemma was about her. And Gabe. Even the mere thought of him had her breathing out long and slow.

Paige waved her hands in front of her face. 'I know in your loved-up state you're seeing cupid's arrows flying all over the place, but it's not like that. I assure you. It's sex. Pure and simple. Well, to be honest it's not so pure or so simple.'

Finally Mae stopped looking at her as if she was trying

to see right into her soul. Her voice a low growl, Mae said, 'Now, you're talkin'. Details. You owe me.'

Paige figured she did, and then some. And gossiping like this felt so good, like the old days. 'So what do you want to know?'

'Do you have actual conversations in between bouts of athletic lust?'

'Sometimes. Sometimes we don't want to waste our breath.'

'Phew.' Mae rested her elbow on the table and her chin on her upturned palm. 'Do you catch yourself daydreaming about him? About his belly button, the whirl of hair behind his right ear, the way his eyes go all dark and dreamy when he sees you?'

Paige raised an eyebrow. 'Clearly *you* do.'

'Ha! So are you seeing anyone else?'

'No,' Paige answered before she'd even noticed Mae's change of tack, or the knowing gleam in her eye. Dammit.

'Do you want to?' Mae asked.

Paige sat up straighter. 'Where's Clint?'

'At the bar.'

'Good, I need another drink.'

'I'll bet you do.' Mae gave Paige's foot a quick nudge under the table. 'I know you, Paige. You are doing your absolute all to avoid even considering it, but I'm living proof that happily ever afters can happen, even to those who don't believe in them. And that's the last I'll say about that.'

Mae mimed zipping her mouth shut tight as Clint returned with a beer for himself, another pink drink for Mae, and a Midori Splice for Paige.

'You looked like you might need it,' he said, before he slumped back onto his stool and closed his eyes as if he was seriously about to have a nap right there in the middle of the bar.

Paige should have thanked her lucky stars that Clint's arrival had saved her from answering any more of Mae's questions. But watching Mae's eyes constantly swerving back to her fiancé, her finger running distractedly across the rim of her cocktail glass, her cheeks warm and pink, a small smile curving at her mouth, Paige felt as if she was witnessing something so intimate she ought to look away.

But she found she couldn't.

Did Mae really believe they could love each other through everything? Through fights and ambivalence? Through having kids and demanding jobs? Through the times they were in each other's pockets every minute of the day and the times they spent apart? Through the times they'd inevitably hurt one another in moments of boredom, exhaustion, self-absorption?

Her parents hadn't. Not even close. For them it had simply been too hard. So Paige just couldn't make herself believe. Even when Clint opened one eye and gave Mae a warm lazy smile, and it was like being *this* close to the real thing Paige could almost touch it.

She took a hard gulp of her cocktail, barely tasting it as her mind shifted to the one secret she hadn't dared share with Mae, the secret she'd refused to even admit to herself until that quiet moment in the noisy bar.

She felt things for Gabe. Soft, gentle, warm things.

She didn't believe it would last. She didn't believe it was about anything other than chemistry. But it terrified her to the soles of her boots.

In the end Gabe was gone a little over a week.

Paige was thrilled at how much she got done with all that extra time! She'd done her tax. She'd rearranged her lounge-room, twice. Made her way through every level of Angry Birds. Caught up with Mae, and Clint, another two times. And she'd thrown herself into work with a gusto she hadn't felt for months, shining up her proposal to shoot the summer catalogue in Brazil until the thing about glowed.

Time apart had been a good thing for sure. She was in a good place. Sure again about what she was doing. And that she could handle it. Yet there was no denying the nerves that skittered through her belly the morning of the Monday he was due back.

She donned the new black lacy underwear she'd bought specially, then practically skipped into her walk-in robe to get dressed for the day and—

Instead of reaching for the work outfit she'd hung out the night before, her hand went to the white garment bag poking out from the deepest darkest corner of the cupboard and before she could stop herself she'd unzipped the bag containing her secret wedding dress with a rush.

The moment the weight of the daring concoction of chiffon, pearls, and lace filled her hands, something flipped a switch inside her and she had rough-housed the gown over her head. The satiny lining slid over her curves, cool and soft against her bare skin, then the hem dropped with a gentle swoosh to float over her bare toes. Her fingers shook as she guided the zip up her back until it stopped just below her shoulder blades.

Eyes closed, knees trembling, she turned to face the mirror behind her wardrobe door. She hoped desperately the thing swam on her, or the colour made her look jaundiced, or that she looked as if she belonged on the top of a toilet-paper roll like the doll her mum had in her downstairs bathroom.

'It's just a dress,' she whispered, her voice echoing in the cosy space. Yet when she opened her eyes it was to see herself through a sheen of tears.

Was this how Mae felt when she tried hers on? Beautiful, and special, and magical, and romantic, and hopeful? She didn't know, because she'd never asked. It was always Mae who brought up the wedding. Mae who came over to her place with bridal magazines. Mae who booked meetings with caterers and bands. Mae who had to work so hard to get Paige to even pretend to sound enthused.

Mae had motivation. Mae had found the thing they'd spent so many years convincing one another didn't exist. A man to trust. A man to hold. A man to love.

As if she were having an out-of-body experience, Paige watched her reflection with a feeling of detachment as a single tear slid down her cheek. And then everything came into such sharp focus she actually gasped.

Paige knew the moment it had happened. The moment her work had ceased to satisfy her. The moment she'd stopped dating. The moment her life had lurched out of her tightly held control.

It had happened with the first flash of Mae's pretty little solitaire as Mae had giddily told her Clint had proposed. The diamond dazzling her as the sun caught an edge, piercing her right through the middle, tearing every plan, every belief, every comfort she had that she wasn't alone in believing love wasn't priority number one.

She pressed the heels of her palms into her eyes, heat and tears squeezing past them.

What was *wrong* with her? Her best friend was in love. Getting married. Actually *happy*. Because of *that* her world had crumbled?

She'd always thought the hot spot that flared in her stomach whenever she looked at Mae and Clint together was fear for her friend. She'd been kidding herself. It was envy. Deep, torturous, craving certainty that she'd never experience even a tenth of the love and affection they shared. It had run so deep that for months she hadn't even been able to face going on a date that would only remind her she was destined to be alone.

The tears came so fast she began to sob. And then to choke.

And then she couldn't breathe. Her lungs felt as if they were being squeezed from the inside out. The only way she'd ever breathe again was to get out of the damn dress.

She tugged at the straps, but they dug into her shoulders. She yanked at the deep neckline, but it wouldn't budge. Her trembling fingers wrenched at the zip at her back and—

She stilled, one foot braced indecorously on an ottoman, her arms doing some crazy pretzel move behind her.

The zip was stuck.

Like something out of a movie, the next hour of her life flashed before her eyes. She had to leave in ten minutes if she had a hope of getting to work on time. And first up that day? The final presentation of her Brazilian proposal.

Determination steeling her, Paige took a breath, sniffed back any remaining threads of self-pity, gripped the zip between unwavering fingers, and tugged.

Nada.

Argh! What was she going to do?

Mae and Clint lived only a couple of suburbs over, but in peak-hour traffic it would take for ever for one of them to get to her. The neighbour next door was in hospital getting a nose job. If she called on Mrs Addable upstairs her predicament would be all over the building before she even left the apartment.

Maybe she could wear the thing. She could cover most of it up. Her chartreuse beaded cardigan. Her cropped chocolate jacket. Her fringed grey cowboy boots. And accessories. Lots of fabulous accessories. She pictured the conference room: Callie holding court with the fawning assistants, Geoff hovering over the pastry tray trying desperately not to eat one, her assistant Susie looking up at her as if she were the bee's knees as she waltzed in...*wearing a wedding dress.*

With a sob Paige gave in and slumped to her back on her bed.

* * *

Gabe stood in the ground level foyer of the Botany Building, rubbing a hand across the back of his neck. It had bee
a hell of a week. The two other mobs who'd lined up to hea
out the ramblings of a rabble of tech-nerds on nanotechnol
ogy applications had been the hardest competitors he'd bee
up against in an age. He'd been lit by the honest to goodness
thrill of the chase, and the flicker of brilliance he'd spent hi
career chasing felt, if not imminent, then at least possible fo
the first time in a long time.

And yet Gabe felt unpredictably relieved at being back
The cold didn't seep into his bones like before. The trundl
of trams didn't give him a twitch. And even the Gotham
esque skyline didn't appear quite so unforgivingly stark. I
fact with the morning sun pouring over the jut of skyscrap
ers, glorious Finders Street train station, and the gleaming
snaking river, the city had looked downright pretty.

Maybe he'd missed his bed, with its him-shaped dent. O
maybe he'd missed what could have been in his bed, all long
and warm and languid, a warm smile lighting up her dee
blue eyes, her lush pink mouth—

The lift binged.

Gabe discreetly repositioned himself. Whoever might b
in the lift didn't need to see how a week without Paige in hi
bed had affected him. But without even opening its doors
the lift headed back up without him.

A muscle twitched in his cheek. 'Now, this I didn't miss.

The lift paused on the eighth floor. Paige's floor. He
checked his watch. She might not yet have left for work. He
could drop in. Say 'hi'. Shore up their plans for dinner tha
night. He actually laughed out loud. As if he'd be able t
stop at just that.

No, he needed to get into the office to debrief Nate on th
deal. He needed to get back to the piles of paperwork tha
needing reading before he signed on the dotted line to lis

BonaVenture on the stock market. So that he could get out there again, back amongst the sharks where he belonged.

And yet as he eyeballed the lift his mind didn't wander to the big wide world waiting for him. His fingers twitched at the thought of burying themselves in masses of silken blonde hair. His mouth watered as he imagined the sweet taste of soft pink lips. He hardened at the thought of burying himself deep inside a woman who knew how to take him to the brink and right on over the other side.

He checked his watch again. His feet twitched and he stared at the lift, as if eyeballing it would make it come back to him.

Screw it.

Three long strides took him to the door to the stairs; he pushed through and took them two at a time, a surge of adrenalin all but giving him wings. His blood pumping hard through his veins as he got ever closer to number eight.

He reached her floor, jogged to her apartment, and, before he could talk himself out of it, banged on her door with a closed fist, feeling a connection to his caveman ancestors. If he was able to do more than grunt before kissing that heavenly mouth of hers he'd deserve a damn medal.

She was home. The shuffle of bare feet on her polished wood floor brought on a heavy heat in his groin. 'Paige,' he called, his voice as gruff as a bear's. 'It's me.'

Then, listen as he might, he heard nothing, not even a breath. He hadn't imagined it, had he? Conjuring up sounds of her that weren't even there? He started as the doorknob squeaked and turned in its socket. Then the door opened as if in slow motion.

It had been barely a week since he'd seen her, yet the moment he looked into her beautiful face his heart skipped a beat. He'd heard the expression, but before that moment he'd not known it felt like stepping off the top of a tall building with only a faint hope there'd be a dozen firemen waiting below with a big trampoline.

Paige blinked at him, her gorgeous blue eyes smoky with smudged eyeliner. Her hair was all a tumble. Her skin flushed pink. The woman looked so gorgeously rumpled he throbbed for her, and it took every effort not to throw her over his shoulder and toss her down on the bed and take her before they'd even said hello.

Cleary a glutton for punishment, he slid his gaze down her gorgeous body to find it encased in—

What the—?

He blinked. And again.

Well, he thought as his libido limped into hiding as though it had been kicked where it hurt most, *you don't see that every day.*

CHAPTER EIGHT

'ARE we a tad overdressed for this time of the morning?' Gabe asked.

'What do you think?' Paige asked, before swallowing so hard the tendons on her neck looked about to snap.

'I think you're wearing a wedding dress.' Even as he said the words a pulse began to beat in his temple. 'Is it yours?'

After a long second she nodded, her eyes like those of a puppy who'd been kicked. As if *she* were the one who should be feeling hard done by, not the guy she was sleeping with who'd just come back from a week away to find himself staring down a bride.

Right. Okay. Think. Not an easy thing to do considering he was fighting against the unwieldy mix of raging lust and abject horror wrestling inside him.

'And you're wearing it because…' *You've been married before? You're getting married today? You missed me that much…?*

Wow. Had everything somehow been leading to *this*? No matter all the safeguards he'd put in place, had he been outfoxed again? Should he have paid more heed to Hitchcock's warnings after all? He'd give her a minute to explain. Two at most. And if he wasn't a hundred and ten per cent thrilled with the answers he was outta there.

'The zip's stuck!' She turned, lifted her hair and flashed

him an expanse of beautiful back. And creamy-coloured lace, and pearl looking things and—

Gabe lifted his eyes to the ceiling. 'That's not exactly… I meant why do you own a…you know?'

'Took you long enough to ask.'

Gabe was fairly sure he'd only been at her apartment door for a minute but apparently he'd passed through the looking glass, so who knew? 'Forgive me if my mind's working at about thirty per cent velocity, but what the hell are you talking about?'

'Oh, come on. You knew about the dress.'

Gabe shook his head, hard, hoping it might send him back to the right dimension. 'What precisely am I meant to know about it?'

'That it exists. That it's mine. That I have a wedding dress in my possession.'

'Paige, I'm on the back foot here, with the dress, and the accusations, and the…dress. But I can honestly, hands down, say, I've never seen it before.'

'The day we met,' she shot back, eyes flashing, arms crossed beneath her breasts until they loomed above the deep V of the dress. 'I was carrying it in the lift.'

He opened his mouth to tell her she damn well wasn't, because there was no way in hell he'd have made a play for an *engaged* woman. Who needed that kind of drama? *Was* she engaged? No. He couldn't believe it. He shut his mouth, realising nothing good would come of any question he asked. And she didn't look in the mood for an argument. In fact she looked pretty close to a nervous breakdown.

Not exactly what he'd imagined their reunion might be like. Sure, he'd imagined heat, he'd imagined sweat, he'd not even dared hope to come close to losing consciousness. But right then, the only thing keeping him from bolting was the fact that the terror in Paige's eyes pretty much mirrored his own.

He tore off his beanie, unwound his scarf, rid himself
f his jacket and threw them onto her kitchen diner. Then,
ands shaking a little, he reached out, slowly, and curled
is palms around her upper arms, careful not to touch the
abric wrapped lovingly around her body. Then he pressed
imself inside her apartment and kicked the front door shut
vith his foot.

'Paige. Believe me when I tell you this. I don't recall you
arrying anything that day.'

'You told Nate I tried to shut the door on your hand, but
ou don't remember me carrying a fluorescent white garment
ag with 'Wedding Dress Fire Sale' in hot-pink neon writing
lashed across the front of it?'

'I remember fine.' *The big blue bedroom eyes. The rum-
led blonde hair. The legs that went all the way up. The sparks
ouncing off the walls. The instant intense stab of desire that
ad made a mockery of his efforts to sleep his jet lag away.*
I remember *you.*'

At that Paige blinked. Faster than a hummingbird's wings.
And then she breathed out, long and slow, as if she'd been
olding her breath a real long time.

At the slow rise and fall of her chest his eyes defied him
nd slid down, noting how well the…thing fitted her, dipping
t the front, hugging at the sides, sloping down her beautiful
ips. If a man in a rented tux ever got to see *that* walking to-
vards him down an aisle, he'd have no complaints.

But he would never be that man.

He liked Paige. She was funny, smart, great company,
reath-taking in bed. But if this dress was some kind of sign,
he was signalling the wrong man.

He wasn't a marrying man. Not even long-term-commit-
nent guy. His priorities simply made it impossible. For as
ong as he could remember his ambitions had been clear-cut:
o work hard and make his gran proud. After his one mon-

umental hiccup, he'd poured all of himself into fixing tha mistake. Never making the same one again.

And he wasn't here. Was he? It didn't feel as though h was, but, considering his track record, who the hell knew?

He pinched the bridge of his nose, knowing there was n going forward—to the apartment, to work, or dinner, or eve to her bed—till they cleared this all up.

Gabe slowly removed his hands and tucked them into th pockets of his old jeans and took a small step back. He lifte his eyes deliberately to hers. Her eyes were all liquid-blue her lush mouth down-turned. She looked so forlorn, so…un bridely, it was almost laughable. Almost.

He motioned with his chin to the small kitchen table. 'Sit She sat. Gabe sat too, though far enough away so as not t touch. 'So do you want to tell me what this is all about so can stop looking over my shoulder for the priest?'

'Really?'

'More than you know.'

'Okay,' she said, then after a big deep shaky breath wer on. 'So I'd been shopping with Mae to find her wedding dres the morning before we met, and I saw this dress and felt lik I'd never breathe again if I didn't take it home. Not out o some deep and abiding desire to get married. I've never bee one of those girls who always wanted to get married. On th contrary. So we can clear that up.'

'Okay,' he said, feeling far from clear.

Then Paige looked down, a swing of fair hair falling ove her face, all her usual va va voom seeping out of her as sh stared at some unknown spot on the table. 'Turns out Ma getting married has really thrown me. More than I'd realise until about half an hour ago. I've been completely out of syn since she got engaged. We've been in one another's pocket for such a long time. And now she's…not mine any more. She held out her hands as if she'd lost something then settle back into her slump. 'I've been going through the motions ever since. With Mae. At work. Not dating.' Her eyes slid to his, her long dark lashes all crazy and clumped together. 'You're the first guy I've seen since it happened.'

The emphasis on the word 'seen' brought a flare of heat to his groin. When he shifted on the chair Paige noticed, and her mouth flickered into the first smile of the day.

'Mae had a theory about why I bought the dress,' she went on, 'and it was easier to believe that than to believe the truth. That I was jealous of her. Not the marriage bit, the happiness bit. So I kind of wished for you. And then a minute later you stuck your fingers through the lift door.'

'I'm sorry... You wished for me?'

Sass put some sinew into her slump as she flicked her fringe off her face, and lifted one saucy shoulder. The flare of heat spread till it roared through his blood with the speed and intent of a bush fire.

'Well, not *you* in particular,' she said. 'A man who... Well, a man. Mae's theory for why I bought the dress was that I needed to get some.'

Gabe's mouth turned dry at the thought...for about half a second. Then saliva pooled beneath his tongue and he had to physically press himself back into the chair so as not to go right ahead and give her what Mae thought she needed.

Paige slowly eased herself upright, leaned back in her chair, and looked him dead in the eye, and he realised she hadn't been kidding. If any other man had walked into the lift at that precise moment she would have been sitting at her kitchen table sending some other guy hard with desire with those burning baby blues of hers.

No way. It wouldn't have been the same. The way they fitted was chemical. One in a million. Thus worth pursuing to the edges of his limits. Clearly, or he wouldn't still be sitting there while she wore a wedding dress.

He leaned forward, keeping her gaze connected to his. 'And now that you have…got some, how are you doing?'

Paige tilted an eyebrow, before wafting a hand past her lace-covered curves. 'How do you think I'm doing?'

'Fair enough.' Gabe rubbed his fingers into his eyes to clear the image that was making it hard for him to see straight. 'And do you try it on every morning—? '

'Good God, no! This was the first time *ever*. Don't think I ever had any intention of you finding me like this. This is my worst nightmare. And I can't fathom why *you're* still sitting here and not halfway to anywhere else but here!'

She had him there. He'd help her get the dress off then vamoose. Go home. Go to work. Put some space between them so that he could think.

He shoved back the chair so hard it squeaked on the pale floorboards. He motioned to her with a flick of his fingers. 'Come on.'

'What?'

'You said that thing was stuck.'

She nodded. 'The zip. It's caught on something. I tried tugging, and shimmying it over my head, but it fits like a glove.'

It did that. 'Then let's get you free of it, shall we?'

Paige stood, and turned her back to him.

Swallowing down the bile rising in his throat at the connotations of ridding a beautiful woman of a wedding dress, Gabe forced his eyes to move to the dress to find a paper clip had been bent through the eye of the zip.

His tension melted a little. At least now he could be certain she'd had a go at taking the thing off. As for the rest? Everyone had weaknesses, and if hers was for a combination of lace and pearly-looking things, then it beat smoking. Just

'Do you need me to move at all?' she asked, lifting her hair away from her neck, the scent of her shampoo wafting past his nose for the first time in days. The interplay of muscle across her back made his fingers feel fat and useless as blood left his extremities to pour into his groin.

He reached for the zip, the backs of his fingers brushing across her warm skin. Her muscles twitched at even his slightest touch. A few strands of hair fell to slide against the back of his hand and, God help him, delicate shocks prickled down his arms landing with a rock-hard thud in his pants.

'You want this thing off or not?' he asked, his voice gruff.

'I do.'

'Then stop wriggling.'

She stilled. And there were a few long moments in which the only sound was the shuffle of satin on her skin as the hopeless zipper refused to budge.

'I had an outfit,' she said. 'For tonight.'

'Another one?'

Her laughter was husky, telling him he wasn't the only one affected by the fact that he was, to all intents and purposes, trying to get her naked. The sound vibrated through him, morphing into a *whump whump whump* that pulsed through his veins.

'Quite something, this outfit of mine. Red, sleek, no zip in sight.'

He swallowed down the lust rising from the bottoms of his feet all the way to the back of his throat. The phenomenal pull of desire he felt for her, despite the wedding attire, gave him one last pause.

Did he want her too much? To the detriment of his own sense? His own self-interest? He listened to his gut, and listened hard. But even his deeply scarred conscience couldn't go there. She was habit-forming, but the hold she had over him was unintentional. And all the more dangerous because of it? Not so long as they both knew the score. He'd just have to make sure she never forgot it. Him either.

'Careful,' she cried out suddenly when the sound of overstretched fabric rent the silence. Then like the collapse of a dam, the zip gave way. The dress tipped over her shoulders and she scooped it to her chest, but not before he'd caught a glimpse of a strapless black lace bra and a hint of matching G-string.

'Oh, come on!' she said, turning and staring down at the dress so that her breasts pressed together. 'I'd been working on that damn thing for half an hour! It clearly hates me. Well, I hate it right on back. It's so going straight to Good Will after this.'

'Nah,' he said, his voice rough as sand, 'I have the touch.'

She glanced up at him, her chest pinking as she realised the direction of his gaze. And he was more than half hard. When their eyes met, her bottom lip was tucked between her teeth, and her naked toes curled over one another under the pool of material at her feet.

And Gabe knew he wasn't going anywhere.

A half-second after he moved for her, she let the dress go and was in his arms. Clinging to him as he devoured her with his mouth. Tasting her neck, his tongue tracing the line of her jaw, teeth nipping at her ear. When he slid his hands to cup her backside it was to find the dress was thankfully gone, leaving him with her hot bare skin and a strip of lace.

When he lay her back on the table, atop his jacket and scarf, she was pink all over. A pulse beating fast in her neck. Her lips moist from his kiss. Her eyes so hot he could barely make out a thin circle of blue. She grabbed him by the beltline, tugging him between her legs, wrapping her thighs about him as she whipped his button fly open with one rough yank.

With a growl he buried his face in her breasts. Drinking in the scent of her till his lungs were full. When he palmed her breast she arched off the table.

Lust filled him so thick and rich his vision was a pinprick. His focus concentrated on a bead of perspiration running down her torso. The jump of her muscles as his hands encircled her waist. Her gasp as he pressed a kiss to her navel. The grip of her hands in his hair as he sank his teeth into her hipbone. The way she trembled as he ran a thumb along the strip of soft black lace.

Holding onto the thinnest thread of control, he pressed her thighs apart and kissed her. She flung an arm over her eyes and let her thighs fall apart all the way. He tugged the slip of lace aside and took her in his mouth, tasting, bringing her to the edge before pressing soft kisses to her inner thigh. When she begged him to never stop, he never did, and when she came it was with such abandon he almost came right along with her.

Fumbling for his wallet, he took for ever before he found a condom. Sheathed, he hovered over her, waiting until her eyes found his, glints of fire, before he sank into her. Pressing into her velvet heat, deeper and deeper. The walls of her body gripping him like nothing else he'd ever known. One hand around the top of the round table, the other on his hip, she sucked in short sharp breaths. When pleasure gripped him from the inside out his eyes squeezed shut and he heard himself yell her name as he came.

As the world slowly came back into focus Gabe's head cleared. And it was as if the hard and fast sex had knocked something loose.

He looked into her eyes, to find them dark, liquid, sated, making him hard for her all over again. Knowing it, she grinned, and stretched her arms over her head, letting them dangle over the edge of the table.

Willing himself to keep it together another moment, he asked about the one part of the morning that hadn't made some sort of crazy sense. 'All this time you thought I thought you owned a wedding dress, and you therefore believed that *I* believed you were possibly about to be married.'

She looked up at him from under her lashes. 'Possibly.'

He braced an arm against the kitchen table. 'And that was *okay* with you?'

'Not normally. But remember I was a girl with not a lot of experience in happily ever afters who'd just bought a wedding dress. I needed to do something equally desperate to counteract the first act.'

Gabe blinked at her. A glint had made it through the sexual haze in her blue bedroom eyes. She was making jokes? 'Hell, Paige. Consider what you've put me through so far this morning and give me the slightest break, okay?'

She lifted a knee to brace herself, her inner thigh accidentally sliding along the outside of his leg. Or maybe not so accidentally. He was fast learning the woman had hidden facets.

'Gabe, I've dated guys who aren't jerks and they've still jerked me around. So I figured dipping my toes back into the dating pool with a jerk there'd be no nasty surprises.'

'Did you call me a jerk?' Gabe pushed himself to standing, found his jeans and yanked them up, buttoned them, and ran a hand up the back of his neck. His head was starting to thud.

'No. No!' she said, bracing herself on her elbows, the long, lean, rumpled, semi-naked length of her draped over the table. 'Honestly, there's nothing about you that screams jerk. Or whispers it even. But, come on. You were all big and dark and stubbled and dishevelled from your flight. Could you blame me for not jumping straight to "Mr Nice Guy"?'

His default position, to get annoyed and stay that way, flickered to life. But the thing was she was right. She'd seen him at his irritable worst and thought him unapproachable. He had seen a leggy blonde and thought SEX! They'd both been spot on.

But, just in case, he looked back at her, right into her eyes, looking for something else. The opposite of what he'd always been most afraid of. A sign of hope. Of expectation. A sign that she was deeper into this thing than he was.

'Yikes! Is that the time?' she said before he had the chance and Paige wriggled off the table and made a mad dash for what must have been her bedroom. The shower turned on. Two minutes later she was out. Dressed in tight black pants, black T-shirt, black man-eater boots, a swirly grey jacket that made her eyes look like the clearest summer sky.

With a hairpin between her teeth as she tamed her long hair up into a quick neat bun, she said, 'I have to run. So so late. Big big meeting. Last chance to convince Callie to let me shoot the summer catalogue in Brazil.'

He grabbed her hand as she fled past. She spun to look at him, her brows raised in question. How to put this delicately? 'I was never one of those boys who played "getting married" dress-ups when I was a kid either. Just so you know.'

She cocked her head, a grin sliding onto her mouth. 'Good to know. And considering your namesake, and your extensive knowledge of Doris Day movies, I'd have thought a penchant for playing bride and groom might have been one step too far.'

Damn, he thought. Some girl he'd found himself. Or had she conjured him after all? Either way... *Damn.*

'See you tonight?' she asked.

He nodded.

She planted a kiss on his lips. *Domestic,* he thought, not sure how it made him feel, before she pressed up on her heels, slid a hand into the back of his hair and the kiss deepened until blood was roaring through his head once again.

Who knew how long it was before she unpeeled herself from his front, blew a stray strand of hair from her forehead, and grinned?

'Welcome home. Lock up on your way out.' And she was gone.

When the sound of the slamming front door stopped echoing through the apartment, Gabe looked around, realising belatedly it was the first time he'd been inside. Pale furnishings. Lots of books, mostly coffee table and recipe. No prints on the walls, only photos; blown up, framed well. Photos of her travels, laughing raucously with Mae, with a cool-looking blonde who must have been her mother.

The rest wasn't overly garnished as he had imagined it might be, considering her job and her admitted penchant for scatter cushions. It was soft, elegant, warm. A haven not a showroom. It was her. Which gave him the impression that inviting someone into her home was akin to inviting someone into her life.

A strange feeling came over him then. Tightness. Darkness. Anticlimax.

She'd never invited him in. Not once. He'd had to practically bang her door down like some testosterone-laden caveman to get inside.

He'd thought himself in charge of the tempo of this thing. But from day one she'd come to him, and left him, on her terms. He'd let her because it was easy. He'd let her because it was hot.

He grabbed his stuff before letting himself out, locking the door behind him. As the lift took its sweet time in collecting him he stared unseeingly at his scowling face in the silver doors of the lift.

He told himself that after the rest of the morning's debacles it shouldn't have even registered on his list of things to give a flying hoot about. That since they were having a casual fling it shouldn't damn well matter at all where they were doing the flinging and where they weren't. But if the ball of lead that had taken up residence in his gut was anything to go by, apparently it damn well did.

CHAPTER NINE

GABE sat at his big gleaming desk in his vast and spartan office at BonaVenture later that day, ignoring yet more paperwork. His desk was annoying him too much to concentrate. The colour of the walls was making him twitch. Not that he wanted to shop online for interior decorations ever again. When he'd done so for the party he'd actually felt his balls shrink a size.

Instead he sat there and fumed and wondered, if Paige's apartment was such a clear reflection of her, then what did this office and his apartment say about him that his oldest friend thought he'd find them comfortable?

He sank his face into his hands and rubbed his temples with his thumbs. Since when had he ever wanted to be *comfortable*? For as long as he could remember, he'd sought brilliance in his life. He'd wanted to make an impression. Every way, every day. Nothing like having your parents die young to show a kid that every moment counted.

And somehow that had twisted into a footloose existence where the only thing that had his lasting imprint on it was a bed.

It was a hard truth to admit. Harder still to know what, if anything, he planned to do about it. Because no matter how far his life was from his original plans, it worked. Look at the success that had come of it. Did he even have the right to want to change things now?

When Nate came into his office followed by his assistant and a tray of coffee and doughnuts, like any cornered animal, Gabe lashed out. 'Tell me we're nearly done,' he growled.

'But that would be a lie,' Nate said. The assistant smartly left.

'I've read everything you've put in front of me. Listened to a dozen different experts. I'm not sure what else can be brought to the table. Hell, I'll take a meeting with a bearded lady and her psychic monkey if that'll convince you I'm up to speed.'

The sober leather chair on the other side of Gabe's desk squeaked as Nate lowered himself into it. 'I hoped your time away would eventually wear down the chip on your shoulder. Seems it's burnished it to a shine.'

Gabe glanced across at Nate, a fighting muscle jumping under his left eye, to find Nate looking tired. More than tired, he looked older. As if the years, the business, had taken their toll on him too. Gabe wrestled his inner bear back into his cave, because he knew he was partly to blame.

'I've been working on this move for nearly eight months,' Nate said, his eyes hidden as he rubbed his thumb and forefinger deep into his sockets. 'And all I've asked of you is a few days to play catch up.'

'I've hardly been twiddling my thumbs all this time.'

Nate stopped rubbing his eyes. Instead he looked at the ceiling, a muscle working in his jaw. 'Never said you had, mate. But I can't do this on my own. Well, I can, clearly.'

Gabe opened his mouth to refute that, but the steel in Nate's eyes stopped him.

'More to the point,' Nate said, 'I don't want to do it on my own. When we created this monster together everybody thought we were crazy. But we knew better. And it was fun.

Even through the lean years. Look at what we achieved back then. Look at Alex. He wouldn't be the wunderkind he is now without us. And Harry's little website now practically runs the web. Then there were the McDumbass twins. What were we thinking there? Good times even when they were bad.'

Gabe's chest tightened. It had been so good. Exhilarating. Every decision fraught with risk and they'd only had their guts to guide them. And yet they'd got it so right time and time again. When had it all started to feel like so much work? He knew when. The one time he'd got it so very wrong.

Gabe leaned forward, placing his hands palm down on the table so as not to clench them into fists. 'We agreed back then that I'd take care of the research, you the schmoozing.'

'Mate,' Nate said, his smile wry. 'I let you sacrifice yourself for the sake of the company, because with your over-blown sense of moral justice if I'd asked you to stay you'd have walked in a heartbeat thinking that's what was needed to save us all.'

'I—' Would have, for absolute sure. His gran's voice rang in his head: *Work hard, boy, and make me proud.* It was the compass by which he lived his life. And it felt as if he'd never stopped paying for the one time he'd lost his way.

In frustration, Gabe pushed at a pile of paperwork that shifted and swooshed to the floor. They both looked at it a moment, neither of them with the energy to clean it up.

'This is what it comes down to,' Nate said. 'List, or not. Sell, or don't. Make more money than we'll ever know what to do with overnight, or keep at it.'

'You got any dice on you?' Gabe said, and Nate's jaw clenched so hard pink spots broke out on his neck and cheeks.

'If that's how you want to choose, then that's your business. Just pick.' Nate thumped himself on the chest with a closed fist. 'It's not fun for me any more. How about you? When was the last time you found this fun?'

Gabe stared back.

'Yeah, that's pretty much what I thought.'

Gabe's insides felt so twisted he wasn't sure they'd ever find a way to untwist again. The desire to walk out of that door, only this time to never look back, burned within him. He knew he could go out on his own and survive fine. But something held him back. Whether it was his 'overblown moral compass' or something more elusive he could no longer be sure.

'Let's get out of here,' Nate said, standing and heading for the door. 'Get a drink. We can do this later. There's no rush.'

Gabe, who'd already decided a drink was a damn good idea, pushed himself to his feet. 'No rush? You spent the last ten minutes convincing me to make a decision!'

Nate's shoulders squared from behind as his fingers curled around the door. And with a rush Gabe understood.

Gabe said, 'Did you really think if you kept me here long enough I'd magically begin to realise all that I'd walked away from, and *stay*?'

Nate turned and leant against the doorjamb, a lazy smile spreading across his face, though there was no humour in it. 'Well, yeah, actually. It's time for you to come home. Because if you're not going to run this thing with me, then I'm out.'

Gabe blinked. He thought of what it had taken for him to come home. The red-eye flight. Sleeping on the floor of his apartment. The million memories, good bad and everything in between, clawing at him from every street corner. The bitter winter cold that never seemed to leave his bones unless he was with Paige—

His inner rant stopped there as if it had run head first into a brick wall.

Paige.

No matter the storm gathering around him, he couldn't add her to the fallout. The mere thought of her, warm and willing

and wanton, was enough to quiet the worst of the noise building in his mind. His time with her was probably the reason
he'd made it to this point without imploding. Or simply getting on a plane in the middle of the night. Or noticing Nate's
now patently obvious motivation.

While she'd never even invited him in.

'So, old friend,' Nate said, cutting into his abstraction, 'do
we take this thing out for a proper spin together? Or do we
make more money than Midas and walk away?'

Nate gave the doorjamb a thump, and left, his voice sliding back through the door as if he were on the other side of
the world as he said, 'Now hurry up. That drink won't wait
all day.'

Paige gazed out of the window of the dark and sumptuous
Rockpool Bar and Grill, the lights of the city glittering over
her reflection in the glass. She couldn't remember ever feeling
so relaxed on a first date. It was as if the breakthrough she'd
had that morning about how she felt about Mae's engagement
had unblocked all sorts of things inside her.

And then there was her date, who, for all intents and purposes, should have run screaming the minute she'd opened
her door wearing a wedding dress that morning. But he'd
stayed. Let her talk. Stripped her bare. Didn't flip out. That
took some kind of man. Intrepid. Generous. Rock-solid. A
Grown-Up. A man who knew himself so well he'd never have
asked her on a date if there was anywhere else he'd rather be.

When he'd shown up at her apartment door earlier that
evening in dark jeans, clean boots and tailored jacket over
a grey shirt—his version of dressed up—she'd felt so *full*
it had taken every ounce of energy to appear normal. But
he didn't make her feel normal. He made her feel safe. And
for someone who spent her life waiting for the other shoe to
drop, it was a trip.

She breathed deep, her nostrils filling with the mouth-watering scent of char-grilled beef, her gaze tripping over the mass of shiny black tables, past portraits of cattle hanging on the walls, to snatch glimpses of Gabe as he paced in the bar. After he pocketed his phone, and jogged up the steps to the dark restaurant, his eyes found hers. And her breath left her lungs in a whoosh as it always did when she found herself the subject of that stunning gaze.

'Sorry,' he grumbled as he sat across from her, 'work.'

She shrugged. Not much caring. She was glad to be there with a guy she liked and respected. One whose company, conversation, touch she'd missed acutely when he was away. But she'd survived just fine. She felt so urbane she could burst.

'You picked dessert?' he asked, flicking through the menu.

'You're not going to look at the appetisers first?'

'Never. Rule of thumb is only choose as much pre-dessert dinner as your chosen dessert will allow.'

'How you look like that when you eat how you do is beyond me.'

He glanced up at her, his eyes dark, but a smile tugging at the corner of his mouth. 'God loves me.'

'Clearly.' Her breath caught when he held her a gaze a fraction longer before his eyes swept slowly down her length before landing back on the dessert page. His smile turned to a grin as he said, 'There. Doughnuts. Lemon curd with vanilla apple and ice cream.'

When he flicked back to the steak selections, Paige leant her cheek in her palm and took her fill. The dark shirt straining across his huge shoulders. The golden lamps created gleaming streaks in his dark hair and shadows beneath his slashing cheekbones. Though she was sure the shadows beneath his eyes had nothing to do with the fall of the light.

He'd had a hard day, which she had no doubt had been made harder still by how it had begun. And yet here he was.

A yearning kind of ache blossomed in her chest. And the same fullness she'd felt when he'd appeared at her door. Her heart beat a little faster to compensate.

Gabe looked up from his menu, and caught her staring. His eyebrows rose in question.

'So how is work?' she said, glancing away to find her wine. 'All big secret plans you're here to work on going well?'

A muscle jerked in his jaw and he frowned at the menu. 'Well enough.'

'Nearly done doing whatever it is you came here to do?' she asked.

He folded the menu and grabbed his drink, not even catching her eye as he said, 'Not soon enough.'

Whoa. She rubbed at the bare arm of her one-shouldered dress as she came out in a sudden case of goose bumps. 'So what *are* you working on, exactly?'

Gabe's eyes, darker still, slid back to hers. 'I can't discuss it.'

'Why the heck not?'

All he offered was a stubborn lift of his shoulder, and as the blissful warmth she'd been basking in all the long day took on a decided chill her contrary muscle kicked into full gear. She looked right back as she asked, 'What are you, some kind of spy?'

His mouth twitched, before flattening into a straight line. 'No. But my work can be…sensitive.'

She looked from one dark eye to the next, looking for a glimmer, a spark, something to tell her he was kidding and she'd missed the subtlety of his tone. But all she got was a big old wall. 'But you work in investments of some kind, right? Like a mini-bank.'

The pause before he nodded was so long Paige felt every beat of her heart, thumping short and tight. She waited, impatiently, until his distracted gaze caught on hers. 'I admit it's been a while since I've been on an actual date. But from memory it's the kind of event where people talk, with work being a common topic. So how about I go first? After the Brazil range we're going Parisienne for autumn. Your turn.'

She knew she was pushing him. His stillness couldn't have made it more obvious. But the leap it had taken for her to risk escalating what she felt for him by putting a name on it had been a leap of faith. In *this*. In him. She'd poured out her heart about the whole Mae thing. Something so deeply personal she hadn't even been able to admit it to herself. While he was acting like, well, pretty much the definition of a jerk.

She never should have agreed to do this. This wasn't what she'd signed up for, feeling all anxious and shaky and hopeful. She knew better than to make herself vulnerable to having her emotions screwed with by the actions of some guy.

She tucked her feet beneath her chair, ready to throw down her napkin and get the hell out of there before she did something completely daft, like cry.

Until Gabe casually threw out, 'My work's not a game, Paige. Not all frou-frou and garnish. A lot of money's at stake. And reputations. Hundreds of people's futures.'

Paige's fingers still gripped the table, and, ignoring the *frou-frou and garnish* comment in an effort to stop herself from throwing her drink at him, she said, 'Good for you. But that doesn't explain the stoic silence on the subject.'

'The sharing of privileged information has serious consequences. I have to be extremely careful about who I talk to about my business particulars.'

It was so ridiculous she actually laughed out loud. And then a memory flickered into her head. 'Mae! Is this about that "insider trading" joke she made back at The Brasserie that night?'

Gabe didn't even blink as he said, 'She doesn't seem to be the most discreet person on the planet.'

Wow. Jerk didn't even *begin* to describe how he was acting. While she felt like the world's biggest fool.

'Enjoy your dessert,' Paige said, already on her feet as she grabbed her purse, threw twenty bucks for the drinks on the table. And then, in a last-ditch effort to appear sophisticated and not the trembly mess she felt, she added, 'Call me when you're done. I'll keep your side of my bed warm.'

She stalked out of the restaurant all but blind with rage and hurt and humiliation.

For a moment there, her heart pitter-pattering as she'd watched his beautiful head bent over the dessert menu, she'd actually let herself dream a little that maybe her soft, warm feelings for him meant something. That the fact that he'd seen her in a wedding dress and not fainted was a sign that something special was happening. Something precious. That her luck had changed.

Luck schmuck. For her to think differently about love, she'd need luck, a miracle, and the kind of change of heart for which she'd need a defibrillator, a thousand volts, and a near-death experience thrown in for good measure.

Gabe sat alone at the table long enough to finish his drink, even while it tasted bitter the whole way down. He had every intention of staying till the meal was done. There were doughnuts after all. Until out of the corner of his eye he saw the coat-check stubs, both of them, still on the table, meaning Paige was heading out there, into the freezing cold night, in an outfit that would give her frostbite.

'Dammit,' he growled, throwing a couple of hundred down to cover the table, before he grabbed the nearest waiter, jabbed the coat-check stubs in his hands and offered him another fifty if he got the coats in thirty seconds flat.

There was no denying he was angry that Paige had stormed off. Nothing he'd said had been untrue, even while he'd hardly gone out of his way to mollify her when it became clear she was getting upset. It was only because the urge to tell her everything she wanted to know had been so strong. After his run-in with Nate, the desire to get her take, to see the convoluted mess through her clear eyes, was too seductive.

And he'd been *there* before. Gripped by the need to open up to someone. He'd lost his gran just before he'd met Lydia, and had needed someone soft and warm to listen while he talked. And now he might be about to lose his company, his life's work, and again he found himself turning to a woman. A cool blonde, to make things that much more convoluted, especially when giving into that urge had screwed things up so royally the first time.

Coats in hand, he shot out of the restaurant, down the long hallway, his long strides landing in the circles of golden light. He burst out into the Crown Casino complex, turned back the way they'd come.

Relief poured through him as he saw her on the next level down, halfway across the dark marble lobby and heading for the street. No way he could have missed her; not in that dress. Red, sleek, with a well-placed frill, a split up the side and one-bare shoulder, it had made it nearly impossible for him to keep his hands to himself, even while she pissed him off.

When she hit the busy night-time crowd outside he might never find her. He ran down the escalator, apologising every two seconds, and he angled past the bustling crowd. And he caught up with her at the edge of the cab rank, standing tall, back straight as the valet hailed her a cab.

Gabe threw his coat over his elbow and placed hers over her shoulders. She didn't even flinch. As if she'd known he was there. As if her awareness of him was that attuned. Even as he tried to block out every feeling that realisation lit a spark of desire in his blood.

A cab swept up the crescent-shaped drive and Gabe whipped open the back door before it had even pulled to a halt. Paige slid inside and Gabe followed.

'Where to?' the cabbie asked.

When Gabe barked, 'Just drive,' the cabbie didn't argue. He set his meter to running and curved into traffic, whistling beneath his breath.

Paige slid her seat belt into place and looked out of the far window. Moonlight glinted off her hair. The city lights reflecting colour onto the curves of her red dress. It had slid halfway up her thighs, leaving her long legs smooth, tempting, crossed, knees pointed determinedly away from him.

'Paige, look at me.'

She shook her head, and if anything sat straighter. And like a slap to his subconscious he remembered the hurt twisting Paige's beautiful features as she'd thrown money on the table and offered him her bed for the night.

He fought the urge to kick the back of the cabbie's seat, and closed his eyes and prayed for patience. And help. Something he hadn't asked for in a long long time. He'd been so used to doing everything on his own. He'd had no choice. But if anyone out there was listening, he'd take whatever help he could get to make Paige listen.

The only thing close to help it got him was an insistent voice telling him to help himself. He ran a hand through his hair and said, 'I was an ass back there.'

Her shoulder lifted. But had her breath hitched in her throat?

He shifted to face her more fully. 'A stubborn, mulish ass. A jerk, if you will.'

Her shoulders slowly lowered. Silence hovered between them. And she turned, a half-turn, so he had her profile to contend with: long lashes, stunning eyes, red lips, skin like alabaster in the moonlight. She said, 'Too right.'

Okay, so she was talking to him. What more did he want? Hell, if he knew. But the idea of losing her right when things were so unstable at BonaVenture gave him such a tightness in his chest he gripped his fingers into a fist ready to give himself a good thump.

She breathed out long and slow, then in a voice with the kind of calm he'd have killed for in that moment she said, 'You have no idea the secrets I've kept in my life. I'm just saying.'

Gabe leant his arm along the back of the seat. 'Such as?'

She glanced at the cabbie, who was singing 'O Sole Mio' at the top of his lungs by then, before she realised the trap. Her blood-red lips curved into a smile, even while her forehead puckered into a frown. 'The big ones aren't secrets any more. Stuff about my mum and dad mostly. About his cheating. Mum knew it, I knew it, and we all pretended like it wasn't happening to keep the peace. Not so peaceful that, actually. Suffocating in fact. Much better now the secrets are out in the open. For all of us.'

Gabe watched her, eyes glinting, jaw tight, doing what she needed to do to rise above what amounted to a right royal mess of an example of what a relationship should be. His parents had died when he was young enough that he'd never had any kind of example of what a real loving relationship meant. His gran had tried to instil in him a sense of right and wrong, and had probably hoped that with that foundation he'd figure out the rest as he went along. Would she be disappointed how profoundly he had *not* figured it out? No doubt.

'It's fine,' Paige said into his silence. 'You don't have to tell me anything about your life if it makes you uncomfortable. Honestly.' But by the down-turned edges of her beautiful mouth he knew it was anything but fine.

Letting him in the cab had been her way of offering him a second chance. And he was going to take it. He needed a mental run-up. Even while the gist of his ignominy was public record, proof that even all these years later there was no getting away from it, talking about that time was...difficult. But if it came down to talking, or saying goodbye then and there...

Gabe wiped both damp hands down the sides of his thighs and talked. 'When I said the sharing of privileged information has serious consequences, it's because I know from direct experience. I talked too much once and it nearly cost me everything. So you can understand how I need to be careful about such things.'

'How did you screw up?'

Those big blue eyes of hers looked right into him. Drawing him in like a siren song. And even as he told himself the song was not meant for him he said, 'A woman. A blonde.'

Paige curled a swathe of her golden hair around a finger.

'No,' he said, answering her unspoken question. 'Not like you at all.'

Her eyes swept back to his, darker now. 'Girlfriend? Fiancée? Wife?'

'Friend. With benefits.'

A smile ghosted across her face. 'A bit like me, then.'

Gabe shook his head. 'Not unless you are my lead for a company I'm investing in, but spying for my direct competition at the same time. '

'Ouch.'

'Indeed. My rival, who couldn't find a good idea with two hands and a flashlight, leaked our relationship to the Australian Securities Commission, which led to an investigation.' Gabe looked out of the window. It had started to rain. The city lights now reflecting off the shining black road, the swish of tyres on the wet surface strangely soothing, considering how fast and frantic his heart was beating. 'We were cleared, but that kind of thing sticks.'

'Why did she do it?'

'Money, and a lot of it, for making me, a complete stranger

to her before that point, look criminal at worst, incompetent at best. She wrote me a year or so after, explaining. Her husband had left her, and taken their kids and their cash and disappeared. She needed the money to find him.'

'She was desperate,' Paige said, as if it was no excuse, but maybe she understood a little.

Gabe turned back to find her knees had swung to face him and were mere millimetres from his own. His gaze fixated on the shadow beneath the stretch of red fabric at her thighs and his solar plexus clenched. 'You don't stumble into that kind of thing all the time in home wares?'

She moved a little, the dress rode higher and he had to grip the seat so as not to slide a hand up her warm thigh. She said, 'We did believe our catalogue images were stolen once. Turned out the intern had let a virus into the system when she was downloading a fake version of Angry Birds and it had eaten every image on file.'

'Not the same thing, then,' he said, his voice dry.

'Not so much.'

The cabbie finished his song, and in the silence Paige's chest rose and fell in a hypnotic rhythm. Now fixated on the silky frill that fluttered over her right breast every time she breathed, Gabe found himself saying, 'We were on top of the world right when it happened, and afterwards so near bankruptcy Nate was living on sandwiches and I was living on the crusts so that every spare cent could stay in the business. My only choice was to take myself out of the picture, while still doing the thing I did best, to give BonaVenture a chance. And I've been travelling ever since.'

Her long lashes swept swiftly against her soft cheeks and she looked long and hard at the middle of his chest. Every muscle within touching distance of that gaze clenched. 'How long ago was this?' she asked.

'Seven years.'

'About the time your gran Gabriella died.' Not a question. A statement. And, hell, if he couldn't remember even having told her.

His voice was gruff as he said, 'About then.'

'You were what? Mid-twenties? That's a lot to deal with. Especially for someone so young.'

Again with the understanding, he thought, but even he didn't fall for the nonchalant act. Instead he remembered with a piercing kind of immediacy how adrift he'd felt at that time. Anchorless. As if he'd lost his moral compass right as he'd hit the jackpot with money and success. Hell, no wonder he'd been easy pickings for the first woman who'd tried.

Her voice sang to him through the murky haze. 'BonaVenture Capital? Like the sponsors of the tennis? And that race before the Melbourne Cup, that's the BonaVenture Stakes, right?'

Gabe nodded again. Not that he'd known any of that before he'd read about it in the prospectus these last weeks.

'Well, it seems to me that, whatever you did, it worked. You lost your glass slipper for a while, but in the end you found it again.' And then she smiled, a soft, perceptive smile, and her eyes turned that particular shade of deep melting blue they only seemed to turn when they found him.

The image snapped something inside him. He felt it lodge in his ribs, like a Polaroid jammed in the corner of a mirror. A moment he should never forget. Then before he could stop himself he said, 'We're listing the company on the stock market. That's why I came back.'

He waited for the cold hard grip of panic to envelop him at what he'd revealed. But it never came. Instead he felt as if a fist that had been clenched deep inside him for as long as he could remember had unfurled and let go.

'Well, there you go. There's your happy ending,' she said, brightly, clearly having no idea what he'd given her. Or what he'd given himself. Then, 'I assume lips sealed on that one? No telling Mae?'

'Paige, about that—'

'Oh, shut up. She's the biggest blabber mouth this side of Antarctica. But I'm the only one who's allowed to say it. *Capiche?* And thanks for telling me.'

She leaned in then, as if it was the most natural thing in the world, and kissed him. Her lips were warm and sweet, the gentle flick of her tongue over his bottom lip incendiary.

When she pulled back she looked into his eyes and grinned. If her smudged lipstick was anything to go on he knew why. He was man enough to own a red pout for a kiss like that any day of the week. She unbuckled her belt, slid across the seat and leant on his shoulder. He belted her in, safe. Her scent curled into his nose, her sweet, luscious body nestled against his side, and he gave the cabbie directions to Docklands in a tone that meant the sooner the better.

He watched the familiar buildings slide by in silence. He'd always thought Melbourne looked its best in the rain. It brought lustre to the dark architecture. That night the city fair glittered back at him, like the facets of a jewel.

And Gabe realised whatever happened after this, without the secrets pressing against the inside of his skull as they had for so very long, for the first time in a long time he could see the flicker of brilliance at the corner of his eye.

Gabe walked Paige from the lift to her apartment door. He stood back, hands in his pockets, as she unlocked her front door, not wanting to fracture the delicate peace they somehow seemed to have carved out of the chaos of the evening.

Once the door was ajar she turned to him, her hand against his chest, small, warm, yet strong enough to make him feel as if it held his heart at bay. 'One more question.'

'Shoot.'

'This blonde who caused you all that trouble. Was she a natural blonde?'

He coughed out a laugh. 'Lydia?' he said, the name not creating the same swell of acid in his stomach as it used to. He thought about it. 'I'm not sure that she was.'

'Then there was your problem,' she said, her eyes meeting his. 'You should stick to natural blondes only in future.'

'I'll take that under advisement.'

They stood that way for a few beats, or a few minutes, how the hell was he to know? He was caught in those big blue eyes, and that gentle barely there touch had him rooted to the spot.

Then she stepped aside. 'Coming in?'

After the night they'd had Gabe wondered if it might be for the best to kiss her goodnight and head up to bed. To let the things they'd shared settle a while.

For about a tenth of a second he wondered, before he stepped over her threshold and sank his hand into her glorious hair, and pressed his mouth, his body, his self as wholly against her as it was possible to do while upright and fully clothed.

He'd been invited after all.

CHAPTER TEN

GABE burst into Nate's office the next morning at eight sharp. 'We're not selling!'

Nate looked up from his position on the floor by the window where he was twisting himself into some kind of pretzel shape on a mat.

Gabe's heels all but screeched on the rug as he pulled to a screaming halt. He cleared his throat and looked away. 'Sorry,' he said. 'I'll come back when you're not…doing that.'

Nate pulled himself neatly to standing and wiped a hand across his sweating brow. Motioning to the mat with an elbow as he downed half a bottle of water, he said, 'Yoga. Good for stress relief. You should try it.'

Gabe looked pointedly around Nate's princely office as he sank into a butter-soft leather couch. 'What have you got to be stressed about?'

Nate snorted. 'Now, what was it you stormed in here so early in the morning to declare?'

'Don't list the company,' Gabe said. 'Don't sell.'

Nate leant his backside against his desk and watched Gabe for a long moment. Then he asked, 'Why?'

'I've been up all night rereading the contracts. All of them.' Well, much of the night. The first half he'd spent in Paige's bed. It was soft, cool, and he'd found it nearly as difficult to leave it behind as his own. But fuelled by a kind of boyish energy he hadn't felt in years he'd felt a need to do the job he'd come there to do. So he'd kissed her goodnight and gone back to his apartment where he'd downed about a keg of coffee and read. 'I needed to understand what we've achieved. And what we'd be giving up. After what we've gone through to get here? To hell with that.'

'Okay, then,' Nate said. He moved around his desk, picked up the phone and asked his assistant to get 'John' on the phone as soon as he was in, then put down the phone with a soft click. 'So you're in for the long haul?'

'That's what it said on the beer coaster.'

At that Nate's cool finally gave way. He grinned from ear to ear. And it was done. No over-thinking, over-talking, making things more complicated than they had to be. Just two men, making a decision that set the course for the rest of their lives.

Nate moved to the far wall where a bar was hidden discreetly inside a bookshelf. Like something Rock Hudson would have had in his apartment in some old Doris Day movie. Gran would have liked that. Would have liked *this*. Gabe's mouth kicked into a half smile.

Gabe took the imported pony-necked beer on offer, even while it was eight in the morning, and the two men clinked bottles before taking a hearty swig. The bubbles burned down Gabe's throat. Cold, sharp, invigorating. As if his body were fresh and hollow and waiting for the filling.

Nate said, 'Would have been more dramatic if you'd waited until the meeting with the Securities Commission.'

'Thought that's what I was doing, hence the volume of my proclamation.'

'They're due at nine. Did you actually read any of the internal memos I CC'd you these past weeks?'

'I figured if there was anything of grave importance you'd make sure I knew.'

Nate ran a hand over the back of his neck. 'Tell me again why I wanted you back?'

'My winning personality.'

Nate's eyebrows lifted till they all but disappeared into his hairline.

And so they continued, offending one another and knocking back beers until they were gloriously sloshed. When BonaVenture's lawyer called back a half-hour later, listening to the poor guy go off his nut was the most fun Gabe'd had at work in ages. And he wondered why it was he'd not come home sooner.

Paige pushed her way through the heavy glass doors leading to the head office of Ménage à Moi. She shielded her eyes against the overbright twinkles from the coloured glass chandelier above, her heels catching in the thick cream carpet as she trudged down the hall towards her office.

Her mind was like mud. Making love to Gabe half the night was only half the problem, as from the minute he'd left she'd had not a wink of sleep. After the drama of the date, the delicateness of the cab ride, and the sweet glorious way Gabe had made love to her all through the night, she'd been consumed by the sudden need to put it all into a neat little box. The feelings, and fears, and flutterings filling her as she'd lain there staring at her dark ceiling were so far beyond the bounds of her experience, if she didn't control them she feared they'd control her.

Crap, crap, crappity-crap!

Susie, her assistant, looked up from her cubicle with a start, and Paige realised she'd shouted that last bit out loud. She was re-e-eally going to have to stop doing that.

'Morning, boss. Guess who got a delivery?' Susie said, leaping from her chair and rushing to sweep Paige's office door open. 'Look.'

As if she could have missed it. A gargantuan bunch of flowers in a vase on her big glass desk—effusive, lush blooms of creams and greens—swamped everything else in the room. The feelings, fears, and flutterings smacking into one another as they went crazy inside her, Paige reached for the card with shaking fingers. Opened it.

The message was simple. Cryptic. And not from Gabe.

I owe you one, it read, signed *Nate Mackenzie*.

Gabe's business partner? What on earth would he be thanking her for—?

Oh, God. The one and only time they'd talked he'd asked for a favour. He'd wanted her to use her influence to get Gabe to stay.

A rush of warm, hopeful, luxuriant, dangerous feelings swarmed her, so fierce and scattered she hadn't a hope in hell of controlling them.

She shoved the card back into the envelope and said, 'Thanks, Susie.'

Susie bounded on her toes, clearly desperate to ask about the flowers, but it was as clear that her boss wasn't about to spill the juice. She shut the door quietly on her way out.

Paige turned the glossy white wooden blinds until they let in as little sunlight as possible, threw her jacket and scarf over the pewter stand in the corner, then slowly sat in her chair. She moved the mouse to bring her monitor to life, clicked on the memo icon on the screen and tried to start her day. But the ridiculous spray of flowers occupying the left side of her vision taunted her. She gave up and reached out and ran her fingers over a pale velvety petal.

Was Gabe staying? He hadn't said anything about it last night. And for him he'd said a lot. So she couldn't dare hope. She couldn't dare discount it either. Either way, the time had come for damage control. To protect herself, as she had done her whole life.

Of course the most sensible thing to do was end it now. She laughed so loud she expected Susie to come running. Who was she kidding? She no more had the wherewithal to end it now than to chop off her own leg. But it would end. Whether quick and painful, or slow and painful, these things always did.

Paige bent over until her head thunked on her desk.

If she had any hope of getting off this roller coaster with an ounce of self-respect, she had to do whatever it took to make sure Gabe never guessed how she felt. She was going to have to remind him what their relationship was all about: *not* dates and feelings and impossible hopes.

She only hoped it wasn't too late.

When Gabe got home that evening he felt as if he were walking on air. He and Nate had spent the better part of the day in Nate's office, laughing, reminiscing, ordering in take-out, while the rest of the office went bonkers. Turned out one of the nice things about being such a success was that they could pay other people to deal with the fallout.

The day only got better when he walked into his apartment to find Paige sitting on his kitchen bench, toying with his flamingo mobile-phone holder. Her long legs crossed at the knees and the setting sunlight slicing between the buildings, creating gold, pink, and hot orange streaks across her body. Her *naked* body.

'Evening,' she said, a slumberous smile playing about her gorgeous mouth. Then she pulled a strawberry from a bowl beside her and slid it between her lips. The ripe red fruit popping in her mouth before her tongue swept out to lick away the juice. 'Want some?'

Heat sliced through his body in a devastating wave and his feet forgot how to move. She was every Sam Spade fantasy any man had ever had but with one big difference. She was real. Flesh and blood. Soft skin and softer lips and— He was so hard so fast he couldn't think any more.

He dropped his laptop bag to the floor, and went to her; the last truly coherent thought was that he ought to speak to Sam the Super about security.

He was so hot for her it should have been over in half a minute, but the second his lips met hers, he tasted strawberry on his tongue, absorbed the warmth in her soft bare skin sliding against his palms, something shifted. And the whole world became still.

His eyes found hers, looking to see if she felt it too, but the sun's rays shimmered too bright in all that liquid blue. He tucked her hair behind her ears, and as she sucked in a short, sharp breath he saw it. Desire, need, anticipation. And something a lot like awe. Hit with an emotional wallop he couldn't hope to decipher in his rigid state, he knew there was no way to tell her how she made him feel. He'd have to show her.

Even as he burned with an ache he could barely contain, he slid an arm beneath her knees, and carried her to his room, his eyes not leaving hers. She blinked fast. Her breaths coming hard. And clasped her hands together behind his neck.

He took her to his big bed and gently laid her down. Her pale skin glowing against the rich dark brown of his sheets, her blonde hair splayed around her beautiful face, her eyes, dark with passion, watching him hungrily. She looked… He wanted… He knew…

Hell.

He tore off his clothes. Too many layers, damnable Melbourne winter. Then naked, protected, he lowered himself over her, carefully. Her eyes not once leaving his, she reached to cup his head, and pulled him down to kiss her. Deeply, slowly, thoroughly.

When she wrapped one long leg around his backside and moaned softly into his mouth, any control he might have had slipped away. He pressed himself against her opening to find her more than ready, and he pushed into her in one smooth stroke.

Skin on skin. Heat on heat. The slip and slide of their bodies created the most perfect friction he'd ever felt. Their eyes remained locked on one another throughout as he buried himself so deep inside her he wasn't sure how he'd ever find his way back.

Her mouth opened on a gasp, the muscles of her neck straining, her eyes drifting closed as he felt her tighten, and tighten, and tighten. The most luxurious torture consumed him right as she came in his arms with a cry that echoed around the room. He peaked while she still convulsed around him, the pleasure slamming to the absolute outer reaches of his consciousness. The devastating pressure eased from his body in slow receding waves, until he was left feeling boneless. Bare.

He pulled out, and lay down beside her, cradling her into him, his arm holding her between her breasts, her beautiful backside pressed against his groin, her hair beneath his cheek. And it wasn't long before her breaths settled to the soft puffs of sleep.

As he lay there, more wide awake than he could ever remember feeling, the world outside slid back into his mind. He was keeping BonaVenture. Which meant working more closely alongside Nate. And not leaving any time soon.

Paige had never hidden the fact that she was perfectly happy for their affair to be a short-term thing. And he'd been right there with her. His staying would change everything. One way or the other.

She shifted in her sleep, the underneath of her foot sliding along the top of his, her cheek rising to press against his lips before she settled deeper into his pillow.

He had to tell her. She needed to know. Not while his

whole body still hummed from the after-effects of making love to her.

He'd lived by his gut for long enough now, he'd know when the time was right.

Paige came back to consciousness slowly. Her body felt so drugged with pleasure she could barely open her eyes. But when Gabe's scent curled beneath her tongue she remembered where she was. In his bed, covered in a big dark blanket, with a big hard man tucked right in behind her.

The big seduction scene she had planned had gone up in smoke the second she'd looked into Gabe's eyes and realised how much she hoped he was staying. And then when, with so much gentleness, he'd stroked her hair from her face, she'd forgotten everything but how he made her feel. Safe, adored, hot as the sun.

All the control she'd planned to take back had slipped through her fingers, and now she felt as if she'd been turned inside out and pulled apart and put back together again wrong. No, not *wrong* so much as differently.

She turned, his big heavy arm sliding across her breasts. She pushed a lock of dark hair away to get a better look at him as he slept. His long dark lashes rested peacefully against his swarthy cheeks. His nostrils flared with each breath. Fresh stubble shadowed his jaw.

A sigh shot past her lips, bringing with it a sense of inevitability.

She'd spent so much time convincing herself that the intensity of their affair had sprung from the situation, her desperation to get laid and quick, his brief stay in town. But in that quiet place, that quiet moment, in his big beautiful bed with its Gabe-shaped dint in the middle that sloped their bodies towards one another, she gave up trying.

She placed her hand over his heart and with her next breath

in she let herself feel the surge of sensations blooming inside her. The pinch in her chest, the warmth in her belly, the way her lungs felt as if they couldn't get quite enough air any more—like spots of ink dropped into a pond, spreading from her centre in little ripples that crashed softly against her skin.

Gabe stirred, the muscles in his chest undulating, sending her hand rolling over the smooth hot skin as if it were riding the crest of a wave.

This. This man. This heat. This *feeling.* It seemed as if there ought to be one word to sum all of that up.

There was a word, she realised as the ripples headed back to her centre and joined in a warm, solid, beautiful ache in her heart. A word she'd spent her life shunning, mocking, fearing.

It was love. And it had been coming on for so long it wasn't even a shock.

What it was was amazing. Beautiful. Consuming. A miracle.

I love you, Gabe, she whispered inside her head. Then, spent, she snuggled under the blankets and fell back asleep.

Paige nibbled on her little fingernail, or what was left of it, and watched Mae's mouth move as she gushed over a pair of sky-high white boots at Bridge Road discount shoe shop. But she heard nothing but the thoughts swimming through her head.

That which she'd only begun to fathom the night before had grown wings and taken flight. She was head over heels, deep and true, in love with Gabe. She'd done things, admitted things, felt things with him she'd never imagined she'd ever do. She'd never been with a man who made her feel safe enough to dare. She wanted to be with him, the way normal people had relationships. She wanted him to stay.

She'd about convinced herself she wasn't a sucker.

Gabe liked her. He trusted her. He wanted her. She knew

all that for sure. There was also the fact that she'd given him more than his fair chances to wipe his hands of her, and something had kept him coming back for more. Didn't all that mean what she wanted was possible, not the fantasy her mother had believed was real?

'What do you think?' Mae asked, jabbing her with a high heel, pain finally pulling her into the present.

'About?'

'These,' Mae said, wiggling the boots in Paige's face.

'For what purpose?'

Mae blinked at her. 'For... My... Wedding. Where are you right now? 'Cause as sure as I'm getting married you're not here.'

Paige pulled her finger from her mouth. 'I'm here. All yours. Now, boots. Well...that depends. Is your theme sexy Christmas elf?'

Mae grimaced and put the shoes back. 'Even though your taste is totally boring, this has been fun!'

'Totally.' And it had been. Shopping with Mae—*only* Mae—was always fun.

Mae said, 'Doesn't it feel like weeks since we've been able to do this, just the two of us?'

Paige laughed, then realised by Mae's blank smile that she hadn't been kidding. It hadn't occurred to Mae that it felt like weeks because it had *been* weeks. Which was why Paige was gripped by this amazing, delicious, petrifying, confusing, churning emotion and had no idea how to tell her best friend.

Paige picked up a hot-pink sparkly sandal and checked the price. 'Lucky you've got this wedding stuff to organise or we'd never see each other.'

'You've been the busy one of late. You and lover boy. In fact you look exhausted. And I think you should tell me in intimate detail exactly how he exhausted you last.'

At the mere mention of Gabe, Paige came over all hot and

squidgy. Ignoring Mae she ran her fingers along the suede fringing of an aqua cowboy boot. Then she looked around and wondered if they'd walked into a shop meant for drag queens. Or hookers.

Mae gave an exaggerated sigh. 'Fine, then answer me this—when's your sexy pirate setting sail?'

Paige slowly put the pink sparkly sandal back in place, lining it up neatly. 'Not sure.'

Mae snuck a bite of a secret chocolate bar she had stashed in her handbag, while skimming a glance at the shop assistant hovering nervously around the array of absurdly expensive shoes. 'But that's still his plan, right?'

'I really don't know,' Paige said as she turned the lurid green pump that had somehow ended up in her hand. There'd been no mention of leaving, or staying for that matter, when she'd headed off around dawn. Just a kiss so lush and deep her toes had curled so hard they'd cramped.

Mae swallowed slowly. 'You haven't thought to ask?'

'No,' Paige said, exasperated. 'I haven't.'

Because she was benevolently waiting for *him* to bring it up? Or because deep down below all the lovely, warm, excited feelings tumbling about inside the spin dryer that was her tummy, she wondered why he hadn't talked it over with her already? Because it changed everything? Or because it didn't make any difference?

'Wow,' Mae said on a slow release of breath.

Paige looked up, expecting Mae to be eyeballing some other crazy pair of wedding-inappropriate shoes.

But Mae watched her, eyes huge. 'You're a goner.'

Paige *pffted* with all her might and grabbed a pair of a tomato-red peep-toed ankle boots and sat on the black velvet ottoman in the middle of the store and toed off her comparatively conservative ballet flats.

'Look at you,' Mae said, sitting right next to her. 'All

flushed and trembly with that faraway look in your eyes. I caught you humming earlier. Some old movie song I couldn't put my finger on. Sandra Dee—no, Doris Day! I think you've even put on a little weight.'

'What?' Paige said, hands going to her hips as she looked down at her thighs splayed on the seat. Mae was probably right there, considering what amounted to a doughnut addiction of Gabe's, and how much she'd come to appreciate the perfect pleasure of dough and warm icing right after sex.

'Careful,' Mae said. 'You might melt right here on the shop floor. And I don't think *la shop girl* over there is big on mess.'

Paige put the boots down and stared at her chocolate brown toenails. 'Look. Gabe and I are… We haven't… I mean, I *like* him. I may even— But I'm not sure if he's—' Suddenly the boutique felt claustrophobic. 'Maybe we should head to that place down the corner. It has two floors and an espresso machine.' Paige had her feet in her shoes and was out of the door and off down the dodgy Richmond footpath, breathing in great gulps of chilly air.

Mae caught up a half-block down, taking her by the arm. 'Paige, wait. Hon, this is me you're talking to. Your best bud. What's going on?'

Best bud? Paige thought, turning to look at her friend. The friend who had no clue how afraid she was in that moment. Afraid of loving Gabe. Afraid that he might not love her back. Afraid that so long as she got to have him she could live with that.

Mae looked back at her. Same wild red hair, same piercing green eyes. The same, but not. No longer all hers.

Finally the pressure built so hard and fast inside Paige there was nowhere for it to go but out. 'You know why it feels like for ever since we've done this? Because the only things we do without Clint nowadays are wedding-related expeditions on which he is not allowed to come.'

Mae took a moment to catch onto the change of subject, before the colour drained out of her face. 'No! *No*. It's not like that.'

Mae looked so mortified, Paige's resentment deflated like a pricked balloon. 'Don't worry about it. It's okay. I get it. Life goes on.'

Mae pulled her out of the stream of foot traffic until they huddled on the stoop of a dark doorway that apparently led to a Brazilian wax clinic. *Of all places,* Paige thought, promising to backhand Lady Fate the next time they caught up.

Mae said, 'You know that nothing's changed between *us*. I'll always be there for you.'

Paige's throat felt as if it was closing up. 'You won't. You're already not.'

Mae opened her mouth but nothing came out. Then she frowned down at her Doc Martens with their red tartan laces. And Paige thought if nothing had changed Mae would wear *them* on her wedding day, not some vision of what she thought Clint might like.

The anger that churned through her at that thought pushed her the final step. Paige said, 'The past few months have been hard for me, Mae. Like I can't seem to get a foothold any more. In the past I'd have found it at work but even that's not enough any more. I think *that's* why I bought the dress. To feel something other than lost. Then along came Gabe. He makes me feel like I've been found. God, that's petrifying. That I might actually *need* him in some way, *any* way…' She closed her eyes, all her foolish feelings hurtling against the inside of her head.

'Tell me about it,' Mae said, her voice dripping with irony.

Paige opened her eyes to squint at Mae. 'Don't. You and Clint make it look so easy it burns.'

Mae threw her hands in the air and swore so loud Paige flinched. 'God, I'm gonna have to come out and say it, aren't I?'

'What?'

Mae's chutzpah faltered for a hundredth of a second before she said in a rush, 'I cheated on Clint.'

Every ounce of blood in Paige's body made a dash for her feet. She pressed her back against the door, the cold glass keeping the uncomfortable heat rushing through her body from overwhelming her. '*When* did you—?'

She couldn't even say the word. Not after what Mae's dad had put her mum through all those years ago. Mae knew the hurt, and had repeated her dad's mistakes anyway. Paige felt panic rising in her throat. Was a failing like that in the blood? Could it not be helped?

'A while back,' Mae said.

'Does he know?'

'Yeah.' Mae started pacing. 'Dammit! He'll hate that I told you.'

'But why?'

'Because it's nobody's business but ours.'

Paige felt as if she'd been slapped. And the cold of the day had nothing on the chill sealing her emotions. Her voice was cool as she said, 'I meant, why did you cheat.'

But Mae was in such a state, Paige wasn't sure she'd even been heard.

Finally Mae stopped pacing and looked down the street. She tucked her hair behind her ears only for the wind to whip it back out sideways again. 'I told you because you need to know that *no* relationship is perfect. Not even the ones that might seem all rosy on the outside. And sometimes relationships can be imperfect *and* still be special and magical. Clint and I know each other's weaknesses and love one another anyway. There's an amazing comfort in that. Like whatever comes our way we know we can handle it. Together.'

Paige suddenly had a raging headache. Thumbs at her

temples, eyes squinting, she said, 'Look, do you mind if we do this another day?'

'Sure,' Mae said, sliding her hands into the pockets of her coat as she stared hard at her shoes. 'There's no rush. Besides, Clint might not even recognise me if I walked down the aisle in white heels.'

At that it all became too much. Without another word, Paige headed off down the street. Her feet felt numb. Her head a mess. Her stomach as if it were trying to turn itself inside out.

She heard Mae's voice trail after her. 'Tell him! Tell him how you feel, Paige. You'll only regret it if you don't. Believe me.'

Paige just kept on walking.

And with every footfall she knew Mae was right about one thing. She couldn't hide her feelings any more. She had to tell Gabe how she felt.

Not because she'd regret it if she didn't but because he was a good man who always tried to do the right thing. She'd tell him because he needed to know how brilliant he was. She'd tell him because not telling was lying, and she never wanted to hurt him as Mae had hurt Clint.

And she'd tell him because if she ever had any chance of making a life for herself, one that wasn't defined by mistakes other people made, it was now.

CHAPTER ELEVEN

WEDNESDAY evening Gabe and Nate leant their backs against the edge of the dark city bar, enjoying the glow of a celebratory thirty-year-old Scotch.

Gabe was exhausted after being in the office most of the past two days knocking out a new company charter with Nate. But a good exhausted. As if he were twenty-five again with the wind at his back and the world at his feet. Only for the first time in years he didn't have to be running across the globe to keep the feeling going.

He closed his eyes to the chatter of Aussie accents, easy laughter, and he let the glow of life in his home town settle over him. There were ghosts—of his parents, his gran, his deepest regret—and always would be. But despite all that, as cities went Melbourne was pretty perfect now he came to think about it. The food, the bars, the sports. Even the strong seasonal weather was kind of lovely so long as you were ready for it.

And then there was Paige.

His eyes flickered open and the crowd swam in front of his vision. Yet for all the hustle and bustle he could still feel the gentle sweep of her finger across his forehead, the curl of her soft hand on his chest, the heat of her skin imprinting upon him, the air scooting over his collarbone as she'd whispered the words, *'I love you, Gabe.'*

His gut clenched the same now, a couple of days after the fact, and no amount of shifting on his stool changed that. At the time he'd pretended to be asleep. Not to have heard. He'd told himself it had been the afterglow talking. He'd come pretty close to nirvana that night himself.

But as the Scotch eased into his blood and the good people of BonaVenture laughed and celebrated in front of him, easing from his shoulders the years of guilt and self-recrimination, there was no deep dark place inside him to hide that moment any more.

It hadn't been the afterglow. Paige was in love with him.

For a moment, a sliver of time, he let the idea find a way beneath his skin. He couldn't kid himself. A good portion of the appeal of sticking around was about her. Being with her hadn't been easy. Hell no. The woman was as stubborn as a mule, and could be a real pain in the ass, but it was her spirit that had hooked him, drawn him in, steadied him. It had been some time since he'd decided Paige Danforth was his karmic gift.

But he'd never imagined it to be more than a beautiful affair. He'd never imagined that she might either. It had only been a few days back that he'd realised she hadn't even invited him into her apartment. When he'd kicked himself for being more invested than she was.

And yet...

He breathed out long and slow.

It was all there if he let himself see it. He'd seen it in her eyes. Felt it in her touch. Knew it in the unguarded way she gave herself up to him every time they had sex. It had been so long since he'd been anywhere near that depth of feeling he hadn't recognised that a gorgeous, seductive, testing dish of a woman *loved* him. The truth of it filled him like a wave of—

'Oh, and the nanotechnology deal fell through,' Nate said.

'I'm sorry?' Gabe said, blinking back into the light as

the wave of sensation turned out to be a prickle of sweat all over his body.

Nate motioned to the waiter dashing past to bring them both another of the same.

'Think hard,' Nate said. 'You spent a few days in Sydney the other week—'

Gabe ignored the drink the barman slid beside his elbow. 'Yeah yeah yeah. What I don't think I heard right was that I didn't land it.'

'They went another way. Don't sweat it.'

Don't sweat it? Too damn late. The prickles of sweat now felt like a million tiny little needles calling for his blood. Gabe turned on his stool to face the back of the bar, elbows landing on the sticky surface, fingers covering his mouth as he stared unseeingly into the dark mirror.

He didn't *not* land deals. Ever. He was the rainmaker. Failure was not in his vocabulary. It was *the* talent he brought to the table. The only time it had deserted him had been when he'd been distracted by real life—

Paige. Half the time away he'd spent thinking about Paige. The other half he'd been trying not to think about her. He'd called in the work, hadn't he? Because he'd thought it parochial and easy. And because he'd practically had a hard-on all week.

Dammit. He sat forward and rubbed his hands over his eyes.

From the moment Paige had tried to jam his fingers in the lift door, he'd known she was a train-wreck in the making. Yet he'd jumped on board because being with her had been intoxicating. For a man who hadn't felt much of anything in a long time the rush had been impossible to resist.

He'd had an excuse the first time he'd let a beautiful blonde take his eye off the ball. This time he had none. He'd clearly learned nothing since he'd been gone. And the realisation made him feel ten different kinds of reckless.

The ride had been something, but it was time to get off. He'd done what he'd come to Melbourne to do and now it was time to go. The prickles eased the moment he made the decision, and he had to believe that meant something, as his gut was the only moral compass he had left.

His hand found the drink, the ice clinking gently against the glass. And as he lifted it to his mouth he caught his reflection. Distorted by rows of spirit bottles lined up along the dark mirror behind the bar, he recognised his father's jaw, his mother's dark hair, his gran's eyes.

And his own big fat lie.

Moral compass, my ass. He'd been desperate for an excuse to jump ship the second Paige had whispered those four soft words into the darkness. Because they'd tugged hard at something inside him. Something he'd thought lost. Something he'd trusted would stay that way.

Love wasn't something he sought or wanted in his life. All love meant to him was loss.

His memories of his parents were rare, and even then they'd flicker into his mind and fade as fast, leaving a hollow ache in their place. His memories of his gran went deeper. Her toughness and substance and faith had given him the foundation from which he'd built his life. And when she'd died he'd lost his way.

This damn city, he thought. There were too many ghosts after all. He knew he'd stayed away for good reason. This time he wouldn't ever let himself forget.

Not caring to look himself in the eye any longer, he spun back around.

In the end it really didn't matter why. His decision was made. And it was for the best.

* * *

Gabe told himself it was for the best a hundred times between then and when he knocked on Paige's apartment door.

When she opened up music twanged in the background. It faded to a blur as he took in the sight of her: bare feet, hair pulled back into a messy ponytail, faded pink T-shirt stretched across her breasts, old jeans barely clinging to her hips revealing a sliver of flat stomach. Without her usual high heels and eclectic layers she seemed smaller. Softer. Sweet as all hell.

So he told himself again.

'Come in, come in,' she said, her voice breathless, her smile hesitant. But then she tipped up onto her toes and slid her arms around his neck. Pressed her body against his. And let out a long sigh.

And before he even knew what he was doing he slid his arms around her waist and held her tight. Her scent, her taste, her heat infusing him till his blood fizzed with it.

So he told himself *again*.

'You look tired,' she said as she sank back on her heels. She licked something off her fingers as she padded deeper into the kitchen. Something sweet if the warm scents coming at him from her apartment were anything to go by. Sweet because she knew that was how he liked it.

When she glanced back over her shoulder, her chin tilted down, her finger caught between her teeth, her eyes smiling, her feelings for him were so transparent it hurt. Deep behind his ribs.

And he knew he'd never have to tell himself again.

When she realised he hadn't moved, she spun on her toes and faced him, her forehead creased into a frown. 'Something up?'

'I'm leaving.' There, whip off the Band-Aid fast. Better for her. Better for him.

Her finger remained in her mouth a beat before it slowly

slid free. Frown still in place, she reached for a tea towel and slid it through her fingers. 'Where to this time?'

He didn't have an answer. That afternoon he'd scoured his emails and found a couple of early leads in Paris and Brussels. Another in Salt Lake City. But he didn't have a flight booked. He'd take whichever came first and research from there.

Her eyes slid past him and landed on his bags out in the hall—the same bags he'd arrived with weeks before. 'You're leaving? As in *leaving*.'

He nodded. Jaw clenched against the dawning realisation in her eyes. He could see her fighting it. Fighting the inevitability they'd both selfishly ignored.

'But I thought… I mean, aren't you…?' She shook her head, as if trying to clear out the cobwebs. 'When will you be back?'

'Not sure. Depends on the work.'

Her eyebrows slowly lifted as if she wasn't buying that one for a second. 'From what I heard you're the boss. Seems a man in that position can make his own hours.'

'That's not the way I operate. Never has been.'

The tea towel gripped tight about her hands, she placed her fists on one hip. 'Right. Then maybe you can answer this one. How long were you gone last time you ran away?'

'A while,' he said, before realising he hadn't denied he was running.

'Weeks. Months. Years?'

'About that.'

She nodded, hurt, anger, and possibly worst of all resignation twisting her lovely features. She slowly uncurled the tea towel from its death grip and placed it on the bench. 'Is this where you assure me we can take up where we left off when you next swing through town?'

He gritted his teeth against the glimmer of hope in her big blue eyes that belied the sarcasm in her tone. He'd never imagined it would be this hard to do the right thing. But he could do it. If only because he knew if he gave an inch he'd be *her* anchor, only so much as he'd be holding her back when she deserved to be happy. Happy with someone who knew how to be happy with her.

When he said nothing, the glimmer of hope snuffed out. If she could have turned him to ice with a look, he'd have been a frozen solid on the spot. 'Wow. I can't believe I hoped you'd say yes. How close I came to being that woman. The one who accepts the dregs if that's all she can get from the man she—'

She swallowed back the next word, and Gabe was so thankful he hated himself.

Her chin hitched north as she looked him right in the eye and promised, 'I'll *never* be her.'

All warmth, and sweetness, and vulnerability had fled, locked behind an ice-cool façade. The façade she showed other men. The façade she'd let down for him. It should have made it easier, the distance she was putting between them, instead he wanted her to fight back. To let loose a storm of angry heat in his direction.

But if cool was what she needed, then cool she'd get. 'Atta girl.'

A flicker of heat glinted within the wall of ice blue and he pressed his feet into the floor. 'So if this is it, if this is such a simple goodbye for you, why are you even here? Why tell me to my face?'

She had him there. But he couldn't think up an answer that made any sense. So he went with the incontrovertible, 'This was only ever going to be short term. You know that.'

'You choose now to remember that? You, the man who asked *me* on a date. The man whose best friend sent me flowers as he thought it was because of me that he was—' She shook her head again, before it drooped as if she no longer had the strength to hold it up.

Dammit. Gabe took a step inside her kitchen until he was close enough to touch. To catch her scent above the scent of baking; far sweeter than any doughnut, or anything else he'd ever known. 'Paige, you are an amazing woman—'

'Stop. Right there.'

'No.'

She flinched at his tone. Then slowly looked up. The deep sadness and hurt in her eyes killing him. But his decision was made. And it wasn't about what he wanted. It was about what he *had* to do.

He reached out and tucked a stray strand of soft blonde hair behind her ear. 'It's been…' *Dazzling. Tender. Once in a lifetime.* 'A hell of a ride.'

She swallowed. Her eyes flicking between his as if she still couldn't quite believe it. As if she might yet wake up and find it was all a bad dream.

He must have moved towards her because suddenly she was sinking into him with a sigh, her hands splayed out across his back, her head against his chest. He rested his chin on her head, closed his eyes, and told himself *this* was shoring up his karmic balance. And maybe from that point on he could truly start his life afresh.

With an effort greater than himself he pulled away.

'Goodbye, Paige.'

She wrapped her arms around herself and nibbled at her heavenly bottom lip, refusing to say goodbye.

Gabe could barely feel his feet as he walked out of her door. He lifted his bags to his shoulder and pressed the button for the lift. The door opened instantly, he stepped inside. He didn't even get a chance to look back, or not, as the lift door practically bit his backside as it snapped shut behind him and he was going down before he'd even picked a floor.

* * *

Paige went the only place she could think that would stop her from shattering into a thousand pieces. To Mae. So when Clint opened the door to his apartment he couldn't have looked more surprised than she felt. Somehow she'd forgotten he even existed. What a mess.

'Hey, Paige,' Clint said, looking at her chin rather than her eyes, meaning she must have looked an absolute treat. 'Ah-h, Mae's not here.'

'Right.' She sniffed, rubbing at the sore spot under her ribs where it felt as if a chopstick had been jammed for good. 'Can I come in anyway?'

He glanced inside to where the sports channel blared on the TV. 'There's a replay of the Pies game. I was kinda looking forward to unbuttoning my jeans and burping out loud.'

The guy was a human Labrador; it simply wasn't in him to be unkind. So she knew his hesitation could only mean one thing. He knew that she knew that Mae had cheated. But whatever he saw in her face in the end he pushed the front door open and waved her under his arm.

Five minutes later, Paige sat curled up on Clint's faded old tartan couch, a musty-smelling throw tucked around her, a cup of hot chocolate warming her palms as he told his side of Mae's story, which turned out to be the best possible way she could have distracted herself from her own mess of a love life. From the knowledge she'd been moments from telling Gabe she loved him, right before he'd summarily dumped her.

'We'd been going out for about two months when I walked into a party to find her with her tongue down my friend's throat, his hands making a joke of her top.'

'Why?' Paige asked, even while she wasn't sure she wanted to know why Mae had done it, or why Clint had forgiven her. Because if they couldn't get this love thing right what hope was there for anyone?

Clint sat forward, the fire flickering in the old grate creating shadows across his kind face. 'You grow up assuming you'll find the one, but as you get older you realise it's as rare as finding a bar of gold bullion in your cornflakes. Then one day you walk into the same bar you've been in a hundred times before and there she is.'

It seemed too easy to say love conquered all. And too hard all at the same time. 'But she *cheated* on you. With a *friend*. How could that not be game over?'

He twirled his beer in both hands. 'Of course she picked a friend. Love is a scary thing, and she loved me too much already to walk away.'

Paige shook her head, trying to follow the anti-logic, even while it made absolute sense in a way that surprised her to her very roots. 'Are you guys still friends? You and the guy?'

Clint's eyebrows all but disappeared into his tidy crew cut. 'I decked the guy. Broke his nose. It's only that he felt like a right git for what he'd done that he didn't press charges. A man's gotta do what a man's gotta do for the woman he loves.'

The commentators on the screen suddenly went wild and Paige realised Clint was being abnormally quiet considering the Magpies had scored a ripper goal. She glanced across to find him staring into the middle distance, his eyes glassy, the fingers of his right hand flexing, as though sense memory made them feel the pain of the strike. And only then did she notice the knuckles of his other hand had turned white on his beer.

'Aren't *you* scared?'

'Of what exactly?' Clint asked.

'It not working out? Her leaving? Her cheating again? Her not loving you as much as you love her?'

'Sure. I have my moments. But they pass. And they're worth it. Because *she's* worth it.'

The clench in Paige's stomach was the very definition of bittersweet. 'She's really getting married, isn't she?'

Clint could have laughed. She wouldn't have blamed him. But the sweetheart reached over, wrapped a big brotherly hand around her head, and tucked it into his shoulder. And he sat there and let her tears soak into his sweatshirt. Without judgment or advice. Just acceptance.

It seemed he understood, way more than she even had herself, that she was grieving. Had been since the moment she'd seen that ring on Mae's finger. It had meant the end of the most important, strong, invincible relationship of her life.

What she hadn't realised was that it could be the beginning of another. She pulled back. Looked into Clint's kind hazel eyes. If Mae was the closest thing she had to a sister, then that made Clint family too.

She gave him a watery smile. And with a wink he lifted his beer in a salute and served himself a piece of pizza that looked as if it had cooled and congealed many hours before, before pressing the volume button on the remote.

Paige breathed deep through her nose and pulled the blanket up under her chin, knowing he'd be gone to her now for a good bit unless she had something derogatory to say about the umpires.

She grabbed a piece of cold pizza and noticed that the pizza box sat alongside myriad mug rings and a corner of a magazine page that had been stuck there years before by something sticky. Elsewhere, fishing rods poked out of the tall pot in the corner. A bike with muddy wheels leant against the wall in the entrance.

She was surprised Mae hadn't made more of a mark, filling the place with wild cushions and a top of the line espresso machine. Even Paige's place still had touches of Mae about it. It seemed Clint was a man who knew himself. Who knew exactly how far he was able to be pushed. And how far he'd go in the name of love.

Paige's heart clenched again, but left alone with her

thoughts this time there was no fighting it. She had to ride the pain. To own it. To learn from it. And to imagine how it would feel to take Mae by the collar and shake her till her brain rattled for nearly screwing things up with this amazing guy.

When prickles shot down her legs, warning her if she'd waited another five minutes she'd likely have lost all feeling in them, she untucked them. Right as the front door creaked, groaned, and snapped open, and Mae bustled through the door carrying Chinese food and more beer.

'And there she is,' Clint said. 'The woman I love.'

When Mae saw Paige sitting on her couch, beside her fiancé, snuggled under an afghan, she baulked. Paled. Her expression hovering somewhere between a pained smile and a frown.

Paige threw the blanket aside and leaned over and gave Clint a kiss. 'Be good to her or I'll rip off your boy bits and feed them to my ferret.'

'You don't have a ferret.'

'I'll get one.'

Clint smiled. Sweet man. Strong man. Good man. Good enough for her Mae.

Paige stood up, padded over to Mae on wobbly legs. Mae looked as if she'd yet to take a breath. Until Paige reached out and enveloped her in a great big bear hug. With a whimper Mae pressed back with all her might, her version of a hug considering her arms were full.

'You look like crap,' Mae said.

'Feel like it too. I'll tell you about it later, I promise.'

'Chinese is getting cold!' Clint called out.

Mae sniffed. 'Handle it!'

'All righty, then,' said Clint.

Paige laughed, amazing considering the day she'd had. But even while her heart felt as if it had been pounded with a meat hammer, there was enough left to feel happy for Mae. Happy her friend had found the most important, strong, invincible relationship of *her* life.

To Mae she said, 'Be good to him.'

Mae's eyes shifted sideways, landed on her fiancé, who was flapping a hand at the TV, his voice rising by the second, backside halfway off the couch, willing his team forward from his position at wing-via-couch. With a sigh she said, 'Always and for ever.'

Then Mae all but ran to the couch, snuggled in under her fiancé's waiting arm.

The pain beneath Paige's ribs eased a tiny little bit, and she managed to swallow back the tears that had started—happy for them, devastated for herself—before she closed the door behind her.

As she walked along the Richmond back streets to the tram stop, the icy winter wind snuck through her clothes, but she shoved her hands deep into the pockets of her warm jacket and kept walking, Clint's words playing through her mind on a loop.

A man's gotta do what a man's gotta do for the woman he loves.

She'd thought Gabe cared. Even with her limited experience she'd been near certain that he felt the same way. Had she been so completely wrong?

If all he'd wanted was meaningless sex, he could have kept her on a string. And she might have let him. It could have gone on that way for months. Years. But he hadn't. He'd made a clean break, giving up a sure thing to save her from herself.

While she'd been not nearly so self-sacrificing. She'd kept Gabe at a distance from the beginning. She'd made it all about sex while he'd been the one to suggest a date. She'd never told Mae about him, while he'd told Nate about her. She'd never made any effort to let him into her life, while he'd opened his apartment to her on day one.

Even at the last she'd not told him how she felt. Never told him she wanted him to stay.

No wonder he'd found it so easy to walk away. Because she'd stood there and let him.

CHAPTER TWELVE

GABE leant back in the wrought-iron chair in the outdoor café at the edge of St Mark's square, his unfocused gaze touching on huddles of wide-eyed tourists gawping at the architecture, and lean, young, dark-haired Venetian men checking out the female tourists.

Pigeons cooed and fluttered across his vision. He downed the remnants of his espresso, then went back to the dozen new emails from different departments back at BonaVenture HQ: Research, Accounts, PR.

Nate, who'd seemed not all that surprised when he'd left, but had also made him swear in blood he'd be gone no longer than a month, had also made him promise to use BonaVenture's extensive resources rather than try to do everything on his own. Thankfully the guy had an eye for talent because even while Gabe was sure he was halfway to landing the deal, and beating out four other mobs vying for the chance, his level of care didn't amount to a hill of beans.

They'd land it or they wouldn't. And life would, in fact, go on.

What had been keeping him up nights was that he found it near impossible to imagine what kind of life that might be.

Before closing his email, he scrolled down, in case he'd missed any messages. But no. No phone messages missed either. Not the one he was hoping for, anyway.

The day he'd arrived in Venice he'd wandered the meandering streets to get on local time, and had come to a halt at the sight of a pair of battered pink lawn flamingos leaning at an odd angle amongst the junk in the dusty window of a bric-a-brac shop. He'd taken a photo on his phone and messaged it to Paige.

A peace offering, he'd told himself as he'd pressed Send, because he wished he'd handled the dissolution of their affair with more style. But that was hogwash. He'd wanted to know she was thinking about him, even if for a moment. Even if it was to consider him pond scum. Because he thought about her constantly.

He knew he'd done the right thing in making a clean break, and yet he didn't feel righteous. He felt...lonesome.

Gabe slammed his laptop shut, slid it into his satchel, and hooked the strap over his head. He slid his sunglasses onto his face and picked a random corner of the square and set to getting lost in the bewildering twisting cobbled alleyways of Venice once again. Knowing he could never truly be lost. All paths led to the water.

Where Melbourne was full of white noise—Nate, BonaVenture, his parents, his gran, Lydia—every corner turned compounding his alienation, Venice held no memories for him as yet. As such it was quiet. So quiet he could no longer ignore the voices in his head.

He'd convinced himself he'd left Paige so he'd never have to lose her, thus losing her anyway. At a distance that made about as much sense as cutting off his toes when the temperature dropped in case of possible future frostbite. And under the quiet blue Italian sky it had become all too clear: all his adult life he'd avoided intimacy, love, contentment because he felt he hadn't earned it.

Guilt had a way of twisting a person and he'd been twisted for so long he couldn't remember what it was like to be simple and straight up and down. But until he'd heard Paige's gutsy confession in that soft, sweet, sure voice, he'd never known what twisted really felt like.

He pulled up short of skittling a clump of tourists leaning over a bridge watching a gondolier, straw hat at a rakish angle, slide his boat artfully along the canal below, 'O Sole Mio' tripping from his practised lips, and sending all the girls into giggling swoons.

The song tickled at the corner of his memory—the cab-ride through water-washed Melbourne the night of their one and only date. He'd fought for Paige then. As the water twinkled up at him he began to understand why. He'd been falling for her already, and, even while he'd been scrambling to regain traction on his old life, his instincts had told him to stick with her instead.

He grumbled, 'Excuse me,' and bodily lifted a kid out of the way so as to get past. To keep moving. Round and round in circles, twisty, like a rat in a maze.

Soon enough, he hit the water again and the nefarious scent of the canal was enough to have him turning straight up the next alley he found. This one dark, dank, narrowing, as close to being lost in the city as he could hope to be. He walked till sweat gathered beneath his armpits and his bag made his shoulder ache. Until a patch of sunshine filtered through the precariously inclining buildings to either side.

There he stopped. Tilting his face to the warmth. And with every deep breath out he let the quiet in. As everything fell away, every sliver of guilt, and sadness, and regret, the vacant spaces began to fill. With sunshine, with warmth, with hope. And with Paige. Her scent, her skin, her smile, her eyes, her tenacity and her temper. And that one night, wrapped around him in the warmth of his bed, when she had whispered that she loved him.

Something dazzling blinded him—a flash of sunshine,

a reflection off water somewhere. And when he blinked the ground beneath his feet shifted so fast he held out his arms to get his balance.

Sucking in air, he knew the groundswell had nothing to do with the fact that the only things keeping the entire city from falling into the sea were thousands of wet sticks. It was vertigo. Paige-induced vertigo. She made his heart race, and his blood rush, and kept him more than a little off balance. And while it wasn't easy, and nothing was guaranteed, *that*, that energy, that exhilaration, that acute reminder that he was alive, was the exact flash of fire, of brilliance, he'd spent his whole life chasing.

Breathing deep, the impossible scent of orange so strong in his nostrils even the pervasive scent of the Venetian waterways didn't make a dent, he shielded his eyes as he looked up at the pale clear sky and attempted to figure out where he was.

And which direction he had to go to get home.

Paige did a last-minute check on the details of the Brazil recce trip.

Everything was in place—the hotel, the permission to use the beach, the local suppliers, the photographer. Once she was happy everything was right to go, she checked she had her passport, left a message on Sam the Super's phone that she'd be away—for whatever that was worth. Then she locked her apartment door and slid the key into an envelope to leave in Mrs Addable's mail box so her upstairs neighbour could water her plants.

She pressed the down arrow outside the lift and watched the number display above the lift, trying her best to stamp down her rising impatience. But she wanted to get on that plane as soon as humanly possible. She was so tense, when the lift binged almost instantly, she flinched. And when the lift doors slid open—

Her heart skipped a beat.

Because inside the lift, in leather and soft denim and huge scuffed boots, looking exactly as big, and dark, and dangerous as the day they'd first met was—

'Gabe?'

'Morning, Paige.'

The deep rumbling voice clinched it, vibrating down her spine, searing her to the spot so that she couldn't move, and filling her up with so much heartache she could barely contain it.

Because he'd left without even a backward glance. *Protect yourself!* a familiar old voice yelled in the back of her head. But as she drank him in, his dark soulful eyes, his big broad shoulders, his knee-melting scent, she told the voice to sod off.

She was done preparing for the worst. It felt a whole lot better hoping for the best. And if there was even a remote chance she could have what Mae and Clint had, then she needed to be ready for it. Open to it. Even if it meant having her heart broken all over again. The risk was worth it. Gabe was worth it.

'I was hoping to catch you before you headed into work,' he said, all smooth and nonchalant, as if he weren't meant to be on the other side of the world.

Work? As if she'd be let through the Ménage à Moi doors in her airplane uniform of beanie, ten-year-old electric-blue stretchy pants, faded Bon Temps football T-shirt, blazer, fluffy socks and Mae's old Docs.

And then she realised. He hadn't noticed her clothes. Hadn't even noticed the huge blood-red suitcase at her feet. His eyes hadn't once left hers. He'd only seen *her*. Just as he had that first morning in the lift when she'd been carrying a garment bag bright enough to be seen from the moon. And every day since. Bar, of course, the days since he'd told her she was amazing and left.

'What are you doing here?' she asked, heart trying its dandiest to be hopeful, but it was struggling with the new skill. 'You're meant to be in Venice.'

His eyebrow rose, and she realised belatedly she'd given away that she'd found out where he was. 'I am,' he said. 'I was. Now I'm not. Seems I have a whole staff I can get to do the hard yards for me, leaving me to swoop in at the last and look brilliant.'

'Lucky you.' When Paige realised she was gripping the handle of her suitcase so hard the tops of her fingers were becoming numb, she eased off. 'I'm not heading into work, but you did just catch me. I'm meant to be heading to Brazil.'

With what seemed like considerable effort, Gabe dragged his eyes from hers long enough to take in her beanie, her take-no-prisoners boots, her massive red bag. 'Brazil? The catalogue. You won them over. Well done you. You'll love it. What time's your flight?' Even as he congratulated her he moved to the front of the lift, both hands gripping the doors, as if blocking her way.

'I said I'm *meant* to be heading to Brazil.'

His dark eyes slid back to hers. And the twin flints of heat and hope lighting their dark depths had her heart thumpety thumping against her ribs so hard she had to check to make sure her T-shirt wasn't dancing in time.

'Meaning you're not.'

'Not. I too have underlings and sent them in my stead.'

His nostrils flared as he breathed deep. As he considered the connotations of what she'd said. As he leaned an inch out into the hall.

'Look at us,' he rumbled, 'delegating.' And look he did, all

he way down her legs and back up again with such concen-
tration she felt every touch of his gaze like a caress. 'Frees
up the spare time, I find.'

'Whatever will we do with it?'

'Come here,' he said, with a tilt of his chin, moving his
big body aside, 'and I'll give you some ideas.'

Paige didn't have to be asked twice. She shoved her suitcase against her front door, tossing her handbag and key in
the same general direction, then practically leapt into the lift.

Once inside, she scooted to the back before she glanced up
at him, his breadth blocking out the light, making the room
feel so tight with him in it. And, God, he smelled good. Of
fresh air, and clean cotton, and spice, and soap, and every
good manly thing.

The lift doors might have closed at that point. Or they
might not. Paige was trying too hard to find some kind of
rhythm in her breath to notice much of anything but the man
in her sights. The man moving slowly her way.

When he got close enough she had to look up to see him,
she took a step back, but he just moved closer still. So close
her fingers itched with the effort not to slide her hand up the
soft cotton of his T-shirt, scrunching the fabric into her hands,
revealing all that hot male skin as she went. To run across his
overlong stubble. To smooth out the new creases across his
brow. He looked tired.

'Long flight?' she asked.

'Long week,' he said, his eyes roving over her face. Then,
as they landed on her eyes, 'Longest of my life.'

He moved closer. Close enough she could just make out
the rim of dark brown around his bottomless black pupils. 'If
you're not going to Brazil, where are you going?'

Here goes, she thought. *No going back from here.* 'I'm
going to Venice.'

'Are you now?' he rumbled, his voice like velvet as he kept on coming.

She rocked back on her heels till her shoulders hit the lift wall. And Gabe couldn't be any closer without touching her. So touch her he did, his big hand sliding around her waist to settle in the sweet spot of her lower back, his heat wrapping around her like a blanket.

With a sigh she felt to the bottoms of her feet, Paige slid her hands up his arms to curl around his big leather-clad biceps. 'I hear it's lovely this time of year.'

'It rains this time of year. Thunderstorms like you wouldn't believe.'

Had he pressed closer still? She could feel his heart thundering against her chest and one hard thigh nudged between hers. Her eyes fluttered closed and she had to force them to open back up again. 'Is that why you're back? Fear of storms to go with your fear of small spaces.'

He stilled as humour flared in his dreamy dark eyes. Until they came over so serious her chest began to ache in the most beautiful way. He shook his head. 'Clear skies as far as the eye could see.'

'Oh.' She licked her lips. Needing to know, needing to hear him say it. And looking into his face, so beautiful, so close after all those nights when it had been so far, she found the courage to ask, 'So why are you back?'

His dark eyes flickered between hers, and after what felt like for ever, he said, 'I have something for you.'

He tilted sideways and her body followed his like metal shavings to a magnet. Then she saw the bulky item wrapped in newspaper leaning next to her against the wall of the lift and she near leapt out of her skin. It came near to her shoulders, and she hadn't even seen it.

From the second the lift doors had opened she'd only seen him. He grabbed the package and held it out to her. 'For you.'

She took it, peeling away the Italian newspaper it had been hastily wrapped in. The guy really hadn't a clue about garnish. And she loved him all the more for trying.

A black eye peeked out of the newspaper. Then a pink head. A darker pink beak. Two beaks. The newspaper fell to her feet with a scrunch and a shuffle and she was left holding two bruised and battered vintage flamingo lawn ornaments, pink paint worn away in places, their necks curved into a heart as they touched beaks.

Gabe might not have known a thing about garnish but he knew plenty about her. So much so her heart was lodged so far up into her throat she didn't know what to say.

'They're the ones from the photo,' he explained.

She sniffed as discreetly as possible and willed away the tears burning the backs of her eyes. 'What photo?'

'The one I texted to you.'

Her hand went to her phone in the back pocket of her stretchy-pants, only to remember it was in her handbag. Her bag she'd left in the hallway, while the lift was sailing past goodness knew what floor. She was about to find out how trustworthy her neighbours were.

'That? I thought you'd accidentally sent it to the wrong person.' And that fate could be a cruel cow at times.

'But…isn't that why you were coming to Venice?'

Suddenly big bad Gabe Hamilton looked unsure. He'd come all the way from Venice to bring her a couple of used flamingos and he'd done so without any guarantee of what he might find. If she'd thought she couldn't have loved him more than she did after seeing his gift, she'd been dead wrong. And now was the time to tell him.

But she'd planned to spend the next twenty-four hours' travelling to come up with the right thing to say. So that he'd hear her. So that he'd believe.

Paige swore inelegantly as she planted her feet and her

hands flew out to her sides as the lift shuddered and the lights flickered to low. By the cessation of vibration through her legs she realised the lift had stopped. Her eyes cut to Gabe, to find his hand on the emergency button. Gabe who, no matter how he might try to deny it, was at least a little claustrophobic.

He took the flamingos from her hand and leant them against the wall, then grabbed a hank of hair poking out from under her beanie and gave it a tug. 'You know why I'm back, Paige.'

When his hands moved to brush her neck, to run over her shoulders, his thumbs tracing the edges of her breasts before his long fingers curled beneath her blazer and around her waist, Paige's whole body pulsed so hard she wrapped her fingers around the lapels of his thick leather jacket to keep herself from collapsing in a heap.

'I'd like to think so,' she said, 'but I'm not averse to hearing you say it.'

Humour flared in his eyes again. Humour and heat. Then he leant his forehead against hers. 'I'm back,' he rumbled in his deep delicious voice, 'because you love me.'

Paige hiccuped a half-sob half-laugh. Then she croaked, 'Excuse me?' her hand flying to her throat, but Gabe caught it, bringing her knuckles to his lips. His eyes closing as he breathed deep, drinking her in.

'You love me,' he said. He turned her hand to press his lips to the leaping pulse inside her wrist. 'You told me so. Soft and warm and sated in my bed.'

'I didn't say that out loud! Did I?'

'You did. I can all but feel your breath whispering against my cheek even now.'

Paige's spare hand flew to her own burning hot cheek. He knew she loved him. And he was still standing there, kissing the tips of her fingers. 'You knew, and yet you—' *Left.*

Gabe placed her hand over his heart, and then cradled her cheeks to make sure she was looking him right in the eye as he said, 'I knew and I found it hard to believe. Right up until I found it impossible not to believe.'

Gabe didn't make it any easier for her to get a grip on what was happening when he began raining soft warm kisses across her forehead, below her eyes, at the corners of her mouth. Then with a groan he swept his hands to take possessive rights on her backside, and he nuzzled her neck, warm air scooting across the sweet spot below her ear.

His voice vibrated through her as he said, 'I've spent every day since I've known you convincing myself it was all happening too fast to be real. That you were too good to be true. That I needed more time to be sure.'

The old Paige would have said, *Amen* to that. But the new and improved Paige was falling deeper and deeper into a blood haze and she flipped his leather jacket out of the way so she could find a backside to hold. So that she could press her hips into his. To tilt her head to give him all the access to her sweet spots he wanted. 'And now?'

'It only took ten thousand miles and trying to live a life I'd outgrown to realise when it comes to you, Paige Danforth, there's no such thing as too fast.' Gabe lifted his head, his eyes dark with desire. 'I'm in love with you, Paige. And I'm ready for you to love me right on back.'

That was all Paige needed to hear. She ran the back of her hand along his cheek, over his week-old stubble, then threaded her fingers through his dark hair and pulled his head to hers. A groan left his mouth as their lips met and she melted into him, heat on heat, hands everywhere as they couldn't get close enough. He smelled so good, felt so strong, her limbs were so loose, her blood on fire, her heart full to bursting. *This* was what she'd worked so hard to avoid? Never again.

She dragged herself from the fog of his kiss, and, while she could have watched him looking hungrily at her lips for ever, she waited till his eyes left her mouth to look into hers to say, 'I love you more than you can know.'

'I reckon you love me exactly as much as I know.'

Paige pressed onto her toes and kissed him again. Only this time it was soft, lingering, searching, finding. A kiss that had found its home. A tear ran down her cheek as emotion too great to hold back overwhelmed her.

Gabe pulled back, licking her tear from his lips, and wiped a gentle knuckle down the trail. 'Now that we've got that all sorted out, you weren't busy, were you?'

Paige laughed, and thought of the suitcase that was hopefully still outside her apartment. 'Nothing pressing.'

'Good, because I'm in the mind to buy a suit and thought you might be the girl to help me pick one out.'

'A suit? I've never seen you wear a suit. Not once.'

'Turns out I need the right inducement.'

'Such as?'

'I'm not sure my leather jacket quite goes with that dress of yours. The white one with all the beads—'

'Pearls,' Paige corrected, even as her blood began to rush so fast through her system she thought she might be about to faint.

'Hmm?'

'They're natural freshwater pearls. Just saying.'

His mouth kicked up into the beginnings of a smile. A flash of teeth. A crinkling of his eyes. A mere hint of the smile that had got her into this in the first place and she had to swallow down the flood of saliva that poured into her mouth.

'Right,' he said. 'The way I see it, if you hadn't bought the dress with the *pearls* you wouldn't have wished for me. If I hadn't caught you in the dress, hadn't been forced to rid you of it like a groom on his wedding night, I might never have been snapped out of my self-delusion that I'd never want to do it for real. That dress came with a little bit of fairy dust, methinks. Only fair I get me a suit to match. You in?'

Paige tried to think. She really did. But the thought of Gabe fresh shaven, in morning grey, top hat, tails, pearl buttons on the waistcoat and a matching pale cream cummerbund was so ridiculous a picture she laughed out loud.

'Something funny about the idea of you marrying me, Miss Danforth?'

Her laughter stopped quick smart as Gabe slid down onto his knee, just one knee, and lifted her top to place a kiss on her belly. She slid her fingers into his long thick hair and shook her head. Then, her own knees giving way, she sat on his.

'You want to marry me?'

'You don't think I came all the way back here carrying a pair of love-locked flamingos on a whim, do you? You're it. You're mine. I'm done. And I'm already looking forward to seeing the faces of your fan club as they watch you walk down the aisle.'

Not having a clue as to what he was talking about, Paige shook her head. 'I know you, Gabe. You won't see a single person in the crowd but me.'

'True. So you're in?'

'All the way in.' She held up a finger when his smile grew. 'On one condition. I don't want you wearing a suit for me. I love you just the way you are.'

'Yeah,' he said, sliding her beanie off her head and scrunching it behind her neck. 'I know.' Then he kissed her as if his life depended on it.

A few minutes later, feeling as if she were in the middle

of a dream, Paige said, 'Though I have always liked men in suits.'

'Well, you can't have one. Not any more. I'm all you got now.'

She wrapped her arms around his neck and sighed. 'Fine. I think I can handle that.'

'All this? I guess we'll see.'

A flicker of something lit his eyes. Something dark and delicious. A warning, the boundaries of which she knew she was going to thoroughly enjoy pushing again and again and again if the heat that came along with it was anything to go by.

Her voice was husky as she said, 'You've spent the past day in airports or on planes so perhaps we could make a quick stop at home before we do any shopping.'

With a whoosh Gabe lifted her to standing and tucked the flamingos under one arm. 'I knew you were a woman after my own heart.'

Laughing, Paige went to press a button, then paused.

'Eighth floor,' Gabe said, tucking her beanie back onto her head. 'My place never felt like it was really mine. Yours, on the other hand, I like very much. Though it could do with a bigger TV. And I've seen inside your fridge and there's only so much celery and carrot and dip a real man can take. And that girly bed has to go—'

'Yeah yeah yeah,' Paige said, all the while knowing she wasn't letting him near the decorating aspect of her apartment. Except his bed. The thing was so glorious she'd carry that bed down from his apartment herself.

She pressed the emergency stop button, then the button for the eighth floor and leant her head on Gabe's shoulder as his arm wrapped around her waist. And waited for the lift to move. She'd waited her whole life for him, she could wait a few minutes longer.

This big brawny man who'd seen flamingos and thought

of her. The dark, dangerous pirate who was prepared to buy a suit to marry her. The man who, when he went to Venice, or Brazil, or Timbuktu, would always be thinking about when he'd next be home.

A man who only had eyes for her.

EPILOGUE

SAM the Super leant back in his chair, shaking his head at the leggy blonde and the big guy from the top floor as they stared into one another's eyes like besotted teenagers on the lift's security monitor. They were both oblivious to the fact that he'd sent the lift to the penthouse and back to the lobby twice already.

She was hard work, the blonde, the way she couldn't just leave his little bit of fun with the lift well enough alone, but, he thought grudgingly, he admired her chutzpah. The other residents took his antics with the lifts for granted, but she never stopped trying to put things to rights. And while he was in a mood for admitting such things, he thought the new guy was all right too. He glanced at the box of cigars the guy had given him in thanks for helping him track down his bed.

Maybe he'd start to cut them a little slack. Maybe.

When the new guy reached up and cupped the blonde's chin, running his thumb over her cheek, Sam's mouth twitched in what felt like the beginnings of a warm smile.

When the black and white figures on the screen leant towards one another, clearly on the path to kissing, *again*, he mumbled beneath his breath, flicked off the monitor of the security camera. Sure, he liked to have his fun, a guy had to fill the hours of the day somehow, but they could keep their happily ever afters to themselves.

He pushed himself to standing with a groan and headed towards the service lift. It was time he changed the orange blossom mist in the foyer diffuser anyway.

* * * * *

THE MILLIONAIRE'S
MARRIAGE CLAIM
LINDSAY ARMSTRONG

Lindsay Armstrong was born in South Africa, but now lives in Australia with her New Zealand-born husband and their five children. They have lived in nearly every state of Australia, and have tried their hand at some unusual – for them – occupations, such as farming and horse-training – all grist to the mill for a writer! Lindsay started writing romances when their youngest child began school and she was left feeling at a loose end. She is still doing it and loving it.

CHAPTER ONE

JOANNE LUCAS steered her grey Range Rover over the appalling road and shook her head.

Sure, she hadn't expected the drive to a sheep station somewhere south of Charleville in outback Queensland to be a picnic. But the road had been quite good until she'd turned off onto the station track, and it was far worse than anything she'd anticipated. It was also quite a bit further than she'd expected to drive, and the chill dusk of a winter's evening was drawing in.

She scanned the horizon for some sign of habitation but there was none. This was serious sheep country, the Murweh shire—she knew from the research she'd done it carried approximately eight hundred thousand head of them! There were also cattle stations in the area so you expected it to be wide open and isolated.

On the other hand, her destination, Kin Can station, had quite a reputation. So did its owners, the Hastings family, for wealth and excellence in the wool they bred.

How come they couldn't afford to put in a decent road to the homestead, then? And how on earth did the wool trucks cope with it?

Come to think of it, if she hadn't had her wits about her, she would have missed the small, nearly illegible Kin Can sign on a gate—another surprise because she'd been led to believe the station was well sign-posted.

Do they actively discourage visitors? she asked herself, then slammed on the brakes as she topped a rise to see a man standing in the middle of the track aiming a gun at her.

Do they ever! It flashed through her mind, followed immediately by—So what to do now?

Any decision was taken out of her hands as the man loped forward and wrenched her door open before she could lock it. Not only that, he slung the gun over his shoulder and manhandled her out onto the road.

'Now look here,' she began, 'this is insane and—'

'What's your name?' he barked at her as he backed her up against the bonnet.

'Jo…Joanne, b-but people call me Jo,' she stammered.

'Just as I thought, although I was expecting a Joe—of the masculine variety—but perhaps they thought you could seduce me and keep doing it until they tracked me down.'

He paused and a flash of ironic amusement lit his intensely blue eyes as he looked her up and down then murmured, 'On the other hand, you don't look that feminine, Jo, so I'll go with my first scenario.'

Jo, who had gasped several times as he'd spoken, lost her temper and stamped heavily on his toe with the heel of her booted foot.

He didn't even flinch. 'Steel toecaps, darlin',' he drawled. 'So it gets your goat up to be called unfeminine?'

Jo breathed heavily but a small portion of her mind

conceded that, yes, it had—which was just about as insane as the whole mad situation. Nor could she resist a glance downwards, although she did resist the urge to tell this crazy person that most women would look unfeminine in creased cargo pants, a bulky anorak and a knitted beanie that concealed her hair.

She did quell the sneaky little voice in her head that reminded her some men found her height and straight shoulders unfeminine anyway...

'Look here, whoever you are,' she began, 'I'm expected up at the homestead so—'

'I'll bet you are, Jo,' he rasped, 'but we're going a different way. Let's just see what you're packing first.' He started to pat her down like a policeman.

'Packing?' It came out in a strangled way edged with outrage as she tried to evade his hands. 'Will you stop touching me? I'm not packing anything.'

'Take 'em off, then,' he ordered as his hands reached her waist.

Jo gaped at him. 'Take what off?'

'Your strides, lady.'

'I most certainly will not—are you out of your mind?'

'OK! Turn round and lean over the bonnet so I can search for hip holsters, thigh holsters or wherever women carry their concealed weapons.'

Jo stared at him in the fading daylight and wondered if she was the one going mad or—was this a nightmare? But the substance of her nightmare was anything but dream-like.

He was tall, taller than she was, with good shoulders. In a navy jumper and torn, dirty jeans, he looked to be extremely fit in a lean, rangy way. His thick black hair was short and ruffled and his jaw was covered with black stubble. Then there were those furious blue eyes that gave every indication of a man not to be trifled with.

But why? How? What? she wondered wildly. Some modern day bushranger on the loose? Surely not!

It's not unheard of, she corrected herself immediately, but why would he have been expecting any kind of a 'Joe'?

'Make up your mind,' her tormentor ordered. 'We haven't got all day.'

With trembling fingers, Jo unzipped her anorak and started to lower her cargo pants. Then she got angry again and pulled the anorak off and flung it over the bonnet. She ripped her boots off and stepped out of her pants. 'You may look but don't you dare lay a finger on me again,' she ground out, her grey eyes flashing magnificently.

The man grimaced and raised his eyebrows. 'Well, well!' His gaze dwelt on her figure beneath a fitted, fine-knit blue jumper and pale blue cotton briefs, and drifted down her long legs.

'Just goes to show you shouldn't make snap judgements,' he said with humour, looking back into her eyes, 'since it would be fair to say that in other circumstances you'd be welcome to seduce me, love.' The humour left his eyes. 'Turn around.'

If she'd been angry before, Jo was boiling now, but caution had the upper hand. She turned and lifted her arms to shoulder height. 'Satisfied?' she asked over her shoulder.

'Yep.' She stiffened as she felt his fingers on her waist and the elastic of her briefs pinged against her skin. 'Good old Bonds Cottontails, I do believe,' he added. 'OK, get dressed, then we're going for a drive.'

Jo pulled on her cargo pants. 'A drive? How far?'

'Right into—' He paused. 'Why?'

She hesitated, unsure whether to confess that she'd somehow underestimated the distance to Kin Can homestead, and another of her concerns had been that she'd run out of petrol...

'Come on, Jo—' he unslung the gun menacingly '—talk!'

'I don't have much petrol left.'

He swore. 'Bloody women!'

'I believe there's a pump at the house so—'

'Told you that, did they? Well, it's not going to be of any use to me. Get in and switch on so I can see how low the tank is.'

Jo swallowed and finished dressing as quickly as she could. And when she switched the motor on and the petrol gauge was revealed—bordering the red— he swore again, even more murderously, then, 'No spare tanks?'

'No.'

'What are you? One of their molls press-ganged into providing back-up?'

'I have no idea what you're talking about!' Jo cried. 'None of this makes any sense.'

'Oh, yes, it does, sweetheart,' he replied insolently, then rubbed his jaw with a sudden tinge of weariness. It didn't last long, that first faint sign of weakness, however. 'Plan B, then,' he said grimly.

*   *   *

Ten minutes later, Jo was steering her vehicle over another diabolical track, but this time following her captor's directions.

She'd had no opportunity to escape, as he'd made it quite clear he would shoot her down if she made any attempt to run away. Her request to be told what was going on had received a 'don't act all innocent with me, lady' response.

And he'd quashed, with an impatient wave of his hand and virtually unheard, her solitary attempt to explain who she was, why she was on Kin Can station and her conviction that he was making a terrible mistake.

He'd also searched the vehicle before they'd set off, then glanced at her with a considering frown.

So she drove with a set mouth and her heart hammering; he wouldn't allow her to use the headlights and the light was almost gone.

'There,' he said, pointing to a darker shadow on the landscape. 'Pull into the shed on the other side.'

At first Jo thought it was only a clump of towering gum trees, then she discerned the outline of two buildings. 'What is it?'

'Boundary riders hut,' he replied tersely as she nosed the vehicle into an old shed.

'Is it...is this where you live?'

He laughed scornfully. 'Who are you trying to kid, Jo?'

She sucked in a breath. 'I'm not trying to kid anyone! I have no idea what's going on or who on earth you are! What's your name?'

He glanced at her mockingly. 'For the purpose of maintaining your charade, why don't you choose one? Tom, Dick or Harry will do.'

'I have a better idea,' she spat at him. 'Mr Hitler is particularly appropriate for what I think of you!'

'So the lady has claws,' he said softly, with an appreciative gleam in his blue eyes, and switched on the inside light.

'You better believe it.'

Their gazes clashed. It was an angry, defiant moment for Jo, but there was also fear lurking beneath it. Fear and something else—a certain amount of confusion. He might act like a bushranger or a boundary rider gone berserk, but he sounded like neither.

What he said was undoubtedly inflammatory and insulting—let alone the incomprehensibility of it all— but the voice was educated and cultured with the kind of accent that a wealthy, old-money family and a private school steeped in tradition would imbue.

Then there was his navy-blue jumper. If she was any judge, it would have cost a small fortune, being made of especially soft, fine new wool—although they were on a sheep station that specialized in fine new wool, weren't they?

But most perplexing of all was the frisson tiptoeing along her nerve ends in the form of an awareness of him stealing over her. If you discounted his stubbly jaw and his eyes that could be murderous, he was well proportioned, excellently co-ordinated and rather devastatingly good-looking...

'What?'

She blinked at his question. 'N-nothing.'

'Or—thinking of changing sides?' he suggested. 'Believe me, Jo, you'd be well advised to. Being my moll would have infinite advantages over—'

'Stop it!' She put her hands over her ears. 'I'm no one's *moll* and have no intention of becoming one!'

'No?' He said it consideringly with his gaze roaming over her narrowly. 'You could have fooled me a moment ago.'

Jo bit her lip and was furious with herself.

He laughed softly. 'You're not much good at this, are you?'

'If I had any idea what you're talking about—'

She broke off as he moved impatiently.

'Enough! Let's get inside. We'll take all your gear.'

'What for?'

'So I can go through it with a fine-tooth comb.' He clicked off the overhead light and jumped out.

She had no choice but to follow suit. The shed had doors and he pushed them closed and latched them, so unless you knew to look, there was no sign of her car. Then he gestured for her to precede him into the hut.

He did go through her things with a fine-tooth comb, but after he'd secured the hut and lit a fire in the rusty combustion stove from a store of chopped wood and old newspapers.

The wooden hut was small and rudimentary. It had a half-loft storing some bales of old straw, but the ladder to it was broken. There were a couple of uncomfortable-looking narrow beds, a table and two hard chairs, one dilapidated old armchair, a small store of dry and tinned goods and a couple of milk cans filled with water.

There was one high window, but it had been broken and boarded up, and one door. All the same, as a precaution against any light being seen, Jo gathered, he hung a blanket over the door and a rough, dingy towel over the window.

Two things he did she could only approve of: the light and warmth from the stove were welcome against the cold, dark night, and the aroma from the pot of coffee he set on the stove caused her to close her eyes in deep appreciation as she took her anorak off.

On the other hand, two things she noticed while they waited for the coffee added to her confusion. He looked at his wrist, as if to check his watch, then with a grimace of annoyance, pulled it from his pocket and laid it on the table. It had a broken band, she saw, but, although it was plain enough, it was also sleek, platinum and shouted very expensive craftsmanship.

A faint frown knitted her brow. A demented boundary rider with a couple-of-thousand-dollar watch? Then there were his jeans. Torn and dirty they might be, but they were also designer jeans if she was any judge.

'No milk, but there is sugar,' he said presently, and handed her an enamel mug. 'Help yourself.' He indicated a sugar caddy.

She took two spoonfuls and looked around as she stirred them in.

'Take the best chair, ma'am,' he said with some irony and indicated the armchair.

'Thanks,' she murmured and sank down into it. A small cloud of dust rose but she was too tired and tense to care and she realized she was still wearing her beanie. She plucked it off irritably, and turned to look at her captor as he made an involuntary sound.

She raised an eyebrow at him. 'What have I done now?'

'Er—nothing,' he responded. 'Why on earth do you cover your hair?'

Jo ran her fingers through her cloud of dark gold hair. Someone had once told her it was the colour of beech leaves in autumn. True or not, she regarded it as her crowning glory, perhaps her only glory, and it was certainly her only vanity, her long, thick, silky hair.

She pushed her fringe back and shrugged. 'It's cold and dusty out there.'

His blue gaze stayed on her in a rather unnerving manner and she felt a tinge of colour steal into her cheeks because she had no doubt he was contemplating her figure.

She would have died if she'd known that it had crossed his mind to wonder whether that deep rich gold colour of her hair was duplicated on her body...

He turned his attention rather abruptly to her two bags, unpacking the entire contents of the smaller one onto the table.

Jo sipped her coffee and watched as he went through every item of clothing she'd brought, her writing case, books, sponge bag and make-up, her first-aid kit. He upended her canvas tote bag and her diary, her phone, a map and her purse fell out together with a bag of sweets and some tissues.

He picked up the phone. 'This isn't any good to us out here, we're out of mobile range.'

'So I gathered,' she said bitterly.

He smiled unpleasantly. 'Did you try to get in touch with them after you left Cunnamulla? I would have thought they'd have warned you about that—or supplied you with a satellite phone. Joanne Lucas,' he read as he examined her credit card, her diary, her Medicare card and her driver's licence.

'If you go back to the diary, you'll find my address, my doctor, my dentist and possibly my plumber and electrician.' She eyed him ironically.

He didn't respond, but started to repack the bag. The sight of him handling her underwear again annoyed her intensely, however, and she jumped up. 'I'll do that!'

'OK.' He pushed it all down the table towards her and reached for the bigger bag. 'Painting gear, from the earlier look I took at it,' he said.

He took out a collapsible easel, a heavy box of oil crayons, charcoal pencils, a sheaf of cartridge paper and a smaller box of sharpeners and rubbers. 'Now that—' he sat back '—has to be an inspired bit of camouflage, Ms Lucas.'

'You can believe what you like but, as I tried to tell you earlier, I was commissioned by Mrs Adele Hastings of Kin Can station to do her portrait. That's why I'm here.'

'Mrs Adele Hastings is not on Kin Can.'

Jo stared at him. 'But I spoke to her only a few days ago to make the final arrangements!'

He shrugged and folded his arms.

'How do you know she's not there, anyway?' Jo asked.

'I...made it my business to know.'

Jo frowned. '*Are* you some demented, latter-day bushranger? Or a boundary rider gone berserk? Is that what this is all about?'

'Go on.'

'What do you mean, "go on"?' Her frustration was obvious. 'All I'm trying to do is make some sense of it.'

'Fascinating stuff,' he commented. 'Just say I were either of those, what would it lead you to assume?'

She gestured with both hands. 'You…held up the homestead, got sprung maybe, escaped, mistook me for reinforcements and took me hostage—' She broke off abruptly and her grey eyes dilated as she castigated herself for even mentioning the possibility.

He smiled. 'Well, it so happens I did escape, Jo. And not long before I did so, I heard them calling their back-up, by the name of Jo—Joe—whatever, and requesting confirmation of what the back-up vehicle would be. They repeated what they were told— a silver-grey Range Rover.'

This time her eyes virtually stood out on stalks. 'That's…that's—'

'Coincidence?' he suggested sweetly. 'I don't think so.' His mouth hardened. 'Then there's the fact that you drove in by the back gate, as instructed, which took you a long way out of your way but, being a woman, I presume, you neglected to think of the extra petrol you might need.'

Jo opened and closed her mouth a couple of times, then, 'So *that's* why it seemed a lot further than I'd calculated. But—' she stopped to think briefly '—what happened to the front gate?'

His gaze narrowed on her. 'You know,' he said at last, 'you might be whole lot cleverer than I first thought. You're certainly an inspired liar—what the hell could have happened to the front gate?'

Jo gritted her teeth. 'According to Mrs Adele Hastings, the front gate, the main gate, the *only* gate she mentioned should have been about fifty kilometres back from the gate I drove through. And it should have been well signposted. "You won't miss it," she told me. "It's a big black truck tyre with the name painted in white on it." Believe me, I kept my eyes peeled but I saw nothing like that.'

His eyes narrowed but he maintained the attack from a different direction. 'And you just kept on driving all those extra kilometres?' he taunted.

'Yes, I did! But only after I used my mobile phone to contact Kin Can only to find I'd gone out of range. That road was quite good, though, and I thought— what's fifty kilometres to country people?'

A glimmer of a smile lit his eyes but it was gone as soon as it came.

'Nevertheless, you have it right. I do intend to hold you hostage, sweetheart, so I hope you mean something to whoever you're working for, otherwise things could be a little nasty for you.' He stood up. 'Care for some soup? Or there's baked beans, uh, tinned spaghetti—'

Jo went to slap his face, only to end up pinned in his arms.

'Now, now, Lady Longlegs,' he said softly. 'You may be pretty athletic, but you're no match for me.'

'Don't call me that!'

'I'll call you what I like. I'm the man with the gun, remember?'

Jo shivered.

He felt it through her clothes and it crossed his mind again that, in different circumstances, Jo Lucas was his kind of woman—tall, with lovely, clean lines and some fascinating curves. As for her face, perhaps not a face to look twice at in the first instance, he thought, but once you did, it held the eye.

Her skin was smooth and creamy, but her lashes and eyebrows were darker than her hair and they framed her grey eyes admirably. Her nose was straight, her mouth was actually fascinating with a slightly swollen bee-stung upper lip that excited a rash impulse to kiss it he had to kill rather swiftly...

And the whole was completely natural, no trace of make-up, no plucking of her eyebrows into coy arches and, he glanced down at her hands, no painted nails.

So what does that all tell me? he wondered. She's a practical, serious-minded person but rather unexpectedly lovely in her own quiet way?

He chewed his lip and stilled the sudden movement she made to free herself and again their gazes clashed. He smiled inwardly at the proud expression in her grey eyes that told him she was hating every moment of being confined in his arms against her will.

If looks could kill, I should be six feet under, he reflected wryly. I wonder how she reacts to being made love to? Soberly or...

He paused his thoughts with an ironic lifting of his eyebrows, and she blinked in sudden confusion as if she'd been trying to read his mind, and failed.

Just as well, he mused with a certain humour, and attempted to direct his thoughts into a more businesslike channel, only to find himself speculating on how she'd got roped into this diabolical situation.

She was bound to be someone's lover, surely? Brought in on a tide of passion, perhaps—but no, it just didn't seem to fit her. Neither did she look venal, although it was hard to tell with women. But what was left? A grudge? What the hell could she, personally, have against him? A grudge against society, then, or...

That was when he paused to ask himself if there could be some mistake?

But how about all those coincidences? Too many to be believable? Yes. On the other hand, she appeared to have no suspicious equipment, no equipment at all other than a useless mobile phone. But did that preclude her from simply driving a back-up vehicle? It did not and he couldn't afford to take any chances anyway.

He let her go abruptly.

'I've had a thought,' she said quietly. 'While you're holding me hostage here, the real Joe, if there is such a person, is probably making his way to the homestead as we speak.'

His eyes narrowed again. 'Time will tell, lady.'

'Who are you?' It came out unwittingly and she bit her lip but, once said, she decided to persevere. 'At least tell me what's going on. Surely, as a hostage, I'm entitled to know what I've got myself into?'

Several expressions chased across his eyes—did she imagine it or was one of them a trace of perplexity? If so, it was immediately replaced with bland insolence.

'Got yourself into?' he repeated. 'A bed of your own making, I would imagine, Jo. In the meantime, I don't know about you, but it's going to be baked beans and biscuits for me.'

*   *   *

Two hours later, the hut was quiet and dim.

Jo had eaten a few spoonfuls of baked beans, she'd attended to a call of nature in the rough outhouse attached to the hut, and been attended in turn by her captor. When she'd finished, they'd both stood outside for a short time, listening and trying to probe the dense, chill darkness for any sign of life, but there had been none.

In Jo's case, she'd also been trying to get her bearings just in case an opportunity to escape came up.

Then he'd shepherded her inside and told her to go to sleep.

The beds were along the walls at right angles to each other, their thin grey and white ticking mattresses unadorned by sheets, although each bed had one dismal-looking pillow and one hairy-looking blanket.

She took her anorak off again and her boots, and prepared to lie down, but he stopped her suddenly.

'Get your night gear on,' he ordered.

'What for?'

'You are going to bed.'

She gestured contemptuously. 'You call this a bed?'

'It's all there is.'

'Perhaps, but I'd feel much happier in my clothes. There could be fleas, there could be ticks, there could be—anything.'

'All the same, Jo, I'd rather you got into your PJs. I'll get them for you.' He picked up her bag.

'No—hang on!' she protested with her hands planted on her hips. 'If you think I'm going to afford you some kind of a peep show, if that's why you want me to change into pyjamas, you're mistaken, Dick!'

He raised a lazy eyebrow and scanned her from head to toe. Her hands-on-hips posture and her straight back made the jut of her breasts particularly enticing beneath the fine pale blue wool of her jumper.

'What a pleasant thought,' he said softly, eyeing the outline of her nipples and the narrowness of her waist. 'But—' his lips twitched as she looked downwards and hastily amended her stance '—sadly, it wasn't what I had in mind. I fully intended to step outside while you changed.'

'So why...what...?' She stared at him in confusion.

'It's simple, sweetheart,' he said. 'You're much less likely to be running around the countryside in your nightwear, should you devise some devilish plan of escape. Apart from anything else—' he smiled at her with pure devilry '—you'd freeze. Don't be long,' he added. 'I'm not too happy about freezing either.' He stepped outside.

Jo unclenched her jaw and said every swear word she could think of beneath her breath. But there was nothing for it other than to retrieve the least revealing of the two pairs of pyjamas she'd packed, and change into them.

'Decent?' he called.

'*Yes.*'

'Decent and—mad,' he murmured as he came in, closed the door behind him and rearranged the blanket. 'Mmm.' He scanned her from head to toe. 'I see you kept your bra on. Not much protection against—anything, I would have thought.'

Jo looked down at her pyjamas. In a fine white cotton, with bands of filigree embroidery, her bra was visible beneath the top, but the alternative had been a pair of short, sleeveless pyjamas in a sensuous lilac satin.

She raised her gaze to his face. 'I'll get even with you one day for all this if it's the *last* thing I do.'

'Should be interesting. Go to bed, Jo.'

'What…what are you going to do?'

'Wait and watch, what else?'

'If you dare try crawling into my bed—' she began, but he cut her off.

'I don't actually hold with rape, whatever else you may think of me. I prefer my women warm and willing. Unless—' he cocked an eyebrow at her '—a bit of hostility is what turns you on?'

'You're disgusting,' she said through her teeth.

He laughed softly. 'There is quite—a body of evidence that would disagree with you.'

'I can imagine. Gangster molls, no doubt.'

His expression cooled. 'Certainly none of them have been as good an actress as you are, my dear.' He turned away to pick up her boots, her anorak and her bag of clothes and he slung them onto the loft.

Jo could have screamed from frustration. Instead, with an expression of rigid distaste but supreme self-control, she lay down on the bed and pulled the blanket up.

Sleep, of course, was the furthest thing from her mind, although she closed her eyes a couple of times as the fire in the stove burnt low, and her captor lounged back in the armchair—with his gun across his knees.

If she could feign sleep, she reasoned, perhaps he would lower his guard, even fall asleep himself? But what could she do if she managed to sneak out of the hut? He had her car keys in his pocket and he'd locked the car; her clothes and boots were out of reach. And, as he had so diabolically foreseen, running around the rough terrain outside in her bare feet and pyjamas was highly unappealing if not to say inviting pneumonia and injury.

But perhaps I could hide, she mused. He doesn't appear to have a torch and perhaps I could sneak a blanket out with me?

She strained her eyes in the gloom and stared at the door. There was no lock, only a bolt on the inside and—her heart started to beat faster as she remembered—a bolt on the outside as well. How much better if she could not only sneak out and find a place to hide, but lock the man inside the hut as well? If he was trying to escape detection for whatever reason, he'd hardly shoot his way out of the hut...

She took some deep breaths to compose herself and moved slightly. The bed squeaked a bit but he didn't stir.

Gotcha, she thought, but decided to wait a while longer in case he was only cat-napping.

Ten minutes later, she sat up cautiously, and waited. No movement from the armchair, so she eased herself off the bed and flinched at the series of squeaks. Still no movement from the chair, though, but she stood quietly, trying to adjust her eyes to the gloom. The fire was nearly out in the stove but eventually she could see him. He was sprawled out with his head back and one arm hanging over the side of the chair.

The gun was still in his lap and an almost overwhelming temptation came to her—she only had to steal forward and grab it—but she had no knowledge of guns at all. What was there to know, though? Anyone could pull a trigger, not necessarily *at* him, but if he knew she was prepared to fire the damn gun wouldn't that be enough?

Then he moved and she froze. But all he did was turn slightly and bring his arm up so that his hand rested across the gun. And he muttered something unintelligible, but slept on.

Almost weak with relief, Jo stayed where she was for a few minutes, but decided that grabbing the gun was out—she could get herself shot. And she lifted the blanket off the bed and tiptoed towards the door where, with infinite care, she moved the blanket covering it aside and eased the bolt ever so slowly backwards.

'Nice try, darling.'

She nearly jumped a foot off the floor and lurched round to find him standing behind her with the gun pointed straight at her heart. How he'd got there so soundlessly was a mystery.

'Wh-what woke you?' she stammered.

'Don't know. Some sixth sense, maybe. What—' he looked at her ironically '—did you hope to achieve, Jo?'

Her shoulders slumped. 'I don't know. But,' she said with more spirit, 'I couldn't just lie there and accept—fate or whatever!'

He stared down at her. There was an agitated pulse thudding at the base of her throat and her eyes were wide and terrified but also stubborn.

He heaved an inward sigh and lowered the gun. Whatever she was, this woman was getting to him, he acknowledged. There were things he couldn't help admiring about her. You had to be brave to try to escape out into an unknown landscape on a frigid night with no shoes and only an old blanket.

But he still couldn't afford to take the chance that she wasn't who she said she was, however brave and—all the rest.

He turned away to put some more wood in the stove, then he stretched and studied his options. He had no idea what had woken him but one thing he did know—over twenty-four hours without sleep was taking its toll and his gaze fell longingly on the beds.

'OK,' he said, 'here's what we'll do.' He pushed her bed lengthwise against the other one, closing it in against the wall. 'You hop into that one—' he indicated the one against the wall '—and I'll use this one.'

She opened her mouth to protest but he forestalled her wearily. 'Jo, you're in no physical danger from me. However, I should warn you that the only way you can escape from that bed is to climb over me, and you mightn't find me in as conciliatory a mood were you to try. Now will you hop in?'

She hesitated, then did as she was told, to lie with her back to the second bed. He put her blanket over her and lay down, grappling with his own.

He was right, she realized. There was probably two inches' leeway from the other walls at the head and the foot of both beds so she was effectively penned in. She sighed and wriggled a bit to get comfortable.

A sleepy voice behind her said, 'You're right. These are only an apology for beds. You'll be pleased to hear, if you are Joanne Lucas, wandering portrait painter, that the beds up at the homestead are much more comfortable.'

'How would you know?'

'I've tried 'em.'

Jo frowned. 'These people you imagine I'm part of—who are they? And why are you running from them?'

'Kidnappers, as if you didn't know.'

Jo cast her blanket aside and sat up. 'Oh, this is ridiculous! Why would anyone, but particularly me, want to kidnap you?'

'For my sins,' her captor said, 'I happen to be Gavin Hastings the Fourth.'

CHAPTER TWO

Jo WAS struck speechless for several minutes, but her mind was jumping as she recalled her several conversations with Mrs Adele Hastings, his—if he was who he said he was—mother!

She could only describe Adele Hastings as talkative. A child called Rosie had featured frequently in her conversations, but Jo had never been able to work out whose child she was.

Her son Gavin had also featured prominently, so that Jo was in the possession, quite ancillary to the business of doing the lady's portrait, of a store of knowledge about Gavin Hastings.

He was an excellent son, a bit high-handed at times, mind you, a bit prone to getting his own way, but extremely capable, he could turn his hand to just about anything, which he needed to be able to do to run the vast Hastings empire inherited from his father...and so Mrs Hastings had gone on, although admittedly in very well-bred tones.

Jo had done a bit of research on the family and discovered that it *was* quite a dynasty. The first Gavin Hastings had been a pioneer. His grandson, Gavin's father, had not only extended the family holdings, he'd diversified into cattle. He'd also married Adele Delaney, daughter of a press baron. Jo hadn't researched any further since it was Adele's portrait she was doing.

How come, though, she wondered, Adele hadn't told her excellent, high-handed—that bit was quite believable!—son about the portrait? And how come Mrs Hastings wasn't on Kin Can? On the other hand, if he was who he said he was, it explained the fine clothes, the watch, the cultured accent, although it still seemed incomprehensible he didn't know about the portrait.

She looked down at her captor to pose this question to him, but Gavin Hastings the Fourth was fast asleep.

Jo sank back to her pillow thoughtfully. The light from the stove was stronger now and she didn't have to peer through the gloom to make out his features. In repose, he looked younger, but she guessed he was around thirty-four.

Sleep, however, didn't diminish his good looks, although it did present him as much less arrogant. Above the bristles his skin was lightly tanned, his dark eyebrows less satanic, and his mouth that could be so hard or smile so sardonically, insolently, iron-ically—she had a whole range of less-than-pleasant expressions to recall even after such a short acquain-tance—was relaxed and well cut.

One couldn't doubt, she decided, that, all spruced up, Gavin Hastings would be dynamically attractive.

He could also be extremely unpleasant, she re-minded herself. He could be cutting and unforgivably personal even if he was being pursued by a gang of kidnappers—and she still had to prove to him she was no 'gangster's moll'.

Perhaps if she drew his portrait he'd believe her? Not now, of course, but at the first opportunity. As for being in a kidnap situation with him…

Her tired brain gave up at that point, and she fell asleep.

She had no idea how much later it was when she was wrenched awake by a drumming sound. She sat up with her hand to her throat and a dry mouth, only to feel someone's arm slide around her and hear a voice say, 'It's rain. Good news, really.'

'Who…what…?' It all came tumbling back to her. '*Rain!* It sounds like a machine gun!'

'Old tin roof, no insulation, that's all.'

Jo shivered. There was no sign of light coming from the stove and it was very cold. 'Why good news?' she asked.

'Should make it harder for them to find us, assuming they're still looking—I don't know about you, but I'm freezing.'

'You could always build up the fire,' she suggested.

She heard a low chuckle. 'Got a better idea. Lie back, Miss Lucas—I presume it is Miss?'

Jo ignored the question and asked one of her own. 'Why?'

'So we can cuddle up and put both blankets over us.'

'That is not on my agenda!'

'Well, it is on mine.' And Jo found herself being propelled backwards into his arms.

'I always suspected it would come to this,' she said bitterly.

'What?'

She swallowed.

'You have a bad mind, Josie,' he said into her hair. 'Are you off men for some reason? Is that why there's this intense suspicion?'

'Sharing a bed with a stranger—being forced to,' she amended, 'is enough to make any woman suspicious, surely? Not to mention all the rest of it. After all, you were the one who brought up seduction in the first place.'

'For my sins again,' he murmured. 'But you have to admit it's warmer like this.'

It was. It also felt—she couldn't quite work out why—safer. Because she knew who he was now? And knew she was on the side of the 'goodies'? Still very much suspect, of course, she reminded herself, but talk about a series of incredible coincidences!

One thing she was certain of, though, she had not missed Kin Can's main gate, so what *had* happened to it?

She opened her mouth, not only to bring that up, but so much more. Did he have any idea who his potential kidnappers were? How had he escaped them? But his deep, slow breathing and the relaxation of his arm about her waist told her he was asleep again.

She smiled unexpectedly. So much for seduction. But if you could believe what he himself had alluded to, a body of evidence—a whole lot of women who found him attractive, in other words—suggested he was a much safer bet asleep.

What kind of women appealed to *him*? she wondered suddenly. Gorgeous? Definitely. Sexy? Had to be. Joanne Lucas?

She moved abruptly and removed herself from beneath his arm and slid cautiously onto the other bed, still trying to share both blankets. He didn't move at all.

*   *   *

It was barely dawn when Gavin Hastings stirred and lay still again. Then he sniffed and frowned. His cheek was resting against someone's hair, hair that felt silky soft and gave up the faint fragrance of—what?

For some reason, a bottle of shampoo swam into his mental vision, a clear plastic bottle decorated with apples and pears and filled with green liquid—of course! Amongst Joanne Lucas's toiletries had been just such a bottle of shampoo; it was her hair and it smelled very faintly of pears.

Something else from her toiletries swam into his mind; a pink lady's razor with which, no doubt, she shaved those long, lovely legs. He rubbed his jaw wistfully. Even a pink razor would be extremely welcome to someone who hadn't shaved for two days.

Then his mind wandered onto another pleasure—the woman sleeping peacefully in his arms. Her body was soft and warm against his, in fact her curves felt sensational nestled into him and, he reflected ruefully, he had better get himself out of this situation before a certain claim he'd made earlier proved to be incorrect.

But, as he moved Jo Lucas gently away from him, she murmured softly, a small sound of protest, and she buried her head against his shoulder.

A spark of humour lit his eyes. You're going to hate me when I make mention of this, Josie, and if you get on your high horse again, as you most likely will, I shall no doubt bring it up…won't be able to resist it!

The humour died as he stared down at the sleeping

girl in his arms. Not only the perfume of her hair, but her smooth, soft skin and her warm, lovely body teased his senses.

His memory took flight again, not to a bottle of shampoo this time, but the vision of her without her cargo pants and the high, rounded swell of her hips beneath a pair of no-nonsense Bonds Cottontails. If she was a pleasure to study from the front, he thought, it would surely be a sheer pleasure to watch her walking away from you with those hips swinging beneath a flimsy skirt…

He dragged his mind back with an effort. Who the hell was she? Not only that, how often had he used women to make him forget, only to find they were an anodyne but not the real thing?

He got out of the bed less than gently and stretched vigorously. When he turned back, Jo's eyes were open, and completely bewildered.

'Morning, Miss Lucas,' he said briskly. 'Time to get back to the fray.'

Jo stayed exactly as she was for a long moment, then she sat up abruptly and combed her hair back with her fingers. 'Good morning.'

'Sleep well?' he enquired with a mocking tinge of irony.

'I…er…must have. I don't seem to remember much about it.'

'Just as well.' He waited, bastard that he was, as her eyes looked confused again, then he changed the subject completely. 'You may not have noticed but it's still raining. Here's what I suggest—we make use of your fold-up umbrella to visit the outhouse, then you can do what you like while I do a recce.'

'Do what I like?' Jo repeated uncertainly.

'Get dressed in peace, perhaps heat some water on the stove for a wash—I'll build up the fire—or, contemplate your navel if that's what you prefer to do at this hour of the morning.'

Her eyes darkened and he knew it would have given her great pleasure to tell him to get lost, but in much more colourful language. She kept her mouth shut, however, and climbed out of bed.

'Here.' Something made him take pity on her, and he reached for her anorak. 'Wear this.'

She accepted it but refused to look at him, even when he pulled her bags and boots down as well.

Fifteen minutes later Jo was on her own in the hut, bolted in from the outside to her intense annoyance, but he had got the fire going and there were both the coffee-pot and a pot of water for washing simmering on the stove.

After a brief wash and dressing in a fleecy-lined grey tracksuit, she felt a lot better. She brushed her hair and tied it back and made herself a pot of coffee. And she pictured Gavin Hastings reconnoitring with, not only her fold-up umbrella, but the plastic poncho she always carried—neither of which would afford him great protection, but they had to be better than nothing in the downpour outside.

Gavin Hastings, she reflected, who had made a nasty little remark about something it was just as well she couldn't remember—*what*?

She surely couldn't have slept through his taking advantage of her in any way. She surely wouldn't have taken advantage of *him* in any way so…?

She glanced over at the two beds. Only one of them, narrow as it was, still bore the sagging imprint of being slept on. She clicked her teeth together in sheer annoyance.

She must have spent the night in his arms, right up close and personal. Only two bodies in one dilapidated old bed made for one body would cause it to stay sagged like that. To make it worse, the sagging bed was his, the bed on the outside, so she must have been the one to move over.

Clearly a tactical error, she thought, even if I was half asleep. I must have been cold and *scared*—I must have been mad!

The coffee-pot bubbled at that point, so she poured herself a mug and tried to turn her mind away from things she couldn't change. Then she remembered her idea of doing his portrait in a bid to prove she was who she'd said she was.

It turned out to be an exercise with curious side effects as she opened her pencil box and tore a piece of cartridge paper in half...

She'd always been a sketcher. For as long as she could remember, she'd doodled and etched and found it a great comfort, but paints had never particularly appealed to her. She'd tried watercolours, oils and acrylics but found that none of them was her medium.

At eighteen, however, her life had changed dramatically and she'd gone to art school for a year. That was where she'd discovered oil crayons—and it had all fallen into place. It had not been a lack of colour appreciation, her failure with paint, it had been her difficulty in merging the two techniques, drawing and painting.

Oil crayons allowed her to draw in colour, and she virtually hadn't stopped since the discovery. So that now, at twenty-four, she had a small but growing reputation in portraiture.

Of course, doing portraits had its downside. You were often at the mercy of less-than-likeable characters and your fingers itched to portray them that way. It had, however, gained her recognition, and once that reputation was well established she would be able to draw what she pleased and sell it—landscapes and particularly children, whom she loved to draw, although not necessarily as their parents wanted them portrayed.

As she organized herself as best she could, she practised a familiar technique. She breathed deeply and cleared her mind—and she called up her captor.

As always, some emotions came with the image she was seeing in her mind's eye, her reaction to her subject, but what caused her to blink in surprise was the veritable kaleidoscope of emotions that came along with Gavin Hastings's dark, good-looking face.

She discovered that her fingers longed to score and slash lines and angles onto the paper with her crayons in a caricature of the devil with very blue eyes.

Jo, Jo, she chided herself, if he's to be believed, he's been subject to a kidnap attempt so he's bound to be antsy!

Doesn't matter, she retorted. I don't like him, but I especially don't like the way I *do* like some things about this man I don't like. And I resent wondering, actually wondering, what he thinks of me!

She stared down at the still-pristine piece of paper beneath her fingers and was horrified to find herself breathing raggedly. This isn't going to work, she thought. There's only one way I can draw Gavin Hastings with any peace of mind and that's asleep.

She had no idea how much later it was when she heard the bolt being withdrawn on the other side of the door, but some instinct made her throw her anorak over all the evidence of her endeavours.

He came in looking as mean and nasty as any demented bushranger, daubed with mud and soaking wet.

Her eyes widened, then she looked at her watch and realized he'd been away for over an hour. 'Are you all right?' she asked.

'Concerned for me, maybe even missed me?' he queried sardonically. 'No, I'm not all right. Put some water on to boil.'

Jo opened her mouth to take issue with his manner, then changed her mind, and he started to peel off his clothes.

'Uh—what happened to the umbrella and the poncho?' she ventured.

'They were about as useless as a pocket handkerchief so I threw them away.'

Joanne listened to the rain pounding on the roof for a moment. 'Yes, well, they weren't designed for this kind of downpour.' She refilled the coffee-pot and set it on the stove. 'Did you—achieve anything?' She turned to look at him, but turned away abruptly—he was down to his underpants and socks. Then she took hold and told herself not to be spinsterish. 'Here.'

She took a blanket off the bed and handed it over. He didn't thank her as he draped it around him.

Instead, as their gazes met his was full of such chilling scorn that she flinched.

She had to say, 'Look, none of this is my fault. It's no good being angry with me. If anything, it's counterproductive.'

'Really.' He sat down at the table. 'Have you been able to come up with anything *pro*ductive while you've been twiddling your thumbs?' he asked unpleasantly.

She set her teeth.

'Well, I'll tell you what I've been doing,' he said. 'Skulking around my own property, stealing my own fuel, which I then had to carry like a packhorse, while you've been—' his gaze strayed to a corner of the pencil box protruding from beneath her anorak and he swept the jacket aside '—I don't believe this—painting!'

'It's not painting. I don't use paints. I use oil crayons.'

'Nevertheless—' He stopped and studied his portrait, but what he thought of it she was destined not to know because, although he blinked once, he then looked up at her with palpable menace. 'Do you honestly think this proves anything?'

'I…' She bit her lip. 'I was hoping it would.'

'Then you thought wrong, lady. So—' he relaxed somewhat, but the attack didn't relax at all as he studied the portrait again '—you looked your fill while I was asleep, Jo?'

Some colour came to her cheeks. 'It's a habit I have. Bones, lines, angles, muscles are my stock-in-trade.'

'What about cuddling up to strange men?'

The hiss of droplets turning to steam on the stove top told her the water had boiled, but she ignored it. 'I must have been asleep. I certainly don't remember doing it. I must have been cold—that's all there is to it.'

He watched her set mouth and returned her level grey gaze for a moment, then shrugged. 'It was very pleasant, as it happens. Would you be so kind as to clear the table, Miss Lucas, and would you lend me your pink razor?'

Jo parted her lips, but then closed them.

'You're right,' he said as if she'd spoken, 'I need a shave. It might even put me in a better frame of mind. You wouldn't happen to have a mirror?'

She had more. She had a small cake of soap, a clean, slightly damp towel, a toothbrush and toothpaste, but the mirror was tiny.

He used it all the same, squinting at it humorously for any patches of bristle he'd missed. Then he cleaned his teeth with heartfelt relief.

'I like a lady with a good, sharp razor,' he commented at one stage. 'New?' He held it up to the light.

'It was new,' Jo agreed dryly.

He laughed. 'Might not be good for much after ploughing through that beard, but if we ever get out of here, Jo, I'll buy you another one. Ouch.' He fingered his jaw. 'You wouldn't have any aftershave lotion, by any chance?'

'If that's designed to make me feel less than feminine,' she said pointedly, 'it's like water off a duck's back. No, I don't, but you could try this.' She handed him a bottle out of her toilet bag.

He turned it over in his hands and read the label. 'Witch hazel? What's that?'

'A very good, natural astringent that should make your skin feel all tingly and fresh.'

'Ah.' He poured some into his palms and slapped it on his face. 'You're right! A woman of great resource. Incidentally—' he screwed the cap on the bottle '—I thought I'd dispelled that less-than-feminine tag?'

During his ministrations, he'd shoved the blanket down to his waist and she had picked up his wet clothes and hung them on the other chair in front of the fire.

'I don't give a damn about what you think of me in that regard,' she replied, but the truth was the sleek muscles of his shoulders, the springy dark hair on his chest, his tapering, rock-hard torso were all hard to ignore for two reasons. The funny little sensation they brought to the pit of her stomach and a very real desire to capture such male perfection on paper.

There was a little silence. Then he said ironically, 'You're a hard nut to crack, Josie.'

She shrugged and busied herself with making breakfast—this time tinned stew and biscuits. But her fingers stilled as she remembered what he'd said earlier, and she turned to him suddenly. 'Fuel?'

His eyes narrowed. 'I wondered when that would sink in,' he murmured.

'So you got some? How? Did you get up to the house?'

He shook his head. 'There's a machinery shed not that far away.'

She turned back to the stew. 'So we're...we can...go?'

'No. There's a creek up and running between us and the gate we wouldn't get through even in a four-wheel drive at the moment.'

Jo served up breakfast. She handed him a knife and fork, then sat in the armchair with her plate balanced on her knees and chose her next words with care.

'There are some things I don't understand. Were you completely alone on the station when they kidnapped you?'

'No, I wasn't. The head stockman was—immobilized before they came after me.'

'Not killed?' Her eyes were dark with shock.

'No. But captured and tied up and removed heaven alone knows where.' He started to eat with evident hunger.

'And there was no family, no one else?' she asked with a frown.

'Jo—' he paused with his fork poised and glinted her an assessing look '—whoever they are, they'd done their homework. It's a long weekend, it happens to be the district's annual rodeo with all its attendant parties, B and S balls and the like. A lot of people are away from home, in other words. It so happens *I* was supposed to be away from home but I changed my mind at the last minute.'

'Is that why your mother isn't home?' she asked perplexedly.

This time he waved his fork. 'My mother took off for Brisbane two days ago. Some show she'd forgotten she had tickets for. I can only be grateful she wasn't there and neither, particularly, was Rosie.'

Suddenly, his blue gaze seemed to drill right through her.

Jo blinked. 'She mentioned a Rosie several times when we spoke on the phone—a child, I gathered, but I couldn't work out whose.'

He stared at her for another long moment, then finished his breakfast and put his knife and fork together. 'Mine.'

Jo digested this with several blinks. 'Well, what about your wife?' she ventured.

'She died in childbirth.' He pushed his plate away and there was something completely dark and shuttered in his expression. 'Any chance of a cup of coffee?'

'Of course,' Jo murmured and got up to attend to it. 'Would...' she hesitated '...would I be right in assuming your mother is a tad absent-minded?'

He looked heavenwards. 'My mother, God bless her, has developed a memory like a sieve lately.'

'Well—' Jo put a mug of coffee in front of him '—that explains it!'

'You mean it explains why she forgot you were due to descend on Kin Can?'

'Yes!' Jo put her hands on her hips.

'Doesn't explain why she never once mentioned anything about getting her portrait painted—drawn, whatever—to me.'

Jo subsided. 'Perhaps she meant to surprise you?'

'So how do you think she was going to explain you, in the flesh, away?'

'I don't know—she's *your* mother!'

'For my sins—yet again,' he said dryly, and got up. 'I don't suppose you have any men's clothing in your bag of tricks?' he added moodily and hitched the blanket around him again.

Jo merely stared at him steadily.

'Once again, if looks could kill I'd be six feet under. OK, Miss Lucas, assuming you are lily-white, above board and all the rest, do you have any suggestions?'

Jo resisted the urge to give vent to her feelings—she posed a question instead. 'How many are there?'

'Two. They wore balaclavas so I have no idea who they are.'

'How did you escape?'

He sat down on the corner of the table. 'Checking up on me, Jo?'

'I do only have your word for it.'

He mulled over this for a moment, then grimaced. 'They trussed me up like a chicken and locked me overnight in a windowless storeroom. What they didn't know was that under the lino there was a trapdoor—the house is on stilts about two feet above the ground, handy in times of flood. I got away through it.'

'How? If you were trussed up like a chicken?'

He rubbed his wrists and Jo noticed, for the first time, almost red-raw, chafing marks on the inside of each wrist. 'I found a pair of old scissors and managed to saw through the rope with them. Not that easy since my hands were tied against my back.'

'No,' she agreed with a tinge of awe, which she immediately tried to mask by adding, 'Why didn't they take you away instead of storing you in the house for a whole night?'

He glanced at her. 'Well, you see, Josie, I wasn't their target.'

She stared at him blankly.

'No,' he said meditatively and rubbed his chin. 'It was Rosie they'd planned to snatch, my six-year-old daughter—a much softer target.'

Jo's mouth fell open.

'As you say.'

'But…are you sure?'

'I'm quite sure. I heard all the discussion, all the recriminations going on throughout the night, all the new plans being made. They decided since they'd got me they'd take me in her place, but that's why they called for some back-up.'

'Thank heavens for your mother's bad memory,' Jo said a little shakenly.

'All the same, not only do I have to get myself off Kin Can, I have to prevent my mother and Rosie waltzing back into their arms. They cut all the phone lines, you see.'

'Won't that make people—your mother—suspicious?'

'Not necessarily. The system can have its problems out here and it is rodeo weekend.'

'I do have a suggestion,' she said slowly. 'Not to do with how to escape, but I feel pretty sure they must have also removed…any indication it was Kin Can station from the main gate. Perhaps to confuse anyone looking for the place?'

He gave it some thought as well as tossing her a considering look.

'Believe me,' she said quietly, 'that is why you found me on the back track.'

'Hmm… You could be right.' He shrugged. 'The main problem now is—have they given up and gone away? Or, are they waiting to trap me somehow, even out searching for me?'

'They don't sound terribly well organized.'

He stood up, cast the blanket off and reached for his clothes. 'Fate may have conspired against them, the weather certainly has, but they're a dangerous duo—trio if Joe got through. One of them, at least, is using a mixture of drugs and alcohol to keep himself hepped up.'

Jo shivered and watched as he struggled into his damp jeans, T-shirt and jumper. 'Did they offer you any violence? Other than tying you up?'

His lips twisted. 'A kick in the kidneys, a wallop over the head—' he searched his scalp through his dark hair and winced as he obviously found a bump '—and several others, but perhaps I gave them some provocation.'

'You didn't go quietly?' she hazarded.

'No, my dear, I didn't.'

Something in the way he said it chilled Jo to the core. She had no doubt Gavin Hastings would be a bad man to cross.

'As for the rest of it, they had the foresight to immobilize every other vehicle up at the house and they locked the dogs in the shed and threw away the key. The gun was a lucky break for me. Case, the foreman, must have forgotten to put it away in the gun cupboard in the shed. I nearly tripped over it.'

Jo collected the tin plates and empty mugs and stacked them on the floor next to the stove. 'So your plan was to intercept the other Joe and...?' She looked a question at him.

'Force him to drive me to the nearest phone.' He watched her as she swept some biscuit crumbs off the table with her hand, and she became aware that the lurking suspicion was back in his eyes.

'Silver-grey Range Rovers are pretty common, you know.'

'Perhaps. How about a Joe and a Jo?'

She hesitated. 'I—'

But a crack of sound split the air and a bullet tore through one wall and buried itself in the opposite wall.

For a second they both froze, then Gavin Hastings leapt off the table and in a flying rugby tackle crashed her to the floor only just before another shot splintered the door around the bolt. Two minutes later the door had been kicked open and a man with a gun and wearing a balaclava was standing over them.

'Well, lookee here, Joe,' he snarled over his shoulder. 'Gav's got himself a girl. Pretty kinky keeping your mistress stashed away in an old boundary riders' hut, don't you reckon, guys?'

CHAPTER THREE

THE next few hours were the stuff of nightmares.

Jo and Gavin Hastings were tied up and loaded into a van. The second vehicle they were using was almost identical to Jo's Range Rover. But the crudity of the humour levelled at Jo was appalling and she was in no mood to appreciate that she was completely vindicated in Gavin Hastings's eyes. She was far too scared to even glance him an I-told-you-so look.

Nor could she do anything other than blink a couple of times when the kidnappers retrieved Gavin's gun, only to cast it aside in disgust when it was revealed to have no bullets.

Then the humour turned sour when the realization hit the kidnappers that the creek between them and the back gate was not negotiable. A heated argument ensued until it was finally decided they'd have to return to the homestead and take the track from it to the main gate.

But that didn't work for them either. The van got bogged about a quarter of a mile from the house. She and Gavin had their feet untied and were frogmarched up a winding, tree-lined driveway by two of the kidnappers, while the third, using the Range Rover, attempted to tow it out of the mud.

Her first impressions of Kin Can homestead, therefore, were blurred by rain and fear. All she could say was that it looked vast.

And as they reached the front steps a nasty little fracas developed as one of the men put his arms around her and tried to kiss her. Gavin swung his arms tied at the wrist and clouted the man on the head. He went down like a ninepin, but then so did Gavin Hastings as he was punched in the face by the other one.

Finally, they were manhandled up the front steps and into the house. Again her impressions were overlaid by fear, but she couldn't help the startled thought that the house was a work of art, spacious, beautifully furnished and the essence of luxury.

After more argument they were locked into a bedroom. As an added precaution, one of the kidnappers untied the cords around their wrists, but produced a pair of handcuffs and manacled Jo and Gavin together. 'Try sawing that off,' he jeered.

It was a while before Jo caught her breath. They'd collapsed onto the bed after being shoved into the room. But she sat up eventually, and wondered if her companion had blacked out—there was no movement from Gavin Hastings.

'Are you OK?' she asked anxiously and lifted her hand. His came up with it. 'This is ridiculous!' She studied their linked hands joined by the shiny silver cuffs.

'Mmm...' he agreed. 'Right out of a very bad gangster movie.' And with an effort, he heaved himself into a sitting position. 'But before I say any more, may I offer you my apologies, Miss Lucas?'

Jo opened her mouth, then closed it with the faintest smile curving her lips.

'That's being very generous, Jo,' he said gravely.

'I would have forgiven you for calling me all the unprintable names under the sun.'

'Oh, I haven't had time to work out if I've forgiven you or not.'

One eyebrow shot up. 'So why the smile—it looked like forgiveness.'

'It may have looked like it but I was actually thinking that all shaved and cleaned up you were rather— pretty. That is no longer the case.'

'*Pretty!*' He looked genuinely horrified.

'Well, good-looking, then,' she amended.

'What's wrong with me now?'

She shook her head sorrowfully. 'You have all the makings of a magnificent black eye, but I do thank you for springing to my defence the way you did.'

'So I should think,' he retorted, and with his free hand gingerly explored the swollen area around his eye, and he swore freely.

'What are we going to do?' she asked quietly.

'I had a thought—' he ground his teeth '—but the bastards are getting more dangerous by the minute. I get the feeling there's an element of panic beneath the gung-ho attitude—what do you reckon?'

She could only agree but added, 'I did think one of them, the tallest guy, seemed a little less..gung-ho, though. Maybe he'd listen to some sense?'

'Such as?'

Jo shrugged. 'You could point out that you have no idea who they are and their best bet would be to shake the mud of Kin Can off their boots as fast as possible rather than kidnapping *anyone*—let alone two people.'

'Not just a pretty face,' he commented. 'My own

sentiments entirely. I even thought of offering to help them on their way, monetarily, although that goes supremely against the grain. But now you're involved—' He broke off at the sound of raised voices. 'The thieves have fallen out, by the sound of it.'

Jo shivered.

'Can't put my arm around you,' he said humorously, 'but consider it done mentally.'

She smiled ruefully.

'That's better. OK, let's attract their attention and attempt to parley. One, two, stand up!'

Jo stood up with him and moved alongside him to the door. He rapped loudly on it. It was opened after a while by the tall man Jo had taken for being the less gung-ho of the three.

Ten minutes later it closed on them and was locked from the outside.

'Think he bought it?' Gavin enquired. The tallest of the three kidnappers had gone away with the expressed intention of consulting his 'colleagues'.

'I don't know. Only time will tell, I guess.' Her shoulders slumped.

He looked down at her critically. 'In the meantime—and I think you've been wonderful, Jo, most women I know would have had hysterics at least by now—we might as well make ourselves comfortable.' He indicated the bed.

Jo looked down at the soggy mess they both were. 'We'll make a mess.'

He grimaced. 'Who cares? Now, the key to it is for us both to sit down on it and gradually manoeuvre ourselves into a supine position—boots off, naturally.'

Several awkward moments later they were lying side by side on the bed, propped up by some wonderfully full, soft pillows.

'I see what you mean about a superior standard of bedding in the homestead,' she remarked, and looked around the room.

He grinned. 'My mother has very superior ideas when it comes to, not only interior design, but clothes, cars, the lot.'

Jo could only agree with the interior design bit. Although it wasn't large, and most probably a spare bedroom, the décor was lovely and no expense had been spared. A crisp cream waffle bedspread, although not so clean any longer, fuchsia-pink walls, cream woodwork and a tall, gorgeous dresser, cream again with brass handles. There were flower prints on the walls and Roman blinds at the window. There were also security insect screens over the window, fastened from the outside.

'No trapdoor under the carpet?' she asked.

'No, sadly. And no likelihood of any helpful implements in the drawers or cupboard.'

'There could be, surely?'

He shook his head. 'The room was cleaned out completely prior to being redecorated recently.'

'Oh.'

He turned to study her profile. 'I'm sorry I got you into this.'

'I probably would have got into it anyway, bad timing sort of thing.' She flinched and stiffened as the level of voices rose outside the door.

He listened for a while, then took her hand, the one manacled to his. 'Tell me about yourself, Jo Lucas.'

'I...' She made an effort to tear her mind away from the kidnappers. 'I...well, I'm an orphan. My parents died in a train crash when I was six and I went to live with my maternal grandmother. I was twelve when she developed Alzheimer's Disease so I was transferred to a series of foster homes. She died when I was fifteen.'

His hand tightened on hers.

She gestured with her free hand. 'There was a happy ending—of sorts. My father had been estranged from his family, well, his father, and they'd completely lost track of each other. He was English and he'd originally emigrated to Canada but came on to Australia.' She paused.

'Is this painful?' he queried.

'Uh—it's more like water under the bridge,' she said slowly. 'His mother had never stopped trying to find him, though, and she kept him, or his immediate descendants, in her will. When she died it took her lawyers another six years to track me down but they finally did when I was eighteen. So I came into a bit of money and I was able to put myself through art school and support myself ever since.'

'You'd be middle-twenties now?' he hazarded.

'Yep—twenty-four.'

'So how's it been otherwise since you were eighteen?'

'Fine.'

'I meant emotionally, relationships and the like. Sounds like a pretty traumatic upbringing to me.'

'It had its ups and downs,' she conceded.

'And it left no marks?'

Jo hesitated, then swallowed as a loud crash was

heard, and perhaps because of the horror and danger of the situation, she found herself telling him more than she'd told anyone for a long time.

'Ah, I have a slight problem there. Can't seem to bring myself to rely on anyone else. Not that it's a real problem. I mean, I'm perfectly happy as I am.'

'A loner,' he said after a long moment.

'A loner who loves it.'

'But you do have friends?'

'Of course. I went to school with my flatmate, Leanne Thomson. I keep in touch regularly with two of my foster families, as well as one of my art teachers, and so on.'

'What about men?'

Jo opened her mouth, then closed it and stared at the ceiling briefly. Surely there were some things you couldn't tell a perfect stranger even in these circumstances?

'I'm not good with men,' she said at last. 'They— I don't know—seem to find me too independent. I have thought I was in love a couple of times but it came to nought.' She shrugged.

'You—' He stopped as there was another crash, followed by a gunshot and a crescendo of angry voices.

Jo closed her eyes and turned her face into his shoulder as she trembled down the length of her.

He stroked her hair, but she could feel the tension, and the anger in him as well.

'Tell me about you,' she said shakily.

'Me? Well, I thought my life was perfect. I inherited Kin Can, I married the girl of my dreams, we made a baby and—it all fell apart because of an obscure medical condition no one realized my wife was suffering from that took her life just after Rosie was born.'

'I'm so sorry.' Jo clung to him as there was another shot and two crashes. It sounded as if they were wrecking the house. 'Go on.'

'There's not a lot more to tell. Rosie is the light of my life, I can't see myself ever marrying again—and do you think the bastards are killing each other?'

'I hope so, but why wouldn't you ever marry again?'

'I guess, once you've had perfection you just know it's an impossible act to follow. I guess I know myself well enough to know that I'd be holding every other woman up against that…happiness and finding her wanting. I suspect part of me will never forgive fate for what it did to me—and I'm a bad loser.'

'Do you have friends?'

He grimaced. 'I used to. All my friends are married now and they seem to specialize in trying to set me up with blind dates so I'm a bit wary of them. But, actually, my best friend married my sister, so I now have him as a brother-in-law.'

Jo opened her mouth, then shuddered against him as the fracas outside continued.

'What are your favourite things, Jo? Other than drawing? I—' he paused, then grinned '—for example, can't resist roast beef—never, ever eat lamb if I can avoid it. I'm particularly attached to my dogs, an ice-cold beer on a hot day and Nicole Kidman.'

Jo had to smile. 'Let's see, Hugh Grant and Colin Firth run a dead heat for me, chocolate and, above all, I love drawing kids.'

'Why? Don't they squirm and scratch?'

'Yes, but if you get them talking, they tell you wonderful things, their imaginations are marvellous. Although their parents would be horrified at some of the things you hear.'

'I can imagine. Have you had much to do with kids?'

'Uh-huh, especially foster-kids. I—have a very soft spot for them, of course, but all kids really. You often learn a lot from them.'

He hugged her hard, then sat up, drawing her nearer as the noise outside drew closer to their door. 'Time to remember I'm not a good loser,' he said grimly. 'I've just had a spark of inspiration. Why the *bloody* hell didn't I think of it earlier?'

'I don't know. What is it?'

He released and looked upwards. 'There's a man-hole in the ceiling.'

Jo followed his gaze. It was an old, iron-pressed ceiling with floral wreaths all over it, beautifully re-stored. 'Where? I can't see it.'

He pointed to a corner and gradually she made out a square cut into the iron, but her first instinct was that it would be impossible for them to get through it, manacled together as they were.

'We can do it, Jo,' he said when she voiced her concerns. 'All we have to do is push the dresser underneath and climb onto it. If you just follow my orders, we'll be fine.'

She gazed at him, then blew her fringe up with a smile in her eyes. 'Orders?'

'Well, instructions.'

'That's better. But,' she added as he grimaced, 'assuming we do, and don't get caught in the process, how will it help us? Surely they'll hear us moving about the roof? And what if they decide to accept your offer?'

Gavin Hastings rubbed his jaw. 'I could do it on my own,' he said reflectively. 'I've had a bit of practice at crawling around confined spaces soundlessly.'

'How so?'

'Spent some time in the SAS,' he said briefly. 'OK, we'll reserve it for desperation tactics at this stage.' He stopped as footsteps approached the door, and Jo clung to his hand.

'Listen—' he lowered his voice '—whatever happens now, do *exactly* as I say, Jo. Promise?'

She swallowed and nodded.

'The other thing is, there only seems to be one gun between them so whoever is toting it is the guy to be specially wary of, OK?'

She nodded again as the door was flung open.

There were only two of them—no sign of the tall man they'd attempted to bargain with, and that struck more terror into Jo's heart. Had they shot him when he'd tried to talk reason to them?

'Well, Gav,' the man who'd shot his way into the hut jeered, 'how much loose cash do you have stashed here?'

Jo breathed a tiny sigh of relief, although she felt a tremor of savage emotion course through the man she was manacled to.

But he said coolly enough, 'About three thousand dollars.'

The man jerked his head. 'Lead us to it, lover boy!'

Five minutes later, in what was obviously his study,

Gavin Hastings unlocked a cabinet and removed a cash box from it. He took a wad of hundred-dollar bills out of the box and laid the money on an impressive oak desk.

There was a short interlude while it was counted then shoved into the spokesman's pocket. The other man had said nothing and was clearly having trouble staying on his feet.

'Right. Hold up your hands,' the first man said, and when they did so he unlocked the handcuffs. 'There.' He stood back for a moment as they freed themselves but Jo knew that something was wrong. She could only see his eyes, but they had a glazed, un-with-it look that was terrifying and his whole stance was suggestive of a suppressed, horrible glee.

It only took a moment for her instinct to be proved right as their tormentor raised his gun and aimed it squarely at her.

And he said, not taking his eyes off her, 'See here, Gav, we decided there was no reason only you should be so lucky in...*lurve*, so we're taking this bit of hot stuff with us. Now don't you try and stop us, mate, otherwise she'll buy it.'

There was an instant of awful silence. Then Gavin erupted like a coiled spring. He knocked Jo backwards so she fell against the other man and knocked him off his feet. Then he launched himself at the first man—and the gun went off.

Jo shrieked in despair as she picked up a heavy marble antique inkwell and threw it at the man on the floor behind her. He'd been trying to get to his feet, but as the inkwell caught him on the temple he went out like a light.

Jo grabbed it up off the floor and turned to the melee struggling in front of her, which comprised Gavin Hastings and the man with the gun, and she bore down on them with the inkwell raised above her head and something like a banshee cry issuing from her lips.

But Gavin sat up abruptly and put out a hand. 'It's all right, Jo. I've knocked him out.'

She lowered the inkwell. 'Oh, thank heavens,' she breathed. 'So who got...?' Her voice rose as she noticed the blood dripping down his fingers. '*You* got shot! Oh, no!' She sank to her knees beside him. 'No, no, no!'

'I think it's only a flesh wound in my upper arm.' He grimaced and felt through his jumper cautiously.

'But you saved my life! You actually threw yourself in front of the gun. How can I ever repay you for that and what will I do if you die?' she gabbled, her face paper-pale and her grey eyes dark with disbelief and emotion.

'I'm not going to die, Josie.' He pulled his jumper over his head and Jo winced at the sight of the wound in his upper arm. But she immediately pulled off her tracksuit top and then the long-sleeved vest-top she wore beneath it, which she ripped into strips with her teeth and fingernails, then applied them as a pad and pressure bandages to his wound.

Gavin Hastings flinched but there was a suggestion of humour in his eyes as they rested on her, her upper body clad only in a bra as she worked on the dressings.

'What can you do to repay me, Jo? I think it would be a damn good idea if you married me.' He swayed suddenly, and blacked out.

CHAPTER FOUR

LATER that day, Gavin Hastings stirred in his hospital bed, where he'd been air-lifted by helicopter, and examined his disinclination to allow the sedative he'd been given to take effect.

He'd undergone a minor operation to have the bullet removed from his arm and received the good news that the bone hadn't been splintered. He'd been visited by his mother, who'd then flown on to Kin Can to take charge. She might have a memory like a sieve these days, but when she was in control mode she was highly effective.

Which was not to say she hadn't wept a couple of tears over him to think how close he'd come to dying, but she'd recovered swiftly, and had left him saying, 'All's well that *ends* well, darling!'

But had it ended?

He moved again, trying to get comfortable without disturbing the drip in his arm.

You can't ask someone to marry you, and *mean* it, only to black out before she's had a chance to answer, and say it's ended, he told himself.

When he'd come to, it had been to find himself in a chopper on the way to hospital with no sign of Jo, who'd been left behind at the station.

But why was he so sure he'd meant it? he pondered.

Why not say, for example—I think it would be a

damn good idea if you came to bed with me, Jo Lucas, because I've wanted you since you got rid of your anorak and your strides and revealed those lovely clean lines as well as an awful wrath at being importuned like that....

Not the time and place, of course, he reasoned, but perhaps more accurate than telling her he wanted to marry her?

No.

The negative stood out starkly in his mind. For whatever reason, and there were plenty—she was brave, proud, dignified, quietly humorous at times—it was marriage he wanted. But were any of those the right reasons?

They were certainly not the reasons he'd married Rosie's mother. Not the earth-shattering joy of knowing, for whatever reason, you were wildly, madly in love.

He rubbed his jaw. He'd been a lot younger then—when they'd first met at least, he and Sasha. Maybe maturity and the middle-thirties made you see things differently?

Maybe looking for love, as he'd done at times after Sasha's death, had produced a certain cynicism in him—of course it had!—with himself as much as anything.

So why—he gritted his teeth—did he have this firm conviction he needed to marry Jo Lucas? Especially after telling her he never intended to marry again as no other woman could ever match up to his dead wife.

Rosie, he thought suddenly, and his mother, Adele. Did the seeds of this lie with them?

It was true that, for the last couple of years, Rosie

had been unable to understand why she didn't have a mother like all her friends and her cousins. It was true Adele had been a godsend, but how fair was it to her to keep her tied to Kin Can for Rosie for ever?

Especially, now he came to think of it, after she'd established her own life in Brisbane several years after his father had died, and seemed to thrive on it.

It was that life, after all, that called her back to Brisbane so often, and it had been no problem to take Rosie with her. But Rosie started school next year, so hopping off with her grandmother frequently was not going to be possible, unless she moved to Brisbane with Adele for the school term and spent the holidays on Kin Can.

How did he feel about that?

And—why the hell hadn't he thought of this before?—did Adele feel she'd done her stint at Kin Can and deserved to retire gracefully? Was that why her time on the station was spent—he gritted his teeth again—redecorating until there was no corner of the house that hadn't been remodelled, repainted, re-upholstered or re-carpeted? Because otherwise the life bored her now? She wasn't a born country woman, he recalled.

'I see,' he said to himself. 'All this has been lurking at the back of your mind but you've been too damned arrogant to let it see the light of day or—too bloody *something* to admit you need a wife! You need a mother for Rosie, you need to allow your own mother her freedom, and who better than a girl who likes, admires and sounds as if she understands kids?

'At the same time, a girl you want as you haven't wanted anyone for a long time?'

CHAPTER FIVE

A FEW days later Jo stopped what she was doing—
attempting to capture Adele Hastings in oil crayons—
and sank her chin onto her hand as she recalled the
wash-up of the abortive kidnap attempt.

Immediately after Gavin had asked her to marry
him, he'd blacked out and a police helicopter had
landed on the lawn.

What had transpired was that Gavin's mother had
flown into Brisbane, only to suddenly remember Jo's
imminent arrival on Kin Can. So she'd tried to ring
the station in vain over a couple of days and finally
got worried enough to ring the police.

They'd driven out from Cunnamulla and, on finding the Kin Can sign mysteriously removed, they'd
called for back-up.

Gavin had been airlifted to hospital, and all three
kidnappers—the tall one had also been shot but only
wounded—had been taken into custody. A stash of
drugs had been found in their van.

Case, the head stockman, had been liberated from
a shed a few kilometres from the homestead.

The next day the silver-grey Range Rover driven
by 'Joe' had been found to be stolen, which had made
sense of the kidnappers' request for verification of
what vehicle he'd be driving.

Even more sense to it all had come when the man
who had wielded the gun had been discovered to be

61

the brother of a Kin Can employee Gavin had sacked for incompetence and drug addiction. Revenge had been the motive for it all.

Jo had refused the police offer of hospitalization and counselling. Her worst problem, or so she'd thought, was only some spectacular bruising inflicted by Gavin himself when he'd tackled her to the floor in the boundary hut. She'd also been pressed into staying on by Gavin's mother, who'd flown into Kin Can later that day after visiting her son in hospital.

Rosie had been left in Brisbane with Gavin's sister in case the damage to the homestead, the police presence and the absence of her father might upset her.

It wasn't until the next day that Jo was able to ask Adele Hastings why she hadn't told her son about her portrait.

Adele struck an attitude of considerable hauteur—she was a petite, stylish redhead in her late fifties—and she informed Jo that the less Gavin was consulted about anything, the better.

Jo blinked and frowned. 'Why?'

'My dear, he has enough delusions of power as it is. So I usually go ahead and do my own thing, then when it's a *fait accompli*, he simply has to live with it.'

'But why would he object to you having your portrait done, Mrs Hastings?'

'He probably wouldn't have. It's the principle of the matter,' Gavin's mother confided. 'But you see, I also have a secret agenda, Joanne.'

They were having coffee poured from a Georgian silver pot into wafer-thin china cups despite sitting at the kitchen table. Adele, Jo was increasingly to discover, didn't believe in slumming it under any circumstances and the only reason they were in the kitchen was because there were police and workmen all over the rest of the house.

'A secret agenda?'

Adele Hastings eyed Jo over the rim of her cup out of blue eyes very much like her son's. 'Well, I planned to give *my* portrait to my daughter, Sharon, for her thirtieth birthday. She's a bit of a connoisseur and has expressed an interest in your work. She also has everything that opens and shuts so...' She waved an elegant hand. 'But it's Gavin I particularly want you to do. And maybe Rosie, if you have the time. But I especially want Gavin to hang up beside his father, grandfather and great-grandfather.'

Jo put her cup down with a slight clatter. 'Would he approve?'

'I doubt it. I mentioned it once and he said—forget it, he couldn't be bothered! You'd have to do it secretly, without sittings and so on. But I believe you're very clever like that, my dear,' Adele said warmly. 'My friend, Elspeth Morgan—she was the one who recommended you—was so impressed with all the portraits you did of her cats—from photos, apparently!'

Jo closed her eyes briefly. The Elspeth Morgan commission had been a nightmare, although a lucrative one. A formidable Brisbane society matron, she'd changed her mind six times about what clothes and jewels she should be captured for posterity wearing. Then she'd decided to get her four cats done individually as well, and been quite hurt when Jo had drawn the line at cat sittings and insisted on taking photos.

'Uh—I feel a sort of moral obligation not to draw people who expressly don't want to be done, Mrs Hastings.'

Blue eyes engaged with level grey ones. 'I see,' Adele said consideringly.

And, unbeknownst to Jo, Adele found herself recalling her son Gavin's strictures on the subject of Joanne Lucas.

Obviously in pain and looking feverish against a starched hospital pillowslip, he had nevertheless issued a series of instructions to her. No interviews to be given to the press; no press to be allowed on Kin Can at all, even only to photograph; Rosie to be kept in the dark and in Brisbane until he was up and about—and Jo Lucas to be kept on the station until he got back.

'How can I keep her if she doesn't want to stay?' she'd objected, looking mystified. 'It all sounds like a ghastly experience so it's understandable if she—'

'Beloved, use your considerable powers of persuasion,' he'd broken in with a half-smile, and added, as she'd looked more mystified, 'There are some things I need to—make up to her. I thought she was part of the gang at first. Just don't let her go.'

Adele Hastings withdrew her mind's eye from her wounded but still high-handed son and studied the young woman sitting across the table from her with a suddenly accelerated heartbeat. Was there something between them? Had Gavin fallen in love when she'd given up nearly all hope of it ever happening again? What sort of a girl was she?

Good bone structure, good figure if you liked tall girls, fine skin, lovely hair, but not, one would have thought, Gavin's type—why? Too...understated? Compared to the glorious vivacity, the dark flashing eyes, the bundle of fun and essential willowy chic Sasha, Rosie's mother, had been? Perhaps, but all the same...

Adele smiled suddenly with all the considerable charm she was capable of. 'Forget I even mentioned it, Joanne. But you will stay with us and at least do me and Rosie? One thing I do know, he would love a portrait of her. Not only that, I would just love you to be my guest!'

Jo stirred. 'Well—'

'There's also the fact,' Adele hastened on, 'that I feel so guilty about landing you in what happened, but lately I seem to have become quite scatter-brained!' She shook her head sorrowfully.

Jo found that she couldn't help warming to Gavin's mother. 'It's just as well you and Rosie weren't here at the time,' she said. 'Uh...'

'Please, Jo—may I call you that? And may I tell you a secret? My dear friend, Elspeth Morgan, is actually an old bat and for some reason your portrait of her and her damn cats has really turned her head. She's lording it over all of us like royalty and I can't bear to be outdone like that!'

Jo's lips twitched. 'Us?'

'We, a group of us, work on several charities together. She's always been something of a Hyacinth Bucket amongst us but now she's unbearable.'

Jo had to laugh. 'Thank heavens I didn't think of that at the time! I'd have made her look as if she'd stepped right out of *Keeping Up Appearances*.'

'So you'll stay?'

'Yes.'

'Lovely!' Adele sat back. 'Now just tell me what you need and I'll see you're as comfortable as possible.'

That had been three days ago, Jo recalled as she sat at the table in her bedroom late in the afternoon.

Unlike the bedroom she and Gavin had been locked into, this one was modern, spacious and minimalist. That was why she'd opted for it on being given a choice. There were no frills, although plenty of comfort and luxury beneath its cream and olive décor, and plenty of room for the large table that had been moved in for her to work at.

All the same, it had been three days of coming to understand that the kidnapping affair had taken more out of her than she'd anticipated. Three days of being cosseted by Gavin's mother, of giving statements to the police, and being shown round Kin Can.

Days of being unable to draw a thing.

And days in which to ponder the fact that her heart had actually tripped when Gavin Hastings had declared that it would be a damn good idea if she married him.

Not only had her heart tripped but no amount of telling herself it was only a joke, no amount of tossing and turning at night had been able to alter one simple little fact.

From hating Gavin Hastings, she'd gone, in the space of a heartbeat, to acknowledging she had finally fallen in love. Why it had happened, how it had happened—surely not simply because he'd thrown himself in front of a gun aimed at her? But she couldn't take issue with it either, not from her point of view. She could no longer think of him without the knowledge of love in her heart, and a quiver of desire throughout her body.

From his point of view, however, there was plenty with which to take issue. *Had* he only said it in a moment of light relief after appalling tension?

Jo, she told herself, not for the first time, of course he did. Only hours earlier, if that, he gave you, chapter and verse, every good reason why he wouldn't ever marry again. And it's no good telling yourself that if things could change rather like lightning tearing apart your soul for you, the same had happened for him.

'So why am I here?' she asked aloud. 'He's due home today and very shortly, and I should have shaken the dust of Kin Can off my shoes. Not only that, I can't draw a thing because all I want to draw— is him.'

She sat perfectly still for a few minutes. The house was quiet, she was alone in it apart from the housekeeper, Mrs Harper, who worked efficiently and discreetly, she'd discovered. Adele had flown to Brisbane to pick up Rosie and they were to collect Gavin from the Charleville base hospital on their way home.

She got up presently and wandered through the main rooms. Gavin Hastings had been right. His mother, if it was she and not his wife who'd decorated Kin Can homestead, had very superior ideas, not to mention long pockets.

The original farmhouse had obviously been renovated and considerably enlarged. Although there were some wonderful antiques around, modern touches had been introduced and some of them looked rather new. The formal lounge was spacious with deep white cut-velvet settees on a cinnamon carpet and a huge, glorious gold and dusky pink painting on a feature wall—just swirls of colour but riveting all the same.

Jo recognized the work of a Sydney artist and had a pretty accurate idea of the value of the painting—not small change by any means.

The dining room was starkly simple. Rattan chairs, a round glass table on a brass pedestal, a cream carpet, a gorgeous chandelier strung quite low and a huge pottery urn in one corner. But her favourite room was the one Adele called the garden room. It was a long converted veranda with sliding glass windows down its length and linen blinds.

There were basket chairs, indoor plants in terracotta tubs and low tables stacked with books and magazines. There were Mexican rugs on the polished wooden floor and a lovely view of the sparkling pool outside. It was surrounded by an emerald lawn fringed with flowerbeds and a variety of gums, white, red and yellow-barked.

You could be forgiven for forgetting you were in the midst of thousands of hectares of rather flat, arid-looking mulga country—the stunted acacia that nevertheless provided shade for sheep—when you gazed out onto this view, Jo mused. And she shook her head to think of how a virtual cloudburst only days ago had now been absorbed into the soil as if it had never happened.

But on the other side of the house there was ample evidence this was a working sheep station. A huge machinery shed dominated the landscape, plus—possibly the crux of it all—the shearing shed and attendant yards.

Jo had been given a tour of it all by Case. Despite their utilitarian purposes and the evidence that quad bikes had replaced, to some extent, horseback sheep-mustering, she'd felt an almost Banjo Paterson sense of romance. Especially when she'd been introduced to the working dogs, mostly border collies and kelpies.

To be the mistress of it all would be rather like being mistress of an empire.

The thought had crossed her mind while she'd patted a grinning border collie, taking her unawares and shaking her composure considerably. I must be mad, had been her next thought.

A couple of days later, as she stood under the archway leading to the garden room, she heard a light plane buzzing over the homestead, and her nerves tightened. The Hastings clan was due to land shortly. No more mad notions, Jo, she cautioned herself.

It hadn't been the ordeal Jo had somehow expected, meeting Gavin Hastings again. Of course his bubbly mother with her super social skills had helped. And his daughter, Rosie, had turned out to be a charming imp with her father's dark hair but someone else's dark eyes.

So, unless anyone had been particularly on the lookout, they wouldn't have noticed her slightly heightened colour or the evidence of what her heartbeat was doing, and she felt that, otherwise, she'd been relaxed and friendly about it all.

Then Adele had confided that she'd ordered a celebration dinner but they'd be having it early on account of Rosie, and they'd all gone to their rooms to change. Jo had passed through the dining room on her way to her room, to see the table set with silver, crystal and fine bone china, so she'd showered and changed into the best clothes she'd brought.

These were a fine silky-knit pewter top that crossed over her breasts and tied at the waist, a paler grey, three-quarter-length skirt and silver sandals. She put her hair up in a loose knot, changed her mind and took it down, then resolutely pinned it up again.

Relaxed and casual she might have been able to project on re-meeting Gavin Hastings, but inside her something seemed to be spinning...

'So—' Gavin handed Jo a nightcap, and a flicker of humour chased through his eyes, '—alone at last.'

She glanced up at him and accepted the drink. It wasn't that late but Rosie, complaining bitterly, had been taken to bed and Adele had retired to what she called her 'suite'.

'Are you fine now?' she queried as the silence began to stretch between them. They were in the garden room. Outside, the pool was lit and the trees around the perimeter of the lawn were casting some fascinating shadows.

'More or less. Some stitches to come out, that's all. What have you been up to?'

'Trying to draw, but not successfully. I really think I should have gone back to Brisbane—for a break at least—but your mother was very determined to have me stay.' She blew her fringe up.

Gavin Hastings paced up and down the polished floor then stopped to stare out at the pool as a wallaby hopped across the lawn. 'I told my mother to keep you here.'

Jo narrowed her eyes, then pleated her skirt. There was nothing to minimize his effect on her now.

In well-pressed khaki trousers, polished brown deck shoes and a red and white checked shirt there wasn't anything of a demented bushranger about him other than the remnants of his black eye. He also looked relaxed, although perhaps a little pale, but he had undergone an operation to remove the bullet from his arm.

As she mulled over what he'd said a faint smile replaced her frown as she studied her glass.

'What?' he queried.

She looked up to see him standing right in front of her with a question in his eyes.

She shrugged. 'I gather that being shot hasn't diminished your habit of being in command.'

'There was no reason for you not to stay on, was there?'

'How would you know?' she countered.

He pulled up a chair and sat down opposite her. 'Tell me about it. I thought you intended to stay on Kin Can for a couple of weeks at least.'

Jo gestured. 'Perhaps. But it was all rather traumatic. That—' she glanced at him quizzically '—didn't occur to you?'

'Jo—' he paused and their gazes locked '—I meant it. Will you marry me?'

She froze, then placed her glass carefully on a side table. 'Gavin, you couldn't possibly have meant it.

We barely know each other, we both have very good reasons for—'

'We know each other a hell of a lot better than most people,' he broke in. 'What we went through was extremely revealing, wouldn't you say?'

His eyes searched hers until she looked away.

'We also happen to want each other,' he added softly. 'Would you like me to tell you *how* I want you?'

'No,' she said swiftly and swallowed.

He grinned fleetingly. 'You couldn't stop me.'

'I...I could get up and go away,' she pointed out.

'Not very far. Assuming I allowed you to go anywhere.'

'Gavin—' some steel entered her grey gaze '—you used that tactic before, but may I point out you don't have a gun to reinforce it now?'

He grimaced. 'A gun with no bullets.'

'I wasn't to know that.'

'No, you weren't,' he agreed. 'Nor did it stop you from testing my intentions with the damn gun.'

'Well, then.' She folded her hands.

'I don't see why we can't have an adult conversation about it,' he said submissively.

Her gaze sharpened again, this time with acute suspicion, and his next words confirmed her suspicions— it was a highly unlikely state of mind to find him in...

'My mother didn't have a gun to hold to your head, bullet-less or otherwise.'

His words sank into a pool of silence but the inference was loud and clear—why *was* she still on Kin Can if she didn't want to be?

Jo bit her lip.

'See what I mean?' His blue eyes held a trace of ironic enquiry.

'Just as your mother feels you suffer from delusions of power, Gavin Hastings, she is also a powerful persuader.'

'So it had nothing to do with me?'

'Look—' she turned her head to stare out over the lawn for a long moment '—we both know exactly why marriage is not for us and none of those reasons has changed so—'

'Jo—' his voice hardened '—things do change and sometimes when you least expect them to. OK, yes, I fully expected the memory of Sasha to make it impossible for me to marry again, but this is different.'

'How could it be?' she asked with difficulty. 'How could you hold me up against her memory and *not* find me wanting? Tell me something.' It was a shot in the dark but something Adele had let drop forced her to make it. 'Who does Rosie remind you of vividly?'

'Her mother,' he said grimly. 'She always will. That doesn't mean you and I can't create our own world, our own magic. But let's talk about you for a moment.'

He paused, but gazed at her narrowly until she took refuge from his scrutiny by sipping her drink.

As he watched her it occurred to Gavin Hastings to find it incredible that he'd ever thought her unfeminine, even if so briefly.

All the same, seeing her dressed up for the first time was a sheer pleasure. Her sense of style might be understated but the pewter of her top highlighted her creamy skin and made her eyes greyer. As always the gold of her hair was gorgeous, although he objected to it being tied up, he discovered.

Then there were those legs. Her thigh was sculpted by her skirt as she sat, turned a little away from him, and her ankles were slim and elegant in high-heeled sandals.

'Know what I thought while I was in hospital?' he said at last.

She shook her head.

'I thought if, when I get home, Jo Lucas has gone, that'll be her way of telling me it's no go. But if she's still there, it'll be because she's…at least curious…to see if I meant it.'

Jo stared at him with her lips parted.

'Mmm… Not only curious to see if I meant it,' he went on, 'but unable to shake off the physical and mental closeness we shared over those awful hours, the trust we shared while we were manacled together. Believe me, there could hardly be anything more claustrophobic than being handcuffed to a guy you hate and mistrust.'

'You…' She licked her lips. 'You were on the good side.'

'Maybe.' His eyes bored into her own.

'And, of course,' she added in case that sounded ungrateful, 'you did save my life at the possible expense of your own.'

He smiled faintly and shook his head.

'You didn't?' Her eyes widened.

'It was a calculated risk that went slightly wrong. I had no intention of either of us getting shot. My reflexes must have been a bit out of training. Mind you, the science of calculated risks is always—a risky business.'

Jo released a slow breath. 'Whether it was a calculated risk or not, it was still extremely brave and I'm still extremely grateful.'

'Good.' His lips twisted. 'Why don't you apply that thinking to what I could do for you if you married me?'

She stood up abruptly and tossed him a rather tart little look.

'Don't trade too much on that, Gav Hastings,' he murmured, 'in other words?'

This time the look she shot him shouted, You better believe it!

He laughed softly. 'That's my Josie! Anyway—' he stood up '—think about it.'

Surprise caused her to blink before she said cautiously, 'Does that mean I'm off the hook for the moment?'

He shoved his hands in his pockets. 'Of course. Never let it be said I pressured you into anything. Incidentally, if you're worried about your career as an artist, I think it's very appropriate for a wife.'

Jo opened and closed her mouth several times like a fish out of water.

'And talking of thinking about things, there is always this.' His eyes glinted as he moved to stand beside her. 'Definitely worth thinking about, I would have thought.'

She knew in the split second before he did it what was coming, but *her* reflexes let her down. Indeed, she found she couldn't move a muscle as he took her in his arms.

'I wonder if you have any idea,' he said, barely audibly, 'how your mouth tempts me, Miss Lucas?'

'Why?' She frowned in genuine puzzlement.

'Why? It's just luscious and asking to be kissed, that's why. Hasn't anyone told you that?'

She shook her head. 'I...don't much enjoy being kissed.'

'Could be you haven't met the right man yet.' His eyes glinted. 'Have you ever experienced an orgasm?'

Jo opened her mouth to tell him it was none of his business, but changed it to, 'Why?' again.

He frowned faintly. 'I get mixed signals. There's this cool, calm Jo Lucas quite capable of holding her own against any man, one feels, then there's the cuddly girl who slept in my arms and really didn't want to leave them—'

'So that's what you were so smug about!'

'Bastard that I am,' he agreed without the least trace of repentance. 'But there's also—I don't know—something that makes me wonder.' He frowned again.

'If I'm some kind of freak?' she suggested dryly. 'I'm surprised you want to marry me, in that case.'

'Not at all. The prospect of being man enough to do it is highly appealing,' he said seriously.

Jo caught her breath, because this was absolute arrogance if nothing else and therefore intolerable, but just as she was about to tell him so he started to laugh.

'You thought I was serious, Josie!'

Colour flooded her cheeks and he took advantage of her confusion to lower his mouth to hers.

'Won't hurt in the slightest,' he promised against her lips. 'Just leave it to me.'

Far from hurting or being the invasion she'd always found distasteful, it was increasingly fascinating. Then again, Gavin Hastings took his time about really kissing her. He nuzzled the corner of her mouth, her cheek, the side of her throat at the same time as he swept his hands slowly but, oh, so thoroughly down her body.

At the same time, he drew her against him and she had to fight against a deliciously sensuous tide that flooded her at the contact with his warm, hard body.

Then he curved one hand round the back of her neck and began to explore her breasts with the other.

She breathed raggedly.

'Nice?' His lips returned to the corner of her mouth.

She didn't answer, she couldn't find the words to tell him it might be nice but it was also dangerous. But she did find herself hanging onto his arm unexpectedly, until he lifted his head suddenly and grimaced in pain.

'Oh!' Her hand flew to her mouth. 'Your wound—I'm so sorry!'

'It's OK. Here—' he repositioned them so a wall was behind her '—lean back.'

'Why?'

'Just so I can get my breath again.'

'But I feel terrible,' she protested.

'Jo—' he brought both hands up to imprison her between them against the wall '—I'm fine. And all the more fine to be doing this. Just relax.' This time, he lowered his mouth to tease her lips apart.

She did relax, mainly because she was still concerned about hurting him and not wanting to do it again. Or, she wondered, was it an urge to heal the hurt she'd caused that made her really let her guard down?

Whatever, she went from being wary about the way he was arousing her to accepting it. The next step, allowing her senses to participate, came swiftly. Her skin shivered when he moved one hand from the wall to slide it down her arm. Then his fingers moved to her throat and slipped down to the V opening of her top.

She caught her bottom lip between her teeth, and moved forward against him. His other hand came down and he wrapped his arm around her, and she breathed deeply. As she did so the last of her wariness dissolved completely beneath an assault of pure pleasure and pure man.

'Did you know,' he said at one stage, 'that you looked very attractive tonight but stern? I much prefer you like this.'

'Like what?' she breathed.

'Disordered and wanton.'

'I'm no such thing!'

His hands moved deftly and he released her hair from its knot and untied her top. 'No?'

'That's your doing, not mine,' she protested, but with little heat.

He smiled lazily. 'I've been thinking of doing it for days. You do realize that even while I was harbouring the deepest suspicions about you, Jo, I was—unable to keep my mind off your body and all its delights?'

'I did realize—' she moved beneath his exploring fingers '—that you were being rather bloody-minded about women and their intentions, mine in particular.'

He laughed softly and pushed her top back to kiss her shoulder. 'I hope this is a suitable form of revenge.'

She raised her arms and ran her fingers through his hair, then drew her hands down his back. 'Revenge?'

'Mmm...' He slipped her bra strap aside. 'You have me at your mercy at the moment, Miss Lucas.'

She opened her mouth to say that it could be the other way around, but he forestalled her.

'Or, maybe it's mutual.' And this time, as he cupped her breast he started to kiss her in earnest.

She kissed him back. For the first time in her life she really gave herself up to being kissed and was almost unbearably pleasured by the unexpected intimacy of it.

Her senses spun and she couldn't stay still. She couldn't get enough of the fire and heat of his body on hers and his touch on her breasts and hips seemed to brand her and claim her for his own, almost as if she were his creation.

And she was, she realized. This tall man who'd started out by insulting her in just about every conceivable way, then saved her life whether he liked to think it or not, had somehow unlocked the essence of her femininity. So that she longed to beg for more intimacy, the closest no-holds-barred kind of all.

They drew apart at last and Jo had to lean back against the wall for support. He put his hands up to imprison her against it again and stared down at her.

Her gorgeous mouth was bruised and ripe. Her golden hair lay in a swathe across one shoulder with her fringe in her eyes. Her breasts heaved—there was a dew of sweat trickling down the smooth, pale valley between them until she, belatedly, pulled her bra up, and she blew up at her fringe.

For some reason they both smiled at this little reflex gesture of hers, and he decided to complete her restoration himself.

He combed her fringe aside with his fingers and retied her top, smoothing it into place, then he looked into her eyes again.

Her smile had gone and they were dark now, as if with shock, as if the magnitude of the experience was hitting her—or the unexpectedness of her response? he wondered.

And he realized in the same breath that it was going to take a lot of will power to defuse things between them. An almost inhuman effort, in fact, not to take her by the hand and lead her to his bed and keep her there until she shuddered in his arms and came beneath him…

Then she blinked several times as her gaze focused on the sleeve of his shirt, and he looked down to see a patch of blood.

At the same time Jo Lucas came out of her daze into a sudden fever of a different kind—concern.

'Oh, no! Look what I've done! Why didn't you say? I must be mad!'

'Believe me, I didn't feel a thing and you weren't mad at all.'

'Of *course* I was. So were you!' she retorted. 'How could you even think of going around kissing people like that with a gunshot wound in your arm?'

'I wasn't kissing people plural, only one. You,' he pointed out.

'Don't split hairs,' she warned. 'Let me have a look.'

She started to unbutton his shirt with a militant expression.

'I take it this is not a good time to argue with you, Jo?' he drawled.

'It isn't.' She eased his shirt off.

'Would you mind if I swore comprehensively?'

'Be my guest. I've no doubt heard it all before.'

'Ma'am, in that case I'll give it a miss.' He looked down at the dressing on his arm. 'It probably only needs replacing.'

'We'll see. Come with me.' She handed him his shirt and turned away.

He followed her to her en-suite bathroom where she retrieved her first-aid kit from a drawer. She then proceeded, with competence, to remove the dressing, swab the wound where it had opened slightly between stitches, and redress it.

'There.' She patted him lightly on the elbow. 'I don't think you did too much damage, but you should see a doctor if it keeps on bleeding.'

He put his shirt on with a frown in his eyes. 'Are you also a nurse?'

'No, but I did a first-aid course at school.'

'And did it very thoroughly, by the look of it.' His hands paused in the act of buttoning his shirt. 'Why do I get the feeling you do everything thoroughly, Jo Lucas?'

She raised her eyebrows. 'I have no idea.' She suddenly noticed that he'd buttoned his shirt crookedly and with a click of her teeth started to re-button it.

He put his hands on her wrists and stilled her busy fingers. 'See what I mean?' he murmured.

She lowered her lashes in some confusion.

He added, 'All the more reason to marry you.'

The bathroom had cream tiles and olive-green fittings. There was a wide mirror above the twin basins and Jo turned away from Gavin Hastings, to find herself looking into it, and getting a shock.

Her hair was a mess, her face was pale and her eyes looked different, although she couldn't say why. Then it hit her. They were completely bemused.

'That offer is still open, incidentally,' he said. 'Much as you've made a point of changing the subject.'

She stared at him in the mirror and thought of objecting that she'd had good cause. But perhaps there was a more pertinent objection to make?

'All this has happened so…so *fast*.'

'That's because of the way we met. High drama had an accelerating effect. We were sharing a toothbrush only hours after we'd been introduced. We were virtually sleeping together *before* that.'

She shook her head. 'We weren't!'

'No, you're right,' he agreed, 'now I come to think of it. You must have moved into my arms at least— two hours after I introduced myself?'

Jo looked away from the pure devilry in his eyes. 'You're never going to let me live that down, are you?'

'Nope. And, of course, there's the fact that I saw you stripped to your underwear only about five minutes after we met, Lady Longlegs,' he added softly.

Jo made an abrupt movement, then turned resolutely to face him. 'You can't just ask me to marry you like this without some…explanation. Not after what you said.'

'Jo—' he sobered abruptly '—I'm rushing my fences, aren't I? Sorry. The thing is, it suddenly came to me that I needed a wife because Rosie needs a mother and my mother needs a break. But *before* I worked that out, I had this—I don't know—conviction, that it needed to be *you*.'

'Why?' she whispered.

He shrugged. 'The link the whole kidnapping debacle forged between us? You may think I saved your life, but what you may have forgotten is the lengths you were about to go to with a solid marble inkwell to save mine. Perhaps it's that between us. We care about each other, Jo.'

'As opposed to being deeply, wildly, madly in love?'

She thought he flinched as she said the words, but might have imagined it.

'Sometimes the less flamboyant emotions are the ones with the better foundations.'

Her gaze dropped after what seemed like an eternity and she said very quietly, 'I'll think about it.'

He studied her and seemed about to say something, but changed his mind in the end, and dropped the lightest kiss on her hair before he turned away.

CHAPTER SIX

Jo ELECTED not to go to bed immediately.

She pulled on a cardigan and let herself out onto the veranda from her bedroom, then down a short flight of wooden steps onto the lawn. This was not the pool side of the house but the garden was well tended and there were some lovely shrubs against the veranda wall.

There was also a bench and she sat down and hugged herself. Although it was starting to warm up as spring came to Kin Can, the night air was crisp and cold, there was no cloud cover to trap the warmer air of the day or hide the stars, and there were millions of them.

Due to the lack of artificial light, this area of Queensland was renowned for its view of the night sky.

She gazed upwards for a while, admiring the heavens on one level of her mind, but mostly preoccupied with the miracle that had happened to her tonight, the release from an experience that had coloured her whole life.

It was true she'd always found being kissed distasteful for one very good reason. Between twelve and eighteen, she'd lived with three foster families. Two of them had been warm, supportive and gone out of their way to make her feel part of the family. One of them had proved to be a nightmare.

She'd been fifteen when the husband had started to pay attention to her in a secretive, nauseating way. It had started out with compliments on her figure, then he'd started to touch her, accidentally, she'd thought at first, but one day he'd cornered her and kissed her, then issued a warning to her that if she told anyone, no one would believe her, against him, anyway.

She'd packed her bags and run away to the local police station from where she'd been passed on to the Department of Family and Community Services.

At first, no one *had* believed her, there had even been suggestions she might have 'led him on', but she'd stuck to the absolute truth, her record as a 'sensible' girl had come to her rescue and an investigation had been mounted. Two more girls had been found, who'd lived with the same family and had had similar experiences, although they'd been too scared to come forward at the time.

She'd refused point-blank to go on to any family with a man in the house, she'd received counselling and she'd ended up with a middle-aged widow with a social services background herself, and a daughter Jo's age who had become her best friend.

She'd overheard her counsellors agreeing once that she would most likely be able to put the whole experience behind her because she was so—thank heavens!—sensible, gutsy and independent.

They'd been wrong. They'd overlooked that she was also sensitive. It had lingered at the back of her mind ever since. Her memories had come between her and a couple of men she'd thought she might have fallen in love with.

Perhaps, even, the experience of not being believed

at first had been as damaging as anything else in that her independence had become crucial to her. Never again would she rely on anyone believing her or not.

Gavin Hastings had changed all that. Somehow he'd swept it away effortlessly. Because they'd become so close and shared such heart-stopping danger? Because he had thrown himself in front of a gun aimed at her whether he liked to think of it as a calculated risk or not? Because they'd confided in each other the way they had?

Whatever, even although her heartbeat had tripped when he'd suggested she marry him, nothing had prepared her for the flood of sensuality he'd released in her tonight.

She closed her eyes. She was purged at last. She'd fallen in love and she was loving it—only thing, how was she going to cope with the fact that deeply, wildly, madly might never happen again for him when she suspected it had already happened for her? How was her sensible, gutsy, stubborn independence, but also that innate sensitivity, going to cope with that?

CHAPTER SEVEN

THE next morning, Jo awoke to find Rosie sitting on the end of her bed.

'Good day.' She struggled up and peered at her bedside clock. It was six-thirty and daylight was just starting to filter through her windows.

'Hello!' Rosie said brightly. 'We always get up at the crack of dawn, I thought I'd let you know.'

'So I see.' Jo combed her hair with her fingers.

'Nanna says you're going to draw my portrait as well as hers. I'm so excited because I love to draw myself! Would you like to start now?'

'Now? Uh...' Jo trailed off.

'How about I get you a cup of tea? Nanna swears by her first cuppa.'

'Thank you, that would be lovely.'

Rosie went away and Jo showered swiftly. She was dressed by the time Rosie returned with a tray bearing, not only a cuppa but a glass of milk and two slices of toast.

'One for you, one for me,' she said of the toast, 'and the milk's for me. Mrs Harper did it for me, grumbling all the while that I had no right to wake you up so early, but since I had, she might as well make you some tea. I told her that inspiration waits for no man, but we might need something to keep the wolf from the door.'

Jo regarded Gavin Hastings's daughter—and felt

her fingers tingle in response to messages her brain was receiving. Rosie Hastings was a character.

Obviously used to a lot of adult company, she was very articulate but often sounded quaintly old-fashioned. She had also put on what looked like her best outfit, a pink, fine-corduroy, long-sleeved dress with a ribbon sash, white tights and she'd tied her long dark hair back in pigtails.

The presentation was slightly flawed—some of her buttons were undone, her sash was twisted and her hair a bit knotted—but she still looked like a little girl from a bygone era.

'Thank you,' Jo said gravely. 'I haven't had toast soldiers for a while.'

Rosie grinned. 'How would you like me to pose?'

Jo thought for a bit as she sipped her tea. 'Tell you what, since you love it, why don't you do some drawing? I'll give you some of my paper and you can use this second set of pencils I always carry.' She pointed to a smaller box on the table.

'What a great idea,' Rosie enthused. 'Now what shall I draw? I know! Dad's favourite dog had puppies the other day. Let's see if I can remember them.' She screwed up her face.

They drew for about half an hour and Rosie chatted all the time.

If she was the light of her father's life, Gavin was the adored hero of his daughter. Nanna featured as well and obviously was much-loved, but it was Gavin she talked about most. Rosie also indicated that she loved the station life and was very much looking forward to starting school, although she then sighed suddenly and propped her chin on her hands.

'What is it?' Jo asked.

'Well. There's complications.' And Rosie embarked on a multi-stranded explanation.

Apparently, her dearest wish was to join the School of Distance Education. Formerly known as the School of the Air, the local headquarters were in Charleville and she was already enrolled in their preschool.

Jo knew something about the School of Distance Education from her flatmate Leanne, who had worked on the project. She knew, for example, that the Home Tutor played a pivotal role. In the case of Kin Can, which had four school-age children not counting Rosie, Case's wife, Janine, an ex-schoolteacher, filled that role perfectly as well as being a very nice person. Three of the children were hers.

Jo also knew from Leanne what a vital role the school played, not only in educating outback children, but reaching into their isolated lives and bringing them together.

Rosie enlarged on this aspect. Just about every kid in the district she knew was or would be joining the school.

'I mean,' she said, 'I know that *one* day I'll have to go away to boarding school, but until then I want to be a part of the school. This is my home,' she added quaintly.

'Why not, then?'

'Nanna likes to spend a lot of time in Brisbane and I nearly always go with her, but I couldn't do that once I've started school, so she suggested I go to a school in Brisbane and we come back to Kin Can for holidays.'

'That doesn't appeal to you?'

'No. Of course, much as I love Nanna, if I had my *own mother* like every other kid I know, there wouldn't be a problem! It really is quite a blight on my life, Jo,' she confided gloomily.

Jo's pencil paused and remained poised above the paper. 'You seem to get along rather well with Mrs Harper. Couldn't she look after you while your nanna's in Brisbane?'

Gloom was replaced with flashing scorn. 'They won't even hear of it! Anyone would think I was a baby.'

'I see. What does your father say?'

Rosie deepened her voice. '"We've got months to think about it, catfish, and as Gavin Hastings the Fourth, I can be relied on to make the right decision."'

Jo had to laugh. 'Catfish?'

'It's a joke between us.' Rosie paused as there was a light knock on the door and it clicked open.

'Daddy!' Rosie jumped up and ran over to her father with her drawing. 'Look at this!'

'Rosie, what are you doing here at this hour of the morning? That's nice, but—' Gavin glanced at the drawing '—never again, it's too early. Morning, Jo! I'm sorry about this. For some reason I slept in myself.'

'It's OK,' Jo said. 'We have got to know each other a bit.'

Gavin narrowed his gaze on her rather unseeingly, as if searching back through his memory. 'What,' he said at last, 'has she been telling you?'

Jo smiled wryly. 'That's just between the two of us.'

Rosie looked approving. 'I like someone who can keep a secret. Is breakfast ready? I'm starving!'

The morning passed swiftly.

To Jo's relief, the flying doctor called in, on a clinic run, to check Gavin out.

'Listen, mate,' he admonished Gavin as he replaced Jo's dressing and was told the wound had bled a little, 'you've got to give it time to knit. What on earth were you doing?'

Jo held her breath.

'I was—rushing my fences,' Gavin replied, and shot her a wicked look. 'Speaking figuratively, of course.'

'Well, stop rushing damn fences, whatever that means. You're not in the SAS any more.' The doctor repacked his bag, then looked over at Jo, as if somehow he'd caught the vibes of the moment, and he raised his eyebrows.

'Uh—this is Joanne Lucas, Tom,' Gavin introduced. 'She's here to do Adele's portrait. Jo, meet Tom Watson.'

'Ah! The lady we've been hearing about. Good to meet you! I believe you were exceptionally brave in ghastly circumstances.'

'She was,' Gavin said before Jo could answer for herself. 'Therefore, I'm trying to persuade her to marry me.'

Tom laughed. 'I'd think twice about that if I were you, ma'am. Gavin, here, is renowned for getting his own way. OK, got to fly!' But he paused suddenly with a swift frown, then shook his head and climbed aboard his plane.

'How could you do that?' Jo enquired as they watched the trim RFDS plane taxi down the grassy airstrip.

'Do what?'

'*Tell* him you were thinking of marrying me—as if you didn't know.'

'He took it as a joke.'

Jo glinted him a dark little look. 'Then he stopped to think about it, just as he stopped to think about "rushing fences".'

Gavin grinned and took her hand. 'He's no fool, Tom. And it's no joke either.'

'Gavin—'

'Jo, can I make a suggestion?'

She looked at him warily.

'How would it be if we took a week or two to think this through? You could size up country life, size up my family—not to mention me—and you could do my mother's portrait.'

'I…'

'Is that so much to ask?'

'Do you mean—in return for saving my life?'

He gestured. 'No, of course not. Forget I ever said that. Incidentally, what did Rosie say to you this morning?'

Jo was debating whether to tell him when Rosie and Adele hove into view.

'All right,' he said, 'we'll leave that for a moment. Will you stay and case the joint?'

She smiled slightly. 'Gangster talk, Gavin?'

'It is how we met.'

She gazed at the dusty horizon. 'If you promise me one thing.'

'What's that?'

She looked into his eyes. 'If the answer is no, you'll take it.'

'Done,' he replied promptly. So promptly Jo was immediately suspicious.

'Do you mean that?'

'I am a man of my word.'

She frowned. 'Can I add a rider?'

'Let me guess,' he said gravely. 'Something to do with no—undue pressure?'

'Yes,' she agreed dryly.

'Jo, if you're embarrassed about the way you kissed me last night, don't be. It was enchanting,' he said simply.

She coloured.

'It was also as sexy as hell,' he added, 'and—'

'It's not that I'm embarrassed,' she broke in a little hastily. 'It's obviously a factor to take into account, but—'

'A major factor,' he put in, and lifted his hand to trace the outline of her mouth gently.

Jo trembled as she recalled, with breathtaking clarity, the feel of his hands on her breasts and hips. 'Your mother and daughter are nearly upon us,' she said with an effort.

He dropped his hand and glanced over his shoulder. 'OK. You tell me when you feel I'm exerting undue pressure. Is it a deal?'

It occurred to her she should have added all sorts of riders: no further mention of his proposal to others, no public displays of the attraction that existed between them were two that flashed though her mind. But all she had time to say was, 'Uh…yes.'

'Good.' He turned to greet Rosie and Adele.

Two weeks later the time had literally flown as she'd experienced a thorough but very enjoyable induction to the Hastings version of country life. Although, two things had worked in her favour regarding 'undue pressure' at least.

Gavin couldn't be involved in the more active things she did while his arm healed, and she was able to close herself into her room frequently on the pretext of working on his mother's and his daughter's portraits.

But he did spend time talking sheep to her. He told her how Kin Can was experimenting with a new concept—electronic tagging of individual sheep.

'How on earth could that work?' she asked.

He shrugged. 'Electronic tag readers collate information like weight, need for parasite control, et cetera, so you get a much more accurate picture of the sheep's condition.'

'Science is amazing, isn't it?' She shook her head in wonder. They were leaning against a fence watching a 'yarding'—sheep being sorted into different pens. The air was dusty and alive with whistles as the dogs worked their magic, and sheep proved their propensity for jumping over imaginary hurdles.

He eyed her. She wore jeans and a blue shirt and the breeze was lifting her hair.

'You're—' He stopped a little ruefully.

She looked a question at him.

'Er—I was going to make a remark of a personal nature but I could stick to sheep, it's up to you.'

She smiled fleetingly. 'Stick to sheep.'

'I don't know why I asked since I knew damn well that's what you would say,' he grumbled, but good-naturedly, and thought for a moment.

'All right, you asked for it. Fibre diameter is the key to lightweight comfortable woollen products—'

'You mean each hair?'

'I do. The lower the better, and that, amongst other reasons, is why we farm mostly Merino sheep for wool. Staple strength is another factor, so is rainfall, country and so on. The further south you get in the Queensland sheep belt, the lower the fibre diameter in general. Overall there are nine to ten million sheep in Queensland.'

He paused briefly. 'China is our biggest market for Queensland wool and Australia is the biggest producer in the world of "apparel" wool. An experienced shearer can shear one hundred and twenty to one hundred and forty sheep a day—'

'What?'

'It's true, but you've made me lose my train— uh—'

'Thank you,' she said gravely. 'I think that may be enough information to digest for the moment.'

'Are you sure? There's a lot more—'

'Gavin, I'm sure.'

'Then may I say you're amazingly attractive, Miss Lucas? That's all I was going to say in the first place,' he hastened to assure her.

Jo had to dissolve into laughter.

At other times, she learnt to drive a quad bike. She had some wonderful fun mustering sheep with Case, and getting used to all the whistles, calls and gestures needed to control the dogs.

She glowed when Case told 'the boss' she was a natural.

Rosie gave her a guided tour of the shearing shed, displaying remarkable knowledge as well as her love of station life. Rosie rode her own pony and was to be given one of the pups of the new litter as her own dog. The agony of which to choose was causing her a lot of concern.

Jo and Rosie used the pool most days, days that were warming up more and more, and anyway the pool was heated. Rosie was a dog-paddler and quite safe in the pool, but Jo was an accomplished swimmer and, in a couple of days, she had the little girl doing a passable breaststroke much to Rosie's delight—and her father's approval.

Her father's approval didn't only extend to Rosie's swimming, it extended to her coach. He had a way of examining Jo's figure in a halter-neck candy-striped swimming costume that spoke volumes. Especially when she was dripping wet and her nipples were clearly visible beneath the Lycra.

But all he actually said, and only on one occasion, when his daughter was out of earshot, was that legs that went on for ever were now high on his agenda of feminine perfection.

Jo had glinted him an enigmatic little look, and wrapped a towel around her waist so it covered her legs to her knees.

Not, she had to admit to herself, that she was im-mune from being tantalized by him. Talking of legs, he had a long-legged stride that was so essentially masculine, it fascinated her.

He also had a way of shoving his hand through his hair that indicated he was about to be exasperated and difficult, then a completely wicked little smile that told you he knew it but couldn't help himself. Everyone, she realized, from his foreman, his housekeeper, his mother, his daughter and herself included, tended to have the wind taken right out of their sails beneath that smile.

He was also incurably, she knew, used to getting his own way, but in one minor tussle she'd had with him, when she'd simply and calmly agreed to disagree with him, he'd looked so surprised for a moment, she'd had to resist a powerful urge to kiss him and tell him to be a good boy.

She'd learnt swiftly that that would not have been a good idea because he'd obviously read her thoughts.

He'd eyed her then, from head to toe, and murmured, 'Feeling maternal, Jo?'

'Well—'

'Believe me, that's not how I think of you. In fact I often wonder how you like to make love—soberly? Joyfully? Are you practical even in bed? Or generous? Does that lovely body—' his blue gaze stripped her naked '—arch and writhe and—ah!' He paused and studied the colour flooding her cheeks. 'Not motherly, then.'

She swung on her heel and marched away from him.

That night, as was happening to her more and more frequently, she couldn't help fantasizing about making love to Gavin. And it came to her that if just watching the way he walked and being seriously affected by it was any guide, 'sober' would probably not be how she would feel in his bed.

She learnt too, also from Gavin, more about the Hastings 'empire'. Not only did Kin Can produce wool, they bred rams that were sold all over the world, sometimes fetching staggering amounts of money. Then there were two adjacent cattle properties, a horse stud, Gavin's creation, a cane farm in North Queensland and a long list of commercial enterprises.

'You obviously don't believe in having all your eggs in one basket,' she commented as she studied a blown-up map of Queensland with the Hastings properties etched in a rich, royal blue.

They were in his study, a room she still associated with violence and mayhem, although it had been over three weeks ago.

He shrugged. 'You can't really afford to. Drought and flood, but particularly drought, plague this part of the world.'

She frowned. 'It does flood out here, though.'

'Oh, yes. In fact I have a feeling in my bones this season could be building up to it, but in general drought is much more common.'

'Go on,' she invited.

'Well, wool also has its ups and downs. Beef prices can be notoriously fickle, although we're cashing in nowadays. On the other hand, sugar, at the moment, is hard to give away. Which is why I'm toying with the idea of setting up some fish farms on the cane farm.'

'What about horses?'

'Yearling prices, well-bred yearlings at least, have sky-rocketed recently and I happen to have a couple of ''in vogue'' stallions.'

Jo studied him. He was lying back in a black leather swivel chair behind the oak desk looking big but relaxed, and as if all the power vested in him, as represented by the empire on the map in front of him, sat easily with him.

She frowned as she was struck by a sudden thought. 'Did you have any training to take on all this?' She gestured towards the map.

He crossed his hands behind his head. 'I was brought up to it. My father always believed in a very ''hands on'' approach, and he passed that on to me while I was growing up.'

'So you never wanted to do anything else?'

He grimaced. 'Not really.'

'What about the SAS?'

He lowered his hands and shrugged. 'It's a family tradition for sons to do a stint in the Services and I seemed to have the right qualities to get into the SAS, but I never intended to make the army a career. Then my father died—far too young, sadly—and I came back to take over. Been doing it ever since.' He regarded her thoughtfully. 'Do you have a problem with any of that?'

'No,' Jo said hastily.

He smiled. 'You're looking at me as if you suspect me of all sorts of vices.'

She shook her head and turned away. 'Excuse me, Adele has promised me a sitting.'

'How's it going?'

'Fine,' she said brightly.

'What did you do with my portrait?'

'I...I still have it. Why?'

'Just wondered. OK.' He glanced at his watch. 'See you at dinner. I believe we have company.'

Jo groaned. 'You do an awful lot of entertaining!'

'I don't, my mother does.'

'If I'd known I'd have brought more clothes.'

'You always look fine to me.' His gaze drifted down her figure, then moved up to capture her eyes.

'Thanks,' she said, and stirred uneasily.

'Does that come under the heading of "undue pressure"?' he queried wryly.

'No. No, you've been—apart from a couple of times you've been pretty good about that.' She flinched visibly as she said the words and flinched again as he laughed softly, his eyes alight with devilry, and he got up to come round the desk towards her.

'"Goodness" had nothing to do with it, not the way you occupy my thoughts, anyway. Great restraint plus the thought of having to explain to Tom why I'd opened up my stitches again is more accurate, Jo.'

'Oh.'

'How about you?'

She coloured.

'No restraint required?' His blue eyes were perfectly wicked.

'Some,' she conceded.

He lifted a hand as if to touch her, then hesitated and dropped it, and her body screamed in frustration, shocking her with the intensity of the arousal just the thought of his hands on her could evoke.

'Jo?'

She took a step backwards but he followed her, and she wondered dazedly what he would think if he knew that the only portrait going well for her was the one she worked on after everyone had gone to bed. Not Adele, not Rosie, but himself, stripped to the waist and sitting at an old wooden table in a shadowy hut.

The one she worked on from memory as she tried to add up what mattered most to her about Gavin Hastings.

Was that practising restraint? she wondered. Or was that indulging herself in a way she shouldn't if she decided not to marry him?

'What is it, Jo? Surely we can talk at the same time as you come to grips with the lifestyle?'

She bit her lip. 'Of course! Only not right now. Your mother—'

'Blow my mother.'

'Gavin, she is waiting for me.'

'Tonight, then.' He swore. 'After this blasted dinner party. Because I get the feeling you're tying yourself up in unnecessary knots, Jo Lucas. And what is not helping,' he added grimly, 'is this ridiculous rider about no undue pressure. What the hell do you think I'm liable to do to you? Seduce you out of your mind?'

A tinge of annoyance seeped into her veins. 'You wouldn't succeed. And I should warn you not to get too high-handed with me. I may have—' She broke off, then continued, 'I might like some things about you but I will never like that!'

'Or—you may have fallen in love with me, Josie?' he said softly. 'Is that what you were going to say?'

'Jo—oh, there you are!' Adele swept into the room. 'Did I get the time wrong? I was waiting in my sitting room.'

'I'm just on my way,' Jo said thankfully.

'Yes, why don't you toddle off?' Gavin Hastings invited dangerously.

'What's biting him?' Adele enquired as she settled herself in a lovely old oak abbot's chair.

'I have no idea,' Jo replied briefly, still simmering with annoyance as she organized herself.

Adele had given much thought to how she should be depicted in her portrait. And she'd come up with almost the exact opposite in the details to her friend Elspeth Morgan.

No jewels other than a black pearl ring, although it was the size of a pigeon egg, on her right hand. No off-the-shoulder colourful evening gown but a charcoal linen dress with a broad white Thai-silk collar. No flowers in the background, just the Jacobean-print upholstery of the chair, and her red hair simply dressed.

'He's not always sweetness and light, you know, Jo,' Adele offered.

'I had gathered that. Are you comfortable, Mrs Hastings?'

Adele smoothed her skirt. 'I'm fine.' But like a dog to a bone, she returned to her son's ill-humour. 'Sometimes you need to put your foot down with Gavin. I do.'

Jo had started to draw but her pencil hovered suddenly. Why would Gavin's mother feel there was any need for Jo to be putting her foot down? Did she know about her son's intentions?

'Actually, I'm about to put my foot down myself,' Adele continued. 'Over Rosie's schooling. You do know how much I love Rosie, don't you, Jo?'

Jo relaxed. 'Of course.'

'Do you know how long I've been widowed?'

The apparent non sequitur took Jo by surprise, and she shook her head.

'Twelve years. I was very young when I had Gavin and Sharon,' Adele said. 'I'm only fifty-eight now. That's not very old and I've been alone a long time.'

An inkling of where all this was heading hit Jo suddenly. 'Have you...met someone, Mrs Hastings?'

Adele sat forward eagerly. 'Yes, I have. Oh, what a relief to say it! And the thing is, we've really clicked. He's a couple of years younger but still of my generation and—he's asked me to marry him. That's probably why I've been so forgetful lately! I don't know if I'm on my head or my heels—but he lives in Brisbane, you see.'

'Ah,' Jo said, although her pencil had started to fly. 'Hence the problem with Rosie's schooling?'

'Well, I could never abandon Rosie, not after losing her mother like that, but also because I love her so much. But James would be perfectly happy to have her live with us during the school terms. Indeed, he knows that's the only way he's going to get me!'

Adele tossed her head and Jo reached for a crayon as everything she'd been so desperately trying to capture about Gavin's mother, her very spirit, was suddenly all there for her to transmit to paper.

'Uh—Gavin doesn't like the idea of Rosie going away to school?' she suggested.

'He doesn't really. Not yet, anyway. Not that he knows why *I'm* so keen now. And of course I understand his reservations—he adores Rosie. But, well, I could get her into my old school which just happens to be one of the finest. And *I* would be there for her as I always have in the past.'

'So you haven't told Gavin about the man who wants to marry you? Is there any reason not to?'

Adele's blue eyes flashed. 'He's liable to make all sorts of objections.'

'Why?'

Adele hesitated. 'To put it bluntly, well, there's no other way to put it really—I'm a very wealthy woman in my own right, Jo.'

Jo drew in long, flowing strokes, then tiny delicate ones. 'He's afraid you could be targeted by a fortune hunter?'

'Precisely. Anyone would think I came down with the last shower!'

'Rosie does love it here,' Jo murmured.

Adele's shoulders slumped. 'I know.'

Jo glanced at her keenly.

'Of course,' Adele looked indescribably sad for a moment, 'my dearest wish is for Gavin to find someone himself—and a mother for Rosie. He has so much to offer a girl.'

'Provided she can put her foot down,' Jo suggested, and they both laughed.

But as Jo bent her head she didn't see the completely serious look Adele bestowed on her.

Then Gavin's mother said, 'Still, I keep trying. The

people I've invited for dinner tonight have a gorgeous daughter. She's been overseas for a few years. Gavin knows her but he might find her somewhat changed and—who knows?'

Jo's busy fingers stilled at last as she looked up at Adele. 'You're trying to matchmake?'

'Of course. Why shouldn't I? And Sarah Knightly could be just the one to appeal to him.'

Jo blinked, then looked down again.

If that doesn't put the cat amongst the pigeons, Adele Hastings thought, I'd be most surprised. Really, why do young people imagine you're blind and deaf once you reach a certain age? Oh, yes, I'm trying to matchmake, Jo, but it's *you* I'm aiming at for Gavin!

Jo thought seriously about making an excuse not to attend the dinner party.

She told herself she had no desire to witness what his mother might consider suitable wife material for Gavin. She told herself that she might think she was in love with him, but there was also an obstinate little streak in her at war with allowing him to get his own way too often.

She went in the end because some crazy little voice prompted her to think that she'd never seen him in the company of what might be termed a suitable wife, and perhaps she should?

When she went to some lengths to mix and match her limited wardrobe so that she was wearing something a bit different, honesty compelled her to admit she was on her mettle. It made her feel a little forlorn, although she couldn't be sure why.

In the event, she was introduced to Sarah Knightly

and her parents wearing slim taupe trousers and an ivory linen tunic-style blouse. She'd washed her hair and left it loose after blow-drying it, so that it rippled and shone in a silky golden cloud.

She rarely wore make-up but tonight she'd applied eye shadow, mascara and lip gloss.

Her first reaction to Sarah Knightly was—oh, great! One of those tiny, delicate girls destined to make me feel overgrown!

Not only that, Sarah was charming, bubbly but surprisingly mature as she reminisced on her years overseas studying water management in drought-and-flood-prone environments—the last thing Jo would have suspected her of. Her parents, also wool growers, were obviously as proud as Punch of their daughter. Their daughter, on the other hand, was not above batting her eyelashes at Gavin.

As one delicious course followed another—pumpkin soup swirled with cream; tiny, tasty whiting fillets; a magnificent leg of ham, glazed and decorated with pineapple rings and cherries, and a mocha soufflé—Jo counted up all the ways Sarah would benefit Gavin Hastings and Kin Can.

They could discuss in detail, for example, artesian basins and their management. They could do the same with dam placement and how to maximize water runoff. Certainly, Sarah could take her place in any society, not only with her looks and style, but her intelligence. What did that leave?

Rosie, Jo thought, and had to acknowledge that the little girl seemed to be on the back roads of her mind a lot. Of course, she also spent a lot of time *with* Rosie so that would account for it—or did it? Did the

fact that she had been motherless herself have anything to do with the growing rapport with, and the
affection she felt for, Rosie Hastings?

'Penny for 'em?'

Jo turned to find Gavin at her side, offering her a
liqueur. They'd removed to the garden room for their
coffee.

'I was thinking,' she said slowly, and took the tiny
glass. 'Thank you—I was thinking that Sarah would
make a very suitable wife for you.' Sarah was outside,
inspecting the pool and garden with her parents and
Adele.

His gaze was cool as it flickered over her. 'I see.
We're still at war over something, are we, Jo?'

'You started it.'

'No,' he contradicted. 'You started it and are wag-
ing it in a veil of silence. That was never my intention.'

Jo stared at him.

'You have to admit you've been avoiding me, Jo.'

Had she? Perhaps, but with the intention of taking
the long view rather than being overwhelmed by his
physical presence?

'I—' She thought for a moment. 'I'm not avoiding
some of the issues now, am I?'

He glanced over his shoulder towards the pool, and
frowned. 'You seriously see Sarah as an issue? I don't
want her, Jo. Or any of the ''suitable wives'' my
mother keeps parading in front of me.'

Jo blinked. 'You know?'

'Of course I know,' he said impatiently. 'I wasn't
born yesterday.'

'I could be forgiven for thinking I was a convenient

wife, Gavin. Not that I'm taking issue with that as such, but since you are going for suitable, you could find someone more suitable—is what I'm saying.' She smiled briefly.

'She got up your nose,' Gavin stated after a long moment.

Jo grimaced. 'Petite girls do sometimes. They make me feel like an Amazon.'

'I tend to feel somewhat clumsy around very petite girls, myself.'

She raised an eyebrow at him.

He smiled, curiously gently. 'Which is why I like you just the way you are.'

Their gazes locked and her heart started to beat slowly and heavily as something flowed between them that was warm and quite lovely.

Her lips parted but he put his hand over hers. 'Later, Jo.'

'Yes,' she agreed huskily.

But no sooner had the Knightlys left than a call came through with the news that a fire had broken out in one of the staff cottages several miles away from the homestead.

'You can't go, Gavin!' Adele protested. 'Your arm—'

'Yes, I can, I must, but only to direct operations.' He grinned. 'You know how good I am at that.'

'Can we help, though? Or, can I help?' Jo asked.

His gaze softened. 'Thanks, but there are plenty of hands, it's direction that might be lacking and it is my responsibility. Go to bed, girls. I'll see you in the morning.' He paused. 'Jo—'

'It's OK,' she murmured.

He hesitated, then turned away.

'He's just like his father,' Adele commented, when he was out of earshot. 'You know you can rely on him!'

It was a while before Jo went to bed.

Something inside her was spinning again beneath that lovely moment of closeness with Gavin Hastings, and she knew that the time was coming when she would be pressed for a decision. She also knew that she very much wanted to marry him. She might get annoyed with his high-handed ways but the burden of loving him was…

She paused her thoughts and wondered why she saw it as a burden when he could make her feel dizzy with delight. When he was the first man to actually do that for her…

When just knowing him made her spin like a top and crave his company. And when the life on Kin Can appealed not only to her artistic senses, but her practical, get-out-and-do-things nature, not to mention her longing for a real home.

Then there was Rosie. She could honestly say that they'd 'clicked'. They spent hours drawing together and Rosie showed some genuine talent. Not only that, they laughed together and Jo had become a confidante.

How *would* Rosie cope with being transplanted from an environment she loved for chunks of the year, and how would she cope with having to share her grandmother with a new husband?

Come to that, what kind of a burden would a six-year-old child put on Adele's new-found happiness, however much Adele might insist she and Rosie were inseparable?

If nothing else, it added up to a lot of good reasons for Gavin to want to marry her, but something was holding her back—the burden of being the one deeply in love while he was not?

'In a nutshell, Jo,' she murmured. 'All your life you've lost the people who meant the most to you. Remember how you felt when you discovered you had a grandmother who'd spent nearly all your life searching for you, but she was gone too? Could this not be a recipe for the same thing if Gavin were to fall wildly, deeply, madly in love again?'

Who is to say he won't fall madly in love with you, Jo? she asked herself.

Then out of the blue something popped into her mind. Was there any form of protection she could take into a marriage of convenience—that was what it was on his side at least—such as not letting him know how much in love she was with him until, if ever, she was confident he felt the same about her?

But then she couldn't help wondering how a sort of 'hedging your bets' policy would affect a relationship. And how hard it might be not to let him see how he affected her. Obviously, she would have to practise some kind of restraint...

The next day brought a sequence of events that seemed to prove to her it was an excellent idea to hedge her bets.

CHAPTER EIGHT

Jo WAS sketching in her bedroom, for the first time rather happy with Adele's portrait, when Mrs Harper came to seek her out mid-morning to inform her that Gavin would like to see her, if she was free.

Jo blinked, a little surprised that he hadn't come to look for her himself. She hadn't seen him since the previous evening so she gathered he must have had an early breakfast and gone straight out, and that had also surprised her after what had happened between them last night. But Adele had passed on the news that, although no one had been injured in the fire, the cottage had burnt to the ground, so she'd assumed he was still caught up in the consequences of the fire.

'He's down at the shearing shed. He rang a moment ago,' Mrs Harper added and hesitated.

'Oh!' Jo got up. 'That explains it.' She paused and looked at the housekeeper, who, in turn, was looking troubled. 'It doesn't? Explain it, I mean.'

Mrs Harper opened her mouth, closed it, then said, 'It's not a very nice day, Miss Lucas. There's a perishing westerly blowing; I'd wrap up if I were you. The weather sometimes does that out here. You think it's summer, then winter sneaks in a last left hook.'

Jo took her advice and changed into a tracksuit and her anorak, although she had to wonder why she was being summoned to the shearing shed on an unpleasant day.

111

In the event, as she jogged down to the shed she found the wind quite exhilarating. There were clouds scudding across the sky and several old peppercorn trees in a clump were tossing their feathery leaves dementedly. Her cheeks were pink; her hair was whipped into a gold tangle as she climbed to the shearing platform.

The shed was swept and empty, except for Gavin who was inspecting one of the electric combs, and she paused for a moment, thinking that he looked rather forbidding.

'Is something wrong?' she asked as she came up to him.

He dropped the comb so that it dangled from its lead and turned to her, and simply regarded her as she steadied her breathing from her run and attempted to tame her hair.

'Gavin?'

'Jo, we need to make a decision,' he said abruptly. 'We've been shilly-shallying around for long enough.'

'Shilly-shallying!' she said incredulously. 'This could be the rest of our lives we're talking about!'

'It's certainly my intention that it is, but we're getting nowhere like this.' He rubbed his jaw moodily, and although he wore clean jeans and a fine, this-time-mulberry wool sweater, he reminded her rather forcibly of the tough man who had taken her hostage.

'Why…what…has something come up I don't know about?' she asked disjointedly. 'Last night—'

'Last night,' he said precisely, 'I was unaware of my mother's intention to remarry.'

'What's that got to do—?' She broke off. 'Of
course—Rosie.'

'Yes, Rosie,' he said. 'If she thinks I'm going to
entrust Rosie to a man I've never met, who could be
some bloody gold-digger anyway, she's mistaken.'

Jo suddenly recalled Mrs Harper's troubled de-
meanour and made the deduction that, unlike herself,
the housekeeper had been within earshot of 'words'
at least, between Gavin and his mother.

But her next reaction was incredulity. 'Surely you
don't believe your mother would fall for a gold-
digger! Don't you think you should at least give her
credit for—'

'What?' He glared at her. 'Do you know where she
met him? On a cruise. Have you any idea what rich
pickings cruises provide for anyone on the make?
Rich, lonely widows—'

'Gavin, just stop right there for a moment,' Jo ordered. 'Believe me, it doesn't become you to harbour
such scepticism about your own mother!'

'On the contrary,' he drawled, 'it's because I'm
extremely fond of my mother, but a realist at the same
time, that I'm so concerned.'

Jo took a couple of calming breaths.

'However,' he went on before she could speak,
'even if she marries him and he proves to be OK,
there's no way Rosie is going to be involved.'

'Yes, well,' Jo conceded, 'that had crossed my
mind.'

'You know about all this?' he shot at her.

Jo nodded. 'She told me yesterday during her sitting.'

'So?'

Jo stopped combing her hair with her fingers and brushed it behind her ears. 'So—what?' she enquired with hauteur.

'Oh, come on, Jo,' he said roughly, 'don't beat about the bush! How did it affect these *prolonged* deliberations of yours?'

'*You* suggested we take some time to think it through!' she cried.

'As I told you yesterday, not like this, in a veil of secrecy and silence.'

Jo discovered in that moment that you could love and hate a man in the same breath. Fair enough, she reasoned, he'd obviously had a shock. Yes, he was obviously very fond of his mother, and she now had a pretty good idea of the wealth involved that would make a lonely widow extremely vulnerable to a man on the make. But this reaction was intolerable even given the circumstances.

'One of my *prolonged* deliberations,' she parodied coolly, 'tells me that a young governess might solve—all our problems.'

'Oh, yes?' he said dangerously. 'How about the fact that we only have to look at each other sometimes to be set alight with need and hunger? Would you prefer to go to your grave wondering about us, Jo? Are you going to play safe all your life? You know,' he said softly, 'I wouldn't have taken you for a coward, not after the way we met.'

She swallowed a lump in her throat and felt dizzy beneath the rush of emotions that came to her as he stared into her eyes. Not like this, something within her cried, it shouldn't happen like this. Not with us both angry but—is he right?

Or—would I be right to hedge my bets after all, at least against the times he can be impossible if nothing else?

She moistened her lips and cleared her throat. 'It so happens I have made a decision, Gavin. I've decided you'd be a very convenient husband for me.'

His eyes narrowed and he made an abrupt movement.

'Let me explain,' she said quietly. 'Of course, there's convenience on both sides. You need a mother for Rosie and that's fine with me. I think we have a special rapport, perhaps because she's motherless and I know what that's like.' She paused.

'Go on.'

It was impossible to tell from his voice or his stance how he was taking it.

'Uh—I've always wanted a home of my own. I guess being a foster-child does that to you, so that's another plus. And, to be honest, I'd have the financial security to draw what I liked. There's a vast range of subjects that appeal to me right here. Kids, animals, landscape.' She looked around. 'Even this old shearing shed.'

His gaze remained narrowed and intent.

'I never did,' she went on, 'intend to spend my artistic career doing commissioned portraits. I saw it as a way to get my work noticed and, once that happened, I always meant to give it away. If I married you, I could give it away a lot earlier. If we agree to this, though, there's one stipulation I need to make.'

'What's that?'

This time there was a detectable response, an echo of harshness in his voice.

She swallowed and took a moment to compose herself. 'That what is past is past and we don't pretend this is anything *but* a marriage of convenience. I know why a "deeply, madly" love match is out of the question for you. You know that I'm something of an independent loner and I'd find it hard to change. But there would be definite advantages for me—as well as you.'

'Does this all lead you to seeing yourself going to bed with me, Jo?'

Her lips parted.

'I mean to say, you sound so damn clinical, we could be discussing the price of eggs.'

'Gavin,' she said through her teeth, 'since the moment you set eyes on me this morning you've been angry and going out of your way to insult me. You're only lucky I haven't slapped your face!'

Her eyes blazed and as she said it she knew that nothing would give her more satisfaction than to do just that—but he saw it coming and ducked, then caught her wrist.

'Whoa,' he said softly. 'Has it occurred to you we're both under a lot of pressure because, rather than adding up the pluses and the minuses, we'd prefer to be doing this—which might just speak for itself anyway.'

She was far too angry to acquiesce when he pulled her into his arms; she was stiff and furious.

'Reminds me—' his lips twisted '—of another time I had you in my arms and you thought you were hating it. In the hut.'

'I was! I am now.'

'Then let me see how I can redeem myself. Will

you marry me, Jo Lucas, not only because of what we can do for each other, but so that we can share a bed, and each other's company, in unity?'

She stared up at him.

'It would be an honour if you said yes,' he added.

She searched his eyes, but could only find a serious query in them. 'Do you accept what I said, though?'

He shrugged. 'If you want me to. I still like to think we care about each other, Jo. I know *I* do and I don't think it would work otherwise.'

Her anger drained away and it was an almost unbearably poignant moment between them. Two people marked and scarred by life—was that enough to hold them together?

It didn't seem to matter to her suddenly. The truth was, she cared so much she couldn't help herself.

She freed a hand and touched her fingers to his cheek, and the assault on her senses was electric. 'OK,' she said huskily.

He heaved a sigh of relief and buried his head in her hair.

Two weeks later, Adele said to Jo, 'You look simply beautiful, my dear!'

Jo glanced down at her wedding outfit, a slim, long, ivory skirt in Thai silk and a short jacket top intricately trimmed with ribbon and lace. Silk covered pumps and short white gloves went with the outfit and a bouquet of yellow rosebuds, just opening, lay on the bed.

Her hair was up and, instead of a veil, a froth of ribbon secured it. Adele had just secured a string of what looked like priceless pearls around her neck, her wedding present.

Rosie, her flower girl, was being dressed by her aunt Sharon in an adjoining bedroom of Gavin's home on the Gold Coast.

The house was also the venue for their wedding. Jo, Adele and Rosie had arrived that morning from Kin Can, to be met by Sharon. Her husband, Roger, Gavin's best man, had Gavin in his keeping in Brisbane.

The house was majestic with sweeping gardens that overlooked an arm of the Coomera River, along which, during the day, a fascinating variety of yachts and boats of all description had sailed in and out from the Gold Coast Broadwater. It also had its own jetty on the river, and a trim, fast-looking craft was tied up to it.

True to tradition, Jo hadn't seen Gavin since the day before.

That might have been why she suddenly sat down on the bed feeling pale and a little ill. The ceremony was due to start in half an hour.

'I feel rather overwhelmed,' she confessed. 'All this—' she gestured to take in the house '—plus, I wanted to do it much more simply.' She stared down at the dazzling diamond on her ring finger.

Adele drew up a chair. 'Why?'

Jo glanced at her, then away. 'I don't know. Second marriage, for Gavin anyway, perhaps.'

'Jo, you're not having second thoughts, are you?'

Jo hesitated.

'Look—' Adele sat forward '—I know it's all been a bit of a rush and I have no doubt you got the third degree from Sharon, she's like that, but I couldn't be happier about this union. I think you're perfect for Gavin and—' she paused '—whatever reservations you may have about it being a second marriage for him, if you love him as I think you do, it will be fine.'

Jo raised her eyes to Adele. 'You know it's a bit one-sided?'

Adele smiled wisely. 'Is it? It looks to me as if he couldn't wait to get you to the altar. Just be yourself, Jo, which in my estimation is a pretty fine person.'

Jo half smiled. 'Thank you.' She stood up and took a deep breath. 'I'm ready.'

It was a lovely wedding. Everyone thought the bride looked stunning, and there was no doubt that the groom was enough to take your breath away in a dark dinner suit with a blinding white shirt front—he took the bride's breath away, anyway.

Rosie was adorable in a long yellow dress with flowers in her hair, and highly excited—she still couldn't quite believe her luck: a mother! And one she liked very much.

Adele was the epitome of elegance in a lavender lace gown and even the groom's sister dabbed her eyes as Jo and Gavin were pronounced man and wife.

Jo had formed the opinion that Sharon Pritchard née Hastings had all of her brother's 'born to command' qualities with little of his charisma, but she couldn't doubt Sharon's affection for Gavin.

There were about thirty people at the reception in the flower-decked dining room that flowed out to the garden. Case and Mrs Harper attended. So did Jo's flatmate and best friend, Leanne, and a few more friends. Her favourite art teacher was there.

On Gavin's side, it was mostly family, cousins, uncles and aunts, but he'd also invited some of his married friends, and laughingly told them—thank heavens, no more ghastly blind dates!

Adele, in a spirit of mischief, Jo could only assume, had invited Elspeth Morgan and her husband.

Of course, Jo detected some surprise and speculation as Gavin made sure he introduced her to everyone. You couldn't deny it was a rushed wedding; you couldn't deny that most of them had never heard of her until the invitations had arrived.

Two of his aunts had studied her midriff area quite blatantly, then withdrawn to have a cosy chat. One of his uncles had asked Jo if she was a Mount Miriam Lucas. Before she could reply that she wasn't, he'd gone on to congratulate Gavin on making a damn fine connection.

'You'll get used to my family,' Gavin said into her ear at this stage. 'We're a weird mob.'

'What's so good about a Mount Miriam connection?' she whispered back.

'Old, very old money.'

'I'm sorry! I did tell you you could do better for yourself,' she reminded him with a smile lurking at the backs of her eyes.

'Jo—' But they were interrupted and he never got to say it.

One thing did impress itself upon her during her wedding reception. The Mount Miriam connection might be about old, very old money, but the Hastings connection wasn't so far off that mark either.

Of course she'd known it was quite an empire Gavin had inherited, but for the first time she got a real glimpse of the upper echelon, rather rarefied society she'd married into. Some of them might be quirky, but all the Hastingses had one thing in common: the confidence that came from 'old money'.

Then it was over. Instead of her and Gavin leaving, the guests left, including Rosie, who was going to stay with her Pritchard cousins for a few days. Jo didn't change but she threw her bouquet and pale blue garter—Rosie caught the bouquet—and then they were alone, apart from the catering company discreetly clearing away.

'Tell me something,' Gavin said as he led her into a glass-fronted terrace that overlooked the river. 'Do you feel really married to me now?'

Jo looked around. The terrace, the whole house, had a Tuscan feel to it. There were citrus trees and miniature Cyprus trees in tubs on terracotta tiles, there were wooden planter boxes growing a riot of impatiens in every colour; there was a fountain with underwater lights looking like drowned stars.

She turned back to him and said after a moment's hesitation, 'I certainly feel very publicly married to you.'

'Good.' He strolled forward with his hands shoved into his trouser pockets. 'That's what I intended to achieve.'

Jo raised an eyebrow. 'Why?'

He stopped in front of her and studied the exquisite outfit, the gold of her hair, her creamy, flawless skin and the grey of her eyes as well as the pulse beating rapidly at the base of her throat. 'So you, and every-one else, would know it's for real.'

'You thought there might be some doubt?'

'None whatsoever on my part,' he answered obliquely, and studied her carefully again. 'May I make a suggestion? Gorgeous as you look, let's change, and relax out here for a while.'

'Good idea.' She glinted him a little smile, then looked down at herself and touched the pearls. 'I haven't given you my present yet. I'll get it at the same time.'

'Off you go, then. I'm going to organize a bottle of champagne since you had a glass and a half at the most earlier.'

'It seemed like a good idea to stay sober.' She laughed.

All her things had been moved into the master bed-room, she discovered, and she raised her eyebrows as she closed the door and looked around.

Someone—Adele?—had gone to town, here. What looked like acres of fawn carpet, a wide bed beneath a bedspread of unbleached cotton ecru with an intri-cate self-pattern, and heaped with scatter pillows cov-ered in fawn wild silk with pearl beadings.

Behind the bed stood a beautiful folding screen that immediately caught her attention—birds of paradise painted on a mushroom foil background.

At the other end of the room two linen-covered armchairs were set around a coffee-table and there was a magnificent elephant wonderfully carved from green verdite, ears extended, trunk raised, one foot bent on its plinth as if it were striding across the veld. It stood about waist-high.

She walked across to it and stroked the smooth green and brown mottled stone. 'Jambo, jumbo! I like you very much!'

Everything had been unpacked for her, including the wedding present Adele had insisted on giving her—a trousseau. She'd turned a deaf ear to Jo's protests on the matter although she had allowed Jo some say in choice of garments.

Amongst them was a pair of silky apricot long trousers with an elasticated waist, wide legs and a matching loose blouse. Jo chose them and changed into them after one last look at herself in her wedding outfit. She took the ribbons out of her hair and brushed it until it gleamed. She left her pearls on and looked around for her present for Gavin.

It was on a bedside table, beautifully wrapped. She picked it up and hugged it to herself and took several deep breaths.

The time was coming and coming fast when she might have to explain something that Gavin didn't know about her...

The time was also coming when she might discover how she matched up to his first wife.

He was waiting for her, not changed, but without his jacket and tie, with his shirt sleeves rolled up and his collar open.

On the low table in front of a deep, comfortable settee stood a bottle of champagne in a stone cooler, two glasses and a tray of snacks.

'You didn't eat much either,' he said as she eyed the snacks.

Jo fingered her rings—the diamond now had a gold band behind it—and wondered what he'd say if she told him nerves had seen her have difficulty swallowing? Then she remembered she had his present tucked under her arm.

'This is for you,' she said a little awkwardly. 'I hope you like it.' She held it out to him.

'Thank you.' He eased the gold ribbon off and opened the wrapping, and went quite still for a long moment. It was an exquisitely framed oval portrait of Rosie, looking over her shoulder with all the vivacity that made her such a character.

He looked up at last. 'Oh, Jo, you've captured her to a T.'

'It did feel as if it was going well,' she said huskily.

'Thank you,' he said simply.

He put the portrait down and came over to her, taking her chin in his hand. 'Missed me?'

'I...why?'

'You look a little shell-shocked and a bundle of nerves all rolled into one. I wondered if being torn from my side yesterday until you walked down the aisle today had anything to do with it?'

She grimaced. 'I did have a moment of sheer panic,' she conceded.

His eyes narrowed. 'Oh?'

'Your mother talked me out of it.'

'How?'

'She told me just to be myself,' Jo said after a slight hesitation.

He frowned, then shrugged. 'I had my own moment of panic.'

Jo looked up into his eyes. 'You wondered if we're doing the right thing?' she hazarded.

'Not at all. I was afraid that's what *you'd* be wondering.'

Jo blew her fringe up and smiled faintly. 'It's done now. There's just one thing—' She paused, then frowned and turned towards the river as shouts and screams floated across the water, then there was a burst of flame and a loud bang. 'What on earth...?'

Gavin reacted swiftly. 'A boat on fire.' He strode towards the terrace doors. 'Stay there, Jo, I'll—'

'No way!' she protested as, by the light of the fire, she saw people leaping from the burning boat into the water. 'Just let me do this.' She took her pearls and engagement ring off, laid them on the coffee table and ran after him.

Next to the sleek cruiser tied to Gavin's jetty was an inflatable dinghy with an outboard motor. 'We've got to take the tide into consideration,' he said as they climbed aboard. 'It's going out so it should carry the boat towards that mangrove island.' He gestured towards an uninhabited island opposite. 'But it could also carry anyone in the water the same way. Jo, I wish you'd stayed behind!'

He pulled the starter chord of the outboard and it roared to life.

'I can help pull people out of the water,' she shouted over the motor.

'Yes, but, although one fuel tank has exploded, there could be others.'

'Just—there, Gavin.' She pointed at a head bobbing in the water.

They spent the next hour rescuing swimmers, and several non-swimmers, two of whom Jo had to dive in and rescue, and depositing them on the jetty. They were joined, thankfully, by other dinghies from houses along the river and several Coastguard and Air Sea Rescue boats with fire-fighting equipment aboard.

As Gavin had predicted the burning hulk ended up in amongst the mangroves across the river, and a second fuel tank did blow up, showering burning debris into the water, but fortunately no one was struck.

All the same both she and Gavin were wet, filthy and exhausted by the time the rescue operation was complete, and after being interviewed by the Coast-guard, they staggered back to the terrace room, took one look at each other and collapsed onto a wooden bench laughing feebly.

'Here.' He got up and poured them a glass of champagne. 'It'll be flat and warm by now, but we deserve it.'

Jo sipped hers. 'Tastes wonderful.' She glanced down at herself. 'How on earth are we going to get clean without dripping mud and heaven knows what all over the carpets, et cetera?'

'Hmm…well, not a problem.' He walked over to the fountain, or so Jo thought, but he stopped at a panel beside it and opened a door set in the woodwork to reveal a switchboard. At the touch of several buttons, one end of the terrace room was transformed.

Blinds descended blocking the view to the river. What had appeared to her to be a circle of parquet wood tiles on the floor split down the middle and each half of the circle slid back to reveal a spa bath. Underwater lights came on in the spa and it started to bubble.

The last thing he did was switch all the other lighting off except the drowned stars in the fountain.

Jo put down her glass and clapped spontaneously. 'Your mother?'

'My mother,' he agreed. 'Neither the architect, the engineer, nor the electrician and the plumber she badgered into producing this have ever been the same since. She got the idea from a Japanese bathhouse.'

'But it's masterly!' Jo laughed. 'I can't wait to get in and get clean.'

'Be my guest.' He touched another panel and a door swung open to reveal a cupboard of terry towelling robes, bath towels and cakes of handmade soap, loofahs, even long-handled back scrubbers.

Jo pulled her ruined clothes off and stepped into the water in her bra and knickers, still laughing delightedly.

'I would say that,' he commented, 'to get the full benefit one would need to be naked.'

'Naked it is, then,' she conceded cheerfully and, beneath the cover of the foaming, bubbling water, removed her underwear. 'Could you please pass me the soap?'

He did so, plus refilling their glasses and finally stripping to his underpants and joining her.

'Thank heavens no one was killed—thank you.' She took her glass and lay back with a luxurious sigh. 'It could have been a whole lot worse.'

'It could have. And you were exceedingly brave, Jo.'

'Not really. I'm a strong swimmer but—' she paused, then glinted a wicked glance at him '—we make a good team. We could even go into business together.'

'We do—it struck me once before. A sort of Tarzan/Jane partnership?' he suggested.

Her laughter bubbled up again and she sipped her champagne, then put it down and began to soap her arms.

'Actually, I have a better idea,' he said. He took the soap from her. 'Now that is what I had in mind.' And he began to soap her.

'I see what you mean,' she murmured after a while as she lay still beneath his wandering hands, and felt her tired, over-exerted body relax, then come alive to other sensations. 'That's lovely.'

'So are you.' His mouth closed on hers.

It started out slow and languorous, the way he kissed her and held her with their bodies feeling weightless in the water as they blended together. A gentle union after the preceding high drama. A lovely let-down still riding on their friendship and the way they'd worked together so well.

Then the tempo changed as his fingers moved more and more intimately on her until she found herself sitting across his lap with his face in her hands as she kissed him and acknowledged that she was being seduced out of her mind—and loving every moment of it.

'Jo—' he breathed and ran his hands down her back to cup her bottom, '—come with me.'

'In a minute.' She went back to kissing him.

'Jo, now. We need a bed.'

She opened her eyes and looked into his to find they were dark with desire—urgent need, in fact. 'OK.'

She put her hands on his shoulders and raised herself off his lap. He groaned and, despite his urgent need, held her waist and kissed her dripping breasts.

'I thought you said—'

'I did, we do, my lovely wife. Let's go.'

They got out, grabbed two robes and shrugged into them, then, holding hands, ran through the house to the master bedroom.

Had it ever been treated so cavalierly? Jo wondered, as wild silk, pearl-trimmed scatter pillows were thrown aside and the ecru bedspread summarily dispatched to the floor with two white robes thrown on top of it.

As for her 'hedging her bets' policy that had included practising restraint so that he would never know how much she wanted him, talk about throwing it out of the proverbial window!

But she couldn't help herself. She was on fire in a way she'd never thought she would be. She needed his lean, strong body; she needed everything about Gavin Hastings to be her very own, to make her whole, to love her...

'Jo?'

'Gavin?'

They stared at each other across the bed. 'Have I ever told you how lovely you are?' His gaze flickered down her body.

'Yes, but I don't mind how often you do it,' she replied gravely. 'Have I ever told you that you're rather gorgeous?'

'You once told me I was pretty.'

She grinned. 'If you lie down on this bed, I'll amend that.'

'Done!'

In fact they lay down together and quite soon their laughing moment became something else.. red-hot desire but, this time, he took the lead until she was helpless with longing and mindless with rapture.

'Now, Jo?'

'Yes, please,' she gasped.

'Good. I'm just about to die.'

'*You're*—I thought I was.'

'It must be mutual, then.'

It was.

It was also quite some time before they spoke again. By that time they were lying side by side, their heads close on the pillow.

He said softly, 'Wow!' Then he stroked her cheek.

Jo slid her fingers through his, and blew her fringe up. 'Make that a double wow!'

He sat up, but only to pull a sheet over them. 'Of course I always knew it had to be like that.'

'How could you possibly?' She turned to look into his eyes.

He pushed her hair behind her ear. 'There was something about the way you tried to pulverize my toes when we first met that must have alerted me,' he said thoughtfully.

She hid a smile. 'You know what I think?'

'Tell me.'

'You're an impossible know-all, Gavin Hastings.'

'On the contrary, Joanne Hastings—' he caressed her body beneath the sheet '—I'm a very good judge of—character.' He curved his hand possessively around her waist.

'Character?'

'You know what I mean.'

She was laughing helplessly. 'I do know what you mean but I feel it has another name.'

'So you—um—were prey to it right from the beginning?' he queried. 'This thing by another name?'

'To my horror and complete confusion, yes.' She grimaced as she recalled their first few hours together.

He laughed and kissed her. 'Shall we sleep?'

'I think it would be a good idea. I'm bushed,' she confided. 'Not everyone has such an eventful wedding day.'

'Indeed. Comfortable?'

'Yes,' she answered drowsily, and a few moments later she was asleep.

Gavin Hastings watched her for a while, and found himself recalling the minutes before they'd been alerted to the fire on the boat.

What had she said? Something about—*it's done now*.

Hardly an acknowledgement that it had been the right thing to do, getting married, he mused, and wondered why those three words lay like a prickle on the surface of his mind.

Of course, the greater mystery was why she'd elected not to tell him she was a virgin. Or was that what she'd been about to say? *There's just one thing*…hadn't those been her words?

The thing was, he hadn't expected it. She was so cool and confident most of the time, she *was* twenty-four, and even though she'd told him she didn't enjoy being kissed, he'd assumed she wasn't completely in-experienced even if they hadn't been particularly suc-cessful experiences.

So what was in her background to account for it? And how serious had she been about insisting this was a marriage of convenience? Nothing that had happened between them tonight had been 'conve-nient'. There was a basic mutual attraction that was extremely powerful, although, on the other hand, he thought dryly, she'd gone out of her way to keep him at arm's length for the preceding weeks.

He studied her in the lamplight. Her gold hair was gorgeously mussed. Her creamy skin was still flushed and warm. Her mouth— Damn it, he thought, why did she have to have the most kissable mouth he'd ever seen? So that he was almost unbearably tempted to kiss her awake and take her again...

His thoughts ranged back over the evening. She was right—in any kind of a crisis they made a good team, but he'd been trained for it. Yes, he'd always had good reflexes, good co-ordination to start with, but she was also a natural with all the above plus steady nerves. He had to admire that and it made them two of a kind, but...

But what? he wondered. Why do I get the feeling there's a girl within this girl I might never be allowed to know—and that it's going to bug me, and go on bugging me until I do find the real Jo Lucas?

CHAPTER NINE

THEY had five days on their own.

Dreamy, peaceful days for the most part when they swam and went boating, talked, read—and made love.

They had some electrifying encounters when their need for each other got quite out of hand...

He took her out to dinner one night. She dressed carefully in a simple, sleeveless black dress with a square neckline, against which her pearls looked fabulous. She put her hair up, and knew immediately as he narrowed his eyes briefly that he didn't approve. But she was rather pleased with it so she left it as it was. Her finishing touch was to spray some perfume behind her ears.

'Ready?' He was lounging in the doorway wearing navy trousers and a cream linen shirt.

She slipped on her high-heeled sandals. 'Ready!'

They ate on the waterfront at Sanctuary Cove, a resort complex with wonderful shops, a marina and a great variety of restaurants. Jo loved it, and before they sat down they strolled through the village, with its ornate lampposts and flower-decked pavements, window-shopping. Then they walked down one of the marina arms admiring the boats.

And she was really enjoying her dinner when, suddenly, Gavin pushed his Lobster Mornay away and announced that he couldn't do it.

'Do what?' She stared at him with her knife and fork poised.

'Eat.'

She frowned. 'Why not? Mine's lovely.'

'It should be down, not up.'

'How could—' Her grey gaze was mystified as she inspected his plate. 'Are you talking about the lobster?'

He shook his head. 'Your hair.'

Jo expelled an exasperated little breath. She'd forgotten all about that disapproving little glint in his eyes as she'd tied her hair up in a knot. 'I'll take it down when we get home.'

'Why not now?'

She glanced around. 'Don't be silly, Gavin. It— that would be—' she sought the right word '—unhygienic.'

He sat back and fingered his jaw. 'Isn't it clean?'

'It's perfectly clean,' she countered with a touch of asperity. 'You saw me wash it earlier.'

'So?'

She eyed him. He looked *perfectly* relaxed with the line of his shoulders wide and comfortable under the cream linen, but just the thought of them did strange things to her.

As an artist she found the perfection of those broad shoulders and his sleek, muscled torso were an invitation she now knew she couldn't resist transmitting to paper.

As a woman and a lover she knew they were a source of desire and joy and the thought of being in his arms and his bed made her feel weak at the knees—but now, here? Surely he couldn't stir her up in that rapturous way in such a public spot?

'Jo?' He said it softly and watched that delicious pulse beating rapidly at the base of her throat.

'Um...well, it's not a good idea to spread even clean hairs around at the table,' she said a little raggedly.

'I'm not asking you to wave it about, just let it down, slowly and carefully, if you like. Actually, slowly and carefully would be best. For me.'

That's just like asking me to undress slowly and carefully for you—it shot through her mind. And some colour spread up her throat to her cheeks. 'It's not good manners, Gavin.'

'Then we better go home—' he stood up and held his hand out to her '—since good manners mean so much to you.'

'I haven't finished,' she protested.

'I could take it down for you.'

'My hair? No! Not here!'

His lips twisted. 'My point entirely. Come, Josie.'

People were already starting to look at them oddly.

'I...we can't just walk out. You haven't paid or anything.'

He gestured dismissively. 'They know me.'

Jo looked around into what appeared to her to be dozens of pairs of amused, quizzical eyes. She put her napkin on the table hurriedly and stood up.

She also said, through her teeth, 'Does that mean you make a habit of this?'

'No. You're the first woman to do it to me.'

Their gazes locked and there was something unsmiling but electrifying about the way his eyes lingered on her.

So much so she turned on her heel and walked out ahead of him with her head held high but every secret, sensual spot beneath her skin clamouring for his touch.

The ride home was fast and they didn't talk at all. He didn't bother with putting the car in the garage, but pulled up outside the portico, and spun the wheels on the gravel of the drive.

They only just got inside the heavily carved front door before he put a hand on her shoulder, saying grimly, 'Do you know you've been driving me crazy for the last two hours with that stern, prim, bloody knot?'

'Oh?' She examined her mixture of annoyance and intrigue—intrigue that she could drive him crazy simply by tying up her hair. Even so, she reminded herself, he had embarrassed her so the big question was—how to deal with such conflicting emotions?

Something dealt with it for her. Something she couldn't name within her told her that two could play this game.

'How about this, then?' she murmured, and slipped off her shoes. The hall tiles were cool beneath her feet.

She looked around and took her pearls off and hung them from one of the hands of the bronze Hindu goddess who presided over the hall. Then she reached for her zip and her black dress floated down her body and pooled at her feet. She stepped out of it gravely, picked it up and hung it over the other of the goddess's hands.

Then she attended to her hair and, when it was released, shook her head so that it swirled in a gold cloud, and she put her hands on her hips. At the same time she noted how heavily he was breathing as he studied the fascinating play of a delicate black lace bra and hipster briefs on the creamy satin of her skin.

'No Bonds Cottontails tonight,' he said.

'No.'

He looked into her eyes. 'Am I allowed to touch?'

'No-o.' Her voice cracked a little but her gaze was firm. 'Not until you apologize.'

'For what?'

'Embarrassing the life out of me.'

He raised a satanic eyebrow. 'You don't see it as a compliment?'

'I may eventually. Right now—well, would you like me to be honest?'

'Be my guest,' he rasped.

Jo considered for a moment and examined her sudden sense of unreality, even unease. 'I'm far more interested in solving this rather savage state of affairs between us.'

A glint of something different entered his eyes. 'How?'

'I don't know. In the meantime, I'm going to bed.' She turned and walked away from him.

She didn't get very far. He came up behind and put his arms around her. 'Like hell you are without me if that's what you had in mind, Jo Lucas,' he growled into her ear and brought his hands up to cup her breasts. 'OK, I'm sorry, but I couldn't help myself.'

She hesitated.

'Let me show you,' he murmured, and moved his

hands down her waist to slide them beneath the top of her panties.

She caught her bottom lip between her teeth. 'That's…' She couldn't go on as she grew warm and wet with desire.

'Am I forgiven?' he breathed against the side of her neck.

She leant back against him. 'I'm tending towards being more complimented,' she said slowly.

'Good.' He turned her round and swept her up in his arms. 'Let's see if I can compliment you further.'

'These,' he said later, 'also drive me mad.'

They were lying on their sides, facing each other. Once again the wild silk pillows were scattered around the floor and the coverlet lay in a crumpled heap beneath his clothes and her bra and pants.

He pushed himself up on his elbow and stroked the curve of her hip.

Jo stretched her arms upwards and pointed her toes. 'I'd never thought about them particularly.'

'Well, if I suddenly ask you, in the middle of dinner, to get up and walk away from me, you'll know why.'

Her breathing jolted. 'I see that I'm in for some exciting times.'

'Mmm. Like right now.'

From the word go, it became extremely sultry as he kissed her from head to toe and revelled in the perfume of her skin, her secret, most intimate spots. And as she gave herself up to the ever-growing excitement, she made her own explorations of his hard, honed body until there was only one place to go.

They went down that road together in perfect unison, holding, tasting, touching and thrilling each other with the sensations they aroused as never before.

And when it was over they lay exhausted in each other's arms, and fell asleep in a tangle of sweat-dewed limbs.

'Jo?'

Her lashes fluttered up to reveal daylight filtering through the curtains, then she turned her head to see Gavin watching her with a frown in his eyes.

'Yes?' She struggled to sit up. 'Is something wrong?'

'Are you all right?'

'Of course. Why?'

He groaned and buried his head between her breasts for a moment. 'I don't know what got into me last night.'

She subsided and her mouth curved. 'Neither do I—I mean, I don't know what got into me. Oh, no.' She sat up again with her hand to her mouth.

'What?'

Although there was no live-in staff, a middle-aged housekeeper, who went by the name of Sophie, came in daily.

'My dress. My pearls!'

Instant understanding came to his eyes. 'You feel Sophie might get the socks shocked off her to find them hanging up in the hall?'

'Yes! Would you...would you be a darling and get them for me?'

'Too late. I heard her come in by the front door about ten minutes ago.'

Jo looked stricken, so much so, he had to laugh. 'She's a married lady with four children and two grandchildren.'

'She may have forgotten what it can be like, in that case,' Jo replied gloomily.

'What it can be like,' he repeated with a reminiscent smile and pulled her back into his arms. 'I haven't. But rest assured she's too well paid to make you feel uncomfortable about it.'

Jo relaxed against him. 'What if she gossips?'

'She's too well paid for that also, and she signed a confidentiality clause anyway.'

'Do you really have to go to those lengths to protect your privacy, Gavin?'

'Uh-huh. As a matter of fact I've stepped up our security since the kidnap attempt. Everyone we employ is now fully vetted first, not only household staff.'

'I always did get the feeling the Kin Can connection was on a par with the Mount Miriam one,' she teased.

Strangely, a variation of that subject, in the form of other problems great wealth could attract, came up a few days later when their official honeymoon was over.

They were still on the Gold Coast but the embargo Gavin had placed on any business—even phone calls—had been lifted, and Sharon Pritchard came down for a visit with her three girls as well as Adele and Rosie.

They had a fun lunch, then Gavin took the kids for a spin in the speedboat leaving Sharon, Adele and Jo to pore over the wedding photos Adele had brought with her.

'Just look at her,' Adele trilled as she pointed to Elspeth Morgan, captured talking very earnestly to one of Gavin's uncles, the same one who had assumed Jo was a Mount Miriam Lucas.

'She was wasting her time if she was trying to impress Uncle Garth,' Sharon said with a chuckle. 'He's as mad as a hatter and ''new money'' doesn't appeal to him in the slightest.'

Adele agreed but added the rider, 'Mind you, there's an awful *lot* of Morgan money and I guess it's not that long ago that we were all new money.'

Sharon waved a languid hand. 'At least we know the dynasty is secure again. Or *can* be, heaven-willing.'

'Sharon,' Adele reproved.

'Secure?' Jo questioned, suddenly looking up from a photo of her and Gavin. 'In what way?'

'In the way of you having sons, darling,' Sharon said succinctly. 'Gavin looked all set to be the first in a direct line of Hastings not to have a male heir, which was a bit of a worry. Nor have I helped exactly by having three daughters.'

Jo turned to Adele with a frown in her eyes.

'Take no notice, Jo,' Adele commanded. 'That's all nonsense. Sharon—' she turned to her daughter '—you can be as bad as Elspeth Morgan! Things don't work that way these days.'

Sharon grimaced. 'Maybe, but you can't deny it would be a huge burden for Rosie's shoulders. And you can't deny that a girl can be very much at the mercy of the man she marries.'

Jo swallowed and looked down at the photo in her hands. She and Gavin were standing side by side looking into each other's eyes and her first glance at the photo had produced a little thrill. Now, all she could think was, amongst his admitted need of a wife, had he neglected to tell her he needed a son?

And was the rest of the Hastings family thinking along those lines? Two of his aunts had certainly had it in mind at the wedding, she recalled.

'Sons can be just as capable of squandering an empire as sons-in-law not brought up to it,' Adele observed prosaically.

'Well, I can't help thinking you showed such a brave, steady, practical nature throughout that ghastly kidnapping business, Jo, that your genes added to Gavin's would produce fine sons.' Sharon reached for another photo.

Jo, Gavin and Rosie waved Adele, Sharon and her girls off later that afternoon.

'OK, catfish,' Gavin said to Rosie, 'we've got two more days down here, then it's back to Kin Can. How would you like to spend the time?'

'I would *love* to go to Sea World! They have some polar bears there. I saw them when they were babies. Have you seen them, Jo?' Rosie turned to her excitedly.

'No.'

'Sea World it is tomorrow, then,' Gavin said. 'Anything else?'

'No, I'll just enjoy being with you two. I wanted to ask you something, Jo. Should I call you Jo or Mum?'

For some reason Jo glanced across at Gavin over Rosie's head and she saw him narrow his eyes suddenly.

'Oh, I think Jo is fine, Rosie, don't you?' she said after the barest hesitation. 'For the time being anyway.'

'What would you *like* to call her, Rosie?' Gavin intervened.

Rosie drew a deep breath. 'You know how we said goodbye to my mother before the wedding, Daddy?'

'Yes, sweetheart,' he said quietly.

'Well, although I never knew her, she was my real mother and I was worried that it wouldn't be right to call someone else Mum, although I'm thrilled to have a new mother,' she assured Jo earnestly. 'Does that make sense?' she added anxiously.

'Perfect sense,' Jo said softly. 'That's fine with me, Rosie.'

'What about,' Gavin said out of the blue as they were getting ready for bed that night, 'our other kids?'

Jo had wrapped herself in a cotton robe and was sitting brushing her hair at the dressing table. She looked up at his reflection in the mirror and she felt her nerves tighten as she recalled his sister's thoughts on dynasties.

'What about them?'

'We do plan to have a family, don't we, Jo?' He came up behind her and took the brush from her. He hadn't changed yet and he wore jeans and a navy T-shirt.

'We didn't discuss that.'

He'd started to brush her hair but he stopped

abruptly. 'I sort of assumed it went without saying.' His eyes in the mirror were intent and probing.

Jo swallowed. 'So did I, I guess. Although perhaps not immediately.' She frowned. 'Are you saying that I should have encouraged Rosie to call me Mum?'

'I'm just wondering if it won't make her feel a little on the outside if she's the only one not to.'

A fleeting smile curved Jo's lips. 'How many do we plan to have, Gavin?'

'It's up to you.' He resumed brushing.

'Look,' Jo said slowly, 'to be honest, I was feeling my way with Rosie. And you,' she added and shrugged. 'It's a delicate area for both of you—as she proved.'

'You thought I might object to her calling you Mum?'

'Yes, I did. Oh, it would be perfectly natural,' she assured him. 'Your memories—'

'Don't include Rosie calling anyone Mum,' he broke in.

'Gavin—' Jo swung round on the stool and took her brush back '—we seem to be on different wavelengths here. Please tell me exactly what you're thinking.'

He sat down on the end of the bed opposite her. 'I just thought it might be practical—' He stopped and looked down at his shoes. 'The thing is, because of the way it happened, I have no memories of Sasha mothering Rosie. On the other hand I have very clear memories of mentally ranting and railing on how unfair it was that Rosie should have been deprived of a mother.'

'You—somehow or other you took her to say good-bye, though,' Jo said huskily.

'Yes. Sasha is buried in the family graveyard on Kin Can. I thought we both needed to say goodbye.' He looked up suddenly. 'I didn't expect it to hit Rosie that way, however.'

Jo considered it all and found herself feeling as if she'd entered a minefield. For the last five days they'd been so close, she and Gavin, she'd lost sight of what she'd assumed was the underlying reason for this marriage—Rosie.

Then, that very afternoon she'd had the importance of sons thrust at her—and here was Gavin talking about starting a family almost right on cue, however it had come up. Not to mention his concern that Rosie would be melded seamlessly into their family unit.

Naturally she would share that concern, she reflected. On the other hand, why did she have the feeling that the honeymoon was well and truly over and providing sons for the Hastings dynasty was coming at her like a runaway train?

Was she imagining it all? Had it simply been a series of coincidences that the subject should have been touched upon the way it had? Or—was Sharon right in thinking she had been summed up *genetically* and found acceptable? Hadn't they agreed only days ago that they were well matched?

Her gaze focused on Gavin suddenly. Had that been the basis of his conviction that he needed to marry her and her only—not quite as unclear as he'd told her?

And what about the conviction she had right now that he wasn't being completely open with her?

'Jo?'

'Uh…' She made an effort to concentrate. 'So far as Rosie goes, I think it would be wise to take things slowly.'

'How about the rest of our family? Slowly, too?'

'Gavin, we've only been married for six days!'

His lips twisted. 'I know. But it is on your agenda, to have kids?'

She raised the brush and stroked it through her hair. 'Why would you doubt it?' she asked.

'You can be—rather secretive, Jo.'

'In what way?'

'I may be wrong, you're very athletic and active, but I got the feeling you were a virgin.'

'Is that what this is all about?' she asked incredulously. 'You have a grudge about that?'

'Not *per se*. If anything I was—honoured. I just can't quite work out why you didn't tell me.'

'It so happens I was just about to tell you when a boat blew up in the river!'

'And after that?'

'It didn't seem…I mean, I'd planned to tell you because I was afraid I might seem, well, awkward, but that didn't happen, thanks to you.'

His gaze softened.

'Besides,' she added, 'we did agree that what's past is past.'

'So I'm not to be allowed to know why you reached twenty-four without ever having a lover?' he queried.

'No one—' she paused '—measured up to you, Gavin.'

Something sharpened in his eyes. 'Then it wasn't

only convenience you had in mind when you married me, Jo?'

'I never said it was.'

He looked ironic. 'It featured quite prominently, but, anyway—how say you now?'

They stared at each other.

'Why do I have the feeling you've got me in some kind of dock and are pressing charges?' she asked huskily.

'Wouldn't it be natural to examine our feelings now it's—let me rephrase—*it's done now*?'

The words seemed to echo in her mind but she couldn't pinpoint why. And she tried to take hold then, but she couldn't help thinking that her decision to hedge her bets might still be a wise one—until she discovered what this was all about and how desperate he was for a son, at least.

She stood up and walked over to the window, from where she could see the channel markers in the river flashing red and green. In her disturbed state of mind they seemed to mirror her dilemma. Green for 'go for broke' and simply be honest with him? Or, red for extreme caution required, pass this point and you're liable to end up on the rocks?

Rocks such as not being able to produce a son to order, for example?

'No, I don't think it would be wise to get academic at this stage, Gavin,' she said, not turning. 'What we've had so far has been lovely. Let's just go forward and try to build on it.'

He didn't reply for a long time, and then he didn't reply in the spoken word. He came up behind her and put his arms around her, and simply held her until she relaxed against him. Then he started to nuzzle her neck and finally, when she was feeling weak at the knees with desire, he took her to bed.

But although their love-making was intense and wonderful, she couldn't help feeling she'd survived a crisis.

Over the next three months she woke gradually to the realization that she was still living that crisis, and that it might have two names. Not only sons, but memories of Sasha?

CHAPTER TEN

THE weather had warmed up considerably three months after Jo's first arrival on Kin Can. She got up one morning and she dressed in khaki shorts, a pink blouse and slipped on sandals. Gavin had risen before the crack of dawn to supervise a muster.

She reviewed her plans for the day as she and Rosie ate breakfast. They were going to work on the doll's house they were building together. Not that it was a doll's house in anything but concept. Rosie had no time for dolls so this was a miniature shearing shed complete with sheep, since Rosie had adopted an orphan lamb to add to her menagerie of a puppy, a pony and a tame cockatoo.

It was going well, Jo thought suddenly, her elevation to motherhood. Not only that, she was enjoying it. She'd persisted with her plan to take things slowly and not force a motherly presence on Rosie and it was working.

One of her worries had been that Rosie might resent having to share her father with someone else, particularly a wife. It was all very well to yearn for a mother, but at six, and never having had one, all the implications could come as something of a shock, she'd reasoned.

But Rosie had shown hardly any signs of that. She threw herself whole-heartedly into all the things they did together, swimming, drawing, reading, as well as being out and about on the property. She'd begun to consult Jo on what to wear, she'd started to confide in Jo about her friends and Jo's suggestion that they build a miniature sheep shed had been a winner.

On the odd occasion when Jo did detect that Rosie longed for her father's undivided attention, she took herself off to draw, leaving the two of them together, sometimes for a whole day.

Rosie had always been completely restored when she'd returned.

The truth was, she mused, the little girl was twining herself more and more into her heartstrings, and there came, one day, a sign that the same was happening to Rosie—the day they ganged up on Gavin, as he put it.

It started over the orphan lamb. Rosie smuggled it into her bedroom, where it made a considerable mess in the traditional manner of infants, not to mention sheep.

Mrs Harper was so horrified that, despite being a fan of Rosie's, she made mention of the matter to the 'boss'.

The lamb was banished, Rosie was distraught and accused her father of being cruel and horrible. When the fact was pointed out to her that not even her puppy was allowed in the house, she stamped her foot and told Gavin that was cruel and horrible too, and now she really hated him!

Jo went quietly away at this stage and consulted Case. That afternoon a prefabricated enclosure and rather large kennel made its appearance in the garden below Rosie's bedroom.

Jo took both Gavin and Rosie to see it before din-

ner and she made the suggestion that the lamb and
the puppy, on the strict understanding that neither
could be let into the house, might cohabit happily in
the garden, close to Rosie's room.

Before Gavin had a chance to say yes or no, Rosie
flung her arms around Jo and told her, with real affection, she was the best mum a kid could have. Jo
hugged her back and discovered that to see Rosie re-
stored gave her a lovely warm feeling.

Gavin, observing all this, said at last, 'I see.'

'What do you see, Daddy?' Rosie trilled. 'Isn't it
a smashing idea?'

'I see that the two women in my life have ganged
up on me,' he said with unusual solemnity.

Rosie slipped her hand into Jo's. 'But we do love
you,' she assured him. 'Can I go and get them now?'

He nodded and his daughter raced off.

Gavin looked into Jo's eyes.

She grimaced. 'Sorry, but...' She shrugged.

He took her hand this time. 'It's going well?' he
suggested.

She relaxed. 'It's going well.'

He kissed her. 'You've been wonderful,' he said as
he drew away, 'but you do realize that either the
puppy is going to grow up thinking it's a sheep or
the lamb is going to grow up thinking it's a dog?'

Jo started to laugh.

A few days later, Rosie mentioned that she was looking forward to having babies.

Jo and Mrs Harper exchanged startled glances.

'I don't know about brothers,' Rosie continued.

'My friend Julia's little brother is terribly naughty but I wouldn't mind a sister.'

Both Jo and Mrs Harper hid relieved smiles.

Jo came back to the present and went on reviewing her day. Before she did anything else, she would have her weekly conference with Mrs Harper where they discussed what entertaining was upcoming, what needed to be ordered in and the like. Running such a large establishment was quite complex, Jo had discovered, and she would have been quite happy to leave it all to the super-efficient housekeeper had it not been for Adele.

She'd flown in not long after Jo, Rosie and Gavin had got back from the Gold Coast, when Gavin had to leave again to attend a board meeting in Sydney. And she'd been quite adamant that Jo should learn all the ins and outs of Kin Can from the lady-in-charge's perspective.

Of course the Hastings men liked to think they were the ultimate authority, she'd informed Jo, but much of the responsibility for the smooth running of the place would fall on her, she would find.

During the next few days Jo had had to agree with her and she'd come to admire Adele's touch with the families who lived on the station, the household staff and how she'd gone out of her way to make their lives on a vast sheep station, in the middle of nowhere virtually, as pleasant as possible.

She'd initiated a sewing circle, a book club and she'd started a video library. She suggested to Jo that she might like to give art classes. She'd made it quite clear that Kin Can was a show-piece of the wool industry and needed to be maintained as such for the buyers of wool and rams who came from all over the world to visit.

She'd also impressed upon Jo that even when your neighbours were as far-flung as they were in this part of the world, a sense of community was vital.

'So you see, my dear,' she finished, 'it's important for you to get involved and to put your own stamp on things.' A glint of humour lit her eyes. 'Not only for the good of the station, but you yourself. Otherwise there are times when a sheep station can drive you crazy.'

Jo laughed. 'So far I'm loving it. There's so much space and freedom.'

'Good,' Adele approved. 'Any time you need a helping hand, just give me a call.'

'How—' Jo hesitated '—are your marriage plans going? I was only thinking the other day that I felt a bit guilty about Gavin and I rather overshadowing everything else.'

Adele grimaced. 'I'm having second thoughts.'

'Because of what Gavin might have said to you about—' She broke off a little awkwardly.

'Gold-diggers? Fortune hunters? Lonely widows?' Adele heaved a sigh. 'It's awfully complicated when there's a lot of money involved,' she said sadly. 'But yes, he could be right. I may have got swept off my feet.'

Jo said nothing but pressed Adele's hand warmly. Yet her mother-in-law's sentiment brought back the subject of sons and heirs to her mind.

Not that Gavin had mentioned a family again, but those thoughts had stayed with her as she'd experimented with taking up the reins of being the mistress of Kin Can.

Nor had their physical need for each other diminished. If anything it had broadened as she got more and more involved in the life of the station and was able to share it with him.

But there was something she couldn't put her finger on at first. Something between her and Gavin brought her a fleeting sense of unease, and she found herself examining it again as she sipped her coffee that morning.

So far as hedging her bets went, she didn't think she was. Yes, she hadn't told him she loved him; yes, she still, for some reason she didn't quite understand herself, headed off any talk of her past. But she thought she matched him in bed and out of it.

Except for the odd occasion when she sensed a suppressed frustration about him that reminded her of their conversation over what Rosie should call her. Reminded her, come to that, of his mood the night she'd worn her hair up out to dinner.

The more she thought about it, the more she wondered if it had only been desire between them that had got out of hand. Or was there more to the unsmiling electricity they generated sometimes?

Then she started to wonder if there were ways she was not matching up to Sasha, ways she was unaware of?

Of course, they had been in love, Gavin and Sasha, but what more could he expect of her when he himself had made the comment that the less flamboyant emotions were the ones with better foundations?

They got along so well for the most part, until she

found that chasm opening up at her feet when she least expected it, as had happened to her recently.

A couple of weeks ago he'd flown her to Brisbane ostensibly because he'd had some business there. They'd dropped Rosie off with Adele and he'd checked them into a beautiful hotel on the Brisbane River. He'd told her that he would have to leave her alone for most of the day but she might appreciate the opportunity to shop or whatever. Then he'd requested a dinner date with her.

She'd agreed with suitable gravity and they'd parted, but she'd been filled with a sense of anticipation.

She hadn't shopped, she'd taken the opportunity to visit a new exhibition at the Queensland Art Gallery she'd been dying to see. Then, succumbing to an unusual whim, for her, she'd had a facial and got her hair done.

It had certainly made it even more pleasurable to don one of her trousseau dresses—a lovely cream linen shift—knowing she was also well groomed.

They had dined at a restaurant overlooking the river, and perhaps something in the way he'd been watching her had alerted her, so that she said suddenly, 'Oh no.'

He raised an eyebrow. They'd finished their main course and were deciding whether to have dessert or not. 'Something wrong?'

'Well—' she touched her newly washed and styled hair '—my hair is down, so it can't be that.'

He lay back in his chair looking impossibly attractive in a dark suit, a pale blue shirt and a navy tie.

'You're not going to ask me to get up and walk away from you?' she queried.

He sat up. 'I wish you hadn't said that.'

She stayed sober with an effort. 'Something tells me it might not be a good idea to have dessert, though.'

'Your instincts are impeccable, Jo.'

She could no longer hide a smile. 'I must be learning.'

It wasn't far from the restaurant to the hotel, and once in their room, he set about undressing her leisurely.

When there was nothing left to take off, he said quietly but with palpable restraint, 'Now you can walk away.'

Jo thought for a moment. Was this turning into another of those unsmiling encounters between them that disturbed her for all their electricity?

'I think I'd rather help you undress first,' she countered. 'We need some—equity, don't we?'

But was she asking a different question? she wondered. Or making a statement along the lines of—we need to be together in spirit, Gavin, not just physically.

'You always did have a mind of your own, Josie,' he said after a long pause.

'Mmm,' she agreed, and put her hands on his shirt buttons.

There was nothing leisurely about the way Gavin got undressed, and there was nothing leisurely about the way they made love. It was urgent and powerful and their climax was mind-blowing...

'You kill me, you know,' he said into her hair, when they were capable of talking again.

Jo moved cautiously in his arms. 'If it's any consolation I feel as if I've been dropped from a great height.'

He lifted his head and looked into her eyes, with his entirely wicked. 'But it was nice?'

'It was…' she sighed luxuriously '…fantastic.'

'When…?' He stopped and his eyes changed.

'When what?'

'No, nothing. Go to sleep, Lady Longlegs.'

'Gavin—' she hesitated '—tell me what's on your mind.'

'Not a lot.' He reached out and switched off the bedside lamp.

Jo opened her mouth to protest that she could sense a definite change in him, a withdrawal, and she needed to know why.

But it occurred to her suddenly that maybe he was remembering Sasha. Maybe they'd done unexpected little trips like this—perhaps they'd stayed in this very hotel, and it was his memories he was fighting.

If so, there was nothing she could do or say.

He stayed mentally withdrawn from her until they got back to Kin Can, then, as had happened before between them, they got back to normal.

But there was also the day she'd hosted her first dinner party. She flinched at the memory.

She'd invited three couples, all from the district, and it had been going really well until one of the men, under the influence of too much wine, had raised his glass to Gavin and complimented him on the fact that he sure knew how to pick his wives.

A horrified silence had greeted his words. The man's wife had looked as if a handy hole in the ground was her preferred option, and Gavin had shot him a murderous glance.

Somehow, Jo had found the composure to get the evening going again but not with the same level of enjoyment as before and she'd been sincerely relieved when it had been over.

'Remind me not to invite him again,' she murmured to Gavin as they waved their guests off for their long drives home.

'Why? He obviously approved of you.'

She blinked, then turned to him incredulously. 'If nothing else it was the height of tactlessness,' she objected.

He shrugged and turned away. 'I think I'll turn in.'

Jo stayed on the veranda for some time, trying to work out how she'd been made to feel as if she'd invited the comment. That's crazy, she told herself angrily. Or had one highly tactless comment brought Sasha back for Gavin? Sasha, presiding over dinner parties as only she could, perhaps?

Sasha, whose shadow I'm beginning to feel more and more, she thought. Nothing else seems to make sense. On the other hand, he *told* me in so many words he would always be holding another woman up to her memory, so why am I surprised and so hurt?

She went to bed, to find him fast asleep—the first time since their marriage he hadn't reached for her, even if only to hold her in his arms until they fell asleep.

She put her coffee-cup down now and sighed at

those difficult memories. Then she forced herself to contemplate the rest of her day.

Once her session with Rosie was over, she intended to sneak a few hours' drawing. She was building up a series of pictures of the station, and was seriously thinking of giving an exhibition. Adele, who seemed to know anyone who was anyone, had also got interested in the project.

But her afternoon session didn't happen. She ended up going to bed with a hot-water bottle.

She did eventually fall asleep, and although the worst was over when she woke up she felt drained and pale. Gavin was sitting on the side of the bed.

'That time of the month?' he queried, and put his hand over hers.

'Mmm.' But as she agreed she couldn't help wondering if it was a flash of disappointment she saw in his eyes.

'You stay there and relax. I'll bring some supper later.' He bent down and kissed her gently.

She drifted off to sleep again, convinced she'd imagined the disappointment. In fact, at that moment she felt cherished and as if she could forget all her previous concerns. That they were all right.

The next morning she was up and about and back to normal. But she was quite unprepared for the conversation she had with Gavin while they took a break for morning tea, or 'smoko' as everyone on the property called it.

They'd ridden their bikes to one of the lambing paddocks. Rosie had been flown to a neighbouring

property for a birthday party and was to stay overnight.

Jo had been delighted with the lambs, then she'd
spread a blanket under a tree and unpacked the basket
Mrs Harper had provided. There was tea in a Thermos
flask and some slices of rich, dark fruit cake bursting
with cherries.

'I could get fat on Mrs Harper's cooking,' she commented.

Gavin sprawled out across the rug as she poured
the tea into enamel mugs. 'You don't look fat to me.'

'Thank you, Mr Hastings. You should know,' she
teased.

He studied her comprehensively in jeans and a
checked blouse, then looked into her eyes. 'Are you
still happy with the way we "know" each other, Jo?'

She hesitated and frowned—another unsmiling moment coming up? 'The way we know each other is
fine with me,' she said carefully. 'How about you?'

'Ditto,' he said. 'Incidentally, is there anything you
can do for what you seem to go through every
month?'

Jo selected a piece of cake and handed him the
plate. 'Go on the pill or have a baby,' she said humorously.

'Does that mean you aren't on the pill?'

She set her mug down carefully on the lid of the
cake tin and waved away some flies. 'What made you
think I was?'

'It's been three months,' he pointed out.

Jo shook her head to clear her thoughts. 'And
you're worried I'm infertile after only three months?
Or secretly taking the pill?' she asked.

'You did say you didn't want to start a family immediately, Jo.'

It struck her that she hadn't imagined that look of disappointment in his eyes the previous evening, after all. And her fears, all her insecurities bubbled up again in a way that was suddenly impossible to resist.

'And you neglected to tell me, Gavin Hastings—' she got to her feet abruptly '—what this marriage really was about! A son to carry on your line.'

'Nonsense,' he replied roughly and stood up himself. 'What gave you that idea?' he added contemptuously.

'The idea came from several sources, actually. You've just confirmed it.' Her eyes flashed and she planted her hands on her hips, but inside she was feeling cold and incredibly hurt. Here I go again, she thought. Having my motivation mistrusted when— talk about motivation!—his has always been suspect.

'You did stipulate this was very much a marriage of convenience, Jo,' he pointed out lethally, as if reading her mind. 'Convenient in the sense that you can walk away from it whenever you feel like it? Is that what you meant?'

Her lips parted to deny it, but she changed her mind. 'I never intended it to become a child-bearing operation to save the Hastings dynasty.'

'So you aren't planning to have a family?' he shot back.

'Not to order, not like that, no! Incidentally, if I don't provide you with a son, Gavin, will I get my marching orders?'

He crossed the gap between them swiftly and grabbed her wrist in a bruising grasp. 'Stop it,' he ordered through his teeth. 'That has nothing to do with it as you damn well know!'

'No, I don't *know*. Let me go, you're hurting me,' she gasped.

He dropped her wrist, but his expression was still infuriated and menacing. 'Jo—'

She turned on her heel and ran to her bike, evidently taking him by surprise because she was able to switch it on and drive away from him before he could stop her.

And she drove with her hair streaming out behind her, a blur in front of her eyes as tears and a dreadful ache in her heart claimed her.

She just didn't see the kangaroo that bounded out from behind a clump of rocks until she hit it and cartwheeled over the handlebars.

The kangaroo picked itself up and bounded off. She lay unconscious on the ground.

'Gavin,' Tom Watson said, 'I think she's going to be all right. She's sprained an ankle, she has an impressive array of grazes, but I don't believe there are any internal injuries or skull fractures—a bloody miracle, actually. I'm going to fly her to Charleville for more tests all the same.'

'When do you expect her to regain consciousness?'

Tom regarded him for a moment. He'd known Gavin Hastings for a long time but he'd only ever seen him look like this once before, when his first wife had died. 'Hard to say. You better come with us.'

'Yes, you go, Gavin,' Mrs Harper said tearfully as

she bent over Jo's inert form on a stretcher, and patted her shoulder tenderly. 'I'll take care of Rosie when she comes back.'

'Where am I?'

Jo's lashes fluttered up and Gavin immediately pressed the bell beside her bed.

'You're in hospital, Jo, but you're going to be fine.' he said quietly, picking up her hand. 'You had an accident on a quad bike—do you remember?'

'No-o.'

Tom came into the room and drew up a chair beside the bed. And patiently and gently he asked her some questions. It took a while but they eventually established that she knew who she was, she knew who Gavin was—although that brought a frown to her eyes—and the only thing she didn't remember at all was the accident.

The effort of it all obviously exhausted her and she fell asleep.

Tom drew Gavin out of the room. 'That's quite common,' he said. 'Some people never remember the actual incident, but otherwise I'd say her memory hasn't been affected at all.'

He paused and searched Gavin's eyes for signs of relief. But his expression was as hard and shuttered as it had been all through the long day and half a night.

'Gavin? She's going to be all right, believe me, mate. Look, I know what this must be bringing back memories of, but—'

'The thing is,' Gavin broke in swiftly and harshly, 'do you know how I'm ever going to be able to forgive myself?' And he turned and strode away down the corridor.

Tom stared after him, then shook his head and went back to his patient.

A couple of days later, Jo felt a lot more coherent although, at the same time, as if she'd been under a steamroller, and she was still being treated for concussion.

Then Tom came to see her and, while he examined her, he took a light, playful approach.

'Don't know what it is with you two,' he said. 'If you're not getting yourself shot by kidnappers, you're getting knocked out by kangaroos!'

Jo smiled weakly, but after Tom's departure she found herself considering his words with a feeling of irony. What was it between them that had seen them end up in the same hospital, same private ward, at the beginning and quite possibly the end of their relationship?

Although she still didn't remember running into the kangaroo, the events that had led up to it had slowly filtered back.

So how ironic was it, she reflected, that from this very bed Gavin became possessed of the impulse to marry her, and her alone? How—fateful—that she should be in it, not really broken in body but certainly in spirit, because there'd been times when she'd thought—what? That she was winning his love and he hadn't married her only for Rosie and sons to carry on the line?

Five days after the accident, Jo was dressed and ready to leave hospital.

She still felt, although it was lessening, as if she'd

been under a steamroller. She still had bruises and grazes, but her ankle had responded well and she could put her weight on it. Otherwise she was fine.

She grimaced at the thought. She certainly wasn't fine mentally.

Gavin had spent quite a bit of time with her, but had said nothing about the argument that had led to the accident. He'd been gentle and determinedly cheerful. At first, while she'd felt so sick and sore, she'd been grateful, but today she felt different. In about half an hour, he was coming to fly her back to Kin Can. So they could formally dissolve their marriage? she wondered.

Was that what she wanted? What were her options? To continue in the knowledge that her principal role in his life was as the mother of his children? No...but...

She gazed out of the window. It had rained almost the entire time she'd been in hospital and was still raining.

Gavin stood at the door of Jo's private ward and watched her narrowly without her being aware of it.

Her lovely hair was tied back in a pony-tail and the lines of her figure beneath a black T-shirt and loose grey cotton trousers were tense and upright as she sat on the side of the bed half turned towards the window.

What was she thinking? he wondered. Was she still as angry with him as she'd been five days ago? Was she contemplating leaving him?

She was pale, he realized, from the one cheek he

could see, and there was still a bruise on it. Her hands were gripped in her lap as if she was in pain. He closed his eyes briefly and cursed himself yet again.

Then he took hold. 'Jo?'

She swung round convulsively, her eyes widening. 'I…I didn't hear you,' she stammered.

'I haven't been here long. How do you feel?'

'Fine! Fine.' She gazed at him with, he got the odd feeling, expectation.

'Shall we go, then? I've had a slight change—'

'Gavin, we need to talk! I need to know where we stand.'

'This isn't,' he said quietly, 'the time or the place. Anyway, you can't be all that fine yet and it's best that we just take things slowly for a time.' He glanced out of the window and grimaced.

'I'm perfectly able to talk,' she said tautly. 'I—I'm not a porcelain doll, but that's what you're making me feel like!'

'Jo, we could have a slightly difficult trip ahead of us so let's talk when we get home.' He picked up her bag.

She stared at the angles and lines of his face and his shuttered expression, and trembled inwardly. How could they have come to this? He might make her feel like a porcelain doll, but she knew she was banging her head against a brick wall at the moment.

CHAPTER ELEVEN

IT WAS one of the station Range Rovers Gavin led Jo to, and he said, 'Sorry about this, but we're driving.'

She looked surprised.

'Things have got tricky overnight. There's been a lot of flooding and the plane was seconded to fly a pregnant woman to Brisbane. Nor is there one damn chopper in the district that isn't on search and rescue missions. But I've put an extra sheepskin over the seat to make it more comfortable.'

'Thanks.' Jo climbed in. 'How are things out at Kin Can?' she added as he got into the driver's seat.

He switched on and drove out of the hospital car park. 'Wet. We've still got access in and out but we're having to move sheep up to higher ground.'

'That bad?'

'Uh-huh.' He flicked on the radio. 'I was tempted to leave you in hospital for a day or so but they need all the beds they can get. There've been some real emergencies with the floods.'

'I didn't realize it was so bad,' she said with a tinge of guilt.

He flicked her a glance. 'No. Well, you did have other things on your mind.'

Jo gazed at her hands. 'Gavin—'

But he stilled her with an upraised hand, then pointed to the radio.

It was a road and weather report being broadcast,

and he swore fluently. 'The main road is cut. We'll have to go the long way round.'

'Perhaps we should go back to Charleville?'

He grimaced. 'There's not a spare bed for love nor money in Charleville and the Warrego is rising fast so Charleville may not be so safe itself. Don't worry, I'll get you through.'

It was six horses stranded in a flooded paddock that caused their downfall.

Jo noticed them first. 'We can't just leave them,' she said.

He hesitated, glancing at her stricken expression. 'No.' He pulled the Range Rover up beside a huge gum tree. 'I'll have to open up the fence. Stay where you are,' he ordered.

But without wire-cutters it was easier said than done to open up the barbed-wire fence so the horses could reach the relative safety of the higher ground beside the road. And Jo couldn't believe how swiftly the water was rising.

In the end she ignored his order and got out to help him. It was pouring now out of a low, sullen, steel-grey sky as he used the tools from the Range Rover's toolbox to unwind the wire from a corner post.

'They shouldn't have horses in barbed-wire pad-docks in the first place,' he said bitterly at one stage.

'Here.' She'd gone to the vehicle and brought back some of her clothes to wrap around his hands that were scratched and bleeding.

'Thanks. Nearly done.'

'Where will they go, though?' she questioned anxiously.

'Back down the road if they've got any sense—and

they do have great survival instincts when they're not fenced in, plus they're strong swimmers,' he said, breathing heavily. 'Can't believe I'm sweating when I'm so damn wet. There.' He unwrapped the last strand and the fence was open.

In a flurry of hooves and flying manes and tails, the horses galloped out of the paddock, and as he'd predicted, took the road back to Charleville.

'Thanks, it was nice of you to help us but got to go!' he said with some irony and Jo grinned.

But he sobered rapidly as they got back into the car. Water was already lapping the side of the road. 'That little "good Samaritan" act may have cost us, Jo. Let's get the latest info.'

It wasn't good. The flood waters in their immediate vicinity were rising rapidly, both in front of them and behind them.

He switched off the car radio and clenched his fists. 'I must be out of my mind. We won't get through now.'

'You couldn't have just let them drown,' she said shakily.

'It might come down to them or us. Listen, I'm going to check in on the CB radio, and then I'm going to investigate that tree.'

He used the CB radio, talking tersely into it and getting patched through to the SES, State Emergency Services, and one of their helicopters, giving them their position and their situation. Then he moved the Range Rover into position right beside the tree.

'Oh, good heavens!' Jo breathed as she stared out of the window. There was a wall of brown frothy water crossing the paddock towards them.

'Just do exactly as I say, Jo,' he commanded. 'I'll help you up onto the roof.'

If that was a painful experience for her, what was to follow was worse. Gavin managed to throw a tow rope over the lowest branch of the tree and he climbed the tree like a big cat.

'It's quite solid, quite safe, Jo,' he called down to her as he tied the rope onto the branch, then lowered one end down to her with a loop on it. 'Now put the loop over you and around your waist, and I want you to come up exactly as I did.'

'But it's so smooth, I don't think I can!'

'Use all the little knobs and knots you can find for your feet. Don't worry if you slip, I've got you and I can help hoist you as well.'

She hesitated, but the water was up lapping against the car doors now. She put her hands on the tree and felt the rope tighten around her waist. And slowly, agonizingly slowly, somehow she began to inch her way up it.

He talked to her all the time, but as she was just out of reach, with her lungs bursting, she froze and knew she could go no further.

'Jo, grab my hand!'

She looked up to see him lying along the branch with his hand held down to her.

'I can't,' she gasped, clinging to the tree trunk. 'I can't reach.'

'Yes, you can. Jo, I *love* you. I've loved you since that very first day.'

'*What?*'

'I wasn't going to tell you until later, when we got home, but it's true. Just another few inches, Jo.'

'But you've been so...so...'

'I told you I was a bad loser!'

'I know you can't forget her, Gavin—'

'It's you I'm petrified of losing. Please, my darling, just a few more inches. We can do it!'

She did it. She never knew how she achieved it physically, except to know that without his strength and his SAS expertise she wouldn't have made it. But, perhaps, what he'd said had been the most powerful impetus of all, and just as the Range Rover started to float away she was huddled into the crook of the tree, breathing like a train, and he was sitting astride the branch in front of her.

'What did you say?' she panted.

He touched her face. 'I love you, sweetheart. I've been going quietly insane for the last three months wondering when, if ever, you were going to fall in love with me.'

Her lips parted, but before she could say a word they heard a helicopter approaching.

He squinted upwards and then down at the rising flood. 'Thank God—and I mean that. This time you'll have a winch to pull you up, and I'll be with you.'

'Never seen the like of it,' the pilot of the State Emergency Services helicopter yelled over the roar of the rotors. 'If it's any consolation, Gavin, both Charleville and Cunnamulla are on high alert now.'

'How about Kin Can?'

'The news isn't good, I'm afraid.'

'Rosie,' Jo murmured urgently.

'She's in Brisbane.' He held her against him.

'Where are we going?' he asked the pilot.

'Roma. Still dry there, although the Mitchell is rising too. But I'm afraid that's as far as I can take you. I need to refuel and get out again—there are dozens of emergencies.'

'Can you take me out to Kin Can?' Gavin shouted.

'Sure, mate, but it's going to be a fast turnaround!'

'Jo,' Gavin said into her ear, 'I'm going to send you down to the Coast from Roma. I need to get back to Kin Can—can you understand?'

'Of course. But be careful. I just couldn't believe how quickly that all happened!' she said dazedly.

'I know—these things have to be seen to be believed—but I will be careful. You too. I can't imagine how you must feel now on top of all your other sore spots.'

'I think I'll be OK.' She nestled into him, then looked into his eyes with a smile in hers. 'You know, I led a very dull but *safe* life until I met you!'

He kissed the tip of her nose and laughed as he marvelled, 'Kidnappers, boats exploding, floods, helicopter rescues—maybe something about our meeting caused the planets to go on a collision course?'

She laughed back, nestled against him again and they didn't talk any more; it was too exhausting making themselves heard.

She had four days in the house on the river before he came back to her.

Thanks to all the confusion due to the floods, Roma's airport had been no place for any further explanations as he'd gone about organizing a flight for her. But he'd cupped her face just before he'd left and said very quietly, 'Tell me you understand?'

'I do.'

'That's my Josie.' He kissed her, then let her go.

Adele had met her in Brisbane and driven her down to the Coast, where there'd been a doctor waiting to examine her, despite her protestations that she was fine.

'Well, you are, Mrs Hastings,' he said finally, 'apart from some new bruises, grazes and strained muscles. I'd take it very easy for a while. You did have concussion, then having to climb a tree to escape a flash-flood—' He shook his head. 'I'm going to leave you a couple of mild sleeping pills.'

Adele took a long look at Jo when the doctor departed, then insisted she do just that. Go to bed and take a sleeping pill.

'I...' Jo started to say, but the truth was she was mentally reeling from all the events of the day, and one event particularly.

'I'll be here,' Adele continued. 'But have a bath first to help wash away any stiffness. Have a spa! Everyone tried to tell me I was insane over that bath but I knew it would come in handy one day!'

Jo opened her mouth to tell her mother-in-law that the spa had already performed one good deed for her, then she decided against it.

And it did help, so did the sleeping pill, although she woke very early and lay very still as she pictured Kin Can under water—and the miracle and mystery of what Gavin had said.

Did I imagine it? she wondered. Was I hallucinating from sheer strain? Did he say it only to get me to make that vital extra effort? Why can't I altogether believe it?

She stared at the light rimming the curtains as the sun rose and found herself recalling their angry conversation before she'd crashed the quad bike. She remembered how everything had added up to one thing—sons.

She remembered his determination not to talk about their marriage when he'd picked her up from the hospital, and how, so suddenly, that had changed...

She did rest for most of that day, as muscles she hadn't known existed protested at any unwise movement.

Adele insisted on staying with her, saying that Rosie was fine with Sharon and she loved her cousins' company.

But the following day, when Jo was feeling better, she suggested that Adele needn't stay on with her.

They'd just received the news that everyone left on Kin Can was fine except for a lot of it being waterlogged.

'These things happen,' Adele said philosophically. 'Charleville all but disappeared in the last big flood. It's not only the rain in the area, it's the result of monsoon rains in the north. But life in outback Australia was never meant to be easy with its cycles of drought and flood. Uh—no, dear, I'm not going to leave you until Gavin gets back.'

'I'll be fine—' Jo stopped rather abruptly and narrowed her eyes. 'Is this what I think it is?'

Adele grimaced. 'Probably. I've had strict orders to stay with you until he gets here.'

'That's...' Jo breathed rapidly.

'Typical Gavin,' his mother agreed. 'I've also been told to keep Sharon away. Apparently she rather thoughtlessly caused some mayhem between you and Gavin?'

Jo subsided but said nothing.

'On the other hand,' Adele continued after a long moment, 'after what you've been through, Jo, I wouldn't feel good about you being here, or anywhere, on your own. So you're just going to have to make the best of me!'

'It's not that,' Jo protested. 'I thought I might be taking you away from—whatever.'

'Well, you're not,' Adele said comfortably. 'And I have some good news.'

Jo frowned.

'I got a phone call from a friend of mine this morning. She runs an art gallery of some repute. She'd be very interested in holding an exhibition of your work.'

Jo gasped. Then her eyes softened. 'One thing I do know—I couldn't have a better mother-in-law!'

Adele looked set to take issue with the statement, but in the end she held her peace, and said only, 'One thing I *promise*, as soon as Gavin arrives, I'll disappear.'

He came two days later.

It was early evening and Adele had ordered a light, informal meal that they would eat early so Sophie could get away.

It was set out on a table in the terrace room, with a bottle of wine. There were open smoked-salmon sandwiches and tiny quiches; two individual sashimi platters decorated with carrot and onion pickles in a soy and ginger sauce; a heaped bowl of fresh, peeled prawns and Sophie's famous, secret-recipe seafood sauce. There were home-made rolls and, for starters, two lidded bowls of asparagus soup.

Jo, who had several grazed patches of skin on her body that were still healing, had changed into something light and cool—a pair of Miss Saigon wrap-style pyjamas in a dusky pink with plum-coloured blossom embroidery.

She'd just lifted the lid off her soup bowl and was inhaling the lovely aroma, when he walked through to the terrace, taking both Jo and Adele by surprise. They hadn't had any messages from him since the day before.

'Well, what a lovely surprise!' Adele rose. 'I take it things must have improved out west?'

'Yes. It's peaked and subsiding rapidly now. Hi, Jo.'

'Hello!' She put down her linen napkin and stood up herself, and it occurred to her she was drinking his presence in through her pores. She certainly couldn't think of anything else to say.

There was also quite a bit about him to remind her of his bushranger image. His jaw was blue with stubble, his khaki shirt was torn at one elbow, his jeans were stained and his boots were caked with dried mud.

'What's the damage?' Adele asked.

'The only place to escape flooding was the homestead—' he smiled as his mother heaved a sigh of relief '—but the stock losses were more than I'd hoped for. Still, we did the best we could.'

His gaze returned to Jo, standing beside the table like a frozen statue. Then he looked down at himself ruefully. 'I think I ought to take a shower. I could even smell! This seat on a plane came up unexpectedly so I grabbed it. Will you excuse me for a few minutes?'

'Of course,' she said, coming to life at last. 'We'll organize some more food in the meantime.'

'No need for that, Jo!' Adele objected. 'I'm heading off right now—'

'But you haven't had a bite and—'

'Sharon can feed me,' Adele said blithely. 'And as you know I don't have to pack. All I need is my book, my purse and my car keys.'

This was true. Adele kept three complete sets of clothes and cosmetics. One at Kin Can, one on the Coast and one at her home in Brisbane. She'd also advised Jo to do the same—one of the practices of the rich Jo had found amusing at first, until she'd discovered it saved an awful lot of time and preparation.

'Well—'

'Now, you take care of yourself, my dear!' Adele came over and kissed her warmly. 'You too, mate!' She saluted her son, and was gone.

Leaving Jo and Gavin staring at each other with Jo, unknowingly, reflecting all her fears and uncertainties in her eyes.

He moved abruptly, then looked down at his grimy hands. 'Give me five,' he murmured and turned away.

Jo sat down again, and covered her soup. The sun

had set and there was just a lingering soft gold light over the river and the mangroves. But for once in her life, she didn't respond mentally to the colours and shapes before her eyes as she wondered what was to come. For, with each succeeding day away from him, her awful fear that there was some catch to what he'd said had grown.

'Jo?'

She turned to see him standing beside the table in clean khaki shorts. His hair was wet, his beard was still in place and he was pulling down a yellow T-shirt. If he smelt of anything it was soap and clean clothes.

'Uh—that was quick.'

'Mmm,' he agreed and fingered his jaw. 'Sorry about this but I get the feeling I've been away for far too long as it is.'

He picked up the wine and poured two glasses. 'You look as if you could do with it.'

'Thank you.' She accepted the glass and their fingers touched briefly.

He sat down and raked his hand through his hair, scattering droplets. 'What's the problem, Jo?'

She opened and closed her mouth several times, then, 'I...when I thought about it, it didn't seem to make sense.'

'I never—' he captured her gaze '—gave sons a second thought when I asked you to marry me.'

She blinked incredulously. 'You said...I can't help knowing that starting a family is a primary concern of yours,' she stammered.

'Because of some guff Sharon spouted about dynasties? If you're wondering, I got that bit of information out of my mother.'

'It didn't help,' she conceded, and took a sip of wine. 'But it wasn't only Sharon. You yourself led me to believe it.'

'Yes, it was a primary concern,' he agreed. 'But it had nothing to do with sons or dynasties. It seemed to me to be the one way I'd get to keep you.'

Her lips parted. 'You didn't think—I don't understand.'

'I didn't either.' He paused and grimaced. 'I guess it didn't seem possible for me to have fallen madly in love in a matter of hours. Of course I'd also sworn off "deeply, wildly, madly" but not, I now know, for the reasons I told you when we were handcuffed together.'

'No?' Her voice was threadbare as different emotions claimed her. Seeds of hope?

'No. Because what Sasha did for me wasn't to ruin me for any other woman, as I thought. She taught me what the real thing was, and it was a wonderful legacy she gave me. I was just too blind and stupid to see it. But what she did leave me with—was a deep fear that I could lose someone I loved, as I lost her.

'As the months passed,' he went on, 'it all became clear to me—from my point of view anyway. But you—' he smiled, although with no amusement '—stayed the same lovely enigma you'd always been.'

She closed her eyes briefly.

'And I couldn't help wondering if, when our marriage was no longer convenient, you would simply move on. That's why I wanted to start a family, so you wouldn't be able to.'

They stared at each other.

'That's why,' he added quietly, 'I could never tell you how I felt—until I was afraid I was going to lose you to a flood. I couldn't bear the thought of hearing you say it hadn't happened for you.'

'So—' she cleared her throat '—you hedged your bets by not letting me know how you felt?'

'Yes. I'm sorry.'

'So did I.'

There was a little silence as he regarded his glass, then looked across at her with a frown. 'What do you mean?'

'I mean that I fell in love with you when you first asked me to marry you—and then you passed out cold. It just—' she moistened her lips '—it just came like that.'

He stared at her incredulously.

'To be honest,' she said with a shaky little smile, 'I didn't ever think I was hiding it that well.'

'Jo,' he said hoarsely, 'why hide it anyway?'

'It was such a miracle for me, I couldn't bear to think it was so...so one-sided. And I reasoned that if you didn't know how I felt it would be—I don't know—like a form of self-protection.'

'I guess I can understand that all too well,' he replied slowly and with a trace of grimness. 'But why was it such a miracle?'

She sighed suddenly. 'I lost everyone I'd *ever* loved, my parents, my grandmother. My father's mother, who looked for me nearly all my life then died before I was found. It makes you scared—'

'I know that, sweetheart,' he interrupted, 'from my own experience. And you have no idea how often I told myself not to forget *why* you might be such a dedicated loner. It was getting harder to convince myself, though.'

'There was another reason. I swore once never to depend on anyone, and it's the real reason, I guess, why I didn't think I would ever fall in love.'

She took another sip of wine, then told him factually and unemotionally about what had happened to her at fifteen.

'Oh, Jo,' he said softly and with such a wealth of understanding and concern as he covered her hand with his, sudden tears beaded her lashes.

'The thing is,' she said, 'you swept all that away almost as if it had never existed.'

'I did?'

She nodded.

'Almost?' His fingers tightened on hers.

'It came back to hit me when you told me you thought I might be secretly on the pill. Not the revulsion, but the memory of not being *believed* in. That's why I got so angry and felt so hurt. That's why I did something so stupid like running into a kangaroo.'

He got up and came round to draw her to her feet. 'I *love* you, Jo Lucas,' he said intently. 'Deeply, wildly and madly. Will you marry me?'

Her grey eyes widened. 'We are married.'

'Properly. With our hearts as well as our bodies. No more secrets, no more uncertainty—you do realize I'm a nervous wreck?'

Her gorgeous mouth dimpled at the corners, then

curved into a smile. 'Yes, Gavin. I would love to marry you properly.'

'Heaven help me,' he said huskily, staring at her mouth, 'I'll never get enough of you, Jo.'

'I think the same could be said of me!'

Later, he untied the sash of her pyjama top and told her she was extremely well dressed for what he had in mind.

She lay in his arms and chuckled. 'Just be careful of all the grazes and bruises.'

He lifted his head from her breasts. 'Damn, I'd forgotten!'

'Perhaps we could work out a plan whereby they might be avoided?' she suggested.

'A plan?' He scratched his head. 'How?'

'You're the ex-SAS person in the family, and pretty good at that,' she reminded him gravely. 'You've saved my life twice now.'

He grinned, then sobered. 'Would this fall into that category, by any chance?'

'Definitely. How about you?' she teased.

'If only you knew. Uh—well, a full inspection is certainly called for. That's basic SAS training, incidentally. Assess the situation thoroughly.'

'Oh, I'm all in favour of basic SAS training,' she said with a dreamy little smile. 'When do you plan to begin the assessment?'

'I could kiss you again first,' he offered, but they were both laughing and they came together in love and a mental unity that was breathtaking.

Several days later when they were back on Kin Can, Jo showed Gavin his portrait for the first time, his second portrait.

He stared at it. 'But this—this is different.'

'I know. This is the one I've worked on ever since you asked me to marry you, the first time.'

He studied it soberly. The inside of the old boundary hut was almost alive with the glow of firelight, and he was seated at the table, with a gun in his hands and naked to the waist.

'Jo—why?' he queried.

'I told you once, bone structure, muscles—all that is grist to my mill and you're a particularly fine specimen.'

'Is that all?'

'Well, no,' she conceded gravely. 'I wanted a reminder of my very own bushranger.'

He lifted an eyebrow. 'Even one who accused you of being a gangster's moll?'

She nodded.

'Do you plan to exhibit this?'

'Oh, no. Mind you, that's a pity. Even if I say so myself, it's some of my best work.'

'What do you plan to do with it?'

'Hang it up in our bedroom so even when you're away from me I can fantasize about you.'

He took a sudden breath. 'Do you have any idea what that will do to me?'

'Bring you home to me PDQ?' she suggested.

He put the picture down carefully and shook his head. 'You may find you have to prise me away with a crowbar, my lovely Jo.'

'Even better.' She moved into his arms. 'You haven't told me what you think of it.'

He looked across at the portrait. 'Well, I'm actually extremely taken with it.'

'Think you come across as a good-looking guy, or artistically?'

He wrapped his hands around her hips. 'Both.'

'You don't have to humour me.'

'Then—' his eyes softened '—artistically, it's so— I don't know how to put it into words—but it took me right back to the old hut. I could smell the wood smoke for a moment.'

She smiled. 'Thanks.'

'On the other hand, I don't know about the good-looking guy bit, but so long as I'm the guy you fantasize about—I really, truly, madly, deeply—appreciate that.'

Deep satisfaction filled Jo and she raised her mouth for his kiss.

THE CHILDREN'S DOCTOR'S SPECIAL PROPOSAL

KATE HARDY

Kate Hardy always loved books and could read before she went to school. She discovered Mills & Boon books when she was twelve and decided this was what she wanted to do. When she isn't writing Kate enjoys reading, cinema, ballroom dancing and the gym. You can contact her via her website: www.katehardy.com.

For Lee and Lucy,
with love

CHAPTER ONE

'WELCOME back.' Lynne greeted Katrina with a broad smile. 'So how was Italy?'

'Fabulous. Italy in late September is just perfect. It's my new favourite place in the world,' Katrina said. 'Pompeii was stunning. And the Blue Grotto. And…' She laughed. 'That isn't what you really want to know, is it? Yes, I brought Italian biscuits back for the ward. Seriously nice ones.' She dangled a carrier bag in front of the charge nurse. 'A big tin of them.'

'Good girl.' Lynne patted her on the back. 'Just what we all wanted to hear. Though I'm glad you had a good time on holiday.'

'How's Sadie doing?' Katrina asked, walking with Lynne to the kitchen and placing the biscuit tin on the worktop along with a note saying, *Help yourself, with love from Kat.*

'Fine. Though she's been missing your stories and wants to know when Doc-a-rina's coming back.'

'Oh, bless.' Sadie, a two-year-old with a clicky hip that had been reset by the orthopaedic surgeon, was one of Katrina's favourites; even though lying on a cot in traction must have been uncomfortable for the little girl, she never once complained and always had a huge smile for the medical staff. 'I'll go and see her in a minute before I start the ward rounds.'

Katrina switched on the kettle, then she slapped a hand to her forehead. 'I almost forgot. The new consultant.' He'd started the day after she'd gone on holiday, and she'd been off duty the day he'd come for his interview and a look round the ward, so she hadn't yet met him. 'What's he like?'

Lynne nodded with obvious approval. 'Gorgeous. And as soon as you hear that voice you just want it to start whispering sweet nothings to you.'

'Except he's unavailable because, like you, he was snapped up as a teenager?' Katrina teased.

'Nobody has a clue, but I'd say probably not. He's excellent with the children, he's polite and pleasant to the parents and the staff, but as for what makes him tick…' Lynne shook her head ruefully. 'Your guess is as good as mine. He's refused every single invite to a team night out so far—politely, but very definitely.'

Katrina frowned. Most new consultants would accept every invitation going in the first couple of weeks, to help them get to know the team outside work and bond with them. 'He's not one of those who spend the bare minimum of time here and as much as possible in private practice, is he?' she asked.

Lynne shook her head. 'Far from it. He puts in the hours. He stays late—and if he does leave early, he'll either ring in or come back to chase up some results.'

A workaholic, then, Katrina thought. Just as long as he didn't expect everyone else to follow his lead—it wouldn't be fair on colleagues who happened to have young families. 'What's he like to work with?' she asked.

'Quick, intuitive and—well, you're about to find out for yourself. He's just walked in.' Lynne glanced towards the door. 'Morning, Dr Morgan.'

'Rhys,' the doctor corrected with a smile.

And what a smile.

Lynne was right, Katrina thought. Rhys Morgan was absolutely gorgeous. Tall, with dark hair and fair skin and blue, blue eyes—pure Celtic colouring. And with a name like Rhys Morgan, she would've been very surprised had his voice not had that faint Welsh lilt.

That incredibly *sexy* Welsh lilt.

And an incredibly sensual mouth.

She pushed the thought away. Rhys Morgan was her new colleague, and she didn't date colleagues. Not since Pete. She didn't make the same mistake twice.

'Good morning, Lynne,' he said.

'Rhys, this is Katrina Gregory, our senior house officer.' Lynne introduced them swiftly. 'Kat, this is Rhys Morgan, our new consultant.'

'Hello, Rhys. Good to meet you,' Katrina said, and stretched out her hand.

When he took it, she was surprised by the jolt of awareness that shot through her. One that was clearly mutual and just as surprising for him, judging by the way his eyes widened very slightly. But then he seemed to regain his control and gave her a polite smile, releasing her hand. 'Hello, Katrina.'

'The kettle's about to boil and our rounds don't start for another ten minutes. Coffee?' Katrina asked.

'Thanks. Black, no sugar, please.'

She spooned instant coffee into three mugs, adding sugar to Lynne's and milk to her own before pouring on boiling water and handing the first mug to Rhys. 'Help yourself to biscuits while you still get a chance. As soon as Lynne spreads the word, they'll be gone.' She glanced at her watch. 'And if you'll excuse me, I want to pop in and see Sadie before we start, to let her know I'm back.'

'Sadie? The little girl with the clicky hip?' he asked.

Katrina nodded. 'Lynne tells me she's been missing my stories.'

He looked slightly disapproving. 'As a doctor, you need to keep a certain amount of distance. Don't get too emotionally involved with your patients.'

'I hardly think telling a story to a little girl who's bed-bound is getting emotionally involved.' And just who did Rhys Morgan think he was, telling her what to do? He may be the new consultant and, strictly speaking, her senior, but that didn't mean he could tell her how to do her job. In her experience, taking a little extra time with their patients often did wonders—it helped them to settle, and she believed that anything that made the hospital a less scary experience for them was a good thing. 'I enjoy my job, and I'm not going to apologise for taking five minutes of my own time to make a child's day that little bit brighter. Excuse me,' she said coolly. 'I'll be back in time for ward rounds.'

When Katrina walked into the cubicle, Sadie's delighted smile took away that rattled feeling she'd had since meeting Rhys Morgan. 'Doc-a-rina!'

'Miss me, poppet?' Katrina sat on the chair beside her, and ruffled her hair. 'What a lovely welcome-back smile.'

'Story?' Sadie begged.

'Later today. After you've had your lunch and I'm on my break,' Katrina promised. 'Hello, Jo,' she said, turning to Sadie's mother. 'I'll be doing the ward rounds in a few minutes, but I wanted to pop in and see you first. How's it going?'

'Dr Morgan says she's doing really well. Hopefully we can go home at the end of the week—not that it's horrible here,' Jo hastened to add.

'But there's no place like home,' Katrina finished, understanding just what Jo meant.

'Good holiday?' Jo asked.

'Brilliant, thanks. I must be three inches shorter after all that walking, but it was worth it.'

Jo laughed. 'If I'd known you wanted to be three inches shorter…'

'Sorry. My cousin Maddie has first dibs on my spare height,' Katrina teased back. 'I'll see you later. And my story for you today, Miss Sadie,' she added, smiling at the little girl, 'is all about a princess. Because when I was away I actually saw a magic cave—the one where a princess met the prince from under the sea.'

'Mermaid,' Sadie said happily.

'Something like that,' Katrina said. 'See you soon.'

When Katrina joined Rhys for the ward rounds, she discovered that he was exactly as Lynne had described. Pleasant to the children, polite to their parents and patient enough to answer every single question and explain in more detail when it was needed. Professionally, she couldn't fault him. And yet there was a reserve about him. Some kind of invisible wall. Like Lynne, Katrina couldn't quite work out what made him tick.

She put it out of her mind so she could concentrate on her patients in the children's assessment clinic for the rest of the morning, and then caught up with her cousin over lunch.

'Welcome home, hon.' Madison hugged her. 'You look fabulous. Though I still think you were mad, going on a walking tour of the Amalfi coast.'

'I saw a lot more than I would've done if I'd been stuck on a beach,' Katrina pointed out.

'So did you meet a gorgeous Italian prince while you were away?'

Madison really was incorrigible, Katrina thought. 'No, but I'm making up a story for Sadie. About the prince from under the sea.' She laughed. 'Right up your street. Or it would have been, had you not met Theo.' She paused. Madison had her finger on the pulse. She might know more about Rhys Morgan. 'Have you met our new consultant yet?' she asked, trying her best to sound casual.

'Rhys Morgan?' Madison nodded. 'I called him into Theatre last week during a difficult birth—and the baby was absolutely fine, before you ask. He's a nice guy. Knows his stuff but doesn't throw his weight around.'

Oh, doesn't he? Katrina thought, remembering what he'd said about Sadie.

Madison's eyes sparkled. 'Since you're asking about him, Kat, does that mean you're—?'

'No, it doesn't,' Katrina interrupted, guessing what her cousin was about to ask. Since she'd found happiness with Theo, Madison had been trying to find the same for her cousin, and the matchmaking was driving Katrina crazy. 'He's nice enough, as you say—a good doctor—but he's a bit reserved. And he told me off this morning for getting too emotionally involved with my patients.'

'He has a point, hon. You *do* get too close to your patients,' Madison said gently.

Katrina rolled her eyes. 'I love my job. I love the ward. And, actually, telling stories to the kids is good for *me*. It's the best stress-reliever I know, going off into a world of make-believe and seeing all these little faces smiling back at me.'

'But you still worry about them when you get home. You never quite switch off.'

'It goes with the territory.' Katrina glanced at her watch. 'I'd better get back. I promised Sadie a story over lunch, and I don't want to upset the new consultant by being late for ward rounds this afternoon.'

'Sounds to me as if you just got off on the wrong foot with each other. Give the guy a chance. He's OK.' Madison paused, looking concerned. 'Not all men are like Pete, you know.'

'I know that.' Katrina rolled her eyes. 'But not all men are potential partners, either. I'm happy to keep men as friends and colleagues.'

'Hmm. When you find the right one, you'll change your mind.'

Katrina ruffled her cousin's hair. 'I know you've found Mr Right, but it doesn't happen for everyone. Anyway, I like my life as it is. I love my job, I have good friends, and I have the best family in the world. Not to mention the fact I'm going to be an auntie and godmother to the most gorgeous little girl in about four months' time.' Madison's amniocentesis results had come through just before Katrina had left for Italy; to everyone's huge relief, all was well. 'I don't need anyone, Maddie. I'm happy as I am.'

'If you say so,' Madison said.

'I do.' And the fact that she couldn't get Rhys Morgan's incredibly blue eyes out of her head, the fact that they reminded her of the colour of the sea on the Amalfi coast—well, that was just post-holiday silliness, Katrina told herself sternly. 'I'll see you later.'

She had enough time to tell Sadie a story about the princess and the merman meeting in the magic grotto, and then it was time to face Rhys again.

'I see you admitted a couple of patients from the assessment clinic this morning,' Rhys said.

He'd been in a different clinic that morning—so when had he had time to check what she'd been doing? Or maybe he'd just caught sight of the ward's whiteboard where they listed the patients and their named nurses and he wanted a quick rundown on what she'd done before they did the ward round. Fair enough. She didn't have any doubts about her clinical judgement.

'There's Jennie Myerson—the GP sent her in because her face was swollen, her blood pressure and temperature were up, she said her joints hurt, and there was blood in her urine,' she explained. 'She's not on medication for anything, so it's not an allergic reaction, but apparently she did have a sore throat a couple of weeks ago. So I wonder if it's a staph infection causing interstitial nephritis.'

'You've given her something for the blood pressure and paracetamol to deal with the pain and get her temperature down,' he said, reading swiftly through the notes.

'I also took bloods and I asked if her urine output could be measured. Are the results back from the lab yet?'

'Not according to these notes.'

'Then I'll chase them after the ward round. But if I'm right and her ESR and urea are up, I'd like to do a renal ultrasound.'

'I think you're going to be right,' he said, surprising her. 'Her urine output's way below what it should be. Did you ask if she's allergic to penicillin?'

'Yes, and there's no family history, so they don't think so.'

'Good. You talk to the lab while I sort the ultrasound on her kidney. If the blood results are what you think they'll be, we'll start her on penicillin. This sort of condition can make a little one feel really rough.'

He went through the other patients on their list equally thoroughly, taking account of what Katrina said and also of the observations recorded by the nurses. Definitely a team player, Katrina thought. Someone who listened to others. Which was a good thing, as far as the ward was concerned.

So why was there still that wall between them?

Because, although Rhys was great to work with—intuitive,

quick to sum up what was going on, understanding how their
patients felt and calming the parents' worries as they went
from bed to bed—she was aware of a definite barrier between
them. He barely even made eye contact with her.

Had it not been for Lynne's comment earlier, she would've
thought maybe it was just her. Although he hadn't seemed to
have a problem with her clinical judgement, he'd made it
clear earlier that he thought she was too emotionally involved
with their patients.

And there had been that weird prickle of awareness when
he'd shaken her hand, which she was pretty sure he'd felt, too.
Maybe this distance was his way of telling her that he had no
intention of acting on it.

Well, that was fine by her. Because she didn't want to act
on it, either. She'd learned her lesson well: getting involved
with a colleague was the quickest way to heartache. Never,
ever again.

Later that afternoon, Rhys was walking past the ward's playroom to his office when he heard laughter. Loud laughter. As
if the children in the playroom were watching some kind of
show, rather than being the general hum of noise of little ones
playing independently. He couldn't remember anyone talking
about a visitor coming to entertain the children, and he knew
there wasn't a television in the playroom. So what was going
on? Curious, he looked through the doorway.

And there at the far end of the room was Katrina. Sitting
on a beanbag, with her feet tucked under her, surrounded by
the more mobile children from the ward and what looked like
most of the children from the waiting room. At first he thought
she was reading them a story—and then he realised that she
wasn't holding a book. The story she was telling was straight

out of her head, illustrated by a couple of glove puppets. She was getting the children involved, too—asking them questions so they made suggestions to shape the story, and persuading them all to join in with a simple song or a chorus.

He glanced at his watch. She should have been off duty half an hour ago. Yet here she was, entertaining the children.

This went beyond dedication.

Katrina Gregory clearly loved her job.

And the children clearly loved her all the way back. He'd noticed on the ward rounds how the newer parents turned straight to her for comfort, how the older ones greeted her as a friend. How the children brightened when they saw her and even the sickest ones could summon up a smile for Dr Katrina. Her warmth suffused everyone.

Even himself.

And, lord, he was tempted. Katrina was gorgeous. And it wasn't just her personality: her midnight-blue eyes were stunning and her mouth was lush enough to make any man sit up and beg. When she'd shaken hands with him that morning, he'd been incredibly aware of her—of the softness of her skin, the light floral scent she wore, the quiet yet clear voice.

Irresistible.

He'd wanted her immediately.

And had held himself back, because it was highly unlikely a woman that attractive would still be single. Even though she didn't wear a ring at work—he'd actually caught himself checking, during the ward round—she probably kept it on a chain round her neck, tucked inside her shirt for safety and staying close to her heart. And even if he'd got it wrong and Katrina was free, he was hardly in a position to offer her anything. His last girlfriend had told him he was so distant he might as well have been in Australia when they'd gone out together—and he knew she'd had a point. He was lousy at re-lationships, so it was best to stick to what he was good at. Work.

Katrina Gregory was his colleague—full stop and end of story.

Quietly, Rhys left the doorway and headed for his office.

CHAPTER TWO

THE following morning, Katrina was on her way out of Sadie's cubicle when she saw Rhys in the corridor. 'Morning,' she said brightly, hoping that he wasn't going to give her another lecture about being too close to her patients but quite ready to battle her corner if she had to.

'Morning.' He gave her one of the slow, sweet smiles he'd given Lynne in the kitchen the previous day—the smile that had made Katrina's knees go ever so slightly weak—and all her annoyance melted away. 'I'm with you in the children's assessment clinic this morning.'

'I thought I was on with Tim,' she said. Their first-year foundation doctor was working mainly with her in the assessment clinic and she was enjoying his enthusiasm and freshness.

'He called in sick this morning—he's caught the tummy bug that's going round. So I'm afraid you're stuck with me,' he said lightly.

'I think I can manage,' she said, equally lightly. Funny how the look in his eyes was making her heart beat that little bit faster. She really needed to get a grip. 'Not that I'm trying to patronise you, but have you worked in the assessment clinic here before? I mean, you know how the system works?'

'It'll be my first time,' Rhys said, 'but I gather our patients are referred by their GPs or by the emergency department staff.'

She nodded. 'We have a couple of paediatric nurses who do the usual checks when the children are brought in—height, weight, temperature, pulse, breathing rate, urine sample—and take a medical history, then we see the children in the order in which they arrive. Unless there's an emergency, of course,' she added, 'but we do warn parents that emergencies take priority.'

'Sounds like the same set-up we had back at the Cardiff Memorial Hospital,' he said. 'That's fine by me. Do you want a coffee before we start?'

She glanced at her watch. 'We haven't really got time—not unless we make it with half-cold water. Who's doing ward rounds this morning, if you're not?'

'Will.'

Will was the senior consultant: a tall, jolly man who had a fund of terrible jokes and even more terrible ties that their patients all loved. She grinned. 'The poor nurses—not to mention the patients—will need sunglasses! At least your taste in ties is bearable.'

'I wouldn't bet on that.' His eyes glittered with mischief. 'This is my third week here. I think it's time to start a competition with Will in neckwear.'

She groaned. 'Don't tell me your wife and kids find them for you, too.'

'Not married. No kids. No intention of having either.'

His voice was suddenly cool, breaking the light-hearted mood, and Katrina winced inwardly. Hadn't Lynne said yesterday that the man was very guarded about his private life? 'Sorry. I wasn't fishing. Just that Will always says his wife and kids buy his loudest ties, and I assumed if you had a collection like his it'd be from the same kind of source.' She raked a hand through her hair. 'Look, I didn't mean to pry. I apologise.'

'No offence taken.'

But that invisible barrier was back between them again. And this time it felt a tiny bit wider.

Katrina tried her best to keep it professional in the assessment unit, though she was very much aware of Rhys's presence—far more than she usually was with Tim or whoever else worked with her. Even when her back was to the room, she knew the precise moment that Rhys left his cubicle and went to call his next patient. And that was worrying. Why was she so aware of the man?

Her third patient that morning worried her even more. Petros was six, and looked very poorly.

'He's been a bit off-colour for the last two days, tired and feeling sick,' his mother said. 'And his back hurts.'

'His temperature's up and he's a bit short of breath,' Katrina observed.

Mrs Smith nodded. 'And his wee's very dark, even though I've tried to get him to drink plenty of water.'

The little boy had olive skin but there was a definite pallor around his mouth, and the whites of his eyes were slightly yellowish. 'Hello, Petros. I'm Dr Katrina,' she said softly. 'Would you mind if I had a little look at you, please?'

He shrugged listlessly.

'He's really not himself,' Mrs Smith said, biting her lip. 'He's always on the go. He's never this quiet and still.'

Katrina squeezed Mrs Smith's hand. 'Try not to worry,' she said gently. 'He's in the right place. Has anyone else in the family or any of his friends had similar symptoms?'

'Everyone's fine.'

So it was unlikely to be a virus, then. The most likely

culprit was a urine infection, but the paediatric nurse had already done a dipstick test and it was clear. She didn't like his breathing rate or temperature, though. 'I'm going to listen to your heart and your breathing now, Petros. And afterwards, if you like, you can listen to Mummy's.'

Petros shook his head but didn't say a word.

'OK. I'll be as quick as I can,' she said, and listened through the stethoscope. 'Big breath in? And out. And in. And out. That's lovely. Well done, sweetheart.' His heart, at least, sounded fine. She was still thinking infection, though. 'Can you open your mouth for me and say "ahh"?' she asked.

Petros did so—the quietest 'ahh' Katrina had heard from a child in a while. There was no sign of infection in his throat, but his mouth and tongue definitely looked pale. 'I'm going to need to take a blood test,' she said to Mrs Smith. 'I think he might be slightly jaundiced, because his eyes are a little bit yellow, so I want to check for that and anaemia.'

'He had jaundice when he was born,' Mrs Smith said. 'But the midwife said it was really common with babies.'

'It is—usually, if they get a bit of sunlight, the jaundice goes away within the first week,' Katrina said.

'It did.'

There was something nagging in the back of Katrina's mind, but she couldn't quite place it. 'It's been a lovely sunny few days, hasn't it?' she asked. 'Have you been doing anything special, Petros?'

'I went to Granddad's garden,' Petros said. 'He grows magic beans.'

'Like *Jack and the Beanstalk*? Wow. Did you meet the giant?' Katrina asked.

The little boy didn't even crack a smile, merely rubbed at his back.

'OK, sweetheart. I'm going to give you something to take that pain away,' she said gently, and gave him two spoonfuls of children's paracetamol syrup. 'This will help you to stop feeling quite so hot, too. Do you like your granddad's garden?'

Petros nodded.

'My father-in-law got an allotment this summer,' Mrs Smith explained. 'He's been growing vegetables and Petros has been helping him. We call the broad beans "magic beans"—you know what it's like, trying to get little ones this age to eat vegetables.'

'Don't I just.' Katrina had played the 'magic' card herself before now with a variety of vegetables and a variety of patients.

'Can I interfere?' Rhys said, coming over to Katrina's workspace.

Well, he was her senior. He had several years' more experience than she did. And if he had any bright ideas, she was willing to listen: in Katrina's view, the patient took priority. 'Be my guest.'

He introduced himself swiftly. 'Mrs Smith, these broad beans you mentioned—has your little boy eaten them before?'

'No. Do you think he might be allergic to them?'

'Not allergic, exactly. Petros is a Greek name, yes?'

She nodded. 'It's my grandfather's name.'

He smiled at her. 'May I ask, which part of Greece does your family come from?'

'My husband's from the East End—well, with a name like Smith that's pretty obvious,' she said wryly, 'but my family's originally from Cyprus. My grandparents came over to London just after the war and started a restaurant.'

'Katrina, when you do that blood sample, can you get it tested for G6PD as well?' Rhys asked.

'Of course.' The pieces clicked into place. 'You think it's favism?'

'Yes—I've seen a few cases in Wales,' he said.

'What's favism?' Mrs Smith asked. 'And what's G6PD?'

'G6PD is a chemical in your body—it stands for glucose 6 phosphate dehydrogenase, but it's a bit of a mouthful so it's known as G6PD for short,' Rhys explained. 'Some people have less than normal amounts in their red blood cells, and it's quite common in people who have a Mediterranean origin. If you don't have enough G6PD, then if you get a fever or take certain medicines or eat broad beans—what they call fava beans in America, which is why it's called "favism"— then the body can't protect your red cells properly and you become anaemic.'

'With this condition, you might also get jaundice—and the symptoms mean you get backache and your urine looks the same colour as tea before you add the milk,' Katrina added.

Mrs Smith nodded in understanding. 'Like Petros's does right now.'

'Obviously we need to check the results of the blood tests,' Katrina said, 'but I think Rhys is right.'

'So can you give him this G-whatever stuff in tablets or something?' Mrs Smith asked.

'I'm afraid there aren't any supplements,' Rhys said. 'We'll check how much iron is in his blood, and if there isn't enough he might need a transfusion—but the good news is that Petros will feel a lot better with some rest and a little bit of oxygen to help him breathe more easily.'

'The condition's not going to affect him day to day,' Katrina explained, 'but he'll need to avoid certain medications— aspirin, some antibiotics and some antimalarial drugs. I can give you a leaflet explaining all that so you know what to avoid.'

'You'll need to tell your GP as well so it's on his medical record and he isn't given any of the medications he needs to avoid by mistake,' Rhys added. 'And we should warn you now that if he gets an infection in future, it might mean his red cells are affected and he'll get anaemia and jaundice again.'

'And *definitely* no more broad beans,' Katrina said.

'Best to avoid Chinese herbal medicines, too,' Rhys continued. 'And, would you believe, mothballs? They contain a chemical in that can affect people with G6PD deficiency.'

Mrs Smith looked anxious. 'But he's going to be all right?'

'He's going to be absolutely fine,' Katrina reassured her, ruffling Petros's hair.

'You said earlier it's common in people from the Mediterranean—so I might have it too?' Mrs Smith asked Rhys.

'No, it's more likely that you're a carrier—the condition is linked with the X chromosome, so women tend to be carriers but because men only have one X chromosome they end up developing the disease,' he explained.

Mrs Smith bit her lip. 'So it's my fault my son's ill.'

'Absolutely *not*,' Rhys said emphatically. 'It's a medical condition and you had no reason to suspect there was a problem. Whatever you do, don't blame yourself.'

'And, anyway, you were the one who took him to the doctor—you did exactly the right thing,' Katrina added. 'Now, Petros, I need to take a little tiny sample of your blood so I can test it—but I have magic cream that means it won't hurt at all. Is that OK?'

The little boy looked up at his mother and then, at her encouraging smile, nodded.

'Wonderful. Now, you have to say a magic word as I put the cream on. Do you know a magic word?'

'Please,' Petros said.

'Oh, honey. That's lovely.' Katrina's heart melted. 'And do you know another one that a magician might say?'

'Abracadabra?' the little boy suggested.

'That's perfect. Now, let's say it together. After three. One, two, three…' She took the pot of local anaesthetic gel. 'Abracadabra.' She applied it to his inner elbow. 'Now, it takes a little while to work, so I'm going to let your mummy tell you a story while I see someone else who's feeling a bit poorly, and then I'll come back and see you, OK?'

The little boy nodded.

'You might see a bit of redness on his skin,' Rhys said to Mrs Smith, 'but that's nothing to worry about—it's part of the way the anaesthetic works.'

'Thank you both so much.' Much of the strain had gone from Mrs Smith's face.

'That's what we're here for,' Rhys said with a smile.

Mrs Smith took Petros back over to the waiting area. After Katrina had seen her next patient, she called Petros back and took the blood sample, chatting to him and telling him some of the awful jokes she'd learned from Will to keep him distracted while she slid the needle into his vein. 'All done. That's brilliant,' she told the little boy, pressing a piece of cotton wool over the site and holding it there for a few seconds before taping it on. 'Did it hurt?'

He shook his head.

'Good.' She turned to Mrs Smith. 'The results should be back later this afternoon—then I'll know a lot more and we can talk it through. I'll come and find you as soon as they're back. I know it's a pain having to wait around, and I'm sorry we can't speed the procedure up at all. But there's a coffee bar just outside the department if you want to go and get a drink, and across the corridor there's a play area—there are loads of books and toys and what have you there.' She smiled at Petros. 'So we'll see you a bit later on, OK, sweetheart?'

He nodded.

'And then I'll be able to make you feel a lot better,' she said.

After the clinic had finished, Rhys looked round for Katrina. She wasn't there, but when he stepped into the corridor he saw her near the double doors. 'Katrina,' he called, 'are you heading for the canteen?'

She ignored him completely, letting the doors swing shut behind her.

Rhys stopped in his tracks, staring after her. She'd just blanked him. Had he upset her by butting in on her patient that morning? She hadn't seemed upset at the time…but maybe she'd put on a professional front for the patient's sake. Fine. He'd have a word with her later, explain that he hadn't intended to cast any aspersions on her ability. From what he'd seen, Katrina was good at her job, and the last thing everyone needed was a personality clash to disrupt the harmony of the ward.

Rather than going to the canteen, he went to the 'grab and go' bar for a coffee and a sandwich that he ate at his desk while sorting out some paperwork.

Mid-afternoon, the same thing happened: he saw Katrina about to enter the staff room, called her name—and she completely ignored him.

Oh, great.

Was she still sore about that morning? Or maybe from the previous day, when he'd reminded her about the importance of professional detachment?

He couldn't let this go on. He didn't want to tackle her about it in the staffroom, though. It would be too public and embarrassing for both of them. No: after their shift, he'd have a quiet word with her in his office and hopefully he'd be able to reach some kind of truce with her.

Lynne called him to examine a patient; on his return, he saw Katrina sitting on the bed next to one of their patients, talking to the parents. Both parents had red eyes, and the child was white-faced. He frowned. Ruby Jeffers had been admitted with meningitis the previous week. He knew she'd been having some hearing problems and she'd had an appointment in the audiology department earlier that day in case the virus had caused damage to the cochlea or inflammation of the auditory nerve. Clearly the news wasn't good, and he wasn't that surprised because he knew that meningitis caused deafness in around seven per cent of children who'd had it.

But what did surprise him was when Katrina pushed her hair up on her left side. What was she doing, showing the little girl a pretty earring or something? Or maybe doing some kind of distracting magic trick, because she pulled something from her ear.

But the little girl still wasn't smiling.

He frowned, drawing closer, and heard a snatch of conversation. 'See? It's really easy to take out. And easy to put in. It doesn't hurt because it's made to measure.'

What was?

'What they do, they have some special stuff to make a mould. It looks like play dough and it's pink and purple. They mix it together—and then they put it into your ear. It feels a bit weird, but it doesn't hurt. You can feel it getting a little bit warmer, and then when they take it out they've got the exact shape of your ear and they can make you a special mould that fits your ear only.'

Ear? Mould?

Everything suddenly fell into place.

Ruby's audiology test must have shown that she had hearing loss—if a further test in six weeks didn't show a marked improvement it was very likely that she would need a hearing aid. But the way Katrina was talking felt personal—as if she knew exactly what it felt like, rather than what the audiology team had told her.

'And you know that test you did, where you had to listen for the beeps? That showed the audiologist what you could hear. So then they can programme the hearing aid to help you hear the bits you can't hear right now, but they don't make the bits that you *can* hear any louder.'

'And it doesn't hurt?' Ruby asked.

'Nope. Once it's in, I forget it's even there—like I said, it's made to fit you perfectly, and only you. Feel. It's not heavy, is it?'

Rhys realised then that Katrina was definitely talking personally.

She wore a hearing aid.

'And watch this.' Katrina lifted her hair again, took the aid from the little girl's hand and slipped it back into her ear. 'Push this switch to turn it on—and, hey, presto, I've got a bionic ear. I can hear the same as your mum and dad now—well, almost.'

'So you can't hear, like me?' Ruby asked, looking surprised.

'Nope. And it hasn't stopped me doing anything I want to do.' She laughed. 'Well, obviously I don't wear it if I go swimming. It'd be like putting your handheld game console in the bath.'

Ruby giggled. 'That'd be silly. It doesn't work if it gets wet.'

'Exactly.' Katrina smiled at her. 'So if your next test shows that you do need a hearing aid, you'll know not to worry because you'll be fine. And you can get special help at school if you need it.' She looked at Ruby's parents. 'There are support groups, and the audiology team can work with Ruby's school. And, believe me, a hearing aid takes a lot of the struggle out of lessons. There won't be any difference between Ruby and everyone else in her class.' She smiled at Ruby. 'Except you can show people exactly what the inside of your ear looks like and really gross them out. Oh, and you can choose your colour. I had to have a clear mould because I'm a grown-up, but you can have a pink sparkly one if you want.'

'Really?' Ruby's face brightened.

'Really. Or a purple one. I really wanted a bright blue one to match my eyes, but grown-ups don't get to have the fun ones.'

Rhys withdrew, feeling a complete and utter heel. Now he understood why Katrina had ignored him: she hadn't heard him. And because he'd called out from behind her she hadn't seen him either, so she'd had no idea he'd even spoken. Considering he'd been about to accuse her of deliberately ignoring him and being petty… Guilt flooded through him. Admittedly, he hadn't known Katrina Gregory for very long, but in that day and a half he'd really been aware of how warm and sweet she was. She wasn't the type to be petty or to bear grudges and give someone the silent treatment.

He really should stop judging people by his own family's behaviour.

And he most definitely owed Katrina an apology.

Katrina dropped by his office later that afternoon. 'I've got Petros Smith's blood results back. You're right—it's G6PD. Thanks for picking that up. There was something nagging in the back of my mind but I couldn't quite place it.'

'That's what colleagues are for,' he said lightly. 'Do you want me to come and talk to them with you?'

'No, that's fine. I can see you're busy.'

'If you're sure. The offer's there.' He paused. 'Actually, before you go, can you close the door a second?'

Her eyes narrowed. 'Why?'

'I'd like a quick word with you.'

She looked wary, but did as he asked. 'What is it?'

'Sit down. I'm not going to bite your head off. It's just…' He sighed. 'I owe you an apology.'

She blinked, but sat down. 'An apology? Why?'

'I called you earlier. On two separate occasions. You ignored me.'

She flushed. 'Sorry, I—'

'Let me finish,' he cut in. 'I thought it was deliberate, so I was going to ask you into my office for a quiet chat and sort out whatever the problem was. Then I overheard you talking to Ruby Jeffers and her parents—and I realise now you didn't hear me.'

She winced. 'Sorry. Sometimes it's difficult at work, especially in an open area—it gets a bit noisy and I have to rely on lip-reading a lot more than I do at home.'

'Don't apologise. You've done nothing wrong—but now I know about it, I'll make sure you're facing me and that I've got your attention before I talk if it's noisy.'

'Thank you.' She stood up. 'I'd better go and see the Smiths.'

He knew he should leave it there. They had a truce. But something seemed to take over his mouth, and he found himself saying, 'Before you do—would you have dinner with me this evening?'

She looked surprised. 'But you don't…'

'Don't what?'

'Don't do team nights out.'

'I'm not very good with crowds.' He rubbed a hand across his face. 'I'm not much of a drinker, I loathe karaoke and that sort of thing, and I'd rather go out for a good meal and a decent conversation than sit at the end of a huge table, not really knowing anyone and being only too aware that I was only invited because everyone's being polite and it's cramping their style having the consultant around.'

'I see.'

Her expression intrigued him. 'Why did you think I said no to team nights out?'

'You mean, when most new consultants would go on absolutely everything to try and bond with the team?' She spread her hands. 'No idea. Maybe you have a complicated home life.'

'There's just me,' he said softly. 'No ties of any sort. So it's pretty simple.'

'Well, thank you for asking me,' she said politely, 'but I'm afraid I'll have to pass. I don't believe in dating colleagues. If it doesn't work out, it makes life very awkward for everyone else on the ward.'

His brain registered her refusal—but her reason told him something else. She hadn't refused because she was already involved with someone else or because she wasn't interested in him: she'd refused because he was her colleague.

'You're right, it can make things difficult,' he agreed. He'd seen it happen with other people rather than experienced it himself; in the past, he'd dated people who worked in the same hospital, but never colleagues from his own ward. 'I'm asking you out to dinner because we've got off on the wrong foot and I'd like us to start again as colleagues—and it's a more civilised way of starting a good working relationship.'

'The wrong foot.' She pursed her mouth. 'You were telling me how to do my job yesterday.'

He'd wondered if she'd bring that up. 'I was concerned that you're getting too emotionally involved with your patients. That's not healthy for you *or* for the patient.' He smiled to soften his words. 'But I saw you telling a story in the play-room yesterday afternoon.'

'On my time, not the ward's time.' She folded her arms. 'And I assume you want me to stop?'

'No. Actually, I was thinking you'd be a natural as a teacher.'

Her face relaxed. 'My best friend from school's a primary school teacher. She uses a puppet to tell stories to her class and it works well, so I borrowed her idea for the ward.'

'And it's a good one. The children seemed to enjoy it.'

'Anything that makes hospital easier for them and reduces the stress on their parents means that they can spend their energy on getting well. And it helps the brothers and sisters, too.' She spread her hands. 'And I enjoy it. If we've had one of those days where everything's gone wrong, seeing the smiles on the faces of the little ones always makes me remember that life's good.'

'So you're a glass-half-full person?' he asked.

'Definitely.'

'Then have dinner with me tonight. As colleagues—and potential friends,' he said.

She looked at him for a long, long moment. 'Not a date.'

'Not a date,' he confirmed. 'And you can choose where we go.'

'All right. Thank you. Do you want to go straight after work?'

'After,' he said, 'you've done your story.'

Her smile was the sweetest reward he could have asked for. 'I'll come and collect you, then. See you later.'

'See you later,' he said softly.

CHAPTER THREE

THIS wasn't a date, Katrina reminded herself as she walked from the playroom to Rhys's office. It was the beginning of a working relationship. And, as she'd told Madison, she was perfectly happy with her life the way it was.

She rapped on Rhys's open door and leaned against the doorjamb. 'Ready?'

He looked up from his computer. 'Can you give me three minutes while I save this file and switch off the computer?'

He was as good as his word, saving the file immediately, logging off then and switching off the machine. 'So where are we going?' he asked as he stood up.

'Do you like Moroccan food?'

'Yes.'

'Good. There's a really fabulous Moroccan restaurant a couple of streets from here called Mezze—Maddie and I go there a lot.'

'Maddie? Ah, now I know why you looked familiar when I first met you. Madison Gregory in Maternity—she's your sister?'

'As good as, yes,' Katrina said. 'Technically, she's my cousin, but our dads have a family business and our mums are best friends, so we grew up together.' She laughed. 'Because she's two years older than I am, Maddie likes to point out that she's the *big* sister. Even though she's still shorter than I am when she's wearing spike heels and I'm barefoot, bless her.' She paused. 'What about you—do you have any brothers or sisters?'

'I'm an only child.'

His voice was neutral, but Katrina was used to watching faces and picking up visual clues to compensate for years of not quite being able to hear someone's tone. She was sure that Rhys was masking something. Though as they were still getting to know each other, now wasn't the time to push him to talk to her, the way she would have pushed Will or Tim or any of the nursing staff on the ward.

She kept the conversation light until they reached Mezze. As they walked in, Rhys took in their surroundings—the rich saffron walls, the ruby and terracotta silk cushions, the tealight candles in stained-glass holders in the centre of the glass-topped tables. Katrina thought he looked as impressed as she'd felt when she and Madison had first discovered the restaurant.

'Good evening, Katrina. Your usual table?' the waiter asked.

'Thanks, Hassan. That'd be lovely.'

When they were settled at a table with menus and had ordered a sparkling mineral water, Rhys raised an eyebrow. 'I know you said you come here a lot…but the staff here actually know you by name?'

'I love Moroccan food,' she said simply. 'Maddie hates cooking, so we tend to come here most weeks. Either here, or there's a really fabulous pizzeria in the next street.'

'So you know the menu well.' His eyes took on a teasing glint. 'Or are you boring and pick the same thing each week?'

'I tend to choose the same pudding, I admit,' she said with a smile, 'but I've tried everything on the menu.' And there was a long, long list of dishes.

'So what do you recommend?'

Katrina leaned back against her chair. 'We could be boring, and order a starter each and a main course. Or…' She paused. 'We could order a huge pile of starters and share it like a *mezze*.'

He laughed. 'I can guess which you'd prefer. A huge pile of starters it is.'

She talked him through the menu and when Hassan brought their drinks over they were ready to order a selection.

'So tell me about yourself,' Katrina said when Hassan had gone.

Rhys shrugged. 'There's not much to tell. I'm Welsh— well, with a name like Rhys Morgan and my accent, that's pretty obvious. I grew up in South Wales, I trained in Cardiff and I moved to London just over three weeks ago.'

That didn't tell her much about him at all—his dreams, his passions in life—but before she had the chance to ask anything else, he said, 'Your turn.'

'I'm English, I grew up in Suffolk and I trained in London.' The same bare facts that he'd given her. Although maybe telling him more might encourage him to open up to her, she decided. 'I never wear pink—my cousin Maddie has the girly gene in the family—and I loathe the romantic comedies she insists on dragging me to.' She smiled wryly. 'She hates the kind of films I like. And going to an arthouse cinema on my own feels a bit…' She wrinkled her nose. 'Well, I prefer to go with someone so I can talk about the film afterwards. That's half the fun of a cinema trip.'

'What would you define as arthouse films?' he queried.

'This is where you can officially label me weird,' she said. 'Not modern ones—really old ones. Films like *Citizen Kane* and *Vertigo*. I have a bit of a soft spot for *film noir*.'

'Good choice,' he said. 'I really like the ones written by Cornell Woolrich as well as the Raymond Chandler films.'

She blinked, then fiddled with her hearing aid. 'Nope, it's working,' she said. 'Tell me—did I imagine it or did you really just say "Cornell Woolrich"?'

'I did.' He smiled. 'I've got all his short stories, too. I discovered them when I was a teenager and loved them—mind you, after one particular story it took me two years before I could order lamb again. And in a Welsh pub that's a bit difficult.'

She laughed, knowing exactly which story he meant—a tale with a twist that had had exactly the same effect on her. 'I think,' Katrina said, 'you and I are going to get on very well together.'

He lifted his glass. 'I'll drink to that.'

Her fingers brushed against his as they clinked glasses, and that same weird awareness she'd felt when she'd first shaken his hand seemed to fizz through her body.

An awareness she wasn't going to act on. She already knew first-hand what happened when you dated a colleague and it went wrong. The awkwardness of having to work together afterwards, trying not to think about just how intimately you knew each other. The embarrassment of everyone knowing what a failure your relationship was, thanks to the hospital grapevine. And, worse still, in a break-up as messy as hers had been with Pete, your colleagues on the ward feeling forced to take sides... No. She wasn't risking that happening ever again. Her relationship with Rhys was going to be a friendship—and nothing more.

Their food arrived, a huge platter containing little dishes and a heap of rustic bread.

'Lamb.' She gestured to the skewers of meat rubbed with spices and then chargrilled.

He laughed. 'That's a barefaced attempt to get me to leave it all for you to scoff.'

'Rats. My dastardly plan has been foiled,' she said, laughing and breaking off a piece of bread so she could scoop up some of the roast aubergine purée. 'Mmm. This is good.'

He tried the tabbouleh. 'So's this. Is that cinnamon I taste?'

'And watercress.' She paused. 'Is your palate honed that well by eating out a lot, or do you cook as well?'

'I eat out a fair bit,' he admitted. 'I can cook—but if I've worked late it's quicker and easier to stop somewhere on the way home.'

If? From what Lynne had said, it was more like 'when', she thought.

'How about you?' he asked.

'Cooking relaxes me. I like experimenting.' She smiled. 'And anything involving chocolate.'

He gestured to the table. 'No chocolate here.'

'Ah, but you wait until you try the chocolate and cardamom ice cream from the dessert menu.'

As they worked their way through the little savoury pastries stuffed with cheese, the stuffed vine leaves and the felafel, Rhys asked, 'So how was little Petros Smith?'

Katrina wrinkled her nose. 'His haemoglobin levels weren't brilliant, but nowhere near bad enough to need a transfusion, and I think it would've been more stressful for him if I'd admitted him—so I let his mum take him home. I gave her a leaflet about Petros's condition and told her what to look out for; she's promised to bring him straight back to us if she's worried at all. He should pick up with a bit of rest—and the main thing is that his family knows now that there's a problem and what he needs to avoid in future.'

'That's good. What about the Jeffers family?'

'They're coming to terms with the situation,' Katrina said. 'They have another audiology appointment in six weeks' time, but they were warned this morning that Ruby's fairly likely to need an aid.' She smiled wryly. 'I wish health screening had been as good when I was a kid.'

Clearly Katrina had had hearing difficulties for a long time, Rhys thought. 'So how long have you been deaf?'

'I'm not profoundly deaf—it's moderate to severe hearing loss,' she explained. 'Looking back, it started when I was about seven, but nobody picked it up until Maddie was at med school and did a module on audiology. I was in my first year, she was in her third, and you know what it's like when you're a med student—you read up on symptoms and you spot them in yourself or other people.'

'Yes, I remember doing that myself,' he said with a smile.

'Anyway, she nagged me to go and get my hearing checked. She even came with me to the audiology department for moral support, bless her. And that's when we found out.'

'Why didn't anyone pick it up earlier?' he asked.

'I was a bit of a dreamer as a child—well, I still am, from time to time—so everyone thought I was just on Planet Katrina and wasn't listening.' She shrugged. 'And you know what it was like when we were young. They simply didn't do the kind of screening they do now.' She rolled her eyes. 'I say "we". I'm twenty-eight, and I assume you're not that much older than I am?'

'I'm thirty-two,' he confirmed. 'So it was a bit of a shock when you got the results?'

She nodded. 'All I could think of was that I was too young to be going deaf—that it was something that only happened to geriatrics.' She gave a mirthless laugh. 'And that's despite the fact that there were several children in the waiting room for the audiology test. I have to admit I was struggling a bit to hear in lectures, but I thought it was just the acoustics of the theatre—that the place was full so it swallowed up noise. You know, in the same way that empty tube trains are much noisier than ones that are stuffed with people in the rush hour.'

'So having an aid fitted made a difference?'

'And how.' Her face was suddenly animated. 'It was incredible. I discovered I could hear better from the back of the auditorium than I'd ever been able to do from the front. And the dawn chorus…I'd never been able to hear it before. Well, not that I remember, anyway. I drove everyone bananas for the first couple of months, wanting to know what each new sound was.' She smiled. 'I was really lucky and had one of the digital aids straight off—the microprocessor is programmed to fit my personal pattern of hearing loss. It's never going to be quite as good as having full hearing, I know, but it's made a big difference to me and I don't get so tired—I don't have to concentrate quite so hard talking to people, or rely on subtitles on a television screen.'

'I had no idea you had a hearing difficulty until I saw you take your hearing aid out and show Ruby,' he said.

'I suppose I should have told you.' She shrugged. 'But, then again, just because I can't hear that well, it doesn't mean I have to be treated differently.'

He blinked in surprise. 'Why on earth do you think I would have treated you differently?'

'Some people can be a bit funny about it when they find out. They start talking really loudly—as if that makes any difference—or they treat me as if I'm slow and can't understand what they're saying. Which, I have to admit, drives me crazy. If you talk to me and I'm not facing you, I don't always realise that you're talking to me and I might not pick it up, but otherwise I'm just your average person.'

Average? No, she wasn't just your average person. There was something special about Katrina Gregory.

Rhys suppressed the thought as quickly as it arrived. He wasn't looking for a relationship. There wasn't room in his life.

'So I don't tend to tell people unless they notice,' she finished. 'It avoids the fuss.'

He could understand that. He didn't like fuss either. 'Do you know what caused your hearing loss?' he asked.

She nodded. 'I had a CT scan because there was a spike in the higher frequencies and they wanted to rule out anything nasty, like an acoustic neuroma.' She grinned. 'I asked if I could have a picture. I thought they'd print something on paper, but they actually gave me a film. It's fabulous. Maddie says I only did it so I could show everyone and prove that there was a brain in my head—but that's because I got higher marks in my exams than she did.'

Katrina's expression told him that this was mutual affectionate teasing rather than a bitchy swipe. Rhys found himself wondering what it would've been like to grow up with a sibling or close cousin teasing him like that.

His family didn't do teasing.

If the truth were told, they didn't do anything except avoid each other.

'I take it the scan was clear?' he asked.

'Yes. And after talking to me the registrar said he thought my hearing loss was probably caused when I had mumps as a child. Maddie still has the odd guilty fit about it, because she says she's the one who gave me mumps so therefore it's her fault I can't hear properly.' Katrina flapped a hand. 'But that's just *ridiculous*. She's also the one who gave me my hearing back, because if she hadn't nagged me about it I probably wouldn't have bothered getting a referral to audiology—I would've carried on as I was, assuming that I was completely normal because I didn't know any different, and struggling a bit more than I'd ever admit to because I didn't want to be treated differently.'

Rhys went very still. A child with a virus causing a serious condition. It was a little too close for comfort to his past. 'So your family blames Maddie for your hearing loss?' he asked.

'No, of course they don't!' She frowned. 'How on earth can you blame a child for falling ill? It's not Maddie's fault that she picked up a virus at school—the same as it wasn't my fault that I caught it too and it affected me in a different way to the way it affected her.' She shrugged. 'These things just happen. You can't let it ruin the rest of your life.'

These things just happen.

How very different his life might have been if his family had chosen that line of thought. If they'd been strong enough to pull together instead of letting his little sister's death tear them apart.

'Are you all right, Rhys?' she asked, looking slightly concerned.

'I'm fine.' You couldn't change the past, so in his view there was no point in talking about it. 'And you're right about this food. It's fabulous.'

Katrina realised that Rhys had deliberately changed the subject. Something was clearly wrong, but he didn't want to talk about it. Not here and now, at least. Maybe he'd open up to her when they got to know each other a little better.

They spent the rest of the evening talking about food and films and books, and Katrina was surprised by how much their tastes meshed. But it wasn't just that. There was something about Rhys. Something in his blue, blue eyes that made her heart beat a little bit faster and made her wonder what it would feel like if that beautiful mouth slid across her own. Which shocked her, as she hadn't wanted to kiss anyone—hadn't even *thought* of kissing anyone—since Pete. Hadn't thought of a man in terms of anything other than as a colleague for the last couple of years.

This was crazy.

Particularly as Rhys worked with her.

Been there, done that, worn the T-shirt to shreds. She certainly wasn't going to risk a repeat of what had happened with Pete—the horrendous atmosphere that had, in the end, forced her to move hospitals to get away from the awkwardness. She loved working at the London Victoria—really loved the way everyone on the ward was like a huge extended family. No way would she be stupid enough to forget that lesson now, have an affair with Rhys and end up having to leave here, too.

Finally, after hot sweet mint tea and tiny pastries soaked in honey, she leaned back in her chair. 'I'm almost too full to move.'

'You should've left me the lamb,' he said with a grin.

'Baa,' she retorted. Then she glanced at her watch. 'Do you know, we've been here three hours?' And yet it had felt like minutes.

'I'd better get the bill,' he said.

'No, we're going halves,' she protested.

'Absolutely not. This was my idea—my apology to you.'

'Ah, but we're friends now. And friends *share*.'

He folded his arms. 'Don't argue with me, Dr Gregory, or I'll pull rank.'

'Bossy, huh?' But she wasn't going to argue—she'd had much a better idea. 'Tell you what. You can pay this time, but next time's *my* bill. We can go and see a film in Leicester Square or something and talk about it over tapas afterwards.'

'That,' he said, 'would be lovely. I'd like that.'

After Rhys had paid the bill, he insisted on seeing Katrina home.

'There's no need, you know,' she said. 'I've lived in London for ten years now. I'm used to being independent.'

'Humour me. It's a Welsh thing.'

'So you're Sir Lancelot?' she teased.

'Lancelot was French. Gawain, on the other hand, was Welsh.'

She laughed. 'Oh, I can see I'm going to enjoy being friends with you, Rhys Morgan.'

He laughed back. 'So are you going to let me see you home?'

'If you insist. You could probably do with walking some of this food off, too,' she added cheekily.

They left the restaurant and walked through the back streets. Eventually, Katrina paused outside a small Victorian terraced house. 'This is mine. Would you like to come in for a coffee?' she asked.

Although Rhys knew it would be more sensible to refuse—things were already going fast enough to set alarm bells ringing in his head—at the same time he didn't want the evening to end just yet. 'Thanks. That'd be nice.'

'Good.' She unlocked the door, then ushered him into the sitting room. 'Take a seat. I'll be back in a moment.'

Katrina's house radiated calm. Pale walls, plants everywhere, and shelves of books and films. No music, though, he noticed. That was clearly one of the areas where he and Katrina differed. And that probably had much to do with her hearing.

There were framed photographs on the mantelpiece and he walked over to take a closer look. A picture of Katrina with her cousin at what was obviously Madison's graduation; another of Katrina in graduation robes with people who he assumed were her parents; another taken of Katrina, Madison and both sets of parents in a garden; more photographs of Katrina's parents. The warmth of the family relationship was so obvious that Rhys felt a twist of envy: it was the complete opposite from his own family background.

Though in the circumstances he couldn't blame his father for walking away and trying to find happiness elsewhere. And, given that she'd lost a child and her marriage had disintegrated, he couldn't blame his mother for the way she was either. As Rhys had grown up, he'd come to terms with the way things were. And he'd worked out that it was much, much easier to be self-sufficient and keep people close enough to be professional, but far enough away so there was no risk of losing them from his life and getting hurt.

It wasn't as if there was a gap in his life. He had a job he was good at, a job he really, really loved; he had his music and his books and his films to fill his spare moments; and that was all he needed. Becoming involved with Katrina Gregory would just complicate things. He needed to get them back on the right sort of footing—colleagues and acquaintances only—and fast.

Katrina, walking back into the living room with two mugs of coffee, noted the expression on Rhys's face. Polite but distant again. Where was the man who'd chatted with her in the Moroccan restaurant, who'd relaxed enough with her to tease her back and laugh with her?

'One black coffee,' she said.

'Thanks.' He gave her a polite smile.

She couldn't think of a single reason why he would suddenly be so reserved with her, not after the evening they'd shared. Knowing how easily a small communication lapse could turn into something huge, she decided to face it head-on. 'Rhys, is something wrong?'

'Wrong? No.'

'But you've gone quiet on me.'

'I've just realised how late it is. And I'm afraid I'm a lark rather than an owl.'

'Me, too,' she said. 'Which means I end up drinking huge amounts of coffee on team nights out to keep me awake.'

'Sounds like a good plan.'

She sighed inwardly. He was definitely back to being polite and reserved. And she couldn't think of a single thing to say without it sounding inane or babbling.

The silence stretched until it was almost painful. And then he drained his mug. 'Thank you for the coffee.'

'Thank you for the meal,' she said, equally politely. 'And I hope you weren't just being nice when you said about going to the cinema with me. It's so rare to find someone who likes the same sort of films I do.'

He looked torn, but then he shook his head. 'No, I meant it.'

'Good. Then maybe we can check the listings together tomorrow, see what's showing later in the week. If you're not busy, that is.'

'That'd be nice.' He stood up. 'Goodnight, Katrina.'

'Goodnight.' She saw him to the door. 'See you on the ward.'

And when she washed up their coffee mugs, she was frowning. What had made Rhys suddenly clam up on her like that? Unless… She swallowed as the memories came back. Unless Rhys had had time to think about things and took the same view as Pete had. That her hearing was going to be an issue.

She'd thought she'd learned from her mistakes—but it was beginning to look as if she hadn't.

CHAPTER FOUR

WHEN the going gets tough, Katrina thought, the tough get cooking. And as she was on a late shift the next day, she spent the morning at home baking brownies. Lots of them. The combined scents of chocolate and vanilla lifted her mood, and by the time she'd walked into work she was feeling a lot more serene.

She left a note on top of the tin in the staffroom, telling everyone to help themselves, and was about to head for the ward when Rhys walked in.

'Good morning,' he said.

'Morning.' She gave him a polite smile, reminding herself that she was going to keep it professional between them.

'What do you know about choanal atresia?' he asked.

'The nasal passage is blocked by bone or tissue, so the baby can't breathe properly,' she recited. 'Has the neonatal unit asked us to look at a baby?'

He shook his head. 'We've got a little girl in, four months old—one of her nasal passages is blocked, which is why it's taken so long to diagnose her. But I noticed yesterday you're very good at reassuring parents. The Gillespies are pretty upset, and I could do with a calming influence. As in *you*.'

She blinked. 'So you're being friendly again this morning.'

He flushed, clearly aware of exactly what she meant. 'I'm sorry, Katrina. What can I say?'

'Well, it'd be nice to know if I did or said anything to upset you last night.'

'No, of course you didn't.' He raked a hand through his hair. 'I'm just not very good at this friendship business. I've always been a bit of a loner and I'm more used to dealing with people on a professional basis. And I guess I panicked a bit because I was more relaxed with you yesterday than I've been with anyone in a long, long time. I'm sorry.'

He was being honest with her. She could see it in his face. And it must have been difficult for him to open up that much to her just now. 'Apology accepted.'

'Good. So, the Gillespies—walk this way, Dr Gregory,' he said, 'and I'll talk you through baby Rosanna's notes.'

By the time they reached the cubicle, she knew the full patient history. Rhys introduced them both to the Gillespies.

'Oh, she's gorgeous,' Katrina said, stroking the baby Rosanna's cheek and smiling at Mrs Gillespie. 'You must be so proud of her.'

'We are.' Mrs Gillespie bit her lip. 'But…'

'You're worried sick about the operation. Of course you are,' Katrina said. 'But you're in the best place. I've worked here ever since I qualified, and Will's a fantastic surgeon.'

'Obviously you'll have a chance to meet him and talk to him before the operation,' Rhys said, 'but as he's in Theatre at the moment and we'll be caring for Rosanna after her operation, I wanted to talk you through what's going to happen this afternoon and answer any questions you might have.'

'Thank you,' Mr Gillespie said quietly.

'Rosanna has a condition called choanal atresia—what that means is her nasal passages are narrower than they should be and she can't breathe properly, because babies can't breathe through their mouths until they're about six months old. It's usually picked up just after a baby's born, but in Rosanna's case only one passage has narrowed so it's taken us a bit longer to realise there's a problem,' Rhys said.

'Is she going to be all right?' Mrs Gillespie asked.

'Absolutely. She'll have an operation to widen her nasal passages and Will can then put a little plastic tube called a stent up each nostril. They won't hurt her, and the stents will keep her nostrils open while her nose heals,' Rhys explained. 'They'll stick out just a tiny bit.'

'The surgeon will take the tubes out in about three months' time, and she'll be able to manage perfectly without them,' Katrina added.

'The operation takes about an hour,' Rhys continued. 'It's under a general anaesthetic, so you won't be able to be with her during the operation, but you're very welcome to wait here on the ward or in the coffee bar, and we'll come and find you as soon as Rosanna's out of Theatre so you can give her a cuddle.'

'We can touch her afterwards?' Mr Gillespie asked.

'Definitely—talk to her, cuddle her, hold her hand. She'll be hooked up to some monitors, which might look a bit scary, but they're there to help us look after her,' Katrina reassured him. 'We'll check her breathing, her heart rate and oxygen levels, and she'll have a drip in to give her pain relief, but over the next few days we won't need them. As soon as she's feeding well and gaining weight, and we've taught you how to keep the stents clean, you can take her home and carry on as normal.'

'About six weeks after the operation, the surgeon will give Rosanna a check-up—again under a general anaesthetic—to make sure her nasal passages are still wide enough for her to breathe properly,' Rhys said. 'If you're at all worried in the meantime, you can talk to your health visitor or your family doctor, or ring us here on the ward.'

Mrs Gillespie dragged in a breath. 'But she's going to be all right?'

'She doesn't have any other health problems, so she'll grow up able to lead a perfectly normal life,' Rhys reassured her.

'We've got a leaflet about the condition we can let you have, just to ease your mind a bit,' Katrina offered.

'It's a lot to take in, and if someone else in the family asks you about it, it might be hard to remember everything we've said,' Rhys added. 'Is there anything else you'd like to ask us?'

'I don't think so,' Mrs Gillespie said, looking doubtful.

'If you think of something later, just have a word with one of the nurses and they'll come and get one of us,' Rhys said. 'Rosanna's going to be in excellent hands. And you'll find that feeding her is a lot easier when she can breathe properly through her nose again.'

'She's such a tiny scrap. All my friends' babies are getting huge—I thought I was doing something wrong.' Tears welled up in Mrs Gillespie's eyes.

Katrina took her hand. 'You weren't doing anything wrong at all. You did absolutely the best thing, talking to your health visitor about it instead of struggling on your own and worrying.'

'My mother-in-law said I should have weaned her ages ago, that's why she isn't growing and why she isn't sleeping through the night yet.'

'Absolutely not,' Rhys said. 'We don't recommend weaning any earlier than four months. Rosanna was finding it hard to feed because it was hard work for her; she's been eating little and often because it's been easier for her. And babies decide when they're going to sleep through the night—every baby's different.'

'Though that's made it harder for you,' Katrina added. 'When you've had a lot of broken nights, you're tired and everything feels much more of a struggle than it would if you'd had enough sleep. Things are going to be a lot better after today.'

Mrs Gillespie brushed away a tear. 'Thank you. Sorry, I'm being stupid,' she said shakily.

'Not at all. You're human, and you've had a lot on your plate.' Katrina gave her a hug. 'Would you like me to get you some water or something?'

Mrs Gillespie shook her head. 'I'm all right. But thank you.'

'We'll come and see you again later,' Rhys promised. 'If you need anything, just ask. You're not making a nuisance of yourself—it's what we're here for.'

The Gillespies, clearly still overwhelmed, just nodded, and Rhys shepherded Katrina out of the cubicle. 'You,' he said, 'were brilliant. Thanks for your help.'

She shrugged. 'It's my job.'

'That's not how it comes across. You really care.'

'It's hard enough for parents to come to terms with the fact their baby's not well or needs an operation—the least we can do is make it easier for them. And Will's always taught the staff on this ward to treat patients as if they're our own family—so we show them respect, dignity and kindness.'

'Not all families are like that,' Rhys said.

That, Katrina thought, sounded personal. Not that she was going to try to get him to talk about it. She knew he'd only back away from her again. 'This one is,' she said simply. 'That's why I love working here so much.'

Later that afternoon, Katrina was having a coffee break when Rhys walked into the staffroom.

'Just the person I wanted to see,' she said with a smile.

'You want a second opinion on a patient?' he asked.

She shook her head. 'I've been looking at the listings. There's a film festival on this week—and there are some really good ones showing tomorrow evening. Shall I book tickets for us?'

'Tomorrow evening?' He looked regretful. 'Sorry. No can do. I'm absolutely up to my eyes in paperwork. If I don't get some of it shifted…'

Katrina had the nasty feeling that he was making a polite excuse. Rhys's predecessor had been a little bit slapdash when it came to paperwork, but things couldn't be that bad, surely?

Well, she wasn't going to push herself in where she clearly wasn't wanted. 'I understand,' she said. Her mistake, thinking a shared love of film would be the basis of a good friendship. She could accept that he didn't want to be more than friends— that suited her, too—but it was obvious that Rhys wasn't interested in even that. 'And I'd better get on,' she said, glancing at her watch.

'You're not finishing your coffee?'

No. Knowing that she'd just made a fool of herself, she wanted to get out of there as fast as possible. Not that she was going to tell him that. 'I've already had too much caffeine today. I don't want to be still awake at 3:00 a.m.,' she said lightly, then rinsed out her mug and left the room.

She managed to keep a lid on her feelings until Friday evening, when she was leaving the ward after a late shift. The light was still on in Rhys's office; she knew he'd been in early and he should've gone home hours ago.

She rapped on the open door and he looked up. 'Yes?'

'Are you OK?' she asked.

'Fine.' He spread his hands. 'Why shouldn't I be?'

'It's just…' Even though part of her knew she should keep

her mouth shut, the words spilled out. 'Apart from Tuesday, you've worked late every night this week, even if you came on duty well before 9:00 a.m.'

He shrugged. 'I'd rather spend my shifts actually treating patients on the ward or in clinic, and I need to catch up on the paperwork at some point.'

'Fair enough, but you're taking it to extremes. Working these sorts of hours really isn't good for you.'

He folded his arms and leaned back in his chair. 'So what are you saying, Katrina?'

'There's more to life than work, and maybe you should cut yourself some slack.'

'Thank you for your concern, but it's really not necessary.'

Her mouth really didn't know when to stop. 'Actually, I think it is. Because you're working ridiculous hours, everyone else is starting to feel they ought to work late, too—and that's not fair. Especially on colleagues who have young families.'

His expression was unreadable. 'I wasn't aware I'd asked anyone else to work late.'

'You haven't,' she admitted, feeling her face heat. 'But you do it, so they feel that if they don't they're not pulling their weight.'

'As you're clearly their spokesperson, you can go back and tell them I said I don't expect them to work the same hours as I do. If anyone has a problem with my hours, they can talk to me themselves.' He frowned. 'And if you'll excuse me, I need to go and check on a patient.'

'The night staff are perfectly capable of dealing with things. If there's a problem where they need your help, they'd be straight in to see you, and you know it.' She folded her arms. 'I think you're just avoiding the issue.'

'There isn't an issue.'

'Yes, there is. You're working crazy hours and it isn't good for you—or for the patients.' She shook her head in frustration. 'You have to be tired. Nobody can put in that amount of hours without wearing themselves out.'

'I'm fine. And, just for the record, I would never, *never* put a patient at risk.' His voice was very cool.

She sighed. 'You really won't let anyone close, will you? On Tuesday, you said we were friends. Since then, you've avoided me—and you've used work as an excuse not to go to the cinema with me. My mistake for taking your words at face value. You were obviously just being polite at the restaurant.'

When he said nothing, she shrugged. 'Well, now I know. I'll leave you to it. Sorry to have bothered you.' She turned away.

'Katrina, wait.' Rhys left his desk and put his hand on her shoulder as she reached the doorway.

She turned to face him. 'What?'

'I have the social skills of a rhinoceros. I'm fine with patients and their parents because it's work and I know what I'm doing. But…' He removed his hand from her shoulder and raked it through his hair. 'I'm not particularly good at this friendship stuff. I'm sorry.'

Katrina had known several people at university who had been practically geniuses in the lab, but utterly hopeless in social situations and hadn't had a clue what to say in the bar. Rhys was clearly the same type: talk about facts and food and film and medicine and he was fine. Talk about something personal, and he was all at sea. And right at that moment he was looking awkward and as embarrassed as she'd just felt. He was trying, really trying, at something he obviously found difficult. The least she could do was acknowledge that. 'Apology accepted.'

'I probably do put in too many hours. But I happen to like my job.'

'Including paperwork?' Now, that one she didn't believe.

'It's not quite the kind of paperwork you're thinking of. Right now I'm reviewing all our patient leaflets and updating them, and working out how we can make our department's website pages easier for parents and children to use. I could do it at home, but from a technical viewpoint it's a lot quicker to do it at the hospital. And,' he added, 'I might point out that you stay late, too, or you come in early to read stories to the children.'

'Half an hour at the beginning or end of my shift,' she said. 'That's reasonable. What you're doing *isn't* reasonable. It's practically doing a double shift. And don't protest, Rhys—you know it isn't reasonable.'

'So I'm a workaholic.' He spread his hands. 'It's not a crime. Plenty of other people work as hard as I do.'

She flushed. 'I'm not nagging.'

'Actually, you are.' He smiled ruefully. 'But I suppose you have a point. All right.' He glanced at his watch. 'Do you have to be somewhere, or do you fancy going for a drink?'

He was asking her out?

Her thoughts must have shown on her face, because he raised an eyebrow. 'As colleagues.'

'And then you'll blank me on Monday morning?' she asked wryly.

He sighed. 'I'll try not to. So. Do you want to go for a drink?'

'Thanks, but at this time of night everywhere's going to be crowded and noisy.' She wrinkled her nose. 'Not to mention dark.'

'Which means it'll be difficult for you to hear or lip-read.' He grimaced. 'I'm sorry. I didn't think.'

She shrugged. 'Not your problem. But thanks for the offer, anyway. It was nice of you to ask.' And even though she was tempted—severely tempted—she didn't suggest an alternative. Because it would be all too easy to let herself fall for Rhys Morgan, to want something from him that he clearly wasn't prepared to give. 'I'd better be going. Have a nice weekend.'

'You, too.'

CHAPTER FIVE

RHYS was polite and pleasant over the following couple of weeks, treating Katrina just the same as his other colleagues. But Katrina found herself looking at his mouth when he talked, and not just to read his lips—half the time her attention strayed and she found herself wondering what it would be like to feel his mouth travelling along her skin. Every time her hand brushed against his, she felt that weird prickle of awareness down her spine, and the feeling grew stronger every single time.

Oh, lord. She should know better. Somehow she had to stop that weird, flipping-over sensation in the area of her heart every time she looked at him.

The worst thing was, she was pretty sure it was the same for him. Because she'd seen him looking at her mouth, too. She'd noticed his colour heighten when his hand brushed against hers—and she'd seen the way his eyes widened for just a fraction of a second and his mouth parted very, very slightly.

Signs of attraction. Of arousal.

And whenever she thought about it her temperature went up another notch.

Katrina was beginning to think that not acting on that mutual attraction was going to make life just as difficult as if they gave in to it and had an affair. And even though it was going to be awkward and embarrassing, she was going to have to talk to him about it. Be honest. And see if he had any better and more sensible ideas than the ones that were running through her own head.

She managed to keep her mind on her work—just—when she was talking to young Kevin Lacey and his mum. Though it really didn't help that Mrs Lacey had a very soft voice, and kept her head bowed so her hair fell in her face and obscured Katrina's view of her mouth.

Oh, lord.

She couldn't hear a single one of Mrs Lacey's questions, and she really wasn't sure that either Kevin or Mrs Lacey had taken in what she'd been saying about Kevin's condition and the operation he was going to have the following day.

Katrina definitely looked strained, Rhys thought. Which was unusual: normally she was brilliant with parents, relaxed and comforting. And although young Kevin Lacey had a serious condition, it was one that could be controlled rather than something terminal, so it wasn't one of those conversations where you knew the parents' hearts were breaking and you felt completely helpless and wondered what use all those years of training were.

A second look made him guess what the problem was: Katrina couldn't see Mrs Lacey's face to lip-read. The lunch trolley was coming round, so the ward was at its noisiest, with cutlery scraping against plates and everyone raising their voices correspondingly. Katrina must be really struggling to hear, he thought, especially if Mrs Lacey's voice was particularly quiet—and, judging by her body language, he rather thought it was.

He walked over to them. 'Hello. I'm Dr Morgan. How are you doing, Kevin?'

'All right,' Kevin replied bravely, through from his pallor and the way the child was wincing Rhys realised that he was far from all right. Clearly his enlarged spleen was causing him pain.

'Mrs Lacey?'

'Dr Gregory's being very helpful,' Mrs Lacey said.

He could barely catch what Mrs Lacey was saying, and his hearing was perfect. So, even with the hearing aid, Katrina didn't stand a chance. Not that he'd bring up her deafness, particularly in front of a patient or parent: he knew she was sensitive about it. But there was something he could do to make things easier for her. 'It's pretty noisy out here because it's lunchtime,' he said, 'and I know you must have a lot of questions about Kevin's condition and his operation tomorrow. Dr Gregory, I'm on a break now. Would you like to use my office so you've got somewhere a little quieter and less distracting to run through all the procedures with Mrs Lacey?'

The relief in her eyes made him sure he'd done the right thing. 'Thank you, Dr Morgan. That'd be good.'

He smiled back at her. 'My pleasure. I'll be back on the ward in half an hour or so, but take all the time you need. And if anyone needs me, they can bleep me.'

'I'll pass the message on to Lynne,' she promised.

'See you later,' he said, and left the ward.

'Would you like a sandwich or anything, Kevin?' Katrina asked. 'Dr Morgan won't mind if you have a snack or a drink in his office.'

He shook his head. 'Hurts too much.'

'I think you need more pain relief. When did you last give him paracetamol, Mrs Lacey?'

The woman whispered something Katrina didn't catch.

'I'm sorry, Mrs Lacey, it's really noisy out here and I can't hear you properly. Let's go to Dr Morgan's office.' Once she'd established that it had been four hours since Kevin had had any pain relief, she was able to give him more and wrote it up in the notes. She also made sure that both Mrs Lacey and Kevin had a drink, although both refused food.

'It's quite a lot to take in,' she said, 'so I'll go over it all again, if that's all right with you. Kevin's got a form of anaemia called spherocytosis—what that means is that his red blood cells don't have their normal covering to hold them in shape and they become sphere-shaped.' She drew a quick sketch on the whiteboard by Rhys's desk to show them the difference between a normal blood cell and Kevin's. 'Because of their shape, the spleen decides they're abnormal and destroys them too early—that's why Kevin's pale and gets really tired after exercise. It also makes the spleen grow more than normal, which is why you're getting the pains in your tummy, Kevin.'

'And it will all go away when the doctor takes my spleen out?'

Clearly the little boy had been listening. She smiled at him. 'You'll stop being tired and you won't have the tummy pains, though unfortunately it won't make your red blood cells go back to normal.'

'And then he'll be all right?' Mrs Lacey asked.

This time, Katrina was able to hear her. 'Removing the spleen does cause some problems,' she said. 'Without a spleen you're more likely to pick up infections. Kevin will need to take antibiotics for the rest of his life to help avoid infections, and you need to make sure he gets vaccinated. I can give you a leaflet which will help you spot any signs of infection—if you see them, you need to take him to your GP straight away.

He'll also need to carry a card with him at all times to say he has no spleen; then if he has to go into hospital or needs treatment the medical staff will know what to do.'

'So will it hurt, having the operation?' Kevin asked.

'You'll be asleep,' Katrina said, 'though you might feel a bit sick and dizzy or have a sore throat when you come round from the anaesthetic. It won't last long, though. It's going to be a bit more scary for your mum—we'll need to put a tube in from your nose to your tummy in case you don't feel like eating or drinking at first, and you'll also have a drip to give you pain relief.'

'Does the operation take long?' Mrs Lacey asked.

'Somewhere between ninety minutes and three hours,' Katrina said. 'You'll be able to stay with him until he's had the anaesthetic, and there are plenty of places where you can have a cup of coffee while you're waiting. He'll be able to go home in about a week, and because the stitches will dissolve on their own he won't need to come back to have them removed.' She smiled at Kevin. 'You'll be back to school in a month—but I'm afraid no sport for the next three months.'

'No football? But…' He looked dismayed. 'But I have to play. I'm in the school team.'

'Sorry, sweetheart. You need time to heal,' Katrina said. 'But I bet you you'll be able to play even better after the operation than you do now, because you won't get so tired.' She smiled at Mrs Lacey. 'Now, I'll get the surgeon and anaesthetist to come and have a word with you later this afternoon, and they'll be able to answer any detailed questions you might have about the procedure. But if there's anything else you want to know, no matter how small it might seem, I'm here to help.'

'No football for three months.' Kevin's lower lip wobbled.

'It'll go by really quickly,' Katrina said. 'What with Bonfire

Night and Christmas coming up, you'll be ready to play again before you know it.'

She answered Mrs Lacey's final questions, then shepherded them back out to the ward and sweet-talked Hannah, the auxiliary nurse, into finding Kevin a sandwich—with the pain under control again the little boy had recovered his appetite.

Katrina didn't see Rhys again until the end of her afternoon clinic. 'Thanks for rescuing me earlier,' she said. 'I really appreciate it.'

'No problem. I could barely hear her myself—the ward isn't exactly a quiet place, and if someone keeps their face covered you can't lip-read.'

Katrina grimaced. 'I should've said something.'

'Not necessarily.' Rhys frowned. 'I'm pulling rank. Come on. Coffee.'

'But I have paperwork to do,' she protested.

'Paperwork can wait. You've finished your clinic and I've done the ward rounds—it's time to take a break.'

'Rhys—' she began.

'I want to talk to you about something,' he said.

He wanted to talk to her? Her heart missed a beat—and then she berated herself silently. Of course he didn't want to talk to her about their relationship. They didn't *have* a relationship, other than that of colleagues.

But she let him shepherd her to a quiet corner of the hospital canteen and buy her a latte.

'It's noisy enough in here for people not to be able to overhear us, but is it too noisy for you? Can you hear me OK?' he asked.

He'd automatically sat so his face was in the light; despite the hubbub around them she knew she'd be able to lip-read anything that she missed hearing. 'Yes.'

'Right. Now, I'm going to tell you something important, so I want you to pay attention. Katrina Gregory, you're a damn good doctor. And your hearing doesn't change that at all.'

She dragged in a breath. 'It's just that sometimes... No, forget it.'

'Talk to me, Katrina,' he said.

She smiled wryly. 'Isn't that a bit like pots and kettles?'

He acknowledged her point with a smile of his own. 'People who keep themselves to themselves probably notice it more in other people. You need to talk about this.'

'As I said, pots and kettles.'

He flipped a hand dismissively. 'My personal life isn't spilling over into work.'

Katrina lifted her chin. 'Neither is mine.'

'I didn't mean that.' He sighed. 'I'm making a mess of this. What I'm trying to say is that I get the feeling you're worried about your hearing affecting your work—but from my point of view it doesn't. At all. You're good with the children and you're good with the parents. This afternoon, *anyone* would've found it difficult to hear Mrs Lacey. I couldn't hear her either. So it wasn't *you*.' He frowned. 'Has someone said something to you about it?'

'Not here.' The words were out before she could stop them.

His frown deepened. 'Do you mean you don't want to talk about it here, or that someone's said something to you elsewhere?'

She squirmed. 'Do we have to discuss this?'

'Yes. It's important. Katrina, nobody can overhear us,' he reassured her. 'And if someone's said something to upset you, I want to know.'

'It's in the past. I'm over it.'

'Are you?'

She lifted her chin. 'I don't mope about things.'

'I realise that, but if someone knocks your confidence, whatever they said comes back into your mind when you have a not-so-good day—like the one I think you've had today. You wouldn't be human if it was otherwise.'

'No.'

'So talk to me. It'll help.' He reached over and squeezed her hand. Just for a moment. And the need that surged through her took her breath away.

'Katrina?' he prompted.

'All right. Since you must know, it was my ex,' she said. 'Pete. Maddie calls him "Pete the Toad"—actually, that's her politest name for him.' She swallowed hard. She may as well tell Rhys the truth. And then he'd back off and she'd be able to get control of her emotions again. 'He left me because I was damaged goods. Because he was afraid that if he stayed with me and we got married and had a child, I wouldn't hear the baby crying—that I wouldn't be a good enough wife and I sure as hell wouldn't be a good enough mother.'

Rhys looked shocked. 'What? That's ridiculous. Katrina, look at the way you are with the kids on the ward. You're the one we rely on to calm kids down and tell stories and distract them, and you're an excellent doctor, too. Pete didn't have a clue what he was talking about.'

'No? We worked together. I was the SHO and he was the registrar on the children's ward.'

'Here?' he questioned. 'So it was the guy who was consultant before me?'

'No. Different hospitals. I moved here a couple of years back.' She dragged in a breath. 'Everyone knew what had happened when we split up. And it was awful, Rhys. The atmosphere on the ward was terrible. Nearly everyone took my side, apart from this one woman who… Well, it turned out she fancied Pete and thought that if she took his part he might, um, show some interest in her.'

'It sounds as if they deserved each other,' Rhys said.

'Probably. I have no idea if they got together or not and I really don't care. But I hated going into the ward every day and facing everyone. People were sympathetic, even kind, but I could see the pity in their eyes, and I loathed the fact they saw me as "poor Katrina" instead of who I am. By the end, I wasn't sure if they pitied me for the way Pete behaved or because I can't hear. And working with Pete was just sheer torture. I never want to be in that situation again.' She grimaced. 'It was so hard to face him, when I'd loved him so much and he'd rejected me. It made me start thinking that I was as useless as he said I was—useless at my job as well as my personal life. Everyone said that he was in the wrong, not me, but it made me question my judgement in men. If he was that awful, why had I been stupid enough to fall for him in the first place? Next time round, would I pick someone who'd treat me just as badly?'

'Useless? *You?* I know violence doesn't solve anything, but right now I'd love to break the guy's jaw,' Rhys said through gritted teeth. 'It's not true, Katrina. You're *not* damaged goods and you're very, very far from useless. You're kind and you're clever and you're a damned good doctor and you make the world a brighter place. Don't ever, *ever* think otherwise.'

The expression on his face told her he meant it. That he was livid with Pete on her behalf.

If he could feel that protective towards her, that had to mean something. And the way he'd looked at her over the last couple of weeks…she was pretty sure he felt the same way that she did. Longing. Attraction.

But she couldn't act on it.

She had to explain—but, then again, how could she? It wasn't an easy subject to broach—and Rhys was such a private man, it made things even more difficult. She swallowed hard. 'Rhys. I don't… Look, this is awkward.'

'I'm not going to betray any confidences, if that's what you're worrying about. What you just told me stays with me and only me.'

She could feel the colour flooding into her face. 'Thank you. But Pete…that's why I never want to date a colleague again. I don't want to go through that horrible mess when it's over, of people taking sides and talking about me, even if they mean well.'

'Perfectly understandable. I'd feel the same.'

'Is that what happened to you, too?'

She'd told him a confidence. Something she clearly didn't talk about very much. And right now Rhys could tell that Katrina felt really vulnerable. The only way he could think of to ease that was to tell her a confidence in return. 'Not exactly. I never dated anyone on the same ward. But…' He paused. 'This is the same deal. What I tell you stays with you and only you.'

'Of course.'

'My parents split up when I'd barely started school. I don't want to go into details, but it was pretty messy, and I promised myself I'd never let that happen to me.' He smiled wryly. 'Of course, when I grew up, I realised that marriage doesn't necessarily end in divorce—not everyone's from a broken home.'

'My parents have been married for thirty years,' Katrina said. 'And they can act embarrassingly like teenagers— Maddie's parents are the same.'

'They're the lucky ones.' He shrugged. 'As I said, I realise that relationships can work—but mine don't tend to. I've tried to make a go of things with other relationships. But it's never worked out in the end.'

'Is that a warning?' she asked.

'No, it's a statement of fact. Even though I know the odds are probably on my side, I suppose emotionally I'm not prepared to take the risk. Which is probably why I keep people at a distance because it's a hell of a lot easier that way. Less stressful. Work, I can deal with. Personal stuff…' He propped his elbows on the table and rested his chin on his clasped hands. 'Can I be honest with you?'

She nodded.

'I'm attracted to you, Katrina. Very attracted. I haven't felt like this about anyone since…' He shook his head. 'Since I don't know when. Though I'm not going to do anything about it because I agree with you that relationships between colleagues are a bad idea. But, just so we're clear on this, I want you to know that your hearing difficulty has absolutely nothing to do with why I'm not going to ask you out. It's part of you, and I think because of it you're more aware of other people's feelings. You read body language better than anyone else I've ever met, so no doubt you've already guessed what I was going to say.'

'I did wonder.' She bit her lip. 'And you're perceptive. You saw when I was struggling today and you sorted it out without making me feel stupid, the way Pete did.'

'Stupid?' Rhys blinked. 'What the hell was wrong with the man? You're not stupid. You're practically ready to be registrar now. You'll ace your exams.'

'I hope so.'

'I *know* so,' Rhys said, taking her hand again and squeezing it.

She licked her lower lip and it set his pulse racing.

'Don't do that,' he begged, releasing her hand.

'Do what?'

'Lick your lip like that. Because it makes me want to…' He dragged in a breath. 'It makes me want to kiss you. And, quite apart from the fact I'm trying to stay away from you, we're in the middle of the hospital canteen. If I do what I really want to do right now, the rumour mill will zip into action so fast it'll practically explode.' He forced himself to take a sip of his coffee, but the cup clattered against the saucer as he returned it. 'You could have me on a harassment charge for admitting that.'

She shook her head. 'Like I said, you're perceptive. So you must have guessed it's the same for me. Right from when I first met you.' She raked a hand through her hair. 'I can't take that chance either, Rhys. I can't risk it all going wrong—I love it here and it'd break my heart if I had to leave, the way I did in my last job.'

'I'm not Pete, so it wouldn't come to that,' he said, 'but you're right. We can't do this. Because you deserve the kind of happiness I don't think I could give you. I mean, sure, we could have a wild affair.' It was a mistake, putting it into words: he could already feel his body's reaction to the idea of making love with her, and the way Katrina's pupils dilated slightly told him that it was the same for her.

Oh, lord.

He needed to get some control here. And fast.

'But I'm not looking for marriage and a future,' he continued, 'and it's not fair of me to ask you to give up the chance of meeting someone who can offer you what you want.'

'So where do we go from here?' she asked.

'We stay as we are. Colleagues. We're both strong enough to put our careers and our patients first.'

'And that's the right thing to do. The sensible thing,' Katrina agreed.

'Good. So we're clear on that.'

'We're clear,' she agreed.

He should have been relieved. But he wished things could have been different. 'When we've finished our coffee, we'll go back to the ward. You go your way, I'll go mine. We work together. And eventually we'll both get over this blip and we'll be able to look at each other without…'

'Wanting to rip each other's clothes off?' she suggested.

He groaned. 'I think I should've ordered a cold shower with that coffee. But, yes. That's what I mean. And I know I've already said it, but I think it bears repeating: just so you know, this has absolutely nothing to do with your hearing.'

'Thank you,' she said solemnly. 'I appreciate it.'

He was still angry on her behalf. Her ex had really done a number on her. Part of him wanted to kiss her better, to show her just how desirable she was. But then they'd end up with a complication they could both do without. Katrina deserved to find happiness with someone who could give her what she needed—which ruled him out.

Right now, they had a deal. And he had every intention of sticking to it. No matter what his body thought.

CHAPTER SIX

THEY managed to keep things on an even keel for the next few weeks—though Katrina knew the second that Rhys walked into the room, even if her back was turned and she couldn't hear him, and she was pretty sure it was the same for him, too. The awareness. The longing. The wondering.

We could have a wild affair. His words echoed in her head. Maybe they should. Maybe it would get things out of their system and then they could go back to being colleagues.

Or maybe it would just make things worse—because although she could imagine what it would be like to kiss Rhys, to make love with him, the reality would be even more intense. Something she wouldn't want to give up.

She was going to have to start taking long, cold showers. Or doing a few lengths of the local pool—which was always freezing—before work.

She was still thinking about it when she saw Rhys walk into the department, carrying a rolled-up sleeping bag and a suitcase.

Was he going away somewhere straight after work? As far as she knew, he wasn't off duty the next day. Odd. It didn't make sense.

Until she walked into the staffroom during her break and

saw him ending a call on his mobile phone and crossing something off a list.

'Everything OK?' she asked.

'In a word, no.' He rolled his eyes. 'You know that storm we had last week? It took some tiles off my roof, and my landlord sent someone round to fix it—except they found some asbestos. I have to move out while it's being fixed. And because the landlord's panicking about health and safety, that means today.'

She glanced at his list—a printout of local hotels and their phone numbers. Most of them were crossed through. 'No luck finding anywhere?'

'Everywhere's fully booked, with it being Bonfire Night, half-term and then that big charity concert at the end of the week.' He sighed. 'I have a feeling I'm going to be sleeping in my office for a few nights. That's why I brought my sleeping bag in.'

'Rhys, you can't. I mean…I know there are showers and what have you at the hospital, but living out of a suitcase would be awful. And you won't get much rest.'

'It's not ideal, I admit,' he said, 'but I can rough it for a few days.'

Her mouth went into gear a moment before her brain did. 'Look, I have a spare bedroom. Why don't you come and stay with me?'

He blinked. 'Katrina, that's really generous of you—but I can't possibly put you out like that. I have no idea how long it's going to take to sort out my flat. It could be days, it could be weeks.'

'It's not a problem.' Apart from the fact that they'd been trying to stay apart. But they'd managed it so far. If they could do it at work, they could do it outside work, surely? And she couldn't see him in a hole like this. She would've made the same offer to any of her colleagues.

'Then thanks—I owe you one,' Rhys said.

'So that suitcase and the sleeping bag is all you've got?'

'I don't travel *quite* that light.' He smiled wryly. 'I have a flat full of books and films. But at least the place is furnished, so it's only a couple of carloads.'

Her mouth was really on a roll. 'I'll give you a hand. If I drive over to your place this evening, we can load my car up as well as yours and it'll only take one trip.'

'Katrina, you're putting me up. I can hardly ask you to do all that lugging about as well.'

'It isn't a problem. Anyone here would do the same—you help each other out if you're stuck.'

'Then thanks. I really appreciate this, Katrina. And I'll buy us a take-away tonight,' he promised.

'You're on.' She smiled. 'Pizza, salad and the nicest rosemary flatbread in the world.'

'That,' he said, 'is a deal.'

After work, Rhys made two quick stops on the way home, stored one of his purchases in the passenger footwell of his car, then took the packing tape indoors and retrieved the flat-packed removal boxes from underneath his bed. He'd made up the boxes and packed the rest of his clothes by the time Katrina rang the doorbell.

'Come in. Coffee?' he asked, ushering her inside.

'Thanks.'

He quickly went into the kitchen and switched on the kettle. 'I've emptied my bedroom and the bathroom. It's just the kitchen and living room to do now.' He smiled. 'I'm glad I moved most of my music over to a hard disk system a couple of years back, or it'd take twice as long to pack.' And he'd only unpacked a small proportion of his sheet music in the first place, which helped.

Her eyes widened as she saw his cello case and the music stand in the living room. 'I would've guessed that you can sing well, being Welsh, but I had no idea you played an instrument.'

He laughed, disassembling the music stand and putting it on top of the sheet music. 'Don't believe the stereotype—not every Welshman can sing. School assemblies used to be torture, with half the kids singing out of tune.'

'Have you been playing for very long?' she asked.

'We always had a piano and I used to bang the keys when I was a toddler. I started proper lessons when I was, what, three and a half.' Before everything had gone wrong. And afterwards he'd found he was happiest when he was playing music. Filling the silence in the house. 'Later I learned to play the cello as well.'

She glanced round. 'You don't have a piano now?'

'Not any more. It's not quite as portable as a cello,' he said wryly. 'Though I admit I miss the piano. When I get round to buying a place in London, the first thing I'm going to do is buy myself a piano.'

'So you left your piano back in Wales?'

'Moving it was going to be a hassle—I didn't know if there'd be room in a rented place or how long I'd end up in a chain if I bought somewhere of my own. My colleague's daughter wanted to learn, and they're friends so I gave it to them.' It had been a wrench, but at least he'd known his piano would have a good home and be looked after.

'Nobody in our family plays an instrument,' Katrina said. 'Dad and Uncle Bryan always have music on in the garage, and Maddie's really into 1950s stuff—Dean Martin and Julie London and soft jazz—but none of them do anything more than sing along and dance around the place.'

Remembering the absence of music in Katrina's living room, Rhys had a feeling that she didn't join in. Unless she, too, kept all her music as digital files…but somehow he didn't think she did. 'What about you?' he asked.

She wrinkled her nose. 'I normally go along with the kind of stuff everyone else likes. I don't tend to bother with having the radio or what have you on in the house, or if I'm driving somewhere on my own.'

So his guess had been right. 'Maybe,' he said, 'I can introduce you to the stuff I like. Though I should warn you it's classical, rather than pop or rock.'

'I'm not sure I'll be able to appreciate it that well,' she said, 'but thanks for the offer.'

Of course. She'd said that she had a problem with high-frequency sounds; she might have a problem at the lower end of the scale, too.

'So shall I start with the films?' she asked. 'Any particular order?'

'Just however you can fit them into the boxes,' he said. 'I'll start on the books.'

'So did you ever think about becoming a professional musician?' she asked.

'Sort of. I almost studied music instead of medicine. It was a pretty hard choice to make.'

'What made you pick medicine in the end?'

'I wanted to make people better,' he said simply. 'Though my music teacher was pretty upset with me.'

'You have to follow your heart. And you can still play for pleasure.'

'That's what I said to her. And paediatrics is really rewarding.' He shrugged. 'So I know I made the right choice.'

It didn't take long to finish packing Rhys's books and films. He refused to let Katrina carry anything heavier than the briefcase containing his laptop, so he packed the boxes and cases into both cars while she finished putting his kitchen things into a box.

And one thing she'd really noticed about his flat was the lack of personal things. Sure, he had books and films, but there was nothing to give a clue to Rhys the man. There hadn't been a single photograph on his shelves or mantelpiece. No postcards held on to the fridge with magnets. Nothing personal at all.

She knew he was an only child and his parents had split up when he'd been young, but she'd expected to see a picture of at least one of his parents in a frame, like she had on her own mantelpiece. Or maybe a shot of a much-loved family pet. Or even one of Rhys as a student, in the middle of a group of friends.

He'd warned her that he kept people at a distance. He had said that he'd given his piano away to a colleague and friend, she remembered. So he was obviously able to connect with people.

Nevertheless, she'd never met anyone quite so self-contained as Rhys Morgan, and she had the distinct impression that she would barely know she had anyone staying in her home while he was there. Which, in a way, would be a good thing—it removed temptation. Part of her thought it was a seriously bad idea, offering Rhys a place to stay when she knew how hard they were both fighting their mutual attraction, though how could she possibly have left him to sleep in his office when she had a spare room?

Luckily there were two parking spaces just outside her

house, so they were able to transfer the boxes quickly without having to carry them halfway down the street. Again, Rhys refused to let Katrina lift anything heavy, so she busied herself sorting out a visitor's parking permit for him.

'Is that the last?' she asked, when he brought another box in and stacked it in the hallway.

'Almost. One more.' To her surprise, he returned with the most gorgeous bouquet of white roses and freesias.

She blinked. 'Those are for me?'

He nodded. 'I picked them up on the way home from work—I wanted to say thanks for coming to my rescue.' He smiled. 'I told the florist you didn't do pink.'

'Rhys, they're absolutely beautiful.' Her eyes filmed with tears. She couldn't remember the last time someone had bought her flowers. Pete had stopped buying her flowers a long, long time before their relationship had finally ended. 'Thank you,' she said, her voice breaking slightly.

'If I'd known they'd make you cry, I would've bought you chocolate instead,' he said, and gently wiped the single tear from her cheek with the pad of his thumb. 'Don't cry, *cariad*.'

'Sorry. I just wasn't expecting...' She swallowed hard. Lord. Having him touch her like that—it would be, oh, so easy just to turn her head slightly, press a kiss into his palm.

She got a grip on herself. Just. 'I'll put these in water, then show you to your room. There should be enough space for some of your boxes there, and we can stack the rest in the dining room—that's probably the best place for your cello, too.'

'I don't want to take over your house,' he said, looking awkward.

'You're not. You're staying here as my guest.'

'Actually, I wanted to talk to you about that,' he said as he followed her upstairs, carrying his cases. 'I want to pay you rent while I'm here.'

'Don't be daft. Besides, it's not as if I've ever let the room or anything.'

'Even so, your bills are going to be higher with me staying here, and I want to contribute. And I'll do my share of the chores and cooking.' As if he guessed what she was about to say next, he added, 'No arguments, because you'd say exactly the same if you were the one staying in my spare room while your place was being fixed.'

She couldn't disagree with that. 'All right. Thank you.'

'Good—and I'm going to start by ordering that pizza for us tonight.'

'The number for the best local take-away is by the phone in the kitchen,' she said, showing him into the little guest room. 'And if you want to let your parents or whoever know that you're staying here, feel free to give them my landline.'

'No need. I have a mobile,' he said. 'But thank you for the offer.'

Katrina couldn't quite catch his tone, but she noted the set of his shoulders. It looked as if Rhys's 'don't let anyone close' attitude included his parents. She remembered he'd said his parents had split up; she could understand him being slightly more reserved with the parent who'd left, but surely he would've been close to the one he'd lived with?

Obviously not.

By the time Rhys had unpacked, the pizza had arrived. Katrina was careful not to talk about anything personal, and he seemed to relax again while they ate.

'So do you play your cello very much?' she asked.

'About half an hour a day, to keep in practice—sometimes more, if it's been a rough day,' he said.

Clearly it was how he unwound at the end of a day. Like the way she lost herself in a book. 'Would you play for me tonight, or are you too tired?'

He looked at her in surprise. 'You'd like me to play for you?'

'As I said earlier, I probably won't appreciate it as much as I should do, but…' She wrinkled her nose. 'I suppose I'm curious. I'd like to know what kind of music you enjoy.'

'Sure. I'll play in your dining room, if you don't mind—it has a wooden floor, so the acoustics will be better,' he said.

'Do you need your sheet music and a stand?'

He shook his head. 'Only if it's something I haven't played for a long while. Most of the pieces I've played for so many years now I know them by heart.'

Katrina watched, fascinated, as Rhys moved a chair into position, removed the cello from its case and tightened the bow.

'I love this one,' he told her. 'It's the second movement of Bach's cello concerto in G minor.'

He really lost himself as he played, she thought, leaning into the instrument as he moved the bow across the strings. The fingers she'd seen gently treating a child on the ward were just as precise as he pressed each note. And when she looked at his face, it was as if the wall he usually kept between himself and other people had just crumbled away. She was seeing Rhys at his most open—and it brought a lump to her throat. Made her want him even more.

He finished playing and looked up at her.

'Very nice,' she said politely.

'But you had to concentrate.'

She stared at him in surprise. 'How do you know?'

'Because of the pitch being so low. I wondered if you'd be able to hear it properly or if it'd be in your difficult zone.' He looked thoughtful. 'Can I ask you something weird?'

'Weird?'

'Come and sit by me and put your hand against the cello's body, just here.' He touched the lower left side of the cello. 'If you can feel the vibrations, it'll help you hear the music.'

'But won't I get in the way of your bow?'

'No, because my arm will be above your head and the bow's going down to the left.'

'And it won't, um, damage the polish or anything? You know, with the natural oils on my fingertips and what have you?'

He laughed. 'It's not a Stradivarius or a museum piece, Katrina. Just a cello. Touching it won't hurt it at all. Come and sit with me.'

She took a cushion from the sofa, then came to sit at his feet, resting her hand against the cello as he'd directed.

'This is probably my favourite piece by Bach.' He began to play again, and she discovered he was right about the instrument. Feeling the vibration of the note helped her to hear it.

'That's lovely,' she said when he'd finished. 'And I know what that was—the Air on the G String. Dad's got a version of it.'

He nodded.

'Don't stop playing,' she said softly.

The next piece was so beautiful she found herself almost in tears. 'That's amazing. What is it?'

'The *adagio cantabile* from Beethoven's Pathétique Sonata. Strictly speaking, it's a piano piece—but I think it works on the cello, too.' He shrugged. 'I used to drive my cello teacher crazy, transcribing my favourite piano pieces.'

'But you play so well. I think I'm beginning to understand why Maddie loves music so much.'

'Music's food for the soul,' he said softly.

'Would it be greedy to ask for more?'

'You want more, young Oliver?' he teased.

She took her hand from the cello. 'Sorry.'

'I was teasing.' He switched the bow to his other hand, then reached down with his right hand to take hers. 'If you'd like me to play a bit more, it'd be my pleasure.'

Lord, the touch of his hand against hers… She couldn't help curling her fingers round his. For a long, long moment they said nothing, just looked at each other. And Katrina found herself wondering what it would be like to feel his hands against her skin. Would he touch her with the same precision as he played the notes? Would he coax the same kind of response from her body that he coaxed from the cello?

It was, oh, so tempting.

But there would always be a morning after the night before. And given that they both had issues, she really needed to take a metaphorical step backwards. Right now.

'So Bach's your favourite composer?' she asked brightly, uncurling her fingers.

She saw the acknowledgement in his eyes: that he'd been thinking exactly the same thing. Wondering what it would be like to touch her properly. Wondering how she'd react to his hands, his mouth.

'Definitely. Actually, I ache a bit from lugging boxes around. I'll play you more another time.'

'I'll go and put the kettle on,' Katrina said. And the awkward moment was avoided, she thought.

For now.

CHAPTER SEVEN

THE following morning, when Katrina got up, she could smell coffee. Clearly Rhys was up already. She showered and dressed swiftly, and walked into the kitchen. 'Good morning.'

'Morning,' he replied.

'And you've made coffee. Wonderful.' She smiled. 'I think I could get used to this.'

'Ah, no. It'll be your turn to make the coffee tomorrow,' he said lightly.

'Did you sleep OK?'

'Very well, thanks.'

'Good.' She rummaged in the cupboard. 'Cereals or toast?'

'You don't have to make breakfast for me or wait on me, Katrina.'

'I know. But I'm making toast for myself, and it's as quick to stick four slices of bread under the grill as it is two,' she pointed out.

'Then toast would be lovely. Thanks.' He poured them both a mug of coffee, adding milk to hers. 'Well. Cheers.'

'Cheers.'

It had been a long time since Katrina had shared her space like this. But she actually found herself enjoying it—and it would be was good to have company on the walk to work.

After breakfast, she enjoyed walking in to work with Rhys; in the weeks since Madison had moved, Katrina had missed walking in to the hospital with her cousin.

Sharing a house somehow made them more in tune at work, too. 'Can I borrow you for a minute?' Katrina asked one afternoon, leaning against the doorjamb to Rhys's office.

'Sure. What's the problem?'

'Little girl, four years old, history of UTIs. No history in her siblings, but I'm wondering if there's an underlying problem.'

'Are you thinking VUR?' he asked.

VUR, or vesico-ureteric reflux, was when the valve between the bladder and the tubes that led from the kidneys to the bladder didn't work properly, allowing urine to flow back towards the kidneys.

'It's only a suspicion. I haven't done any tests yet.'

'Start with an ultrasound,' he said, 'though it's very easy to miss any signs of scarring, depending on what grade of VUR you're looking at and whether your patient has a fever. You might have to do a cystogram.'

'I hope not,' she said. 'It's unpleasant for little ones, even if you do some play therapy with them first to prepare them for the procedure.' The cystogram meant putting a catheter in the little girl's urethra and filling her bladder with a liquid that showed up on X-ray, then doing a scan to see if all the liquid was going through the urethra or if any was going back towards the kidneys.

'Want me to come and have a look?' he asked.

'Please.'

Katrina introduced him to her patient, Annabel, and her mother, and Rhys explained what they suspected.

'We're going to take a magic picture of your tummy,' Katrina said to Annabel. 'It won't hurt, but it might tickle a bit because I have to put some special gel on your tummy to help me take the picture.' She showed the scanning head to the little girl and let her hold it so she wasn't scared, then swiftly did the scan.

Rhys looked at the screen. 'There's definitely some scarring there,' he said.

'So the good news is that we don't have to do any further tests that Annabel might find uncomfortable,' Katrina explained to Annabel's mother.

'And even better news is that although it's vesico-ureteric reflux, I can't see any distension. We grade the condition from one to five, with one being the mildest,' he said, 'and this looks like a grade two to me. So it should clear up on its own without surgery.'

'What causes it?' Annabel's mother asked.

'With small children, it's usually caused by the tunnel through the bladder wall not being long enough,' Rhys said.

'As she grows, the tunnel will get longer and the condition will improve,' Katrina added. 'But we need to make sure Annabel doesn't get any more urine infections, or it might cause some damage to her kidneys.'

'And to make sure she doesn't get an infection, we'll give her long-term antibiotic therapy—a very low dose every day until she's five,' Rhys said.

'But doesn't using antibiotics lead to bugs becoming resistant?' Annabel's mother asked.

'If you don't complete the course properly, yes. But this is slightly different,' Katrina said. 'She'll need to give regular urine samples to your GP, and we'll call her in for an ultrasound every six months to check that her kidneys are growing properly. And if you get any signs of a urinary infection, you need to take her straight to your doctor.'

'So that's if she starts needing to have a wee more often than usual or has accidents that just aren't like her,' Rhys said. 'Or if she's not very well and you can't put your finger on what's wrong, she gets a temperature, or her urine smells unpleasant or has blood in it.'

'Will giving her cranberry juice help?' Annabel's mother asked.

'Should do, but look out for the other signs as well,' Katrina advised.

'So she'll definitely grow out of it?'

'I'm pretty sure she will,' Rhys said. 'If not, we'll need to give her an operation to correct the valve problem—but try not to worry. In most cases the antibiotic treatment works really well and it's more than likely she'll outgrow the condition.'

'We'll need to scan her big brother and her little sister, just to check they're not affected,' Katrina added.

'Because about a third of patients with VUR also have siblings with the condition,' Rhys explained.

'I can book them in for the scans now, if you like,' Katrina said.

'Thank you.' Annabel's mother smiled. 'You've worked together for a long time, haven't you?'

'A little while,' Rhys said.

'I thought so.'

'Why?' he asked.

'Because you finish each other's sentences.'

'Do we?' Katrina blinked. 'I hadn't—'

'Noticed,' Rhys continued with a grin. 'It's called teamwork.'

'Everyone on the ward does it,' Katrina said. Though even as she spoke, she wondered. Did they? Or were she and Rhys just that little bit more in tune?

She was still wondering on the Saturday morning, in a world

of her own, when she walked into the bathroom, shrugged off her robe, pulled the shower curtain back from the edge of the bath—and saw Rhys there, showering off the last suds.

'Oh, my God. I'm so sorry. I didn't realise…I didn't hear…I'm *so* sorry.' She felt colour shoot into her face; mortified, she grabbed her robe and fled from the room.

It felt as if everything was happening in slow motion. The curtain being dragged back, the look of shock on Katrina's face as she saw him, followed swiftly by embarrassment, and then she rushed away.

Clearly he hadn't locked the door properly and she hadn't heard the water running. And the last thing Rhys wanted was for Katrina to feel embarrassed about her hearing or be awkward with him because of it. He turned off the shower with one hand and grabbed a towel and wrapped it round himself with the other as he climbed out of the bathtub. Heedless of the fact he was still wet, he went after her, catching up with her in the corridor by her bedroom door. 'Katrina, wait.' He put a hand on her arm to get her attention and make her face him.

'I'm sorry,' she said again, biting her lip. She looked embarrassed and close to tears, and he hated it. He couldn't let her shut herself away in her room, feeling that upset and miserable.

'It's all right,' he said, making sure that she could see his face. 'It's my fault—I couldn't have locked the bathroom door properly. You didn't hear the water running?'

'No. I wasn't concentrating.' She gulped. 'I'm so sorry.'

'*Cariad*, please don't keep apologising. It isn't your fault. You weren't expecting me to be there and I should have made sure the door was locked so you knew I was there.' He stroked her face. 'I'm sorry—you said you weren't profoundly deaf, and I didn't realise quite how much hearing loss you have.'

'It's the family joke that I'm always the one who sleeps through thunderstorms.' She gave him a brittle smile. 'It's just as well I'm a lark instead of an owl like Maddie, or I'd never hear the alarm and be up in time for work. Mum bought me one of those ones that uses a light instead of sound and gradually gets brighter like the sun, and Dad made sure my smoke detectors are really loud so I'm safe, and Maddie bought me one of those gizmos that flashes when the phone or doorbell rings.'

She was gabbling, and they both knew it.

'Maybe you should sing in the shower in future or something,' she said. 'Very, very loudly.'

Katrina was clearly trying to make light of the situation, but Rhys heard the slight crack in her voice. She was really upset. And embarrassed. And feeling she was lacking in something. No doubt she was thinking about Pete and his cruel, unfair comments.

'Katrina, never, *ever* apologise for being you. You're fine just the way you are.' Even though he knew it was dangerous and he really shouldn't do it—he wanted to comfort her and make her feel better. Which meant putting his arms round her, holding her close.

She was wearing a soft white towelling dressing-gown; when he pressed his cheek against hers, her skin felt even softer.

Irresistible.

He couldn't stop himself. He turned his face very, very slightly until the corner of his mouth was touching hers. The lightest, sweetest, gentlest kiss. And then everything seemed to blur. He wasn't quite sure when or how it happened, but then Katrina was holding him back, her arms wrapped just as tightly round him as his were round her, and her mouth was against his properly. Warm and sweet and soft and responsive, opening under the pressure of his mouth so he could deepen the kiss.

He could feel the blood pulsing through his veins. Feel his heart beating, strong and quickening as he kissed her. Feel every sense magnifying, blooming.

This was exactly what he'd thought it would be like, kissing Katrina.

Amazing.

Even though part of him told him to stop, that he was in grave danger of making the situation much worse, his need for her was stronger. He couldn't remember ever wanting anyone so much. And it was as if a dam had broken, the feeling rushing through him, powerful and unstoppable.

She'd put her bathrobe back on but he knew she was naked underneath. In that brief moment when she'd slipped off her robe in the bathroom, he'd seen just how lovely she was. And he needed to see her again. To touch her. To taste her. He needed that so very, very badly. Still kissing her, he undid the belt of her robe in one fluid movement and pushed the fabric off her shoulders—and then he broke the kiss. Brushed his mouth against hers, just to tell her he had every intention of kissing her again. And then he stepped back far enough to look at her properly.

Lord, she was gorgeous.

He stroked his palms over her shoulders and down her arms, gliding his hands upwards again over her hips and settling in the curve of her waist.

He made a small sound of pure pleasure. '*Cariad*, you're so beautiful. You take my breath away.'

She said nothing, just looked at him, her blue eyes huge and full of wonder and fear; and Rhys knew in that moment that she felt exactly the same as he did. Wanting this so much, but scared in case everything went wrong and crashed down around them.

Maybe it was time to be brave.

He dipped his head and traced a line of kisses round her throat. Her skin was so soft, so sweet. And he wanted more.

As she tipped her head back, he let his mouth drift lower, then took one nipple into his mouth.

She breathed a little, 'Oh' and slid her fingers into his hair. The gentle pressure of her fingertips against his scalp urged him on, telling him she liked what he was doing; he switched his attention to her other nipple, teasing it with his tongue and his lips until she was pushing against him, clearly wanting more.

'You're gorgeous,' he said huskily, stroking over her rib-cage to the flat planes of her stomach. Her breathing was fast and shallow, much like his own. 'And I want you, Katrina. I need…' He straightened up again so he could look her in the eye. 'I think we *both* need this.'

'Yes,' she whispered. She opened her door and walked through it, leaving her towelling robe where it lay on the floor in the hallway.

The soft light filtered through her bedroom curtains and he could see her very clearly. 'You're amazing, Katrina,' he said, following her and closing the door behind him. 'Stunning.'

She actually blushed.

Did she really not know how lovely she was?

And then she smiled and he lost his head completely. He pulled her back into his arms and kissed her again, stroking her back and the curve of her buttocks. She felt perfect. 'I want to touch you, Katrina. I want to touch you all over,' he said between kisses. He wanted to learn what she liked, what gave her pleasure, to make her feel as amazing as she made him feel.

Almost shyly, she tugged at the edge of his towel. It fell to the floor—and then at last there was nothing between them. Skin to damp skin. And it felt so very, very good.

He wasn't quite sure how they got there or who led whom, but then they were lying facing each other in her bed, the cotton sheet cool against their bodies. Right at that moment he felt as if he was burning up with need for her. He let the flat of his hand slide over her curves, moulding itself to the dip of her waist and the swell of her hip.

'Perfect,' he breathed. Then he remembered: she wouldn't hear what he was saying. He shifted so she could read his lips, and repeated, 'You're absolutely perfect.' His fingers trailed along her outer thigh, then gently brushed upwards again, this time against her inner thigh. Katrina shivered and moved slightly, allowing him the access he craved so badly. He cupped her sex, then let one finger glide along the soft, sweet folds.

She gasped as his fingertip skated across her clitoris.

'You like that?' he asked.

'Yes.'

He did it again.

'Oh-h-h.' The word was a breath of pure pleasure.

He bent to kiss her, still stroking her and teasing her until she was making little incoherent noises.

And then a truly awful thought struck him.

'Katrina.' He touched her shoulder to get her attention.

'Hmm?' She opened her eyes, blinking to help her focus. 'What?'

'Do you have any condoms?'

'Condoms?' she echoed. Her eyes widened; clearly she realised exactly what his question implied. 'No.'

'Ah.'

'Are you telling me you don't either?'

'I don't either,' he said ruefully.

'And I'm not on the Pill.' She took a deep breath.

But there was a slight wobble in her voice, telling him that she was as disappointed as he was. That he'd brought her to this pitch of arousal and now he was going to let her down.

Well, he wasn't going to let her down.

'There's another way,' he said softly, and leaned over to kiss her, sliding one hand back between her thighs.

'Rhys…'

'Shh. It's OK,' he soothed, and kissed his way down her body, nuzzling all the way down her sternum, drawing a line of teasing kisses around her navel and finally stroking her thighs apart.

He drew one finger along the length of her sex, and she quivered.

He did it again and again, taking it slowly, feeling the heat build between them.

When he pushed one finger inside her, she gave a gasp of pleasure. 'Yes,' she whispered. 'Oh, Rhys—please, yes.'

He circled her clitoris with his thumb as he moved his hand, gradually quickening his pace, kissing her deeply until he felt her go rigid.

'Open your eyes, *cariad*,' he said, stroking her cheek with the back of his fingers.

She did. And it gave him such a kick to see the wonder in her eyes, the sheer pleasure, followed by the soft, sweet aftershocks of her climax rippling over his skin.

'Oh. My. God,' Katrina said, her voice shaky. Her pupils, he was pleased to note, were absolutely huge. 'Rhys, that was… I mean…'

He loved it that he'd been able to reduce this clever, capable woman to incoherent mush. That he'd made her feel so good she lost it completely.

'Good,' he said, and stole another kiss.

She dragged in a breath. 'My turn.'

'You don't have to.' He moved so that he was lying on his side. 'That's not the way it works, *cariad*.'

'But I…Rhys, you made me feel amazing just now.'

'Good. That was the point. Because you *are* amazing, Katrina.'

'And I should do the same for—'

He silenced her with a kiss. 'There's no shoulds in this.' He couldn't resist kissing her again. 'That wasn't actually supposed to happen. It certainly wasn't planned. I just couldn't keep my hands off you. Once I'd touched you, kissed you—I couldn't stop.'

'So what now?'

That was the big question. And trust her to face it head-on rather than skirt round the issue. 'I like you, Katrina. A lot. And I feel different when I'm with you.'

'But?' She said the word for him.

'But I don't know if I can offer you what you deserve.' He grimaced. 'I'm not good at relationships. I start out with good intentions and then somehow there's this glass wall between me and the woman I'm falling for, and it all goes horribly wrong. I don't want to do that to you—especially after what happened with Pete. I don't want to hurt you.' Even though he knew he really ought to resume the distance between them, try and go back to how things had been before, he needed her back in his arms. He wrapped his arms round her and shifted so that she was lying with her head resting on his shoulder and her arm wrapped round his waist. 'But we've crossed a line here. I don't think we can go back to how it was. Not now I know how it feels to touch you.'

'Me, too,' she admitted. 'And I want to make you feel the way you just made *me* feel. Incredible.'

'You don't have to.'

'I want to.' She stroked his hip. 'I want to touch you, Rhys. I want to make you lose it, the way you made me lose it just now. I want to blow your mind.'

'Carry on like this, *cariad*, and I'm going to forget all about being sensible,' he warned her softly.

She removed her hand. 'Sorry.'

'Don't be.' He stole another kiss. 'We discussed it. We agreed to stay apart. And it didn't work.' He paused. 'So let's try it the other way.'

'You mean—be lovers?'

'Yes. I want to be your lover,' he said, drawing the pad of his thumb along her lower lip. 'I want to take you to the very edge of pleasure.' He wanted to lose himself within her and forget the world.

'Lovers.' She shivered slightly as she said the word, but he knew she wasn't cold. Very, very far from it. The thought clearly excited her as much as it excited him. Her pupils were huge and her lips were parted and it was all he could do not to kiss her again.

She dragged in a breath. 'This scares the hell out of me, Rhys.'

'Me, too,' he admitted. 'But maybe it's time we were both brave. See where this takes us.'

'But keep it just between us for now,' Katrina said.

While this was all so new. He knew exactly where she was coming from. 'Yes.' He kissed her lightly. Just to seal the deal. 'If I stay here with you any longer, Katrina, I'm going to do something reckless.' He kissed her again. 'So I suggest we get up. I'm going to finish that shower. I'd prefer it to be with you wrapped round me, but I'm going to show restraint and shower on my own—because I'm rapidly running out of will-power where you're concerned.'

'Uh-huh.'

'And that wasn't the first brick going up in the glass wall,' he reassured her, seeing the sudden worry in her expression. 'Because, after you've had a shower, we're going out. I don't mind where we go or what we do, but I'm going to make a very necessary purchase at some point today. And then I plan to take you out to dinner. And tonight, Katrina Gregory, I'm going to make love with you properly. The way I've wanted to since practically the first moment I met you.'

She looked at him, half-shy and so achingly sweet he very nearly forgot himself and made love with her anyway. 'I sincerely hope that's a promise,' she said.

He smiled. 'Oh, it is. And, Katrina?'

'Mmm?'

'Just so you know…I always…' he kissed her, just for emphasis '…*always* keep my promises.'

CHAPTER EIGHT

AFTER his shower, Rhys dressed, headed for the kitchen and made a cafetière of coffee. He was sitting flicking through a medical journal, nursing a mug of coffee, when Katrina strolled into the room. Dressed casually in jeans and a light sweater, she looked absolutely edible; and when she gave him a shy, sweet smile, he really had to stop himself scooping her up, settling her on his lap and drinking the rest of his coffee with one arm wrapped round her.

Instead, he put the journal on the table and wrapped his hands round his coffee mug to keep them occupied. 'Hi. Coffee's still hot if you want some.'

'This is getting to be a habit, you making me coffee.' She smiled. 'But it's one I could get used to.' She poured herself a mugful, adding plenty of milk. 'Have you had breakfast yet?'

'I waited for you.'

She smiled. 'Then humour me. I'm going to experiment.'

'Experiment?' Oh, the thoughts that word conjured up.

She flushed to the roots of her hair, and he smiled. 'You're delicious. And I like the fact that your mind works the same way as mine.'

'Stop it. I'm going to make breakfast. Get on with reading your journal.'

Was she trying to keep her hands occupied, he wondered, just like he was, so they didn't end up ripping off each other's clothes again?

And then he wished he hadn't thought of that. Because he really, really wanted to take Katrina back to bed and spend the day discovering just where she liked to be touched, where she liked to be kissed.

She busied herself whipping up something in a bowl and heating butter in an omelette pan.

Pancakes for breakfast? he guessed. Sounded good to him.

'I'll get plates and cutlery,' he said. Mainly because it meant he had to walk right past her and that gave him the perfect opportunity to drop a kiss on the nape of her neck. Just so she knew he hadn't changed his mind while she'd been in the shower. That he still wanted her.

And then, when she tipped the contents of the bowl onto a board, rolled it out and cut out rounds, he realised what she'd just made.

Dough for Welsh cakes.

Not quite traditional ones, as she hadn't added sultanas. But he could smell the sweet scent of cinnamon. And something else.

'These are gorgeous,' he said after the first bite. 'Cinnamon?'

'Sorry, it's not quite traditional—but I loathe sultanas,' Katrina said. 'And the vanilla's my mum's trick.' She smiled. 'I love the scent of vanilla. And you can't beat a really good vanilla ice cream.'

Eaten in bed, he thought, from one of the small half-litre tubs, sharing the spoon and feeding each other and…

'Rhys?'

He shook himself mentally. 'Sorry. Just thinking.' But the

picture was still there in his mind, and he couldn't help the words sliding out. 'You. Ice cream. Bed.'

She dragged in a breath. *'Rhys.'*

Her expression mirrored the longing in his head. Clearly she could imagine it, too.

'We can't.' Lord, it was hard to call a halt when his whole body was crying out to him to just pick her up, carry her to her bed and make love with her until they were both out of their minds. 'We need…'

'Supplies,' she finished.

'Waiting's going to make it even better,' he said. Though right at that moment he wasn't sure he believed that. Every sweet-scented bite of the Welsh cakes made him think of the sweetness of Katrina's mouth and how much he wanted to kiss her.

Katrina had just about managed to get her libido back under control by the time they'd finished washing up. Though the look in Rhys's eyes made breathing difficult. It made her remember just how it had felt when he'd kissed her, touched her, stroked her until her body had surged into a climax.

He'd expected nothing in return. Even turned down her offer to reciprocate.

Later tonight, she promised herself, she'd make it up to him. And how.

She dragged on her fleece while he shrugged on a battered leather jacket. Added to his worn jeans and black sweater, it made him look dangerous. Sexy as hell. Katrina actually had to remind herself to breathe.

He held her hand all the way to the tube station. All the way on the tube. And all the way while they walked on Hampstead Heath, kicking through piles of autumn leaves.

'I've missed this,' he said, looking wistful.

'So Cardiff is full of trees and parks?'

'Not quite in the same way as London,' he said. 'I was thinking more of the village where I grew up. There's a ruined castle with a huge park. I had a holiday job in the tearooms. And, best of all, it meant I got free entrance, so on a dry day I could study under the shade of a tree in the park. Just me, my books and the fresh air.' He smiled. 'And I used to really love walking there in the autumn. Crunching through the leaves and collecting the odd conker.'

Why hadn't he studied at home in comfort, like she and Madison had? Katrina wondered. And if Rhys loved the countryside that much, it seemed odd that he'd chosen to work in a city hospital, rather than as a country GP where he'd get a chance to do house calls and be outside a lot. Or maybe it was something to do with the difficult family life he'd mentioned. A place of escape.

They had lunch, a panini and coffee, in a small café, then spent the rest of the afternoon browsing in the antique and bric-a-brac shops. When he spotted a chemist's shop, Rhys excused himself, and Katrina felt her face heat. She knew exactly what he was going to buy. And she knew that getting 'supplies' was the right thing to do—but she also knew that she was going to spend the rest of the afternoon thinking about what they would do that evening when they got home.

Making love.

The ultimate in closeness.

The weight of his body over hers.

His body moving inside hers.

Excitement and desire shimmered down her spine.

When he walked back out into the street, she couldn't think straight. And clearly she had some kind of goofy look on her face, because he asked softly, 'Are you all right, Katrina?'

'I'm fine,' she fibbed.

'Good.' He took her hand, drew it up to his mouth and kissed the backs of her fingers. 'I think,' he said softly, 'we should have an early dinner.'

She felt her eyes widen. 'Rhys, we're not really dressed…'

'For an expensive restaurant, no.' He drew her close to him and bent his head so he could whisper in her ear. 'Katrina.'

She loved it that he'd thought to check she could hear him. 'Yes?'

'I would love to see you all dressed up. Especially knowing that I'd have the privilege later of undressing you again.'

His words sent a lovely shivery feeling all the way through her.

'But the thing is, if we go back now and change, we might not get past the stage of taking *these* clothes off.'

Oh, lord. The pictures that put in her head.

His mouth brushed the sensitive spot by her ear. 'So let's go somewhere a little more casual. Eat. And then I'm taking you home.'

In the end they found a small trattoria. With candles and flowers on the table, the place felt incredibly romantic. Especially as their table was in a quiet corner, Katrina thought.

Every time she caught Rhys's eye, every time her fingers brushed against his when they dipped their bread in the little dish of olive oil, a little throb of excitement pulsed through her. She could see on his face that it was the same for him. And when the waiter brought the dessert menu to them and asked them if they wanted coffee, Rhys glanced at her. She gave the tiniest shake of her head. She didn't want pudding or coffee. Just him.

'Just the bill, please,' Rhys said with a smile.

Every second they waited seemed to take for ever. Every

step back to the tube felt like a mile. And the wait on the platform for a train, watching the clock and willing the minutes to speed by instead of drag by…

'It's a pity the train's so empty,' Rhys said when it finally arrived.

'Why?' she asked, mystified.

'Because if it was full you'd have had to… Ah, what the hell. We'll do it anyway.' He sat down and pulled her onto his lap, catching her off balance so she had to put her arms round his neck for support.

'Now, that,' he said with a smile, 'feels better.'

They didn't talk on the train. Didn't need to. And Rhys held her hand all the way from the tube station to her house. With every step, Katrina's heart was racing. And the second the front door closed behind them, he spun her into his arms, dipped his head and kissed her.

She felt him slip her fleecy jacket off and drop it on the floor. His leather jacket followed.

'Leave them,' he said softly. 'I'll deal with it later. We've been sensible all day and I just can't wait any more. I want you so much, Katrina.' He took her hand again. Held her gaze. Kissed the tip of each finger, drawing it briefly into his mouth. She could see the flare of desire brighten in his eyes. And then he laced his fingers through hers.

'I could do the caveman thing.'

'You could,' she agreed neutrally.

'But I need to be sure you want this as much as I do. That I'm not pushing you.'

In answer, she drew his hands up to her mouth and kissed them. 'You're not pushing me. And I do want this. And I'm quite happy to be carried off by a gorgeous Welsh knight, even if his white charger isn't actually with him.' She stroked his face. 'Except I'm not little, like Maddie, so I don't want you to do your back in.'

He laughed. 'Ah, now, *cariad*, you're impugning my masculinity.'

She smiled and pressed herself against him. 'I'm well aware that you're a man, Rhys.' All man. And how.

He dragged in a breath. 'And you are irresistible, Katrina Gregory. Not girly—but you're definitely all woman.' He cupped her face, holding her very tenderly, as if she were something infinitely precious. He dipped his head, brushing his mouth against hers in a sweet, gentle kiss. And the second their lips touched, the kiss turned explosive, his tongue sliding against hers and mimicking the way his body would fill her later. Promising and demanding, at the same time. Cherishing and possessive. Claiming her as his and yet making it clear that what they were about to do would be very, very mutual.

She'd never wanted anyone as much as she wanted Rhys Morgan.

And when he finally broke the kiss, ending with a sweet, gentle caress and pulling back enough to look her in the eye, she whispered, 'Now.'

She laced her fingers through his and led him up the stairs.

At the top, he paused. 'And this is where I carry you to my room.'

Katrina shook her head. 'My bed's a double. Yours is a single and I'm too old to behave like a student.'

'Old? Twenty-eight is hardly old.' But he humoured her, let her draw him down the corridor to her room. At her doorway, he paused again. 'Katrina.'

'Yes?'

'Caveman or knight. It's the same thing.' He pushed her door open, scooped her up and carried her over the threshold.

He set her on her feet next to the bed, drew the curtains, then took the hem of her sweater and drew it upwards. She lifted her arms, letting him pull off her sweater; he traced along the lacy edges of her bra with one fingertip, a look of wonder on his face, clearly enjoying the contrast between the stiffness of the lace and the softness of her skin.

'You're so beautiful, *cariad*.'

She felt her face heat, and tried to cover her confusion by saying, 'And you're wearing way too much.'

'Want to do something about it?'

She nodded, and he let her strip off his sweater. She stroked his arms, his shoulders, glorying in the feel of his skin under her fingertips, then let her hands trail down over his chest to his abdomen. 'Rhys Morgan, you're beautiful, too.' She couldn't remember desiring anyone so much. Rhys was just perfect. He wasn't lean and skinny, but he wasn't fat either—just beautifully toned, with powerful shoulders and strong biceps and narrow hips and strong thighs. He really did look like the Welsh knight she'd teased about being—noble, beautiful, his dark hair in sharp contrast to his pale skin and blue eyes. Perfect Celtic colouring. She could just imagine him as a knight, hundreds of years ago, his hair slightly longer. Sexy as hell.

'*Cariad?* What are you thinking?' he asked.

She told him, and he grinned. 'Now, as the knight I'd have the honour of bedding my maiden fair.' His expression sobered. 'And that's exactly what I want to do with you right now, Katrina.'

He drew one finger along her breastbone, then with his other hand he unsnapped her bra and let it fall to the floor. When he cupped her breasts, she tipped her head back, baring her throat to him. He took full advantage, kissing his way down her throat and stooping lower so he could take one nipple into his mouth. She dragged in a breath as he teased the hard peak with the tip of his tongue and then sucked hard. 'Rhys.'

He stopped immediately. 'You don't like this?'

'Ye-es.'

'But?'

She swallowed hard. 'It's not *enough*. I need you, Rhys. Now. All day I've been thinking about you. About us. About tonight. And if you don't make love with me this very second, I think I'm going to spontaneously combust.'

'Your wish,' he said, 'is my command.' He undid the button of her jeans, slid the zip down, and gently pushed the soft denim over her hips. She shimmied out of her jeans and kicked off her socks at the same time, so she was standing before him in nothing but a tiny pair of white lace knickers.

She was pleased to note that his pupils dilated and colour bloomed in his cheeks. 'Katrina. I…' He shook his head, as if clearing it, then stripped off the rest of his clothes in three seconds flat, picked her up and laid her on the bed.

His hands were sure yet gentle as he tipped her back against the pillows, and when he kissed his way down her body, she could feel the faint rasp of stubble. And somehow he found erogenous zones she hadn't even known existed, making her wriggle beneath him, desperate for more. He circled her navel with his tongue, nuzzled her hipbones, and finally, finally slid his hands between her thighs, parting them. But when his hands moved lower, caressing the backs of her knees, she almost whimpered.

'Rhys. Stop teasing me. Please. I need…'

'I know. So do I. Hold that thought,' he whispered, and stole a kiss before climbing off the bed.

Despite being completely naked, he was totally unselfconscious; Katrina couldn't help watching him as he moved. He really was beautiful. Perfect musculature beneath that smooth skin. And she *wanted*. Lord, how she wanted.

He rummaged in his jeans, took the packet of condoms he'd bought earlier from the pocket and removed one.

'My job, I think,' she said, taking it from him as he joined her on the bed again. She undid the foil packet, then slid the condom over his erect penis, and she was gratified when he gave a sharp intake of breath. So he was in the same state as she was? Good.

He knelt between her thighs, and she sank back against the pillows. Just as she'd done that morning, when he'd tipped her over the edge of pleasure, unselfishly making sure that she was sated even though he hadn't been.

And now…

Rhys kissed her again, then whispered, 'Katrina?'

She opened her eyes. 'Yes?'

'Now?'

'Now,' she confirmed.

Slowly, gently, he eased his body into hers.

Katrina had had sex before. Made love before. But nothing had been like this. The way Rhys made her feel…

'This feels like paradise,' Rhys said softly.

That pretty much summed it up for her, too.

He slid his hands up her thighs, gently positioning her so that her legs were wrapped round his waist, and then he pushed deeper. Katrina couldn't help giving a little 'oh' of pleasure. Rhys smiled, but not as if he was smugly pleased with himself—more that he was pleased he was making her feel so good.

He kissed her throat—hot, wet, open-mouthed kisses that had her quivering and clutching at his shoulders, wanting him even closer, needing the ultimate contact. She was aware of the hardness of his chest against the softness of her breasts, and the friction of the hair against her sensitised nipples was driving her crazy.

And then, as if Rhys knew she was right near the edge, he slowed everything down. Slowly, incredibly focused, he withdrew until he was almost out of her, then slid all the way back in again, putting pressure on just the right spot and making her feel as if she were floating.

When her climax hit, it felt like being in the middle of a storm, the dark skies lit by sheets of lightning.

'Now,' he whispered, and jammed his mouth against hers; she felt his body surge against hers, and knew that he too had just fallen over the edge.

Afterwards, she lay curled in his arms. 'Any regrets?' he asked softly.

'No.'

'Good.'

Part of her was almost too scared to ask, but she needed to know. 'You?'

He stroked her face. 'No.'

'Good.'

'But?'

It amazed her that he could read her so easily. That he'd picked up on the tiny, tiny fear. 'I was just wondering...were you planning to go back to your own room?'

'If you want me to.' He shifted so he could look her in the eye. 'But if there's a choice of sleeping with you in my arms and waking up with you tomorrow morning...I'd definitely pick that one.'

Exactly what she wanted, too. 'Yes,' she said softly.

While he was in the bathroom, dealing with the condom, she removed her hearing aid and placed it in the case that she kept next to the clock. When he returned, he said something she didn't catch.

'Sorry. I'm minus sound,' she said, feeling her face heat. 'I, um, don't sleep with my hearing aid in.'

He kissed the tip of her nose. 'No need to apologise. I asked if you were sure about this.'

'I'm sure.'

'Good.' And, with that, he slid into bed beside her, switched off the light and gathered her into his arms, holding her close.

Katrina felt her eyelids droop; safe and secure in Rhys's arms, she drifted off to sleep.

CHAPTER NINE

KATRINA woke twice in the night. Once when she kissed Rhys awake and, while all his defences were down, repaid him the pleasure he'd given her that morning. And once when she was startled out of a bad dream, and cuddled into him as if having his arms round her would protect her from the nameless fears that still lingered. As if he sensed it, he tightened his arms and murmured something she didn't catch but which made her feel safe again.

And then it was morning.

Sunday morning, when neither of them had to be at the hospital.

When she woke, she half expected Rhys to be up already, reading the paper or a magazine at the kitchen table and nursing a cup of coffee, but he was still curled around her, holding her close.

It felt very, very odd.

She wasn't used to waking up in someone's arms. Not since Pete.

And today was a whole new day. Despite what they'd shared the previous night, would it be different now between them? Would Rhys have had time to think about it and come to the same conclusions that Pete had? Would he back away?

She stretched, very slightly, and was rewarded with a kiss in the curve between her neck and shoulder.

Oh.

So he was awake.

How long had he been awake? Had she snored or embarrassed herself by talking in her sleep or anything? The fears flurried through her mind.

'Good morning, sleepyhead.' His voice was clear, slightly amused. 'I thought you said you were a lark?'

'I am.' It couldn't be much past seven.

Then she glanced at the clock. 'Nine o'clock?' she asked in horror. 'But I never sleep in this late!' She twisted round to face him.

'Neither do I. But I didn't want to move,' he admitted. 'I liked waking up with you in my arms, all soft and warm.'

So he hadn't changed his mind. He'd been awake for ages and he'd just wanted to hold her.

Warmth spread through her and her worries faded away. Maybe, just maybe, she thought, this was going to work out just fine.

'So what now?' she asked.

'I thought we could take a shower. A long one. Together. And it's miserable weather outside, so I'll make us some breakfast. If there's something on at the cinema, maybe we could go out.' He stroked her face. 'And if there's not... Well, I'll just have to lie with you on the sofa and watch a film here.'

A lazy Sunday afternoon in autumn spent with Rhys. She couldn't think of anything she'd rather do. 'Sounds good to me.'

The shower took a long, long time, and Katrina knew afterwards that she'd never be able to see her bathroom in quite the same light again. She'd always remember the way Rhys had lifted her against the tiles, the way the water had poured over their bodies as her body had tightened round his, the way he'd soaped her all over afterwards and dried her in a warm, fluffy towel.

Breakfast was forgotten; it was more like lunchtime when they finally made it downstairs. When they checked the cinema listings, there wasn't anything on that either of them was keen to see. Glancing out of the window at the kind of drizzle she knew from experience was miserably penetrating, Katrina didn't really want to go out anyway. They ended up cooking Sunday lunch together and having a quiet, domesticated day indoors—one of the sweetest, loveliest days Katrina had ever spent. They closed the curtains against the rain to watch a *film noir*, curled up together on the sofa, and afterwards Rhys played the cello for her before making love with her again.

If she'd been able to stop time and bottle it, she thought, she would've chosen that day. Because it was just perfect.

The next few weeks were the happiest Katrina had ever known. At work they kept things strictly professional, only having lunch together if it was a case conference on a patient, but outside she spent nearly all her free time with him.

Madison was right, Katrina thought. She *had* been missing out. And she knew without a doubt that Rhys was The One.

He hadn't actually told her he loved her. Just as she hadn't told him. But she knew. It was in his eyes, in the way he touched her, in the way he surprised her with tickets to a rarely shown film, in the way he made sure she could see his face when he said anything to her.

And even though Rhys moved back into his flat when the landlord had given him the all-clear after the roof repairs, he still spent his nights with her—either at his place or hers. She even kept a toothbrush and spare clothes at his places, as he did at hers.

Life didn't get any better than this, Katrina thought. And he was gradually letting her close. Maybe, just maybe, things were going to work out. For both of them.

'I'm the one who's supposed to be glowing,' Madison remarked, adding far too much pepper to her mushroom and avocado pizza.

'You are glowing.' Then Katrina realised what her cousin meant. 'If you're asking if I'm pregnant, don't be daft. Of course I'm not. Clearly these cravings for disgusting pizza toppings are addling your brain.'

Madison rolled her eyes. 'There's nothing disgusting about avocado on pizza. And I wasn't saying that you were pregnant. Just glowing. As in the glow that means you're having absolutely loads of fantastic sex.'

'Maddie!'

Her cousin grinned, totally unrepentant. 'Well, you are, aren't you?'

Katrina felt herself blushing to the roots of her hair. 'Yes.'

'Excellent. It's good to see you happy, Kat. He's the one, isn't he?'

Katrina had quietly confided to her cousin that she was seeing Rhys. 'We're taking it day by day.'

'But you're in love with him, aren't you?'

'I'm not saying the words.'

Madison raised an eyebrow. 'Take the risk. It's worth it, I promise you.'

'Not yet.' There was still something holding Katrina back. She wasn't sure what, but she couldn't say it just yet. It was too new. And she'd only recently realised herself just how deeply her feelings went for Rhys. It was as if a missing piece of her life had slotted quietly into place.

'Well, I'm pleased for you anyway.'

'You haven't said anything to anyone, have you?' Katrina asked, suddenly worried. Now her cousin was ecstatically happy with Theo, she was trying to make sure that everyone else was, too.

'Of course not. You told me in confidence.' Madison sighed. 'When your mum rang me the other day to find out if there was a special reason why you sounded so happy nowadays, I said it was because you loved your job and you're doing well in your exams and you're probably going to make registrar quicker than I did.'

'Thank you.' Katrina toyed with her own pizza. Though she wasn't surprised that her mother had called Madison for a quiet word. Madison's mother always called Katrina when she was concerned about Maddie, knowing they were close and always looked out for each other.

Madison reached over and squeezed her hand. 'Hey. Remember what you said to me about Theo when I was scared? You told me to hang in there because when he'd sorted out whatever the problem was in his head, he'd be worth the wait. And you were right. He was.'

'This is different.'

'It isn't different at all. It's merely that Rhys hasn't got around to telling you what's in his head yet. And have you told him about Pete the Toad?'

'Yes. And he says my hearing's part of who I am—he doesn't have a problem with it.'

'Good. Otherwise I'd break every bone in his body. Twice,' Madison said, very coolly and very seriously.

'Maddie!' Katrina said, shocked.

'Well, I love you,' her cousin said, looking completely unrepentant. 'And anyone who hurts you has me to deal with.'

'He's not going to hurt me, Maddie.' She bit her lip. 'At least, not intentionally. But I don't want to be the first one to say how I feel,' she admitted, knowing that her confidence to her cousin would go no further. 'In case I've got it wrong.'

'For the record,' Madison said, 'I don't think you've got it wrong. He's quiet and deep, but you're the quiet one of the family so he suits you perfectly.' She smiled. 'And I'm expecting to be a bridesmaid, you know. Or matron of honour, whatever you want to call it.'

'You,' Katrina said, 'aren't just counting your chickens, you're giving them all names! But if—and I mean *if*—I ever get married, of course you're walking down the aisle behind me. Except your dress won't be pink.'

'The colour's negotiable. But I want high heels,' Madison said with an irrepressible smile.

'Anyway, we should be planning *your* wedding, not mine.'

'It isn't going to be until late spring—probably the first week of May—and we have loads of time to plan.' Madison spread her hands. 'It's the same deal. Well, almost. I can't marry Theo in a church, so you won't be walking down the aisle behind me... But you'll be there, in a dress—and very, *very* flat shoes.'

'How about a trouser suit?' Katrina suggested hopefully.

'Dress,' Madison said firmly. 'As a bridesmaid *or* a bride. But I might let you off with a trouser suit at the christening.' She paused. 'Christening. That reminds me. Christmas. We're having it at ours this year. Mum and Dad are coming down, Theo's parents are flying over from Greece, and I want you to meet them.'

Katrina looked ruefully at her. 'Sorry, hon. I'd love to be there, but I'm working on Christmas Day.'

'Early or late shift?'

'Early.'

'Good, that makes it a bit easier. Then this is how we'll do it,' Madison said. 'I'll invite Aunt Babs and Uncle Danny up for the day, too, so they get to meet Theo and his family before the wedding, and they can see you on Christmas Day instead of making do with a phone call—and you can come round to our place straight after your shift.'

'Don't hold Christmas dinner up for me,' Katrina said. 'I'll grab something on the ward. Just save me some turkey and salad for a sandwich and a big bit of Christmas cake.'

Madison laughed. 'Stop worrying. Theo's cooking, not me—and, actually, I was hoping you'd make us your special chocolate Christmas cake.'

'Course I will. But I mean it. Don't wait for me to get there before you have lunch. I'll join in when I get there.'

Madison coughed. 'Actually, the invitation was for "you" as in plural. I meant Rhys as well. Unless he's going back to Wales?'

'I'm not sure.' They hadn't discussed it. 'I'll check and let you know,' Katrina promised.

'Good. Because this is going to be the best Christmas ever,' Madison said.

Rhys could hear the screams from the other end of the ward. Quickly, he reassured his patient and his mum that he'd be back in a second, and headed straight for the sound. Katrina clearly had the same idea, because she arrived in the cubicle at the same time.

Denise—a four-year-old who'd been patched up in Theatre following a car accident and had been brought to the ward from the recovery room thirty minutes previously—was thrashing on the bed and screaming.

'All right, sweetheart. It's going to be OK,' he soothed, holding the little girl's hand.

Lynne was in the doorway. 'What happened? I did her obs five minutes ago and she was asleep.'

'My guess is she just woke up to find herself in a strange place and she's scared and she wants her mum,' Katrina said. 'Plus there was the trauma of the accident—it might just have hit her. Does anyone know the situation with her parents?'

'I'm on it. Back in a tick,' Lynne said.

'Check her notes,' Rhys said. 'Could be pain, too.'

Katrina flicked swiftly to the drug chart. 'According to this, they gave her pain relief in the recovery room. So if she's hurting…'

She didn't need to say the rest of it. They both knew that it meant Denise's injuries could be more severe than the emergency and surgical teams had thought and the little girl needed to go back into Theatre.

'Can you tell me where it hurts, *bach*?' Rhys asked.

But Denise was still wailing too much to listen to him.

'Let me give her a cuddle,' Katrina said. 'I'll tell her a story, and if I can calm her down a bit she might be able to tell us what's wrong.'

Rhys had seen how children responded to Katrina—how she'd calmed nervous and upset children on the ward before. There was something about her that made the ward feel like a still, calm place when the world was raging and spinning outside.

And that was how she made him feel, too.

So he let Katrina take his place at the little girl's bedside and lingered a while to watch her as she cuddled the little girl and started talking to her about fairies and princesses and a magic star that could guide everyone home. Gradually, the little girl's screams subsided to noisy tears, and finally to the odd hiccuping sob as she listened to Katrina's quiet, soothing voice. Katrina rocked the little girl gently, stroking her hair and calming her.

Seeing her like that, Rhys suddenly realised the unthinkable.

He loved her.

Really loved her.

Being around Katrina was like being bathed in spring sunshine. And his world had been a much, much brighter place since she'd been in it.

Oh, lord.

This was seriously scary.

He'd never felt like this before. He didn't know how to tell Katrina—where to start, even. Though he knew that in the middle of the ward when they were looking after a distressed child definitely wasn't the right time or place.

'So can you tell me what's wrong, sweetheart?' Katrina asked. 'Does it hurt?'

'Want my mummy,' the little girl hiccuped, her lower lip wobbling.

Katrina glanced up at Rhys, her eyes full of questions.

He knew exactly what she needed to know. Whether Denise's mum was out of Theatre and when she'd be able to visit. He nodded. 'I'll go and find Lynne and see what's going on.'

He met the paediatric nurse halfway back to the reception desk. 'Any news on Denise's parents?'

'Not good,' Lynne said. 'Her mum's still in Theatre, and her dad's not answering his mobile phone.'

'How about grandparents? Aunts and uncles? A family friend, even?' he asked. 'Denise's mum must have had an emergency contact number somewhere—even if the paramedics couldn't find one on her mobile phone, maybe there was something in her diary or a notebook. Even a scrap of paper. There has to be *something*.'

'They're snowed under in the emergency department. I had a word with Eve—' one of the senior nurses in the emergency department '—and she says she'll get one of her juniors on it as soon as she can. She suggested trying the GP.'

'That's assuming we can get in touch with the GP in the first place. And even then it doesn't necessarily mean they'll have emergency contacts.' Rhys shook his head impatiently. 'Katrina's doing a brilliant job, but she can't stay with Denise indefinitely. She's due in clinic in half an hour and we don't have anyone to cover her—Will's in surgery and I'm in clinic myself. I know Tim's shadowing Katrina, but we can't chuck him in the deep end and make him do a clinic without supervision or back-up. It isn't fair to him or the patients.' And cancelling the clinic wasn't an option either.

'If Denise has bonded with Katrina, she's not going to want to let someone else take over,' Lynne said with a sigh. 'And screaming the place down really isn't going to be good for the little one, let alone the fact it'll upset the other kids.'

'She needs a familiar face,' Rhys said. And although they could probably send someone down from the ward to try and find a contact, it'd be quicker for him to do it because he could give an update on Denise's condition at the same time and answer any questions for anyone he managed to get in touch with. He folded his arms. 'I'll go down to the emergency department myself. Bleep me if you need me, warn Reception that this afternoon's clinics are going to be running late—and if there's a problem, I'll take the flak. I'll let Katrina know the situation on my way out. Can you ring Eve and tell her I'm on my way down?'

'Will do.'

'Thanks, Lynne. You're a star.' And it was good to know he could leave everything in the nurse's more than capable hands.

This was definitely a scenario where Katrina's hearing loss came into its own, he thought. Because he'd be able to mouth the message to her so the little girl didn't hear and get worried, but Katrina would be able to understand him. He dropped by the cubicle to explain the situation, then headed to the emergency department.

Eve, who'd been primed by Lynne, got Denise's mother's handbag out of the department safe for him.

'The paramedics tried the ICE number,' Eve said, referring to the 'in case of emergency' number that some people had included on their mobile phones. 'But apparently it's the same as her husband's number. There's just no reply.'

'Let's try the diary.' He flicked through the pages until he found the addresses section. 'Oh, hell. Either she hasn't written down her parents' number because she knows it off by heart, or she's not in contact with them. But there's a number here under "Nursery".' He gave Eve a relieved smile. 'That means they'll know Denise—and they're bound to have emergency contacts in addition to Denise's father.'

He managed to get through to the nursery manager and explained the situation. 'So do you have an emergency contact number we could use, please?'

'I'm sorry,' the nursery manager said, 'I can't give out a number.'

Rhys sighed. 'I rather think that a car accident ending up with a frightened little girl in a hospital bed following surgery, while her mother's still in Theatre and her father's not answering his mobile phone, counts as an emergency. Surely you can give me someone I can contact?'

'We can't give out a number,' the nursery manager repeated. 'It's a breach of the data protection rules and we'd get into a lot of trouble.'

Rhys was very tempted to yell at the woman that sometimes rules needed to be broken, for the sake of common sense and kindness, but kept a lid on his temper. 'Then would you be prepared to call your contacts on my behalf? And, just so you know this isn't some kind of stupid prank, you can call the children's ward here and check. I imagine, as a local nursery, you'd have our number anyway—but, just in case, do you have a pen?'

'Yes.'

'Good.' Rhys gave her the number for the direct line to the ward. 'I'm Dr Rhys Morgan. Ask for me—or if I'm not back from the emergency department you can speak to the senior sister, Lynne Brearley. Right now my senior house officer's with Denise and keeping her calm, but Denise really needs someone she knows with her as soon as possible.'

'Is she going to be all right?'

'She's comfortable,' Rhys said dryly.

'Um. Data protection.'

He'd just bet the woman's face was bright red. And right at that moment he didn't have much sympathy with her. 'Indeed. Thank you for your help. And I'd appreciate it if you could call someone for Denise right now.'

When he got back to the ward, Lynne accosted him.

'I've just put the phone down to Denise's grandparents. They're on their way in,' she said. 'You're a star.'

'Hey, I'm not the one who's managed to make a little girl feel that the whole world hasn't completely collapsed on her. Our Katrina's the one who deserves the credit.'

'She's so good with the little ones. Really lights up their world,' Lynne said.

She lit up his world, too. And Rhys decided that he would tell her that night.

CHAPTER TEN

'THAT poor little girl,' Katrina said later that evening as they left the hospital. 'Just as well her grandparents are going to be able to look after her while her mum's in hospital.'

'She's going to be in for observations for a few days yet,' Rhys reminded her.

'It was lucky she was on the same side as her mum, strapped into her car seat in the back of the car rather than the front,' Katrina said. 'Ed in the emergency department told me the car was pretty much flattened on the passenger side.' They'd also learned that Denise's mother had taken the brunt of the damage, with internal injuries, a broken arm and collarbone and a broken leg.

'And why do I get the feeling that a certain doctor is going to be spending her lunch breaks taking Denise to visit her mother?' Rhys asked wryly.

Katrina spread her hands. 'You could pull rank and tell me not to.'

'You'd simply ignore me and do it anyway,' Rhys said. 'So I'm not going to waste my breath.'

'Good, you're learning.' She paused. 'Rhys, you're working on Christmas Day, too, aren't you?'

He nodded. 'It's not fair to make staff with children do it when they could be at home with their kids.'

Her view exactly. Although she missed spending the day with her family, there weren't any children to be disappointed by her absence and she usually managed either an early or a late celebration with her parents instead. 'I wondered if you were going back to Wales for Christmas.'

He shrugged. 'I'm perfectly happy here in London. Maybe we could spend the evening together after our shift.'

Part of Katrina was delighted that Rhys wanted to spend the holiday season with her, but part of her realised how estranged he was from his family, if he wasn't even planning to see them at the time of year when most people made the effort to see their families. It was a far cry from her relationship with her own family, whose closeness more than made up for its small size. She usually managed to get home once a month to see her parents, whereas Rhys hadn't returned to Wales to see his family ever since she'd known him. And as far as she knew he hadn't spoken to his parents in weeks, whereas she spoke to hers or had a conversation by text or email at least every other day.

Or maybe she'd got it wrong. Maybe this was his way of asking her to spend time with him and meet his family. 'Is your family coming up to see you in London?'

'I doubt it.'

She couldn't quite get her head around that. 'But surely they'll want to see you at Christmas?'

'I doubt it,' he said again. His voice had become very cool, warning her to leave it alone.

But how could she? If Rhys was estranged from his family, that was probably why he was so reserved, she was sure. In his shoes, barely on speaking terms with her family, she'd be utterly miserable.

So maybe she could help him heal the breach. 'How do you know unless you ask?'

He gave her an exasperated look as they reached her front door. 'I just *do*.' He paused. 'You know what, Katrina? I think I'll go back to my place, tonight. On my own.'

On his own? Katrina felt her eyes widen. She really hadn't expected him to react like this, to push her away. 'But, Rhys—'

'Just leave it, Katrina,' he cut in quietly. 'I need some space. Not every family's like yours, you know. And some things are best left as they are. Trust me on this.'

'Rhys, I'm—'

But he'd already turned and was striding purposefully away down the street.

Katrina let herself indoors, but didn't bother cooking anything. She'd lost her appetite.

How could she have misjudged this so badly?

She was tempted to ring him, to apologise for pushing him too hard, but she had a feeling that he'd meant exactly what he'd said.

He needed space.

And the best thing she could do right now was accept that. Take him at his word. Give him what he needed.

Even though it made her miserable.

It was the first night they'd spent apart in ages. Katrina slept badly, missing the warmth of his arms round her and wishing she'd never opened her mouth. For the first time she could remember, she actually felt deaf. Cut off from everyone. Rhys was quiet, but his presence had filled the house.

She missed his music.

Missed his slow, sexy smile.

Missed *him*.

Rhys, too, spent a bad night. And although he was tempted to call Katrina as he sat drinking coffee in his kitchen at 6:00 a.m., knowing that like him she'd be awake, he also knew that she found the telephone difficult—he'd watched her at work talking to a patient's relative on the phone, pressing the earpiece as close as possible to her right ear and switching her hearing aid off in the left so she wasn't distracted by the noise of the ward.

No, a phone call wasn't the right thing to do. There was a better way. He flicked into the text service of his mobile phone and tapped out a message. *Katrina, I'm sorry. I shouldn't have snapped at you. See you at work. Will apologise properly in person. R x*

Half an hour later, his phone beeped to signal her reply. *I'm sorry too. Was too pushy. See you later. K x*

She'd added a smiley face.

So she forgave him. She'd even taken part of the blame herself, though it hadn't been her fault. That, he thought, was a lot more than he deserved.

Katrina was her usual professional self with him at work when they did the ward rounds together, and, as he'd expected she was unavailable at lunchtime because she'd grabbed a chocolate bar and taken little Denise to the general ward in a wheelchair to visit her mother. Which was fine by him, because it meant he had enough time to go and buy something. Strictly speaking, he knew he ought to give her a floral apology—but if he brought a huge bouquet onto the ward and then Katrina left with it, tongues would start wagging. He didn't want his personal life being the subject of hospital gossip and he knew how much she'd hated being talked about at her previous hospital when she'd split up with Pete, so he chose something rather less obvious than flowers—but something he hoped she'd like as much.

When their shifts had finished, he caught up on some paperwork while Katrina did her usual end-of-day story in the children's playroom, and timed it so that he walked out of his office at the same time that she left the playroom.

'Can I have a quick word?' he asked.

'Sure.' She allowed him to shepherd her back into his office and close the door behind them.

'I, um, wondered if I could take you to dinner at Mezze tonight. If you're not busy. To say sorry.'

'Rhys, you don't have to do that.'

'I'd like to. And I want to apologise properly…which is a bit difficult here, under the eagle eyes of our colleagues.'

'Uh-huh.'

'So are you free?'

She smiled. 'Yes. Thank you. And I'd love to go to Mezze.'

'Good.'

He waited until they were seated at the restaurant and had ordered a pile of different dishes to share—all Katrina's favourites—before he gave her the paper carrier bag.

Her eyes widened as she saw the name on the outside. 'Rhys, these are hideously expensive!'

'But you like them?'

She smiled. 'I *love* them. They're my absolute favourite chocolates—the kind of thing I buy as a birthday treat. Thank you. But you really didn't have to.'

'Yes, I did. I shouldn't have lost my temper with you last

night.' He sighed. 'Not everyone has the kind of close family you do, Katrina. And I guess I'm a bit sensitive about it.'

'A *bit*?' she asked mildly.

'All right. Very,' he admitted. 'And I'm sorry.'

'I was too pushy. So I'm as much to blame, which means you really need to share these with me,' she said. Then she bit her lip. 'Um. Speaking of being pushy… Look, I understand completely if you say no, but the thing is that Maddie's having a big family Christmas do at hers. She wants me to go there as soon as I finish work on Christmas Day. My parents are coming up just for the day, because they know I normally work over the holiday—but having lunch at Maddie's is a chance for them to see me too, and to meet Theo…and…' She wriggled in her seat. 'Look, there's no pressure. If you prefer, I'll introduce you to everyone as my friend and colleague who's been on shift with me on Christmas Day. Everyone knows that Maddie, being Maddie, believes that the more the merrier. And…' She took a deep breath. 'I'm gabbling. Sorry. I just wondered if…if you'd go with me.'

She wanted him to go with her. To share a proper family Christmas. Something he hadn't had for years and years and years. Rhys had always made sure he was working over the holiday season, ever since he'd qualified, to avoid the sheer grind of the day.

A big family Christmas at Madison's with Katrina's parents, Madison's parents and Theo's family. The idea of it filled him with dread—he just wasn't used to that sort of thing. But he also knew he needed to make an effort, for Katrina's sake. Her family was important to her.

As for introducing him to them as her colleague—he knew that Madison was as close as a sister to Katrina, and he was pretty sure that Katrina had confided in her that they were seeing each other. Even if Katrina hadn't told the rest of her family, Madison—with the best of intentions—might have already done so.

But if he wanted to be with Katrina—and he knew he did—then he was going to have to compromise. Do this one thing she'd asked of him. 'OK. I'll come.'

'Thank you.'

She held him close, and the dread started to melt away. With Katrina by his side, anything was possible. And he was beginning to believe that maybe with her he could have the relationship he'd never had in his life before. A truly loving partner and a family who'd always be there for him.

On Christmas Eve, Rhys stayed overnight at Katrina's. It unnerved him slightly—he never bothered decorating, other than putting up cards, but Katrina had gone the whole hog. A real tree which scented the air—she'd persuaded him to go with her, three days before, to choose it—covered with white twinkling lights, a holly wreath on her front door, more greenery draped round the mantelpiece, cards everywhere and candles which filled the room with Christmassy scents of orange, cloves and cinnamon. And, just for a dash of roguishness, she had a sprig of mistletoe hanging from the ceiling in the hall before the front door. 'It's not real mistletoe,' she explained, 'it's environmentally friendly silk mistletoe. But it still works the same.'

How could he resist kissing her underneath it?

After dinner—which they'd cooked together—Rhys produced a small box.

'What's this?'

'Welsh Christmas tradition—it's taffy. It's usually made on Christmas Eve, though I made it yesterday morning when I was off duty. And I set it in a tin rather than doing it the traditional way of dropping spoonfuls into ice-cold water,' he explained.

She tasted a square. 'Mmm. It's wonderful.' She tipped her head slightly to one side. 'Does it take very long to make?'

'Half an hour or so.'

'Do you know the recipe off by heart? Just, if you do…maybe we could make some to take to Maddie's tomorrow.'

Trust her to be thinking of someone else. 'Already done, *cariad*, and it's in my briefcase,' he said with a smile. 'This is only a taster for us tonight. But I can make more any time you want.'

'Rhys, I… Thank you.' She walked round to his side of the table and hugged him. 'I know it's going to be weird for you tomorrow, and I understand if you want to change your mind.'

Part of him still didn't want to go. But he really, really didn't want to hurt her by not going. 'I'll be there,' he promised.

'You're probably not going to have time to open your present from me tomorrow morning,' she said. 'So I thought maybe you might like it tonight.' She went over to a cupboard and, to his surprise, brought out a Christmas stocking. 'Happy Christmas,' she told him, kissing him lightly.

'Katrina…' There was a huge lump in his throat. When was the last time he'd had a Christmas stocking? Too long ago to remember. Though he understood why Christmas was always so difficult for his mother. The same reason why he loathed the days between Christmas and New Year, marking the anniversary of his little sister's death and the time when his life had been turned upside down and nothing had been the same again.

He pushed the memories away. Not now. Not here. Katrina clearly loved Christmas, and even though he knew he ought to tell her, he wasn't going to spoil her pleasure in the season. 'Thank you. But I didn't make you a stocking.'

She shrugged. 'That's OK. I wasn't expecting anything.'

'I did buy you something,' he said. Though he'd cheated, putting the presents in a Christmas gift bag or having them wrapped in the shop. 'Wait.' He retrieved them from his overnight bag. 'Happy Christmas, *cariad*,' he said.

'Thank you,' she said, kissing him. 'Let's open them one at a time.'

She loved the film encyclopaedia he'd bought her, the digital photo frame, the new restored special edition of one of her favourite films, a large box of the exclusive chocolates he'd bought her previously as an apology and the only girly indulgence he knew she liked—some exclusive chocolate-scented toiletries.

And he was blown away by what she'd given him. Inside the stocking was an envelope containing a year's membership to the British Film Institute, a CD by one of his favourite cellists, seasonally shaped chocolates which she'd wrapped individually, and a tiny musical box that played the first part of Bach's Air on a G String. And a rare first edition of one of his favourite Cornell Woolrich tales—something that had been missing from his collection. 'Katrina, I've no idea where you managed to find this, but it's fabulous. And you're wonderful,' he said, meaning it.

The following morning saw Rhys dressed up as Father Christmas, Katrina and Tim as Santa's helpers—both in elf costumes—and Lynne as a Christmas fairy, complete with wings and a magic wand. Thanks to the Hospital Friends Group, they had small parcels to give out to all the children on the ward and their siblings: a touch-and-feel board book and socks for the babies; colouring pencils and joke books for the older ones; and small gift tokens for the over-tens to put towards music or video games.

Katrina noticed that little Tommy Price, in with idiopathic thrombocytopetic purpura—a condition involving bruising and a rash that didn't disappear when pressed, showing that there was bleeding under the skin, and they were busy checking out the cause—didn't have any visitors. Although he'd said thank you for the present from Father Christmas, the eight-year-old hadn't moved from his bed to join the other children in the playroom. And she'd noticed that although all the other children in the bay had cards stuck to the wall above their beds, Tommy had nothing.

Her heart ached for him. Seeing how the other children's families had made a special fuss of them must have made him realise what he was missing, and as a result he'd withdrawn completely.

Was this how Rhys's childhood had been, too? And, if so, was he going to be able to cope with a Gregory family Christmas? she wondered.

She stopped by Tommy's bed. His family had been the only ones not to respond to her request for permission to give all the patients a seasonal chocolate lolly. She'd decided to take the line that silence indicated consent, so she handed Tommy the reindeer-shaped chocolate with the red nose. 'Hey. Happy Christmas,' she said.

'Yeah. You, too. And thanks,' he added swiftly.

Tommy's eyes were a little too bright; Katrina, realising that he was near tears, began telling him atrocious jokes until she made him smile. She made a point of pulling a Christmas cracker with him at lunch and slipping him an extra chocolate lolly at the end of her shift.

'I can't believe Tommy Price's family didn't even bother

coming to visit him on Christmas Day,' she said to Rhys, glowering as they left the hospital together. 'That's so *mean*.'

'Don't you think you're being just a tiny a bit judgemental?' Rhys asked mildly. 'Maybe his parents are desperately scared of hospitals. Maybe home life's tough—maybe his parents are caring for an elderly parent or a small child with special needs as well, and there just aren't enough hours in the day.'

'You're right. I'm sorry.' She sighed. 'But sometimes I really wish I had a magic wand. I don't want fabulous riches or eternal youth.'

'You just want to fix things for people,' he finished. 'But you can't fix everything, *cariad*.'

'No. I just wish I could.' She shook herself. 'Right. Enough. We're going to Maddie's.'

The nearer they got to Madison and Theo's house, the more Rhys's stomach churned with nerves. This was important to Katrina, and he was going to do it. But, lord, how he wished he were on a desert island instead. Especially when Madison ushered them inside and he realised how many people were there, how everyone was talking and laughing and acting as if they'd known each other all their lives despite the fact that, as far as he knew, this was the first time Theo's family had met the Gregorys.

This was so very different from the way he was used to spending Christmas.

He managed to smile and be polite to everyone, and Madison seemed pleased with the home-made Welsh taffy and the champagne he'd brought as his contribution to the day. She was definitely delighted with the chocolate Christmas cake Katrina had made; clearly Katrina's love of chocolate was shared by her family.

He found himself a quiet place on the edge of the room, but from the moment they arrived Katrina was right in the centre of things, clearly a much-loved part of the family. But the more he watched, the more he realised how close everyone was. Katrina's parents finished each other's sentences. Madison's parents kept catching each other's eye and smiling. Theo's family, being Greek, were noisily and openly affectionate with everyone, and Theo fussed over his pregnant fiancée.

Katrina's mum was doing her best to make him feel welcome, talking to him about his job—though he noticed that she avoided the normal questions about missing his family at Christmas, so he had a feeling that Katrina had primed her parents not to ask.

Katrina.

Although he responded politely enough to her family, he couldn't keep his eyes off her. She was reading a story to Theo's niece and cuddling Theo's nephew, sitting on the floor by the Christmas tree and looking as if she belonged.

Well, of course she belonged. This was her family.

She fitted into the extended family, too. She'd fit in anywhere. Even his mother, Rhys thought, would find it hard to resist her.

And then it hit him.

Between them, the three sets of parents had clocked up close to a century of happy marriage. They'd support their children, help them through any rough patches so their marriages would work, too.

And their love was unconditional.

So maybe, just maybe, he could afford to take the risk with Katrina. If Katrina was willing to take the risk with him.

He was still mulling it over when Theo's niece came over to him. 'You come and have a story too,' she said in accented but perfect English, taking his hand.

How could he resist following her over to the Christmas tree?

Though Rhys was aware of a very weird feeling in the region of his heart when he sat down next to Katrina and little Arianna insisted that he cuddle her baby brother, Petros, while she and Katrina did a puppet show with her new toys.

Rhys was used to cuddling babies and children. He did it all the time at work, to soothe them when they were in pain or to explain what was going to happen next in their treatment. So holding a toddler shouldn't make him feel so odd—a feeling he couldn't pin down.

'Sorry,' Katrina mouthed.

'It's fine,' he mouthed back, and settled back with the toddler, making appropriate noises of appreciation during the puppet show.

To his surprise, he found himself relaxing and enjoying the whole family thing. Pulling crackers and telling terrible jokes, laughing at the even more terrible ones Theo's niece had clearly learned especially, and mucking in with everyone to set the table for tea and clear up afterwards and play charades.

And then finally it was time to leave.

Katrina's mother hugged him goodbye, Katrina's father shook his hand warmly, Theo clapped him on the shoulder, Theo's family all hugged him—but Madison was the one who floored him. 'Thank you for coming,' she said, holding him close. And then she added in a voice so low it was clearly not meant to be heard by anyone else, 'And especially for doing this for Kat. She's special.'

Yeah. He knew that.

'And I think you are too,' Madison added, 'if you'll let yourself.'

He knew then without a doubt that Katrina had confided in her cousin—a confidence Madison had kept. Given how

close they were, he had a feeling that Madison was very protective about her younger cousin. So the fact she thought he
was good enough for Katrina...

He had a lump in his throat for a good five minutes after
they left.

'I'm sorry. Was it so awful?' Katrina asked when they were
on the tube.

'No. Your family's lovely.'

'I'm glad you liked them.' She bit her lip. 'Just...you've
been a bit quiet since we left.'

'I was a bit overwhelmed,' he admitted. 'It's not the kind
of thing I'm used to.' And right then he didn't want to tell her
what Madison had said. He was still trying to come to terms
with it himself. The feeling that this woman was so right for
him, that she was the one he wanted in his life.

But there were a few things he needed to sort out before
he could ask her to share his life—to take the risk with him.

She curled her fingers round his. 'Thanks, anyway.'

'Any time.'

She smiled. 'So does that mean I can ask you to come to
Maddie's wedding with me next May?'

Wedding.

He took a deep breath. 'Sure.'

'Good.' She paused. 'I told her about your cello. And we
were kind of wondering...it's going to be a civil wedding, not
a church do, so she won't have an organist to accompany her
down the aisle. And...'

He guessed what she wanted to ask but was clearly holding
back. 'You want me to play the cello at her wedding?'

'Only if you want to. Not if it's going to be...' She paused.
'If it's going to be difficult for you.'

Being part of her family? Rhys stopped, spun her round to

face him and brushed his mouth over hers. 'If you want me to play, of course I'll do it. Tell her to pick whatever she likes—no, I'll tell her that myself. Just as long as I have time to practise and polish any pieces I don't already know.'

He'd go to her cousin's wedding. Play the cello during the ceremony. Let her family draw him into the charmed circle.

And maybe, just maybe, he'd ask Katrina a question of his own. In the new year. When he'd sorted out a few things in his head.

CHAPTER ELEVEN

THE first hurdle was two days before New Year. A day Rhys
loathed. Even after all these years, he found his skin always
was a bit too thin on that day. The anniversary of his little
sister Gwyneth's death. He knew he ought to tell Katrina
about it, but he just didn't have the words. Maybe tomorrow,
he told himself, when things were less raw again. And he
managed to act as if things were completely normal—until the
middle of his shift, when a six-week-old baby was admitted
with pneumonia.

The coincidence was harsh enough, but it was one he'd
faced before and knew he could deal with. What he couldn't
deal with was what happened right at the end of his shift—
when the baby's mother, clearly worried sick, was shouting
at her little boy. Blaming him for bringing home the virus that
had made little Felicity ill and caused her to be susceptible
enough to pick up pneumonia on top of it. The little boy's face
was white, pinched, and he was weeping silently.

And Rhys, remembering the child he'd been and the way
he'd felt, was furious. He just about kept a lid on his temper
as he strode into the cubicle. 'Problem?' he asked abruptly.

Mrs Walters stared at him, clearly shocked at the way he'd
walked straight in, but the stethoscope hanging round his

neck and his hospital ID card pinned to his shirt told her she was dealing with a senior doctor—one who wouldn't be fobbed off. Though she was obviously too angry to let it check her. 'Of course there's a problem! My daughter's lying there, seriously ill. You've got eyes, haven't you?'

Rhys wasn't bothered by her rudeness, but he was bothered by the little boy's tears. Today of all days. He was aware that his fists were clenched in anger, and deliberately flexed his hands. 'I think,' he said carefully, 'we need a word in my office.' He glanced around—luckily Lynne was in the bay opposite. 'Lynne?' he said to the nurse. 'Can you do me a favour and keep an eye on Felicity and her brother for me?'

'Simon's not going anywhere,' the woman said.

'No, but you and I are. And your little boy's already upset—he doesn't need to hear this,' he said.

Mrs Walters's face whitened—clearly she thought he was going to tell her something drastic about Felicity's condition. And although Rhys knew he ought to do the decent thing and reassure her before they went left Felicity's cubicle, right at that moment he wasn't feeling particularly nice. Not after the way the woman had treated her little boy. It was too close to his own childhood experience. So he merely shepherded her to his office and closed the door behind them.

'Mrs Walters, I realise you're upset because Felicity's ill, but shouting at your son isn't going help make her better. She needs quiet and rest—as do the other children on the ward.'

She lifted her chin, looking belligerent. 'Don't you talk to me like that,' she said. 'I'm going to report you.'

'You do that,' Rhys said, knowing it was an empty threat— he'd done nothing wrong. 'But I suggest you focus your thoughts a little closer to home first. Felicity should recover without any lasting effects, though she's likely to pick up coughs and colds a bit more easily than most little ones for the next year or so. So although it's worrying for you, seeing her in here—and she'll get a little bit worse before she improves, because that's the nature of the disease—she'll be on the mend very soon.' He folded his arms. 'What I'm concerned about is your little boy. Even though we try to make our ward as comfortable as possible for children, the hospital's still a very scary place for them. Simon's already worried about his baby sister, seeing her here in hospital. You've shouted at him and told him that it's all his fault, so he's probably feeling scared and guilty as well right now.'

Mrs Walters said nothing, but her face went a very dull red.

'I might add that it's highly unlikely Felicity caught the virus from her brother—a virus tends to do the rounds and spread very quickly. She could have caught it from a dozen or more different people. So right now I think your son needs a bit of reassurance—a hug from his mum—and to know that he's loved.' Something he hadn't had at Simon's age—though he was old enough to be over that.

Mrs Walters glared at him, but he could see the guilt starting as his words sank in. Even though he wanted to yell at her, he was aware of his reasons, and reined himself in. Time to be kind. Show a bit of sympathy, he reminded himself. Do what Katrina, with her warmth and sweetness, would do. 'And I think you'll find it'll help you, too. Because Simon will hug you back and give you a bit of comfort in return.' Katrina had taught him the power of a hug.

Mrs Walters's face crumpled and she burst into tears.

Oh, lord. He'd wanted to stop her yelling at her little boy, but this hadn't been quite what he'd intended. Awkwardly, Rhys took the box of tissues from his desk and offered it to her. And when she'd calmed down again, he took her back to the ward.

He'd expected Lynne to be sitting with Simon and Felicity, but instead the little boy was sitting on Katrina's lap.

'Thanks for looking after Simon for us,' he said to Katrina.

'No problem. We've had a lovely time.' She smiled back at him. 'And Felicity's holding her own.'

'Good.' Rhys crouched down so he was at the little boy's height. 'Are you all right there, Simon?' he asked softly.

The little boy nodded, wide-eyed. 'Dr Katrina told me a story.'

'She's really good at that.' Rhys ruffled his hair. 'Hey, I know it's a bit scary, seeing your baby sister here with all these tubes and wires and machines beeping, but she's going to be absolutely fine. And I want you to know that it's not your fault your sister caught pneumonia.'

'Mummy said…' The little boy's lower lip wobbled.

'Your mummy was very worried and scared, just like you are, and sometimes people say things they don't mean when they're worried and scared,' Rhys said. 'But I'm a doctor. My job is to make people better, and I'm going to make Felicity better. Your mummy understands that now. And it really isn't your fault. It's the time of year when there are lots of bugs about, and Felicity's very little, so she can't fight the bugs as well as you and I can.'

The little boy dragged in a breath. 'So she's not going to die?'

'She's not going to die.' Not like Gwyneth had. Advances in medicine would make sure of that. 'All those tubes and wires you can see are there to help her breathe more easily, to help her get enough food, and so we can keep an eye on her and give her medicine when we need to, to make her better,' Rhys said gently. 'And she's not the only one in the ward like this. There are five other babies in this bay who have a similar sort of thing to your sister. Some are more poorly, and some are a bit better because they got the bugs a bit earlier than Felicity did and they're already on the mend.'

The little boy nodded, but said nothing.

'I think your mummy wants a word,' he said, and looked at Mrs Walters.

She followed his lead and crouched down by the little boy, hugging him. 'I'm sorry I shouted at you, Simon. Dr Morgan's right. I was worried and I took it out on you and that was wrong of me. It isn't your fault—and I do love you. I really do.'

Rhys gave an approving nod—and then walked quietly to the safety of his office, knowing that he needed five minutes to himself before he could face the ward again.

Something was definitely wrong, Katrina thought. Even though Rhys had been perfectly in control and hadn't even raised his voice, she'd seen something in his eyes. And he'd been even quieter than usual for the last couple of days.

She went to his office, and blinked in surprise. Since when had Rhys shut his office door?

Worried, she knocked on the door, but she also walked in without waiting for him to say anything and closed the door behind her.

'You're not all right, so don't tell me you are,' she said, seeing the expression on his face. 'What's happened?'

He turned away; she was fairly sure he said something but she didn't quite catch it. 'I can't hear you, Rhys. You were mumbling and I couldn't see your mouth to read what you just said. Please, can you look at me and repeat that?' she asked, her voice soft but clear.

He looked at her. 'Nothing. It's not important.'

This time she wasn't going to let him off the hook. 'It's not nothing,' she said. 'And it *is* important.'

'I don't want to talk about it here.'

That last word gave her hope. It meant he was going to open up to her. Not at the hospital—but there was a real chance that he'd talk to her. 'Look, you should've been off duty twenty minutes ago and so should I. Let's go back to my place. It's quiet and we won't be disturbed.'

To her relief, he agreed.

He was silent all the way back to her house; she respected it, not pushing him to talk about the situation in public. But as soon as they were in her kitchen and he was sitting at the table with a mug of coffee in his hands, she directed, 'Talk to me, Rhys.'

He sighed. 'I just let a case get to me.'

'Felicity Walters?'

He nodded.

'Even I could hear her mother yelling—from the other side of the ward, at that.' She gritted her teeth. 'I was just on my way over to see if I could sort it out when I saw you'd beaten me to it. And I don't know how on earth you got her to apologise to him, but you were brilliant.'

'Mmm.'

His voice was flat, and she frowned. 'There's more to it than that, isn't there?'

He twisted the mug round and round on the table. 'Yes.' He was silent for a long, long moment, and then he looked up at her. 'I was about the same age as young Simon when my little sister Gwyneth was taken to hospital with pneumonia.'

But he'd said he was an only child.

Her questions must have shown in her face, because he said quietly, 'Gwynnie wasn't so lucky.'

'Oh, Rhys.' She put her mug down, went over to him and held him close.

He shifted so that he could pull her onto his lap. 'You're

the only thing that stopped me wanting to strangle that woman. Because you've taught me the power of a hug,' he said.

His voice sounded slightly thick, and Katrina could feel tears in her own eyes. 'I'm so sorry.'

'Not your fault.' He dragged in a breath. 'Though I can remember my mother yelling at me the same way Simon's mother yelled at him. Blaming me for bringing the virus home. If it hadn't been for me, Gwyneth wouldn't have got pneumonia and she wouldn't have died.'

She pulled back just far enough so she could look into his eyes. 'Rhys, you're a paediatrician. You *know* that's not true.'

'I know that now,' he agreed tonelessly. 'But I believed it for a long time when I was a child.'

No wonder he wasn't close to his parents. Did they still blame him? Katrina wondered. 'When did it happen?' she asked.

'Twenty-eight years ago.'

She had a nasty feeling he meant *exactly* twenty-eight years ago. 'It's the anniversary today?' she guessed.

He nodded. 'Any other day, I can deal with it. Today, I was close to losing it and acting incredibly unprofessionally. I was so angry I nearly threw her out of the ward myself.'

'But you didn't,' she said fiercely. 'You rose above it. You understood what drove her to do it and you fixed it. And I'm so proud of you for that.'

His eyes were suspiciously bright as he looked at her. 'Are you, now?'

'Yes.' She nodded furiously. 'And now I understand why you've been quiet, the last few days.'

'I should've told you before. Explained,' Rhys said. 'But…' He broke off.

'You're a very private man. You don't like talking about things.' She bit her lip. 'And I've been nagging you. I pushed you into coming with me to Maddie's for Christmas. Pushed you about playing the cello for her wedding. I'm so—'

'Shh.' He pressed a forefinger to her lips. 'Don't apologise. It's OK. You pushed me, yes, but you did me a favour. You showed me what a real family Christmas is like.'

'You mean, you never…?' She stared at him, stunned.

'Not since I was three. And I can barely remember that.' He grimaced. 'As I said, my parents split up when I was just about to start school. The Christmas when Gwynnie was in hospital was our last together.' He shrugged. 'I guess it's hard for a relationship to survive a loss like that.'

She thought about it. Would her parents have got through it? Would Madison's?

And she was absolutely sure of the answer. 'If you love someone enough, you'll get through it together. I'm not saying it'd be easy, and it would take an awful lot of work, but you'd help each other through it. One of you would have a strong day when the other wasn't so strong, and vice versa. You'd get through it with teamwork.'

'I don't think my parents loved each other enough,' Rhys said. 'And there were problems before my sister died. I remember them shouting a lot. Especially my dad. But then I remember them telling me I was going to have a little brother or sister and the shouting stopped for a bit after that.' He swallowed hard. 'I was so pleased at the thought of being a big brother. Having someone to play with. I had cousins, but we weren't close—not like you and Maddie. My dad didn't see much of his family. And I think he was going through a bad time at work. There were a lot of rows, and then suddenly he was home all the time…' Rhys shook his head. 'Looking back as an adult, I realise that was probably when the mine closed.'

'Your dad lost his job?' Katrina asked.

'Along with most of the men in the village, so it was pretty rough on everyone. Especially around Christmas, when they were upset at not being able to afford to give their kids the presents they'd wanted to buy and worried about how they were going to manage and where they were going to find work.' He sighed. 'And, again, looking back with an adult's wisdom and knowing what I do now about medicine, all the stress probably sent my mum into labour early.'

'Very early?'

'Six weeks.' He shrugged. 'And you know as well as I do that's enough for a baby to be more prone to picking up a respiratory infection—and struggling more with it than a full-term baby. And then I came home from nursery with a really terrible cold.' He dragged in a breath. 'Gwynnie picked it up. The doctor said it was just a cold, but she got worse and worse. She couldn't breathe properly.'

'RSV?' Katrina guessed. Respiratory syncytial virus was one that most children had had by school age—and it was practically epidemic at this time of year. In older children and adults it tended to appear as a really heavy cold, but babies often really struggled. As Rhys had explained to Felicity's brother, the bay where little Felicity was being treated was full of babies who'd tested positive for the virus.

'Probably,' he said, his voice still flat. 'And it turned to pneumonia.'

Just like Felicity's case. It must have hurt a lot every time he walked into the bay or saw the little girl's name on the board, bringing back painful memories from his past.

'The doctor sent her to hospital, but it was too late. She died two days later.'

With premature babies, doctors were taught to err on the side of caution, but clearly it hadn't happened in Gwyneth's case. 'Why on earth didn't your family doctor send her to hospital earlier?'

'Think about it. You're a GP. It's coming up to Christmas. Everyone in the village has got a stinking cold, half of them think their cold's so bad that they need antibiotics—even when they don't—and you're rushed off your feet because of all the people coming to see you with stress-related symptoms since the mine closed and half the men in the village lost their jobs. That, or they're coming to you, telling you in private that their husbands are depressed but refuse to come and see you, and asking what you can do to help men who are too proud to admit they need help. You're swamped and you don't know which way to turn next. Of course you're going to miss things.' He pulled her closer. 'And that's what I think happened.'

She shook her head in amazement. 'You're incredible, Rhys. If I'd lost Maddie like that…it doesn't bear thinking about. I don't think I could ever forgive the doctor.'

'Understanding isn't *quite* the same as forgiving,' he admitted.

'And that woman today… In your shoes, I think I would've strangled her.'

'No, you wouldn't.' He brushed his mouth against hers, very briefly. 'Because you're warm and sweet and nice. And if it wasn't for you, I probably would've lost my temper with her and chucked her bodily off the ward.'

'What do you mean, if it wasn't for me?'

'You taught me the power of a hug,' he said simply.

She swallowed hard. 'Oh, Rhys.'

'I'm just glad you're in my life.'

She reached up to kiss him. 'And I'm glad you're in mine. I know it's been hard for you, telling me. But I'm glad you did. And I want you to know I'm here for you.'

'I know. And I appreciate it.'

She stroked his face. 'So that's why you chose medicine over music? Why you work stupid hours?'

'So other families don't have to go through what mine did, you mean?' He looked thoughtful. 'Probably. I know it wasn't my fault, but I do sometimes wonder, what if? What if she hadn't caught that virus and died: would things have been different?'

'Do you think they would have been?'

He wrinkled his nose. 'I doubt it. I think Gwynnie's death was the catalyst for my parents splitting up, but if she'd lived then they would've split up over something else.'

Katrina was pretty sure of the answer, but she asked the question anyway. 'Have you ever talked to your family about it?'

'No.'

'How long is it since you saw them?'

He shrugged. 'I can't remember when I last saw my father. We haven't exchanged Christmas or birthday cards for quite a while.' He paused. 'He remarried and had three more girls, so I guess he didn't need me around.'

'Rhys, you're his firstborn. Of course he still needed you around.'

'I'm a reminder of bad times for him. Just like I am for my mother.'

'Do you still see her?'

'I visit her every few months, but I don't stay long.' He shrugged. 'It's hard for her, Katrina.'

'It's been hard for you, too,' she pointed out.

'I'm not a little boy any more. I can deal with things. But now you know the truth about my family. They're not like yours, Katrina.'

And she was very, very glad hers hadn't been like that. 'I wish for your sake they'd been more like mine.'

'So,' he said softly, 'do I. But you can't change the past, and I really don't want to drag it up any more.'

'Of course. And thank you for being honest with me.'

'Honest?' He smiled ruefully. 'Not quite. Because there's something I've wanted to say to you for a while.'

Her heart missed a beat. No. She was sitting on his lap, he was holding her close…he couldn't be about to end things between them. Surely not.

Please not.

'What might that be?' she asked.

He raked a hand through his hair. 'I've never said this to anyone before. And there are bits of me that are scared to say it. In case I get it wrong. And my timing's completely out.'

She couldn't read his face at all. And for him to be awkward and unsure… She was starting to worry. But if her world was about to crash down, better to know sooner than later. She lifted her chin. 'Be brave.' Even though she didn't feel brave— at all. 'Say it straight out.'

'I love you,' he said.

She stared at him, hardly able to take it in. 'Did you just say…?'

'Sorry. I told you it was bad timing. I've already dumped enough on you tonight.' He turned his face away.

'No, no, no.' Gently, she cupped his face with both hands and made sure he was looking straight at her. 'Guess what? I love you, too.'

He was silent for a long, long time. And then he said, 'I can't remember the last time anyone said that to me.'

What? She'd been told every single day for her entire life— either in person, or by text, or by phone, or by a card, or by something daft one of her parents had spotted on a day out, decided she'd like and parcelled up for her. It was something she did for her family too—she and Madison often gave each other 'un-birthday' presents, whether it was a fridge magnet or sticky notes or just a postcard one thought would amuse the other.

How could someone never be told they were loved?

It was way outside her comprehension.

'What about your ex-girlfriends?' she asked.

He shrugged. 'I told you, I've never said it before. I couldn't trust myself to commit—I've never had much faith in family and relationships—and my last few girlfriends said I was too cold.'

'You're not cold at all,' Katrina said. 'You're private, yes, but you're warm and you're clever and you're sexy as hell. And I love you.'

'This isn't fair of me. You deserve to be part of a warm, loving family, and I can't give you that,' he warned.

'You don't need to,' she said simply. 'I already have one. And I'd be happy to share them with you.'

There was wonder in his face as he looked at her. 'I never thought this could happen to me. I love you, Katrina. I think I have since the moment I met you. When you went all stroppy on me and informed me that you were going to put a bit of sunshine into a child's life and nobody was going to stop you.' He smiled. 'You've put sunshine back into my life.'

'Good. And I intend to keep it that way.' She paused. 'There's this little thing called teamwork. And I happen to think we make a great team.'

'Yes. We do.' He kissed her. A sweet, gentle kiss that was full of promise—a kiss that told her he'd finally broken down the wall around his heart and let her in.

It didn't stop at a kiss. And Katrina didn't protest when Rhys carried her up the stairs to her bedroom. Right at that moment, she knew they both needed the ultimate closeness.

Afterwards, she lay curled in his arms.

'I love you.' He stole a kiss. 'And I'm going to tell you every day.'

'I'll hold you to that.' She smiled at him. 'And I'm going to tell you, too.'

'Good. I've just discovered I quite like the sentence. Though I might need some practice in hearing it.'

She grinned. 'That sounds like a hint. I love you, Rhys Morgan.'

He smiled, but there was a hint of sadness in his eyes.

'You know, my parents liked you, too. They thought you were a little bit quiet, but I'm the quiet and dreamy one of the family—so as far as they're concerned you match me.'

'Katrina Gregory, no *way* are you quiet,' Rhys said, laughing. 'A quiet person wouldn't perform a glove-puppet story every day in the children's playroom.'

She chuckled. 'I didn't say I was quiet. I said I'm the quiet one *in my family*. There's a difference. They're noisy and bouncy, but they respect that I'm not quite as full on as the rest of them and they still love me. They still value me for who I am. And they'll value you, too. Just as I do.'

He shifted so he could kiss her. 'I love you, Katrina Gregory. And thank you. For…' His words caught in his throat.

'You'd do the same for me,' Katrina said confidently. 'And everything's going to be fine. Because we'll have great teamwork.'

'This isn't all I want to say to you, you know.' He stroked her face. 'There's more. But I need to tie up some loose ends first. Sort out some things that should've been sorted out a long, long time ago.' He kissed her gently. 'And then I can start the new year exactly as I mean to go on.'

CHAPTER TWELVE

THE following day, Rhys was doing the ward round. Felicity's mother was sitting next to the baby's crib and looked up when he took the notes from the basket at the end of the bed.

'Dr Morgan? There's an extra tube up her nose today. And it's taped to her face. Doesn't it…?' She bit her lip.

He guessed immediately what she wasn't saying. 'Hurt? No, it doesn't—the tape means it stays in place and she can't accidentally pull it out.' He sat down next to her. 'It's a lot easier for her having oxygen going through the tube up her nose than having a mask on. What it does is help her to breathe more easily, and that in turn means she'll be less tired. I know it looks pretty scary, but the tube isn't hurting her at all. She's holding her own.'

She nodded, clearly too overcome to speak.

'How's Simon?' he asked.

Tears glittered in Mrs Walters's eyes. 'Last night he told me he wished it was Christmas again, so Santa would bring his little sister home.'

Rhys felt a huge lump blocking his throat. When Gwyneth had died, he could remember doing exactly the same thing— begging Santa to come back and bring Gwyneth with him, and he'd never ask for another toy, ever again.

'You'd be surprised how quickly they bond,' he said gruffly. 'But Felicity's doing fine. We've got her temperature back under control, she's on amoxycillin to sort out the bacterial infection, and because we're feeding her by tube she doesn't have to work so hard and wear herself out drinking her milk.' He smiled at her. 'I'd say she'll be able to manage without the extra oxygen in a day or two, and she'll be back home with you next week, but that cough might linger for a couple of months. And you'll probably find her feeding schedule's gone right back to how it was when she was born,' he warned. 'I'm afraid you'll be up a couple of times a night with her until she's back in a routine again.'

'I can live with that, as long as she's all right.'

'So Simon's not with you today?'

'His dad's taken him to the football to cheer him up a bit. He drew her a picture, though.' She took a sheet of paper from her handbag and unfolded it.

Exactly the kind of drawings Rhys remembered doing at that age. Stick people representing his family. *Mummy, Daddy, me and Flisty,* written in a careful childish script. 'That's lovely.'

'Yeah.' She sniffed. 'And I'm sorry I yelled at you yesterday.'

'You were under a lot of stress. Don't worry about it. It's forgotten,' Rhys said. He checked Felicity, then stroked her cheek. 'Give her a day or two and she'll be off oxygen. But you can pick her up and give her a cuddle, and when she's strong enough to manage without the tubes you can feed her. She's doing fine.'

Later that evening, Katrina was at home, trying and failing to concentrate on the film encyclopaedia Rhys had bought her for Christmas. Rhys was at his own flat, calling his parents. She tried not to feel hurt that he'd chosen to make the calls alone and hadn't invited her to be with him, but he was a private man and she knew it. And he'd said he needed to sort out a few things. There was probably a lot he hadn't told her about his past.

'Stop being so needy,' she told herself fiercely. 'He's told you he loves you. And he's never said that to anyone. It should be enough.'

Then her doorbell rang. When she opened the door, she was surprised to see Rhys on the doorstep, carrying a huge bouquet of flowers and a bottle of champagne.

'Happy new year, *cariad*,' he said with a smile, handing her the flowers.

She let him in. 'But I wasn't expecting…'

'It's New Year's Eve. A time for looking back and a time for looking forward. I was hoping I might be able to spend it with you.'

Tears pricked her eyes. 'I thought…' She'd thought that she wasn't going to see him that evening.

'I love you, Katrina,' he said softly. 'I know I didn't ask you to be there when I called my parents, but I wasn't pushing you away. I was trying to protect you in case things turned nasty. After years of avoiding each other and not talking…I thought it might be awkward, and I didn't want you upset.' He retrieved the flowers from her arms and set them on the floor, along with the champagne, and held her close.

'So how did it go?'

He sighed. 'My mum…well, she is as she is. I don't think even you could thaw her out, *cariad*,' he admitted.

'How about your dad?'

'He'd moved. But luckily the person who bought his house was a friend of his, and gave me his new number.' Rhys paused. 'I'm going to see him on Saturday.'

'Good. Because I think you both need to talk.'

'Yes. He sounded a bit…well, guarded.'

'You probably did, too,' she pointed out. 'And if it's been a long time since you've spoken…'

'It has.' He drew in a breath. 'Katrina, I know it's a lot to ask, and you probably already have plans to see your family this weekend, but I was wondering… Will you come to Wales with me?'

'Of course I will.' There was a lump in her throat which made her words sound husky.

'Are you sure?'

She nodded. 'You're asking me to meet your family. So of course I'll go, Rhys.'

'Don't take it personally if they're funny with you,' he warned.

'I won't.' She slid her hands round his neck and drew his mouth down to hers. 'I have you. Anything else is a bonus.'

His arms tightened round her. 'How did I get to be so lucky?'

'I think,' she said, 'Fate owes you big-time.' She glanced at her watch. 'In a couple of hours, it'll be the new year.'

'Did you want to go to a party?'

They'd had enough invitations. And turned them down. She shook her head. 'Lots of noise, low light and drunken people slurring their words and not moving their mouths properly when they speak isn't a good combination for me. Besides, we're both on duty tomorrow.'

'Then I have an idea.' He kissed again her, then disentangled himself from her arms and retrieved the champagne. 'You, me, this and bed…and the first thing I'm going to say to you in the new year is "I love you".'

And he did.

The following Saturday, Rhys drove them to visit his father. Katrina noted that the nearer they drew to Wales, the less he spoke, and she could see the strain in his face as he drove over the Severn Bridge.

She placed a hand on his thigh. 'Is it that bad, coming home?'

'Land of my fathers, and all that?' He wrinkled his nose. 'Yes. But it needs to be done.' He glanced at the clock. 'We still have a way to go—so as it's practically lunchtime I vote we stop at the next decent-looking pub.'

'Sure.'

The pub in question turned out to have a real open fire, delighting her. And according to the menu all the food was from locally sourced ingredients. 'This looks fantastic, but there are loads of local specialities here and I can't choose between them. As it's your part of the world, what do you recommend?' she asked.

'I'm torn between Glamorgan sausages with mash and red onion marmalade, and lamb cawl.'

His accent had grown more pronounced, she noticed, a soft lilt. Even sexier than normal. 'I'll have whichever of the two you don't have, and we'll share tastes,' she said.

He smiled. 'Fabulous idea.' He went to the bar and ordered their meals and a drink, the food was every bit as good as Katrina had expected, but by the time they'd finished eating and were back on the road, she had a huge knot in her stomach. 'I think I'm beginning to realise how you felt, meeting my family,' she admitted.

'A bit overwhelmed, *cariad*?' he asked softly. 'Don't worry. It won't be that bad. Remember, it's teamwork—we're in this together.'

And then at last he parked outside a small cottage. 'Ready?'

Katrina took his hand and squeezed it. 'Ready.'

'Then let's do this.' Rhys took a deep breath, got out of the car, and opened Katrina's door for her. He was aware that his heart rate was speeding up with every step he took nearer to the door, and his stomach was churning. Llewellyn had sounded so guarded on the phone. So did he actually *want* to see his son, or had he only agreed to see Rhys out of some sense of duty?

There was only one way to find out.

He knocked on the door.

Moments later, it was opened by a man who could have been his double, only twenty-five years older and with iron-grey hair rather than dark.

'Hello,' Llewellyn Morgan said softly.

Diffidently, Rhys held out his hand. Llewellyn grasped it firmly, then shook his head and pulled Rhys into his arms. 'My son,' he said, holding Rhys close. His voice was cracked with emotion, and Rhys knew at that moment he'd spent a quarter of a century living a lie. Because the man who held him close, tears choking his voice, was a man who really did want to see his son. Duty had nothing to do with the reason why Llewellyn had agreed to see him today.

'My manners.' Llewellyn shook himself. 'I shouldn't leave you standing here on the doorstep. Come in.'

'Thanks. This is Katrina,' Rhys said.

'It's good to meet you, *cariad*,' Llewellyn said, shaking Katrina's hand.

'You, too,' Katrina said.

'This is Dilys, my wife,' Llewellyn said, beckoning the woman who sat quietly on the sofa, waiting.

'Pleased to meet you,' Katrina said politely.

'And you.' Dilys placed a hand across her heart. 'And Rhys. You're the spit of your father when he was your age. When I first met him.' She flapped her hand. 'Oh, listen to me rabbiting on, and you've come all this way to see us. Can I get you a cup of tea? Coffee?'

'Coffee for me, please. Black, no sugar,' Rhys said. 'Katrina?'

'White, no sugar, please,' she said. 'And can I help you, Dilys?'

Rhys knew exactly what Katrina was doing. Giving him time with his father. And the smile she sent him as she followed Dilys made his heart swell.

'I hoped against hope you'd see me one day,' Llewellyn said when Dilys and Katrina had left the room. 'Though I thought that was it when you stopped sending cards.'

'When *I* stopped sending cards?' Rhys asked. 'Hang on. You forgot my thirteenth birthday.'

'Never,' Llewellyn said fiercely. 'I sent a card every year. Even after you stopped sending them. Every birthday and every Christmas, until you were twenty-one. And then, I admit—yes, *then* I gave up.'

Rhys was still having trouble adjusting to the idea that his father hadn't ignored his birthdays after all. Or Christmas. So did it mean that his mother had got rid of the cards without telling him? He couldn't believe she'd do something so underhand. Yet Llewellyn's tone told him that his father wasn't lying. He really had sent the cards, and as Rhys and his mother had never moved, there was no way Llewellyn could have sent them to the wrong address.

'I was thirteen,' Rhys said. 'I still had a lot of growing up to do. And I was stroppy with it. I thought, well, if you weren't going to bother, neither was I.' Well, if this was going to be a day of revelations, he thought, it was time to be completely honest and open. Get rid of all the misunderstandings—or maybe confirm them. Confront them and put them behind him. 'I thought you'd got your new family, so weren't interested in me any more.'

'That's not true,' Llewellyn said. 'Yes, I have the girls. But I always loved you, always wanted you.' He sighed. 'I tried to see you after your mam and I split up. But whenever I came to the house to pick you up or take you back, there was a fight with your mam and it ended in tears. In the end I thought it was better to stay away, so you didn't get upset.' He shook his head in seeming frustration. 'I can see now it was the wrong thing to do, but I hated to see you cry. I sent cards, and I know it wasn't nearly enough—but back then I didn't know what else to do.'

'We saw you graduate, though,' Dilys put in, returning with a tray with mugs of coffee and a plate of sliced and buttered *bara brith*, Welsh tea bread, and placing the tray on the table.

Rhys blinked. 'You were there? But…how?'

'Myfanwy in the village used to keep your father posted. She knew your mam wasn't going, so she told us. We rang the university to find out where and what time and if we could get a ticket,' Dilys explained.

'I didn't see you there.'

'I didn't know if we'd be welcome,' Llewellyn said, 'so we kept out of the way. But I saw you up there on the stage and I was so proud of you. My son, the doctor.'

'You never said.'

'And *you* never asked,' Llewellyn countered.

Dilys cuffed her husband's arm. 'Don't be awkward, Llewellyn. He's here now, and that's what matters.' She smiled at Rhys. 'We brought the girls up knowing they had a big brother and hoping that they'd meet him some day. If it was up to them, they'd have been here this afternoon, and they've already sent about fifty text messages to my phone between them saying, "Is he here yet?"' She placed a hand in front of her heart. 'Now, there's me running on, and I promised myself I wouldn't put pressure on you. It's just that we've waited so long and wanted so much…' Her eyes filled with tears. 'I'm so sorry, Rhys.'

'It's not your fault.' Rhys swallowed. 'And, just so you know, Dilys, I never blamed you for Dad leaving. I know he left well before he met you.'

'It was hard, with your mam.' Llewellyn grimaced. 'I lost my job when the pit closed. I couldn't provide for my family, so I didn't feel like a real man and I was hard to live with, too. And then…' He stopped.

Rhys knew exactly what his father couldn't say. So he was going to have to be the one to raise it. 'And then Gwyneth died.'

Llewellyn closed his eyes for a moment. 'I felt so helpless. And it got worse and worse. In the end, I had to leave.' He sighed. 'I wanted to take you with me—but you were all your mam had. I couldn't be cruel enough to take you away from her.' He shook his head and rested a hand on his son's shoulder. 'We've lost years. But maybe now we can make a fresh start. Get to know each other—and in time you might come to see me as your father, not a distant stranger.'

'I'd like that,' Rhys said.

'And although I'm not your mam,' Dilys said, 'I've always thought of you in my head as one of mine.'

Rhys was too choked to answer in words. He simply hugged them both.

'Thank you, *cariad*,' Llewellyn said to Katrina. 'Thank you for bringing my boy back to me.'

The rest of the afternoon was a blur, with Dilys showing Rhys pictures of his half-sisters, Llewellyn showing them an old photograph of four-year-old Rhys holding baby Gwyneth and promising to get it copied for them, and Rhys and Katrina telling them both about the hospital and their life in London.

Rhys refused their invitation to stay for dinner. 'Not because I don't want to, but we're going back to London tonight—we're both on duty tomorrow. But I'll call you. And we'll see each other soon. Maybe you can come to London.'

'We'd like that, wouldn't we, Dilys?' Llewellyn said.

'Yes, and the girls will want to see you.' Dilys insisted on taking a photograph of him before they left, and Katrina took one of the three of them together on Dilys's camera as well as the camera on Rhys's mobile phone and her own.

'You have a safe journey, now,' Dilys told them, hugging them both goodbye. 'And we'll see you soon.'

When they drove away, Katrina was quiet.

'What are you thinking?' Rhys asked.

'If you'd grown up with Dilys and Llewellyn, you'd have had a very different life. You'd have been loved, Rhys, and you'd have *known* that you were loved.'

He shrugged. 'But maybe then I wouldn't have come to London. And I wouldn't have met you. And aren't you the one who always looks at the glass as half-full, not half-empty?'

'True.'

His mouth tightened briefly. 'I can't believe my mother actually kept my father's birthday and Christmas cards from me. I mean, what did she gain from it?'

'Maybe she was scared of losing you,' Katrina said. 'Maybe it was her way of holding on to you. If you thought she was your only family…'

'Hmm.' He sighed. 'Part of me wants to drop in and see her. Confront her. But that's not going to achieve a thing, just drive her even further away. I'm not sure you'll ever get the same kind of welcome from her as you did from Dilys.'

'It's OK.' Katrina reached across to cover his hand briefly on the steering wheel. 'Give it some time. No pressure.'

'Yes. Let's go home,' he said.

CHAPTER THIRTEEN

A FEW nights later, the phone shrilled, waking Rhys; he grabbed it and answered it without thinking. 'Rhys Morgan.'

'Now, that wasn't what I expected to hear.' Madison laughed.

Oh, lord. He'd answered Katrina's phone as if it were his own. And if her cousin hadn't known before that they were sleeping together, she definitely did now. 'I, um…'

'Relax. I'm teasing you. Good morning, Rhys.'

'Morning?' He glanced at the clock. Technically, it was morning. One o'clock in the morning. And then reality kicked in. Madison was thirty-seven weeks pregnant, according to Katrina. If she was calling at this time of the morning… 'Is everything all right?' he asked urgently.

'Yes. It's very all right.'

His heartbeat slowed back to normal. 'Good. But you need Katrina,' he guessed. He was pretty sure that Theo rather than Katrina would be Madison's birth partner, but they hadn't actually discussed it…so maybe Madison was in the early stages of labour and just wanted a bit of moral support from her cousin and best friend. He knew without having to be told that if either of them called for help at any time of day or night, the other would be straight there. 'Hang on.' He switched on the bedside light so Katrina could see his face, and handed the phone to her. 'It's Maddie, and she says everything's all right.'

'But?' Katrina's eyes widened with fear as she took the phone. 'Maddie? What aren't you telling me? What? Why didn't you tell me? Well, yes, of course he'd be panicking. Is…?'

Rhys gave up trying to follow the conversation. But the second Katrina ended the call, he looked straight at her. 'What's happened?'

'I'm an auntie.' She beamed at him. 'I'm an *auntie*!'

'Congratulations,' he said solemnly. 'Mother and baby both well?'

'Yes. Helen had a brilliant Apgar score, after an eight-hour labour—well, it was actually a bit longer than that because Maddie was being dopey and spent the whole day thinking she was having Braxton-Hicks' instead of the real thing. Seven pounds, Theo says she's the most beautiful baby he's ever seen, and…' She beamed again. 'I'd love to go and see her now, except the midwives would have my guts for garters. Maddie and Helen need some rest. But I'm going in before my shift tomorrow.' She paused. 'Um…you can say no, but if you want to come too, you'd be very welcome.'

He could see in her face that she really wanted him there.

And, surprisingly, he found that he wanted to be there too. Sharing the moment with Katrina—the first time she held the baby she'd so been looking forward to. 'I'd love to be there,' he said, meaning it.

The following morning, Rhys and Katrina were in the maternity ward at the crack of dawn.

'Congratulations, Maddie.' Katrina kissed her cousin, then hugged Theo. 'You, too, Theo. The florist isn't open yet, so you'll have to wait for the flowers.' She grinned. 'But I'm glad I'm first with a card.'

Theo coughed. 'Second. I was first.'

Rhys smiled. 'Second's fine by us. Congratulations, both of you. We brought you chocolates. And champagne.'

'And something I bought the day you got your amnio results.' Katrina handed Theo a beautifully wrapped parcel, then peered into the cot. 'Oh, she's gorgeous. And fast asleep.'

Rhys could hear the regret in her voice; Katrina was clearly dying to cuddle her new niece.

Obviously Madison could hear it, too. 'Asleep or awake, she needs her first cuddle from her Aunty Kat right this second.'

Katrina needed no second urging. She picked up her niece, sat on the edge of Madison's bed, and smiled.

Rhys had brought his camera, but he found himself unable to focus for a second. Because the sight of Katrina, with a newborn baby in her arms, made him realise what he really, really wanted out of life.

To be a family with Katrina.

To have children with her. He wanted to hear her telling stories to a little girl with blue eyes and a smile that made the room light up. He wanted to see her making sandcastles with a little boy who had floppy dark hair and was secure in his parents' love, the way he'd never been but the way he knew their children would definitely be. He wanted to share the same special kind of smiles with her that Theo and Maddie gave each other when they looked at their newborn.

'Rhys?' she asked.

He swallowed the lump in his throat and took the photographs. Managed to smile and chat to Theo and Maddie. And when it was his turn to cuddle the baby, he was utterly lost.

'You men are such frauds. There you are, doing the big,

tough macho stuff, but give you a baby to hold and you're utter mush,' Madison accused, laughing.

Katrina joined in the laughter, but Rhys caught just a tiny shadow in her eyes.

Now wasn't the time and place to push her, but he'd ask her later. Make her talk to him, the way she'd made him talk to her. And whatever it was, he'd fix it for her, the way she'd helped to fix his own life.

Then Helen woke up, realised she was hungry and yelled.

'She needs her mummy,' Rhys said, and handed her back to Madison.

'And we have ward rounds and clinic,' Katrina said. 'But we'll be back later.' She stroked her niece's cheek, kissed Madison and Theo, and walked with Rhys to their own ward.

'You OK?' Rhys asked.

'Sure.' Katrina gave him a wide, bright smile.

Maybe he'd imagined it.

He put it to the back of his mind during ward rounds and his morning clinic. A bit of negotiation bought him an extended lunch break; he made an excuse to Katrina that he was due in clinic and didn't have time to go to see Maddie and the baby again, and instead went shopping.

For something very, very special.

At the end of his shift, he went to find Katrina.

She blinked. 'You're leaving early tonight?'

'Hey. I've made a real effort not to be quite such a workaholic,' he said.

She snorted. 'You mean you worked through your lunchbreak.'

He didn't disabuse her of the idea but shepherded her to the staffroom. 'Come on. Time to go.'

'We're walking the wrong way,' Katrina said as he led her through the hospital gardens.

'So we are.' And the sun had set half an hour ago. He didn't care. Because he wanted the rest of his life to start right now. He threaded his fingers through hers. 'Humour me.'

She frowned. 'Rhys?'

He found a quiet bench and sat down, tugging her hand so that she joined him. 'I wanted to talk to you about something.'

'What?'

'Don't look so worried, *cariad*.' He smiled at her. 'This isn't brilliant timing, and it's not quite where I had in mind, but I can't wait any longer.'

She looked completely confused. 'Rhys?'

'I love you,' he said. 'And these last few months…I've come a long, long way. I always thought that I'd spend the rest of my life alone, because it's easier—because I didn't believe in family or marriage. But as I've got to know you, I've realised how wrong I was. The way I feel about you is deeper than I ever believed I could feel about anyone, and from seeing the way you are with your family I've discovered what a family really means. What marriage really means.'

He shifted so that he was on one knee. 'I want to be a family with you. So I'm asking you, Katrina Gregory—will you do me the honour of being my wife?'

'You want me to marry you?' she asked, looking slightly bewildered and as if she didn't quite believe that she'd heard him properly.

'I do,' he confirmed. 'Because I love you, Katrina. Heart and mind and body and soul. What you once told me about teamwork is so true—no matter what life throws at us, we'll get through it because we make a great team. My parents weren't lucky enough to have that together, but I can see now that my father has that kind of bond with Dilys. Your parents have it. Theo and Maddie have it. And I think we have it, too. I want to be with you for the rest of my life. Will you marry me?'

'Oh, Rhys.' She dropped to her knees and hugged him. 'Yes. *Yes*.'

Her kiss was as soft and sweet as she was. And all the empty spaces inside him were filled at last.

Eventually, he stood up and drew her to her feet. 'You've made me the happiest man alive, *cariad*. And I'll be a good husband to you, I swear.' He kissed her again. 'And father.'

'Father?'

He nodded. 'Seeing you cuddling little Helen this morning…it made me realise that was everything I want. You, and our children. If we're lucky enough.'

'Children.'

The flatness of her tone worried him. He knew she liked children—if she didn't, she'd hardly be working as a children's doctor and she definitely wouldn't spend her off-duty time telling them stories—not to mention the wonder in her face that morning when she'd cuddled her newborn niece—so it couldn't be that. But then he remembered the shadows in her eyes, earlier that day, and what she'd told him in the hospital canteen. 'Is this something to do with what Pete said?'

'He had a point.' Her voice was still flat, and the sparkle had gone from her eyes.

'No, he didn't. He didn't have a clue. You'll be a fantastic wife—just as I intend to be a fantastic husband to you. And you'll be brilliant mother.' The kind that his own mother hadn't been. Katrina was warm and loving, she listened—and she noticed.

She shook her head. 'Rhys, I sleep through thunderstorms. I'm bound to sleep through our baby crying in the night—and

I'd never be able to forgive myself if I was needed and I didn't hear and our baby…' She dragged in a breath.

'Died?' He said the word she clearly couldn't bring herself to say.

She nodded.

He kissed her, very gently, then pulled back to make sure she could see his face. 'Katrina, that's not going to happen. I know you can't wear a hearing aid overnight, but that doesn't matter because I'm always going to be there. I'll hear.' He smiled. 'I might moan and groan a bit, and prod you and tell you it's your turn to get up and see to the baby, but I'll hear so you don't have to worry. And in the daytime we'll have one of those baby listeners with lights, the sort you can carry round with you and you can even turn the sound off but the flashing lights will tell you that the baby's crying. We'll work it out.' He stroked her hair. 'Remember what you said to me about teamwork? It goes both ways. I'm on your team, just as you're on mine. And if you're worrying about what Pete said, I can assure you that he was talking a load of rubbish.'

'Was he?'

She didn't sound so sure. 'Yes,' he said quietly. 'Because to me you're perfect, Katrina. You've shown me that anything is possible, with you by my side. You're warm and sweet and you're—oh, this sounds horribly corny, but I mean it—you're like sunshine. I love you just as you are. You'll be a fabulous mother, and we'll work perfectly as a team—we fill each other's gaps. You'll tell better stories than I will, and I'll hear crying more easily than you will. Simple.'

'Oh, Rhys.'

'It's all going to be fine. If you want children…'

She nodded. 'I do. Half the reason I'm so pleased that

Maddie and Theo had Helen is because I never thought I'd have the chance to have children of my own—being an aunt to Maddie's baby is the next best thing.'

'I think,' he said, 'we need to work on this. Helen is definitely going to need a cousin—one who loves her just as much as you and Maddie love each other.'

Katrina's voice was slightly wobbly. 'Sounds good to me.'

'And now we've got that sorted…' He kissed her hand. 'I have to apologise to you. I misled you at lunchtime.'

She blinked. 'How?'

'I let you think I was working. I wasn't. But I did have something important to do.' He took the small box from his pocket. 'Something I wanted to give you.'

She opened it to find a narrow band of gold containing six stones.

'It's a cariad ring—the first letters of the names of the gemstones spell out the word "cariad". Which is Welsh for "dearest".' He smiled. 'Citrine, aquamarine, ruby, iolite—' a stone of such a deep blue that it was almost black '—amethyst and diamond. Though if you'd rather have a diamond solitaire then of course I'll buy you one.'

'No,' she said. 'I'd like a cariad ring. Because you call me that. And every time I see the ring I'll think of what you just said. *Cariad.*'

'It's what you are, Katrina. My heart's dearest.'

'Rhys, that's so romantic.' Tears shimmered in her eyes.

'Don't cry, *cariad.*' He brushed his mouth against hers. 'And it's Welsh gold.'

'But…don't you have to be royalty to buy Welsh gold?'

'No.' He grinned. 'Though, of course, to me you're a princess.'

She snorted. 'Wrong Gregory girl. Maddie does pink and

girly.' Just like the tiny dress she'd given Maddie for her daughter, that morning. 'I don't.'

'I know. I was teasing you.' He brought her hand up to his mouth, kissed her ring finger and slid the ring on top of his kiss. 'This is a promise, Katrina. A promise that I'll always love you.'

'And you always keep your promises.' She reached up and kissed him. 'So do I. I'll always love you, Rhys.'

'Good.' His eyes held hers. 'So when are we getting married?'

'End of the summer?' she suggested.

He shook his head. 'Too far away. I love you, Katrina, and I don't want to have to wait for the rest of our lives together to start. Legally we could,' he said, 'get married in a fortnight.'

'We can't get married yet!' At his raised eyebrow, she explained, 'I want Maddie to be my bridesmaid. And she's only just had the baby.'

'True.' He thought for a moment. 'How about an Easter wedding? Though I want a compromise. As in a Valentine's Day dinner with our whole family—yours and mine—to celebrate our engagement.'

'Yes to the dinner—but there's no way we can get married at Easter. Even assuming everywhere isn't already booked solid, we don't have enough time to organise a wedding.'

'Sure we do.' He smiled. 'You leave it to me—all you need to do is the dresses. I assume you'd like a church wedding?'

'I think,' she said, 'as this is the only time I plan to get married, then yes—I can't deprive my dad of giving me away.'

'That's fine by me. So we need to see your parents. And talk to the vicar. And brief your bridesmaid. Ring your parents,' he said, 'and if they're free this evening I'll drive us to Suffolk.'

'Tonight?' she squeaked.

He shrugged. 'It'll take us, what, a couple of hours? That's doable.'

'But it's rush-hour, Rhys.'

'Doesn't matter. Anything's possible, with you by my side.'

'You're mad,' she said, smiling, 'but I love you.'

'Good.' He stole a kiss. 'Call your parents.'

Her parents were in, and Rhys was as good as his word. They were lucky with the traffic and two hours later they were sitting in her parents' house in Suffolk, and the Gregorys were hugging both Katrina and Rhys. Danny insisted on opening the champagne Rhys had brought, and Babs was delighted when Rhys asked if they could get married in the church in the village.

'Katrina was christened there.' She beamed. 'And you want to get married at Easter?'

'I don't want to wait any longer to start the rest of my life with Katrina,' Rhys said simply.

'There's an awful lot to organise in a very short space of time,' Danny said. 'But I can sort out a car for you, if you like.'

'Dad, I'll never be able to get in one of *your* cars, not with a wedding dress,' Katrina protested.

'Not one of mine,' he said. 'A friend of mine owns a white vintage Rolls Royce.'

'And I have a friend who makes wonderful cakes,' Babs said. 'You know Nicky, Kat.'

'Nicky who makes the best chocolate cake in the world?' Katrina checked. At her mother's nod, she smiled. 'Yes, please.'

Rhys laughed. 'Trust you to want a chocolate cake, *cariad*.'

'And we really need to talk to the vicar.' Danny glanced at his watch. 'Do you want me to call and see if we can pop in and see him now?'

'That,' Rhys said, 'would be brilliant. Thank you.'

'Anything we can do to help, just say the word,' Babs said. 'I promise you we won't be interfering in-laws. But as from now you're officially one of the Gregory family, and we look after our own.'

To Katrina's surprise, Rhys simply gave her mother a hug. 'Thank you. I can't think of any family I'd rather be part of.'

Katrina felt her eyes prickle. As Rhys had told her earlier, he'd come a long, long way. And wherever they went from here, he'd be right by her side.

CHAPTER FOURTEEN

'YOU'RE getting married?' Madison stared at Katrina in shock the next day when her cousin dropped in to see how her first day at home with the baby had gone. 'Hang on. When did all this happen?'

'Yesterday,' Katrina admitted.

'And you're engaged?'

'Rhys wants an official family dinner on Valentine's Day—which means you, Theo, Helen, Aunty Rose and Uncle Bryan as well—but, yes.' Katrina waggled her fingers to make the diamond in her engagement ring sparkle. 'This is a cariad ring.' She explained the significance of the gems to her cousin.

'That's *so* romantic, Kat.' Madison sighed. 'He's lovely. I *knew* he was going to be right for you. So have you set a date?'

'Easter.'

'What, this Easter?' At Katrina's nod, Madison shrieked, 'But that's only a couple of months away. No way can you organise a wedding that quickly! Or is it a register office do?'

'No, it's at St Mary's.'

'Our St Mary's, as in where we were both christened?'

'Yes.'

Madison blew out a breath. 'Cake. Reception. Dresses.

Car. Flowers.' She ticked them off on her fingers and shook her head. 'No, you can't do it, Kat. I mean, I'll help as much as I can, but…it's just not doable.'

'You forget, I have two secret weapons. My mother and my fiancé.' Katrina spread her hands. 'Between them, Mum and Rhys already have all the bases covered. She's making the stationery—you know she loves doing that sort of thing—and your mum's doing the flowers. Nicky's making us a white chocolate wedding cake. Dad's sorting the car and Uncle Bryan's going to drive it, Rhys is talking to the King's Arms today and persuading them to do us a marquee and food and a band, and he says all I have to do is sort the dresses.' She smiled. 'Which is where you come in. And thank you, your offer of help is accepted.'

'Um, honey, Helen's three days old today. I don't think she's quite up to a trip to the shops just yet.'

'We're not going *shopping* shopping. We're going to do it online,' Katrina told her. 'No crowds, no hassle.' Exactly how she preferred to do her shopping.

'But you have to see the fabric to know if you like it.'

'No, I don't.'

'And shoes.'

'I *hate* shoe shopping, as you very well know.'

'Oh, you are so impossible, Katrina Gregory. I should set our mums on you.'

Katrina laughed. 'You can't. They're already involved in the plans. So are you going to help me choose our dresses, or what?'

'*Our* dresses?' Madison blinked.

'Well, who else would I ask to be my bridesmaid?'

Madison bit her lip. 'Kat, I've still got a baby belly. I'm not going to lose it by Easter.'

'You don't have to.' Katrina hugged her cousin. 'We'll find

you something glam that looks fabulous. And you know you'd look gorgeous in a bin bag. You got the style gene in the family.'

'Hey, you're going to look fantastic as a bride.' Madison's eyes glittered wickedly. 'In a dress. You're actually going to buy a dress.'

'Don't rub it in.'

Madison grinned. 'Excellent. And I get to have a pink dress.'

Katrina groaned. 'No.'

'Raspberry?'

'No. That's pink.'

'Pale mulberry?'

'That's pink, too.'

'You're so bossy,' Madison grumbled.

'Because you taught me how,' Katrina retorted.

Two hours later, they'd found the perfect outfits. And shoes to match. And everything was going to be delivered to Madison's house to make sure that Rhys didn't actually see the wedding dress beforehand.

Everyone on the ward was just as pleased for Katrina and Rhys as their families had been, and Katrina was surprised by just how quickly everything fell into place between her mother's organising skills and Rhys's.

'One thing,' Rhys said. 'I need to find a best man.'

'How about your best friend from your student days? Someone in Cardiff? Or someone on the ward—maybe Will?' she suggested. 'And I'm sure he'd make an exception and wear a sensible tie for the day.'

'Actually, I was thinking—if you don't mind—of asking my father,' Rhys said hesitantly. 'I mean, it's still early days...but it's kind of a show of faith. To show that in future our relationship will be what it should be.'

'That,' Katrina said softly, 'would be perfect.' Though there was one sticking point—one that had to be voiced. 'Would your mother mind?'

'She's probably not even going to turn up—to the wedding or to our engagement dinner.' He sighed. 'I'm sorry, Katrina. I can't give you in-laws as nice as the ones you're giving me.'

'Yes, you can. There's Llewellyn and Dilys. And I'm looking forward to meeting the girls this weekend.'

'Me, too.' He held her close. 'Right now, life's better than I ever imagined it could possibly be, even in my wildest dreams.'

'And it's going to stay this good,' she promised him.

Rhiannon, Sian and Mair turned out to be just like their mother: warm and open and talkative. Katrina liked them immediately—and they all adored Rhys.

'There was a reason why I asked you to London,' Rhys said. 'Apart from to see you, that is.' He took four envelopes from his jacket pocket and handed one to Llewellyn and Dilys, and one each to his half-sisters.

'We're to open them now?' Rhiannon asked.

'Now,' Rhys said with a smile.

Dilys opened the envelope and scanned the invitation quickly. 'You're getting married at Easter?' Dilys stared at them in surprise, and then beamed. 'That's fabulous. And you're sure you want us to come?'

'Absolutely,' Katrina said. 'It's not going to be an enormous wedding, as my family's quite small—just our family and closest friends—but there'll be more of a party in the evening when our colleagues will be there too.'

'We'd love to come,' Dilys said immediately. 'All of us.'

'There was something else.' Rhys coughed, and turned to Llewellyn. 'I was wondering if you'd be my best man.'

'Your best man?' Llewellyn echoed, looking shocked. 'I…I'd be proud. Really proud and really honoured.' His eyes were bright with unshed tears. 'As long as it won't upset your mam,' he added, looking awkward.

Rhys gave a half-shrug. 'She probably won't be there.'

Llewellyn sighed. 'She's not softened at all over the years, then?'

'You know the situation,' Rhys said. 'But at least you're all going to be there, so my family's going to be part of my wedding day.'

'We wouldn't miss it,' Dilys said warmly, 'not for anything.'

'And one more thing,' Katrina said. 'We'd like to have an official engagement dinner. Just our families. On Valentine's Day.'

The day of the engagement dinner arrived swiftly. The Gregorys and the Morgans took to each other straight away, and Katrina was delighted by the way Rhys seemed to bloom in their company.

But during the dinner Rhys took her hand, nodding at the family sitting a few tables down from them.

She looked, and saw the same thing that he did: a small boy coughing and apparently finding it hard to breathe.

'I think one of us might be needed there, *cariad*,' he said quietly. 'Could be a foreign body, could be asthma. I'll go.'

She watched him walk over to the family and talk to the parents—and then he beckoned her over.

'Kat, it's your engagement. Stay here. I'll go and help Rhys,' Theo offered.

Madison placed her hand over his. 'Let her go,' she said softly. 'They're used to working together.'

'Like we are,' Theo said. 'Point taken.'

'I won't be long,' Katrina said, and went to join Rhys.

Rhys introduced her swiftly, and continued taking the patient history. Katrina noticed that the little boy was wheezing heavily, though in a way that was a good sign. The last thing she wanted to see was a 'silent chest', where very little air was going in and out of the child's lungs and breathing sounds were completely absent—a silent chest was life-threatening, and the child would need high-flow oxygen therapy and steroid injections as emergency treatment.

'Ben's been wheezing a bit today—we shouldn't have taken him for such a long walk in the cold, but we were having such a nice time we didn't think about the temperature,' the woman said, biting her lip.

Definitely asthma, then, and this attack had been brought on by the cold. 'Has he had asthma long?' Katrina asked.

'Since he was about three. The doctor diagnosed him three years ago.'

'Do you have his reliever inhaler?' Rhys asked.

Even as he spoke, the woman was rummaging through her bag. 'Oh, no. It must still be in our room.'

'Can you get it, please?' Rhys asked. 'And do you have a spacer?'

'A spacer?' she asked.

Clearly not. 'Never mind—I can make something. But we need his medication right now, please.'

A waitress came over to them. 'Can I help?'

Katrina nodded. 'Please. Do you have a polystyrene cup and a knife? Or any cup where we can cut a hole in.'

'If necessary, a brown paper bag,' Rhys added. 'And call an ambulance.'

'Ambulance?' The little boy's father went white.

'Precautionary,' Rhys said gently. 'The medications and a

makeshift spacer might be enough to get him through this, but I don't have a medical kit with me and we never, ever take risks with little ones.'

Meanwhile Katrina picked the little boy up, sat on his chair and settled him on her lap. Laying him down would make things a lot worse, she knew; right now he needed to be up-right, to help him breathe. And being unable to breathe prop-erly was making him panic, which in turn made it even harder for him to breathe—a vicious circle she needed to break by distracting him.

'My name's Katrina,' she said, 'and, although I don't look like one right now, I'm a doctor, just like Rhys. I'm going to help you feel better, sweetheart. Is that OK?'

He nodded, clearly not having the breath or the energy to speak. Not a good sign, she thought.

'Now, I'm going to undo the button on your collar to make you feel a bit more comfortable, and then I'm going to tell you a story. Do you like pirates?'

He nodded, and she quickly undid the button, checked his pulse and counted his breathing rate, and palpated his neck muscles to check whether he was using them to help him breathe—which would mean he was really struggling.

'Rhys, his resps are forty and his pulse is one-thirty,' she said quietly. 'Using neck muscles.'

He nodded and she knew he'd got the message. Ben was having a severe asthma attack; his heart rate and breathing rate were both faster than they should be, as she'd expected, but she'd be more worried if his heart rate suddenly dropped.

She began telling a story to Ben while she kept an eye on his respiration and pulse.

'So how often does Ben take the preventer inhaler, the brown one?' Rhys asked Ben's father.

'I don't know. Three or four times a week.'

'And does he have many attacks like this?' Rhys asked.

'Not really—once every few months, but not as bad as this. We try to keep him away from cats and pollen, because we know they set his asthma off.'

'Any other triggers?'

Ben's father shook his head. 'Not that we know of.'

'OK.' Rhys touched Katrina's hand and mouthed, 'Pulse and resps?'

'Still one-thirty and forty,' she mouthed back.

But at least her story was keeping the little boy calm, Rhys thought with relief.

The waitress came back with a polystyrene cup and a knife. 'Is this all right, Dr Morgan?'

'It's perfect. Thank you,' Rhys said.

'And the ambulance is on its way. It should be here in fifteen minutes.'

'That's great. Thanks.' Rhys smiled at her. 'Now, what I'm going to do is make a hole in the bottom of this,' he explained to Ben's father. 'It'll make the medication more effective because he'll get more medicine into his lungs than he would if he just takes the inhaler on its own.'

A moment later, Ben's mother hurried across the room to him with the inhaler. Swiftly, Rhys made a hole in the end of the polystyrene cup that was just enough to fit the opening of the inhaler, shook the inhaler and fitted it in place. 'Ben, *bach*, I'm going to put the end of the cup over your face and I'm going to ask you to breathe while I count. Can you do that for me?' he asked.

The little boy nodded.

Rhys gave him one puff of the medication. 'That's great, Ben. Slow, deep breath in—that's it—and out.' He counted four more slow breaths for the little boy.

'Shouldn't you give him more, to get it into him more quickly?' Ben's father asked anxiously.

'No, if you do more than one at a time the droplets of the spray stick together and coat the sides of the spacer, so Ben would get less medicine, not more,' Katrina explained.

Rhys removed the inhaler, shook it again, fitted it back into the makeshift spacer and repeated the dose of medication.

'Has he been in hospital before with his asthma?' Katrina asked.

'No,' Ben's mother replied.

'So this must be pretty scary for you. They'll put him on oxygen in the ambulance, and they'll put a little cap on his finger so they can measure the amount of oxygen in his blood—it won't hurt him at all, but if you've not seen it before it's worrying to see your child attached to monitors,' she said. 'They might need to give him some additional medication, depending on how quickly he responds to this—and they'll give you an asthma review. If he's using a reliever inhaler three times a week, as you said, his asthma isn't properly controlled, and they'll need to think about giving Ben something different for a preventer inhaler.'

While Katrina talked, she was checking Ben's pulse. It was still too fast.

'So you see this thing a lot?' Ben's father asked.

Katrina nodded. 'We both work on the children's ward. We've seen little ones much worse than this pull round, so try not to worry.'

Rhys was still administering medication, though, as Ben wasn't yet responding, Katrina was very glad he'd called an ambulance.

'Are you staying here,' she asked, 'or are you local?'

'On holiday—it's half-term,' Ben's mother explained.

'It's a nice part of the world. And you have to take him to Walberswick—it's really pretty on the coast,' Katrina said with a smile.

'So you're local?'

'Local-born,' Katrina said. 'We're just staying here for a couple of days.'

'And we've spoiled your holiday.' Ben's father bit his lip. 'I'm so sorry.'

'We're not exactly on holiday,' Rhys said as he shook the inhaler again. 'We're celebrating our engagement.'

'Your engagement? Congratulations. Oh, and this is the last thing you need, the night of your—' Ben's mother began.

'We're doctors. This is what we do,' Rhys cut in gently. 'We couldn't sit by and see Ben struggle like this. Not when we can help.'

'Absolutely,' Katrina confirmed, stroking Ben's hair. To her relief, she felt the wheezing start to ease. Rhys looked at her, got the message she mouthed to him, and the worry left his eyes.

By the time the ambulance arrived, Ben was breathing much more normally. 'He still needs to go in, though, to be checked over,' Rhys warned, and he and Katrina went to the ambulance door with the paramedics to give them Ben's medical history and explain what they'd done.

When they walked back into the restaurant, people at the other tables stood up and clapped.

'It's our job. We didn't do anything special,' Rhys said.

'Yes, you did.' Mair, the youngest of Llewellyn and Dilys's girls, came over to him and hugged him. 'My brother, the hero. I'm *so* proud of you.'

Rhys hugged her back, not saying anything, but Katrina could see in his eyes that finally he felt part of his family, that he was accepted and valued exactly for who he was—and she could feel tears pricking her own eyelids.

'I'm afraid we had to send your puddings back,' Babs said. 'Your ice cream melted and Rhys's apple crumble went cold, but I'll ask the waitress to bring you a replacement.'

Katrina smiled. 'Thanks, Mum. I don't want a pudding now, though. I'm fine.'

'Same here,' Rhys agreed. 'Too full of adrenalin.'

'I wouldn't say no to coffee, though,' Katrina said. 'Especially as I know what the petits fours are like here.'

Danny laughed. 'I'll go and sort it out. Coffees all round, yes?'

When he'd gone, Sian asked, 'So that's the sort of thing you both do all day? Saving lives like that?'

'Not all day,' Rhys explained. 'It's usually the emergency department who'd deal with a severe asthma attack and then once the patient's stable they'd send him or her up to us. But we do have an emergency assessment clinic and the doctors take turns running it.'

'We have other clinics, too. Plus we have ward rounds twice a day to check up on the children we're looking after who are staying in,' Katrina added.

'And my wife-to-be here spends half an hour a day in the playroom on the ward, after her shift, telling stories.' Rhys slid his arm round her shoulders. 'I told her off the first day we worked together. Told her she was getting too involved with her patients. And I'm very pleased to say I've learned that she's absolutely right.'

Shortly after Danny returned to the table, the waitress brought them coffee.

Dilys nudged Llewellyn. 'Now would be a good time.'

'Good time for what?' Rhys asked.

'To give you both this.' Llewellyn took a parcel from under the table and handed it to Katrina. 'It's traditional.'

Katrina undid the ribbon, opened the box and unwrapped the tissue paper to reveal a carved wooden spoon.

'It's a Welsh love spoon,' Rhys said.

'Symbolic,' Llewellyn said. 'With a heart, horseshoe and a celtic knot—it means love, good luck, and everlasting.'

'It's beautiful,' Katrina said.

Dilys nudged her husband again. 'Tell her the rest of it.'

Llewellyn flushed, but said nothing.

'Men,' Dilys said, rolling her eyes. 'He carved it for you himself. He's been working on it ever since we got back from London, after you gave us the wedding invitation.'

'I just wanted it to be special,' Llewellyn said simply.

'It is.' Rhys's voice was slightly cracked.

This was a gift straight from the heart, Katrina knew. 'We'll treasure it always. Thank you.'

CHAPTER FIFTEEN

AFTER that, time seemed to race by, and then it was the day of the wedding. 'We're not going to need confetti,' Madison said, walking into Katrina's bedroom. 'It's snowing.'

'It can't be. It's Easter,' Katrina said.

'And Easter's early this year. Take a look out of the window.'

Katrina did so. Huge flakes of slow were drifting down and settling lightly on the ground.

'Your wedding pictures are going to be absolutely stunning,' Madison told her.

True, but something else was worrying her more. 'What about Helen? She's only two months old.'

'Stop fussing. She's having a wonderful time, being cuddled by her dad and having her grandmother and her great-uncle cooing over her. Besides, you and I have some seriously girly stuff to do. Even if you were too mean to let me have a pink dress.' She smiled at Katrina and tugged at the towel Katrina had wrapped turban-style round her wet hair. 'Starting with this.'

'I need to do something first.' Katrina grabbed her mobile phone and sent a text to Rhys. *I love you. See you in church.*

He must have been waiting for her text, she thought, because he replied immediately. *Love you too. And I can't wait to carry you over the threshold tonight.*

Madison groaned. 'That text was obviously from Rhys. I know brides are supposed to be blushing, but it's going to play havoc with your make-up if you do that now. Think of…I dunno. Stop thinking about whatever your husband-to-be just suggested and start mentally naming all the bones in the body, or something.'

'I'm getting married,' Katrina said. 'To Rhys. Today. I'm really getting married.'

Madison hugged her. 'And you look absolutely radiant. I'm thrilled for you, I really am. But if we don't start getting you ready, hon, we're going to be late.'

Katrina wrinkled her nose. 'Let's skip the make-up, then. Because I promised him I wouldn't be late.'

'You are *not* skipping the make-up on your wedding day,' Madison informed her. 'I'll just be quicker about it than I would have been. Now, sit still while I do your hair. Mum says the flowers at the church are all done, your bouquet's here, the buttonholes for our lot are downstairs and Dad—if we can prise him away from his granddaughter—is going to drop the ones for Rhys's family at the hotel.' She paused. 'So is Rhys's mum going to turn up?'

'I have no idea,' Katrina said. 'I hope so, for his sake.'

'On the other hand,' Madison said dryly, 'if she's going to be a nightmare and make everyone miserable, it might be better if she stays away.'

'Whichever way, he's going to be hurt.'

'Hey. He has you. And when you walk down the aisle to him today, he's going to be lit up from the inside. You make him happy, Kat. And he's the best thing that's ever happened to you, too.'

Half an hour later, Madison pronounced Katrina's hair, make-up and nails satisfactory. 'Don't put the dress on yet,' she warned. 'Right. Final checklist before I start getting ready. Something old?'

'Mum's pearls.'

'Good, that's borrowed we can tick off as well. New's your dress. Blue? Oh, no, I meant to buy you a garter!' She slapped a hand to her forehead. 'I'm so sorry, honey. You picked a rubbish bridesmaid.'

'No, I picked the best. And you've had a brand-new baby to think about. That's far more important than a blue garter.' Katrina smiled. 'Besides, I bought some hold-up stockings. And the tops just happen to be blue lace.'

'Brilliant. I think,' Madison said, 'we're sorted. I'll go down and get us a cup of tea, and then I'll do my make-up and we'll get you into your dress when we've finished our tea.'

As if on cue, there was a rap at the door and Katrina's mother walked in. 'Tea.'

Madison beamed at her. 'Perfect timing. You're an angel. Thanks, Aunt Babs.'

'I don't think I've ever seen you looking so lovely,' Babs said to Katrina. 'I think I'm really going to need tissues in the church.'

'The mother of the bride is supposed to cry buckets,' Madison said with a grin. 'Underneath her fabulous hat. And from what Mum tells me, your hat is astonishingly good.'

Babs laughed. 'That's because Rose came with me to help choose it.'

'So is there anything I need to do?' Katrina asked.

'Just look beautiful. Everything's under control. Bryan's taken the buttonholes over to the King's Arms, and he brought Rose back from the church—she did the honeysuckle this morning just in case it wilted overnight.'

The church was going to be decorated with winter flower-ing honeysuckle from Katrina's parents' garden—the same flower that was threaded through the bride's bouquet of ivory roses—and Rose had also suggested putting little vases of snowdrops and tealight candles in clear glass holders on the shelf on the back of each pew.

'The church is going to look absolutely stunning. The perfect wedding,' Madison said happily. 'Candlelight, snow, roses, and the feel you can only get from a wedding in an ancient country church.'

There was a knock at the door. 'Delivery for the bride.' Katrina recognised the voice as Theo's.

'You can't come in, Kat's not dressed!' Madison called. 'Hang on. I'll come and fetch it.'

'That's just an excuse to give his wife-to-be a kiss,' Katrina teased. Madison and Theo had set a date for their own wedding for the first of May.

'Be quiet and drink your tea, you,' Madison retorted with a grin.

When Madison left the room, Babs hugged her daughter. 'You look so beautiful, darling. And I know how much Rhys loves you—he's put so much into making today perfect for you. This is going to be one of the happiest days of my life,' she said.

'Mine, too,' Katrina said softly. And she really, really hoped it would be like that for Rhys, too. That he wouldn't let his mother's bitterness spoil this for him.

'Delivery from the groom,' Madison said as she walked back in. 'He's sent you a sprig of myrtle, which he says has to go in your bouquet for luck and then be given to me afterwards, so Mum's sorting that. And he also sent this for you.'

It was a single deep red rose, with a card. Katrina recognised Rhys's spiky handwriting and opened it, then smiled.

'What does it say, then?' Madison demanded.

'I love you,' Katrina said simply.

Madison rolled her eyes. 'I love you, too. But... Oh. Duh. Of course he loves you. He's going to get married to you this morning.'

Katrina laughed. 'I love you too, Maddie. And I don't think I've ever been so...' She swallowed hard.

'No, no, no.' Madison crossed her hands rapidly. 'Don't cry, hon. You can't cry on your wedding day, even if they're happy tears.' She hugged her cousin. 'Drink your tea while I get my face on.'

'You've got half an hour before the car leaves,' Babs told them. 'And I, meanwhile, am going to steal my great-niece for a cuddle.'

Twenty-five minutes later, they were both ready. Katrina and Madison stood side by side in front of the cheval mirror, staring at their reflections.

'You look stunning,' Katrina said softly. Madison's dress was made from wine-coloured chiffon with a V-neck, a V-back and a gathered empire bodice that flattered her post-baby figure and also made her look taller. Her stole was in matching chiffon and, with Madison's dark hair worn loose, the outfit looked incredible.

'So do you,' Madison breathed. 'On me, that dress would look appalling. I'm too short and too round. But because you're tall and slender and gorgeous... It's just fantastic.' Katrina's ivory dress was bias cut, with a scoop neckline, ending in a puddle train. With her mother's pearls at choker length round her neck and a simple pearl tiara and a short pearl-edged veil, she looked the perfect bride. 'I'm so proud of you,' Madison said. 'My little better-than-sister.'

'Don't cry. You'll set me off again,' Katrina warned huskily.

There was a rap at the door. 'Are you ready yet? The car's going to have to leave,' Babs called.

'Come in, Mum.'

Babs walked in and swallowed hard. 'Look at you both. I…' She shook her head. 'Our girls, Rose. They look amazing.'

'Our girls,' Rose echoed, coming in with the bouquets. 'Oh, my lord. There's not going to be a dry eye in the church. You both look fantastic.'

'Car,' Madison said. 'Now. Before you make her cry and ruin her make-up.' But she, too, was sniffing slightly.

Danny held his daughter's hand in the car all the way to the church, too overcome to say anything after he'd hugged her and told her how proud he was of her. Madison was waiting for them in the porch, peering out of the heavy oak doors to see where they'd got to.

'Message from the bridegroom,' she said. 'You have a last-minute wedding guest.'

Katrina blinked at her. 'Rhys's mum? She decided to come after all?'

Madison nodded and made last-minute adjustments to Katrina's veil. 'Don't worry. Rhys is fine. He's smiling. I think his mum's going to cry in a minute, but so is your mum and mine and Dilys—it's what mums are meant to do at weddings. Oh, and Rhys says to tell you he loves you.' She stood back for a moment. 'Oh, Kat. You look wonderful. You and Rhys are going to look so perfect together—because you *are* perfect together.' Swallowing back her tears, she moved into her position as bridesmaid.

And when Katrina walked down the aisle on her father's arm a few moments later, Pachelbel's 'Canon' playing softly, and she saw the joy and love in Rhys's face as he turned to look at her, she knew that her cousin was right. She and Rhys were perfect together—and everything was going to be just fine.

MILLS & BOON®
The Sheikhs Collection!

This fabulous 4 book collection features stories from some of our talented writers. The Sheikhs Collection features some of our most tantalising, exotic stories.

Order yours at
www.millsandboon.co.uk/sheikhscollection

MILLS & BOON®
The Billionaires Collection!

This fabulous 6 book collection features stories from some of our talented writers. Feel the temperature rise with our ultra-sexy and powerful billionaires. Don't miss this great offer – buy the collection today to get two books free!

Order yours at
**www.millsandboon.co.uk
/billionaires**

MILLS & BOON®

Why shop at millsandboon.co.uk?

Each year, thousands of romance readers find their perfect read at millsandboon.co.uk. That's because we're passionate about bringing you the very best romantic fiction. Here are some of the advantages of shopping at www.millsandboon.co.uk:

* **Get new books first**—you'll be able to buy your favourite books one month before they hit the shops

* **Get exclusive discounts**—you'll also be able to buy our specially created monthly collections, with up to 50% off the RRP

* **Find your favourite authors**—latest news, interviews and new releases for all your favourite authors and series on our website, plus ideas for what to try next

* **Join in**—once you've bought your favourite books, don't forget to register with us to rate, review and join in the discussions

Visit **www.millsandboon.co.uk**
for all this and more today!